Dedicated with my deepest feelings of love and gratitude to my best friend, my dearest Sylvie who as a real human being made a difference to my brother's life in the darkest years of his life.

Avec tout mon amour
Roxanne M.

THE MAGIC OF FLOWERS

THE MAGIC OF FLOWERS

A NOVEL

ROXANNE M.

iUniverse

THE MAGIC OF FLOWERS
A NOVEL

iUniverse books may be ordered through booksellers or by contacting:

iUniverse
1663 Liberty Drive
Bloomington, IN 47403
www.iuniverse.com
1-800-Authors (1-800-288-4677)

ISBN: 978-1-5320-4233-1 (sc)
ISBN: 978-1-5320-4234-8 (e)

Library of Congress Control Number: 2018902359

Print information available on the last page.

iUniverse rev. date: 08/23/2018

About the Author

Roxanne M. attended the University of Sorbonne and received her PhD in French Literature. She came to United States of America in 1990, and since then, she has been working as translator and teaching at University of Los Angeles. Her first novel "The Heart in My Head," based on a true story, was published in March of 2014, and is optioned for a movie. She currently resides in Los Angeles, California.

US Review of Books

The Magic of Flowers
by Roxanne M.
iUniverse
book review by Gabriella Tutino

"You can't change your past, but you can look at it with different eyes."

Amanda is a psychologist who specializes in talk-therapy, letting her patients express themselves in an unguarded way. Her newest patient, Tatiana Ayoub, however, has a harder time opening up, fluctuating between wanting to work through her trauma and not sharing. Amanda begins to take a personal interest in Tatiana, curious to know what haunts her. As the two women's therapy sessions continue, they grow closer together, forming a deep and intimate friendship of understanding and healing. What happens when they find out their lives are intertwined more than they thought? How does Amanda's perfume, "Quelques Fleurs," affect those closest to her?

Set against the backdrop of Paris, Roxanne M. deftly weaves psychological intrigue, romance, and modern-day events together to form a tale that meditates on the power of human relationships and trauma. The majority of the story takes place in Amanda's office, which runs the risk of being repetitive and heavy due to the nature of therapy. However, Roxanne M. succeeds at using these therapy sessions as the vehicle of the story through Tatiana and her animated storytelling. The novel does not treat Tatiana's emotional and abuse issues lightly; rather, the manner in which the issues are presented and discussed allow Tatiana to be in control, something that fellow readers who may have similar issues will appreciate.

exhausted and feels sadness listening to the life stories of her patients, entirely engulfing her in mixed emotions is extremely well-articulated by the author. Strength granted to her for becoming a psychologist to fix her own issues and I'm sure many may find that relatable. The most intriguing thing throughout this whole book is the mention of Amanda's perfume, both expressed openly by Tatiana and Alexander. Interesting enough to never underestimate the power of an alluring fragrance, it triggered emotions of the characters who got a whiff, a feeling of peace.

The author has provided her readers with an insider's view to the lives of both Tatiana and Amanda. This book is well-written and has articulated moments shared about their lives which allowed for invoked emotions of sadness, unconditional love, warm embraces, trust and understanding. Expressing such empathy for the character's past that they've endured proves we as mere humans are resilient beings. The story's twist truly puts things in a new perspective, as anyone wouldn't have seen that coming. When the plot thickens, I instantly got the sense of remaining at the edge of my seat as I continued reading, impressive on the author's part.

There have been several times that I felt connected to Tatiana on an emotional level and not just because I'm empathic to her past, but some of her feelings are relatable. I commend anyone who has stepped out of their comfort zone, becoming courageous by seeking professional help, as it takes a lot for someone to take that initial step. What both characters have endured is something I wouldn't wish on my worst enemy and I was glad to learn that Amanda is spiritual, which I can agree with. Some moments shared between both Tatiana and Amanda seemed more intimate and a bear-all kind of vibe due to the level of care involved, and I admire it is as an effective method for the sake of psychology patients. I enjoyed the reading experience of witnessing just how 'damaged' an individual can be to need someone loving enough to listen to them and help them heal from internal scarring. I recommend those who might be considering scheduling a therapy session to give this book a chance, even if you don't relate to Tatiana, you can learn much from her talk therapy sessions.

PREFACE

It is extremely difficult to write about the universe of flowers. I discovered this fact only when I started to study about this wonderful and magnificent world. After all, how could we possibly describe the magical universe of flowers in just a few pages?

The relationship of that universe to people is at the center of certain mythological stories, which tell us that human beings were first born of flowers.

We find principles of spiritual expression underlying such stories; Brahma, for example; the prince of creation, was born within a lotus flower floating and moving lightly upon the waters of an ocean.

What a remarkably poetic concept!

The strong connection between flowers and human beings is certain and indisputable. It is undoubtedly true that if flowers are constantly present in our lives, they can engender an atmosphere of optimism and make us happy. We take care of them delicately and skillfully because they are a source of great pleasure and joy, and inducers of positive emotions.

The language of flowers dates back to the eighteenth century and it was originated in Persia where the names of flowers were used to create a system for memorizing poetic verses.

We can read signs of flowers in Shakespeare: There is a talk of the beautiful rose in Romeo and Juliet, of peonies in King Lear, of the magic power of violets in a Mid-summer Night's dream.

In France, the nineteenth century belonged to Charles Baudelaire's dark and bewitching "Les Fleurs du Mal" (The Flowers of Evil), in which the captivating and fatal character of flowers did not miss the opportunity to distress and disturb the tormented and fragile souls.

In his poem entitled "Le Parfum exotique", Baudelaire discovers with Jeanne Duval, the woman who exudes the sensuality and the passion, the charm linked closely to his exotic dreams. The heady and sensuous perfume of this woman transports the poet to the mystical world of his fantasies and provokes happiness, and a sense of good health as well as prosperity.

The sense of smell is directly associated with our memory. The foundation of the perfume industry explains straightforwardly this amazing connection. Thus, the perfumery develops fragrances that seek to convey and transmit a vast display of emotions and feelings.

I find this really magical and thrilling that a perfumer can take a moment created by nature's magnificent and splendid fresh flowers and somehow put it into a bottle. I was unaware of the power and role that a fragrance is capable of playing in our daily life. I discovered that the scent of a perfume possesses this magical power to transport us.

Every day, we wear the perfume because it creates a mood instantaneously. The smell gives us a strange feeling, hard to describe. We are unable to explain exactly what does happen, or when it is going to happen, or what it is going to do to us or somebody else.

There is a message of peace and serenity through each individual fragrance. Colette, the French novelist of twentieth century wrote: "A fragrance is the inexplicable way in which a flower bombards us with astonishing molecules."

A scent needs to be smelled and explored along all possible paths in order to comprehend how it lives and develops in the air and on the skin within a few minutes or even hours. The search for a successful scent is what matters most. Imagine that you are on the street, and a stranger walks past wearing a perfume worn by someone you have known or loved in your life, needless to say it results in a flashback, straight away.

The strength of our sense of smell is really amazing, since it has not only the power to transport us back to a particular time and place, but furthermore it is crucial how your partner smells. If that strong chemistry is missing, thus you can be certain that the relationship will not last long.

Smelling a delightful aroma can be a very pleasurable and satisfying experience. Aromatherapy has been used therapeutically for thousands of years to improve physical, emotional and spiritual health. Many believe our sense of smell communicates with parts of the brain that stores emotions and memories.

As far as I am concerned, "Quelques Fleurs" has such a magical effect and power to overwhelm and the capacity to seduce and transmit its energy to you that I find it inexpressibly tough to explain.

"Quelques Fleurs", an irresistible combination of grace, strength and independence of spirit is the basis on which this story was written. A symbol of feminine perfection, it remains the eternal perfume of the infinite and the imagination.

Where does my inspiration come from? It is very simple, anything and everything. The foundation of my novels is realism. I find motivation everywhere I look especially the world, this mortal and lethal life that has an incredible influence on my novels. I must stick to realities, I am not at all interested in imagining stories that are completely false, invented, and disconnected from the reality.

A story needs to be based on the real world, the one in which we live, composed of everyday events, the kind that we can expect. However, I have to admit that autobiographical fiction seems to me like a totally vain project. You really need to have an extraordinary and amazing life to even dare attempt to write it. Still, I confess that I put a bit of myself, a light touch in my characters. When Flaubert, the French novelist of nineteenth century said, "Madame Bovary, c'est moi", he fully admits the real truth of it even though it is not entirely real.

As a writer of fiction, I am a realist. My imagination needs real and actual people and events in order to work on and to write my story. However, I must confess that I don't have the intention to dishonor and tarnish the reputation of friends or people and those who crossed my path one day.

I need to think about the truth first before I turn it into a tale. My artistic engagement is complete and absolute, and this is this particular zone of the fantasy, without any boundary, that releases the lock and creates freedom, liberty in creativity and imagination, and I find it tremendously fascinating.

ONE

PARIS, DECEMBER 2014

A frosty cold weather took hold of Parisian region for a few days. Under the glacial blue sky, the big wheel of Tuileries seemed to be counting the last days of the year right before Christmas.

We were experiencing below-freezing temperatures, and trying to beat the winter blues, so that we could say farewell to 2014 and welcome 2015 with enthusiasm. It had been a year of change for me, both personally and professionally.

Sitting behind the French walnut desk, set between the two antique armchairs, I enjoyed watching through the floor-to-ceiling windows that flooded my office with natural light, the splendid courtyard blanketed with the snow.

With vast windows overlooking the enchanting and spectacular gardens of avenue Foche and l'arc de triomphe, and a ceiling almost sixteen feet high, covered with a thin layer of gold paint, this area is enhanced by the light blue and white hues used on the walls and upholstery.

Built into one wall is an antique bookcase filled with the works of my favorite authors. There are only two paintings in my office, "the young girls at the piano", by Renoir and "the dreamer of summer evening ", by James Tissot.

The wood-burning fireplace had been made into a shrine with antique Delft tiles for the surround and the eighteenth century blue and white china arranged on the tiered mantel. In winters, it casts a glow on the new oak floor that had been laid and dressed with a custom-wave Aubusson.

Through a sliding glass door at the far end of my office, a large eighteenth century portrait framed in gilded wood and a stunning Louis sixteenth commode come into view. My husband and I used to have an extravagant life style, and we had collected the art collection at our home on various trips around the world. Each piece is connected to a special memory and adds soul to this place.

These two pieces occupy a marvelous space leading down to the main house, the living room decorated with eighteenth century French tapestries and paintings, the Venetian style dining room, the kitchen and up to the two large bedrooms with high ceilings and an incredible view of the city from each room with a lovely outdoor terrace.

The brass bench in the entry hall is more like a piece of jewelry, it certainly will last through generations. As you enter this apartment and walk through it, everything you see there gives you the impression of wealth, glamour and sumptuousness of a modern Parisian luxury of which you might only see in the movies.

The biggest challenge with a place like this that has a colorful past was to preserve the historical importance. When Christian and I bought this apartment surrounded on all sides by terraces planted with flowers and small trees, my husband who had an incredible taste set himself a simple but formidable goal for the renovations. He wanted to create an ambiance that the original owner would have been proud of. This vast apartment belonged to the billionaire, the famous designer Yves Saint Laurent. When we managed to get inside this locked place for the first time, we were truly stunned with admiration.

In fact, the apartment located at 36, avenue Foche was a whole world to me. It had such a pleasant ambiance, and even more important to me, I could still see the consideration that my beloved husband had given to decorating the place; as all the energy and love that he had put into remodeling were still there. So, it is easy to understand why I had a particularly deep connection to the place.

It was a beautiful afternoon. It was cold and the sun was dropping behind the tall trees of avenue Foche, making my office even darker.

The diploma framed on the wall describes that I attended UCLA to study psychology. I have worked with clinically depressed and bipolar disorder men and women, anorexic and bulimic young girls, those who are alcoholic or turned to drugs, and of course there are tragic and heartbreaking stories of those who attempted suicide. What would become of them? What is happening to the world?

Staring at the window, I was thinking about all these lost souls when mademoiselle Solange came through the door and announced that my next patient scheduled at three o'clock had just canceled her appointment.

My eyes fastened questioningly on her as I asked, "Who is it?"

Mademoiselle Solange who was now standing motionless in the doorway, looked at me with her deep brown eyes, and then she said with a sweet smile, "It's a new patient, her name is Tatiana, Tatiana Ayoub".

"Tatiana? Oh! Yes, of course. Didn't she already cancel two times before?" I asked.

"Yes, indeed", she said as she stepped inside and took a few steps towards me. Next, she handed me a letter.

"The mail is already here?" I asked.

"No, but this letter just arrived for you, it's a special delivery", she exclaimed. Then, she exited the office without a sound, pushing the door close.

I looked at the letter, Doctor Luciano's name was on the envelope, and his handwriting was familiar to me. What did he have to say to me this time? I wondered. I opened the letter and read:

"Dear Amanda,

I am writing you to confirm that Ms. Tatiana Ayoub, a forty-year-old woman, commenced psychotherapeutic treatment with me two months ago, for specific phobia with panic attacks. Specifically, Ms. Ayoub has a marked, persistent fear of losing her bearings when commuting to unfamiliar places, either by driving or through the use of public transportation. Experiencing severe anxiety and panic, she recognizes that her pronounced fear is excessive, but is presently unable to control or manage it. The patient also describes longstanding, severe difficulties with breathing and sleeping, which is also neurologically consistent with a phobia of this type and magnitude. Unable to commute outside of her immediate, familiar neighborhood, she describes several incidents over the past few years when she attempted to commute to an unfamiliar destination, but never made it there. Shortly into the commute, she had to turn back because of panic attacks during which she experienced shortness of breath, accelerated heart rate, light headache, faintness, and a feeling that she was going to crash.

Clinically depressed, the patient who attempted suicide about two months ago currently takes Zoloft and Alprazolam to sleep, but they have no effect on the debilitating anxiety. The standard course of treatment for a disorder of this magnitude is typically over a period of eighteen months to two years, and includes not only antidepressants but especially the talk therapy in order to explore the root and the nature of Ms. Ayoub's depression and anxiety, parallel to this process.

I'm happy to discuss the matter further, if necessary. Please don't hesitate to contact me if you have any questions.

Respectfully submitted,

Claude Luciano, Ph.D.

Clinical Psychiatrist of Paris."

Doctor Luciano's letter of introduction captured my attention. I read it twice, folded it and put it in my drawer. I was impatient to meet Tatiana Ayoub, my new patient.

My four o'clock patient had not arrived yet. I picked up the phone and managed to return a few calls as mademoiselle Solange, tall and slender, came back to the office to serve me a cup of coffee.

Mademoiselle Solange, the eldest of a large family from Nice, is an important part of our household. She is a modest and amiable woman and she has been with us since Celine was born. She took care of her and raised her until she was ready to go to school. She loves her as if she was her own child, and still she enjoys every moment she can spend with her. Gradually, with her special wisdom, she got involved with all aspects of my life, and became my assistant and confidante. She is a part of the family and lives in the back of the apartment. We are fortunate to have her since she is devoted to her work and the house always ran impeccably. I have to admit that I would have been lost without her.

My four o'clock patient finally arrived. I hung up the phone as she opened the door and wandered in.

"Hi", said Isabelle, smiling.

"Hi, please have a seat."

She sat down in one of the two famous armchairs, and the session began. Last year, Isabelle, a supermodel in Paris, started showing signs of being bipolar after her husband had left her for a younger woman. Anyone who has been dumped can attest to the deep pain of that first moment of rejection. Isabelle remained immobile for several months; she was not taking phone calls, and was not even showering. Usually, women like her who suffer from depression, or who have low self-esteem, tend to take breakups much harder. She felt helpless, with bouts of unexplained crying.

I have been seeing her regularly twice a week. Isabelle had been referred to me by her psychiatrist who had asked me to keep an eye on her, so I had been giving her security, support and proper medical assistance. We were about to begin her last session of therapy, and I suspected that her decision to discontinue was dictated by her financial situation as much as anything else.

We looked at each other for a moment in total silence. She stirred in her seat and took a deep breath.

I waited calmly, staring at her.

"Time passes and life changes fast. This was quite an experience. Looking back on it now, I can say those were awful days," Isabelle said.

"There had been so much going on in your life, but now I'm happy to see that all is over, you look content with your life," I said kindly.

"I had not been thinking straight, I was lonely and lost. But now, I'm fully self-realized. I have the capacity of carrying within me a deep sense of peace and calmness," she said with grace.

"You are full of soul, Isabelle, and I'm glad to hear that," I said, smiling at her.

She stared at me for a moment; she seemed to be so sure of herself. Letting out another sharp breath, Isabelle went on, "I was so locked in my head that I could not see any light, but I feel great now, never been better. I made an oath to myself to not give up."

"It's important to know what we can do so that our lives become meaningful and joyful," I said, while thinking.

She nodded.

I simply smiled.

"I needed to hear your gentle and soothing words, as I buried myself in spiritual life. Talking to you was certainly beneficial," she said, after a short silence.

There was gratitude in her words towards me; I could sense it and I was so touched by it.

"So, is everything all right now?" I just asked.

"Yes. Don't worry about me. As you know, this is my last session of therapy with you. I need to take a break."

"All right, I wish you all the best. I'm so proud of you!"

"Thank you. We are going to travel across the world, first to Italy exploring the city of Tuscany and then to India to visit the astonishing beauty of the Taj Mahal. We would like also to take a trip to Cuba, I heard a lot about the exotic city of Havana where there is color in everything," Isabelle said with excitement.

"Did you say we? So I suppose that you are not traveling alone," I said, and I insisted on "we".

She mumbled an answer that allowed her to avoid responding to my question. In the silence that followed, we both said no word.

She felt tongue-tied, awkward.

I remained calm and quiet.

She finally decided to talk by lifting the veil of mystery, "Right, I'm irresistibly drawn to a woman named Florence. I met her at the country club. The two of us flirted and talked and I agreed to dine with her after a further couple of evenings. This is the first time I really fell in love. She is unbelievably sexy and intelligent. We have a number of interests in common."

"I'm so happy for you, Isabelle."

"I have so much respect for you that I didn't want to say anything that you would not approve of," Isabelle spoke fast shaking her head, without looking at me.

"Here, as you know, you can say anything you want, it's okay. As long as you are happy, nothing matters."

"I know, and I really appreciate that. Not everybody thinks so!"

The fact of Isabelle's bisexuality had to be kept secret even though in France, she was accepted as the norm. In her mid-twenties, she was aware of her sexual orientation, of her feelings for women as well as for men.

"I'm now in the best relationship of my life, and I've never been happier. I have a hard time remembering why I was so sad."

"This is so great," I nodded in agreement.

Isabelle glanced at her watch and said, "Perhaps we should stop now, I have a lot to do. Thank you for all your help. As usual, the smell of your perfume is all around, I'm going to miss this scent."

I smiled; there was nothing left to be said. She turned and I heard the sound of the door closing behind her.

When Isabelle left my office, I felt my heart and soul being deeply stirred. I put on some music; it revives me after the heavy stories that I usually listen to all day. Half an hour later, I glanced into Celine's room. Everything seemed peaceful there. She was lying on the sofa, watching cartoons.

Then, later in the afternoon, I went for a walk to the park Monceau in quiet meditation. I thought that the more I hold my patients up, the more this flow of support and the positive energy move in my own direction. I knew that I would not be able to solve all the brain's mysteries, but touching just a tiny piece of one soul is all it takes for me to feel great and be happy.

Two

Who and what inspired me to become a psychologist?

As a young girl, I was always interested in people; I mean people's lives. I was sensitive, empathetic to others. I looked at someone's face, and I would feel and study the meaningful expressions, interpreting every single aspect of the person. I loved the poor, the lonely, and the alcoholic people, people with problems in general. I pitied them because they had a problem. I pitied them because they did not pity themselves since they had pride. And I loved anyone, no matter whom with pride.

One day, my mother said to me, "Amanda, you are a terrific listener, you should study psychology to help people and save lives."

In fact, I have always had a strong desire to assist others in need, especially those who, through no fault of their own, have fallen on hard times or suffer from mental health issues.

Born and raised in Paris, I dreamed of one day, making a good life for myself. I was blessed to have a family that was incredibly supportive. My parents always took me under their wing and protected me. From the time I was a teenager growing up in Paris, California held a special place in my heart. I took my mother's advice and moved to Los Angeles to study psychology at UCLA. And here I am today; I knew this was it.

Following the example of America, the practice of talk therapy, to express feelings and thoughts, and share them with a specialist of spirit had become more and more in general practice in France. People going in for psychoanalysis, expect that their problems and thoughts would be analyzed and solved properly by mental-health professionals. Long before, people were scared of getting help, scared of being labeled to be crazy, and they would never have considered a psychologist or psychiatrist. But now, they realize that the talk therapies can help them work out how to deal with negative thoughts and feelings and make positive changes in their lives.

Indeed, I don't remember ever wanting to do anything else. My life long determination is reflected in my practice with my patients, often with satisfying results. Very young, I spoke with assurance and I never asked myself questions about my career. I had the certainty that I would have a fine future and prospects before me.

The most important element that I often use in my work is love. If you don't love what you are doing, it shows. I am passionate about everything I do and I am a big believer in helping people. I love all my patients, I listen to their problems and pay careful attention to them, trying to find solutions in every possible way to console and comfort them.

I worked very hard to get where I am today. I am a confident French woman who keeps an open mind and a warm heart. I have learned that the best I can do is to give my total effort with total honesty and certainly without refutation. And if I conduct myself like that, I don't worry about what somebody else thinks.

I am a famous psychologist in Paris, but I always knew that fame does not last forever. I had to stop and think for a minute and remind myself that I am not the best in the business because there is no such thing, so I stayed grounded in my job that is more of a passion than work.

I am happy with my life in Paris, in this beautiful and exquisite apartment where I live with my daughter, Celine. It feels warm and cozy, like a real home.

It was in this place that my wedding was held on a sunny day of March1995, and it was attended by my family and faithful friends. Dancers wandered and glided through the large reception room passing the astounding art collection.

My husband Christian was handsome and very healthy. He never caught the flu or even a cold, nothing whatsoever, until that fateful day...

It was March8, 2014 that had been the turning point of my life. This was not to be an ordinary journey. Christian took a short business trip to China, so very far away. As usual, I was sitting behind my desk, reading my patient's files when the creak of the door opening broke the silence. Mademoiselle Solange entered my office. I immediately noticed that she was frightened to come in. I found her greatly disturbed, with a distressed face. She sounded worried, "Have you heard the news?"

"What news?"

She asked me to turn on the TV; we said nothing more to each other.

I watched, paralyzed with terror, as the French media reported breaking news that the flight from the Malaysian capital of Kuala Lumpur bound for Beijing was missing. Since Christian had not called or text messaged me to say that his plane had landed safely in Beijing, I assumed that his flight was delayed.

I watched as my body was shaking. I can't describe the next few hours without tears streaming down my cheeks. According to a press statement by airline officials, the Boeing 777 aircraft was missing without leaving a trace. In fact, they had absolutely no clue where the plane or the passengers and crew on board had vanished.

Mademoiselle Solange and I stared at one another in shock. I could hardly bring myself to believe. I tried to convince myself that it was not my husband's flight, but I knew it was. Trapped in the cycle of hope and despair, I kept waiting for news, crying hysterically.

One week later, I heard the unimaginable news that Christian's flight had disappeared forever. Investigations had been launched. The Malaysian and Chinese authorities tried to reassure families that they were trying hard to find the plane. The trauma had been immense. Two weeks later after the flight vanished; officials made a shocking announcement. They believed that the plane came down in the middle of the vast Indian Ocean.

Focusing on my grief, I tried to stay calm at first, but then, I had a panic attack and sobbed in the middle of the night because it was the only time that I had to myself to mourn my husband's death. I wanted to scream, and I wanted him back.

Condolences from all over the world poured in. My whole family went into deep mourning. I felt as though I was suffocating when I came to realize that my husband would never come home again.

We did a memorial for Christian to remember him. I wanted to honor all my years of marriage with him. The day of my husband's memorial was bright and sunny. It reminded me of my wedding day somehow. My family, Christian's family, and our friends congregated at Nôtre-Dame, decorated with oriels, painted and sculpted gables and frescoes. We talked about him to conjure his memory. Christian was a precious present to me, to my life, and he left me a beautiful and priceless gift, my daughter.

Since then, I slept a lot and lost my appetite for food as well as life. Mademoiselle Solange watched over me carefully for a couple of months. I remember when I walked in the bedroom and saw Christian's silk robe still lying on the sofa, my soul revolted. I only wished that my husband died peacefully in my arms. I was overwhelmed with grief for the way that he had died. It was hard to believe it, I had to accept that he was gone forever but he would live on in my heart and will be with us until the end.

I read "Mourning and Melancholia" by Freud, and I knew that one day I would overcome my grief. At said time, I think it had never occurred to me that there might be someone in my life one day. Or perhaps there would be other men, but there would never be a man who would love me the way that my husband did. Certainly, I was not convinced either if one day I would ever love anyone the same way that I loved him.

I was bewildered to tell my seven-year-old daughter who was not capable of thinking rationally, that her father disappeared all of a sudden and would never come back home. I remember, the first day when I gave her a ride to school, tears filled my eyes. I held her in my arms and whispered in her ear as she left me, "Nothing bad will ever happen to us. I will always be with you, sweetheart."

I tried to be brave, but the thought of having to raise a child alone, stole my senses and I could only cry and curse God through my tears.

Now, with holidays around the corner, I can't stand the thought of spending Christmas without him. We shared fabulous time together, and I assumed that I would live a happy long life by his side. It was not meant to be this way!

The most important lesson that life has taught me so far is the fact that the world is not fair. So, I don't take anything personally. I learned that I am perfectly capable to overcome a trauma and go on with my life. My job is overwhelming; I need an immense energy and a phenomenal concentration to run my business remarkably well.

Usually, my day begins with my yoga class. I find that it energizes both my mind and my body. When I practice yoga, I understand the goodness of it within me; therefore I am able to see the world outside as good as well.

My genuinely workaholic schedule is very hectic since everything is about keeping a calendar near me. It is all about planning my days, weeks and months in advance. I don't really have time to relax, but when I do, I like to spend it with my daughter.

During these past few months, since Christian's death, everything in my life took on a different perspective. I would wonder what purpose or meaning does my life has now. I realized that things considered precious and important in life have no more value, except for human relationships. I read Kant, Hegel, Spinoza and the philosophers who commented the non-materialistic side of life. All the success, money or power in the world mean nothing unless you can help others and give back to those who are less fortunate.

Spiritually, I am deeply sensitive and I feel the suffering and pain of others as my own. In this troubled world, where millions and millions of innocent human beings are devastated and damaged by war, terrorist attacks, poverty, anxiety, depression and last but not least the lack of purpose in life, I naturally feel a great concern for the safety and well-being of my brothers and sisters throughout the world. And I often wonder what can I do to make a difference in another's life?

Since my job allows me to meet a variety of people with so many perspectives, I began by introducing to my patients the path to a life that is peaceful and filled with wisdom, understanding and good judgment. I tried to show them how meditation can bring light to their mind, and the wisdom can lead them to enlightenment in life.

THREE

The winter was upon us. It was a cold and windy day. I came to my office at ten o'clock in the morning and saw patients back to back until three o'clock. Sitting at my desk, I looked at the black and white photograph of my family artfully arranged next to the flowers. How quickly time flies! I shared a wonderful time with my parents and my brother, a genius mathematician, between Paris and the South of France.

My brother is two years younger than I, and until I reached the age of fifteen, sometimes we fought like cats and dogs, and other times we imagined ourselves to be native American Indians, hiding behind the trees and shooting plastic tipped arrows at each other. Matthieu is still very close to me and his closeness makes our relationship so special.

We had to be obedient at home, especially to my father, a famous writer and a member of the French academy. Whenever he rolled his blue eyes at me, I thought that I was looking at the ocean right before the storm; he really scared me.

My mother, a brilliant pianist, graduated in classical music, sacrificed her talents for her children and her husband. She belonged to a generation that was happy to stay home and stand behind their man. I liked to see her radiant face beaming with joy; whenever my father was reading to her his daily literary manuscripts in his study.

I was very close to my mother, the pleasant smell of her perfume Courrège stays definitely attached to my childhood. I don't know if this fragrance is still available in the market.

Still waiting for my next patient to arrive, I looked outside the windows. The snowflakes were blowing and whirling slowly in the air. And since it snows rarely in Paris, I remained still for some time to watch when my buzzer sounded.

It was twenty minutes past three. The door swung open, revealing my new patient.

"Tatiana, I presume? I'm happy to meet you," I said, smiling.

"I'm happy to meet you too," she said, faintly smiling and looking coldly at me up and down, from head to foot.

We shook hands.

"Please, sit down," I said, motioning to the famous blue velvet armchair.

She dumped her mink coat sloppily on the couch, and walked slowly to her seat. She shot me a quick smile.

"I want to apologize for being late," she said regretfully.

I was struck by the image of this young woman, tall, slender, and exotic in vintage couture.

She placed her Kelly bag carelessly on the floor. And like a ballet dancer, the posture of her body bent forward horizontally, as she curled up in her seat.

I looked at her face with great attention. The lines of her face were smooth and her wavy strawberry blond hair drew an arabesque in the middle of her cheek.

For a moment, she sat quiet, dropping her eyes on the floor. When finally, she raised them and stared at me, I became aware of how really pretty she was, high cheekbones, full sculptured lips, arched eyebrows, and a perfect nose.

We exchanged glances, but said nothing.

This was Tatiana's first session of therapy. I could easily figure out by the frigid expression on her face that she suffered from deep depression.

Two months ago, she took a handful of sleeping pills and attempted suicide. The housekeeper, desperately upset, had found her, if not she would have been dead. Tatiana, who was mentally sick, has been seeing my colleague Doctor Luciano, the psychiatrist who has been trying to cure her with pills, with no result.

The drugs that Tatiana has been taking did not work the way he had hoped. He prescribed Zoloft, Prozac, and some other pharmaceutical poison. But what Tatiana really needed consisted in being under a very special protection, a moral support and a prolonged psychological care.

Moments passed in silence. It was a very awkward moment. Neither one of us moved or spoke.

Tatiana watched me anxiously.

I kept my eyes straight ahead. There was an uncomfortable silence. Now, she stared around the office with a certain air of loss.

I knew exactly how she was feeling, and she had the sense that I had a pain as well, and that maybe only because I might not be able to help her.

Encouraging my patients to talk is an extremely difficult and delicate task. I finally took the initiative and broke the silence, "I'm listening to you," I said as I cleared my throat.

She did not react, only a weak smile spread over her face.

I smiled at her.

She kept staring at me. She was uneasy and tense.

I looked at her deeply, and saw no particular expressions on her cold face, perhaps only austerity and sternness.

The heavy silence became embarrassing. Perhaps, she was still hesitating; should she speak or not? Her expressive eyes revealed her ineptitude to trust me. I thought my patience was about to crack, even though in my long experience, I knew that soon she would reveal herself fully to me and speak her mind.

"What am I supposed to say here? You should get fed up waiting", she finally whispered.

I listened to Tatiana's voice, an exhausted voice, and replied, "It's okay."

"How twisted and complicated we humans are!" she exclaimed.

I looked at her kindly; I could not understand what she really meant? What was she at?

Once again, the silence stretched on, and I thought that we were completely disconnected.

"Speak to me, I will help you. Trust me on that," I said with determination, raising a bit my voice.

Tatiana finally broke the long silence, "Well, I guess, I have no other choice but to believe you. You never know whom to trust?" she said loudly. Her voice was filled with pain. She did not look at me as she spoke.

Sitting in an attitude of deep meditation, I looked silently and kindly in her face.

"I'm afraid that I won't be able to. What should I say? Where should I start?"

"Talk about yourself. I'm here to help you, Tatiana. You have to want to get help, otherwise I can't assist you," I repeated, and as I promised her with a look of total confidence, I did not know what I was getting into.

"I heard you are spectacular, is that right?" she asked me seriously.

I did not respond. Our eyes locked.

"What is there to say about me?" she interrogated, as she shook her head hopelessly.

We remained in another silence for a short moment. Then, she tried on several occasions to speak, but could not. I felt that she was still having difficulty how to talk. Sure, she had her thoughts and feelings, but perhaps she could not put them into exact words. I waited.

After a little time, she said as she reddened, "What is there to enjoy in that? Listening to people's misery? It's not fun at all," her face became filled with anguish.

"Don't worry about me," I said smoothly.

"You are going to get bored, tell me how you do it? How do you really manage never to be bored?"

"I'm used to it," I answered shortly and smiled with my eyes.

"Being bored?" she exclaimed as she raised an eyebrow.

We stared at each other, she in confusion, and I in confidence.

Tatiana pondered for an instant in uncertainty, and looked in the space with a hopeless expression, and said, "Perhaps you should have said something," her face became pale.

"I do nothing, I just don't think about it. Tatiana, you should know that here, in this office, it's all about you, not me," I replied as I stared at her sad and beautiful green eyes with long and thick eyelashes. It seemed to me that an aura of melancholy was surrounding them.

Now, I felt that she was lost in thought. Then, Tatiana muttered some unclear words in a low tone, but I could not detect them. Her speech was anything more than scattered words. I looked closely at her pale face for a moment to see what she was trying to tell me, and I only saw that her lips were moving, but she made no sound.

Tatiana took a long time before she said, "The words hurt me and I hate them, do you understand?" she said repugnantly.

"Yes."

"Sometimes, some words sound harsh and meaningless," she stammered.

I simply nodded.

"Oh! I bet you will never understand me," she said furiously, raising her voice.

Tatiana fell into tears. I made no comment. Perhaps, she thought for a moment that she had been quite rude, she immediately said, "Sorry, I'm very sorry."

"It's okay; I perfectly understand your feelings, Tatiana. You should know that I'm here to help you," I said gently.

She shook her head and began to cry silently.

The silence returned.

I waited calmly.

Tatiana, who was greatly agitated, soon caught my eye, trying to speak to me, "And sometimes words are complex and multifaceted. For instance, in Sufi poetry, there is a multivalent correspondence between word and spectrum of thought. The poets such as Rumi, Attar, and Hafiz use ordinary words like song, wine, and sweetheart to evoke a vast network of poetic allusions. But what they really want to say is veiled in the mystic obscurity of the Sufi language," she looked at me respectfully; her eyes were cold.

At her words, my eyes expressed astonishment that I only could understand. I thought that Tatiana was a deep person, with deep thoughts. She's got more depth than all my other patients so far, didn't she? There was something more to her, wasn't there?

Impressed, I clearly was kind of surprised and staggered by Tatiana's knowledge.

She breathed deeply and continued as the tears stood in her eyes, "In fact, my relationship with words is much more complex because they can also be the source of misunderstandings. People interpret incorrectly my words and judge me very unfairly."

I lifted up my eyes from my notes, smiled, and said, "Tatiana, you should know that I'm not here to judge you."

After a moment's pause, she spoke with calmness, "I've kept my feelings to myself, because I could find no words to describe them. My words are plain and simple."

"I'm sure with your simple words, you can still express your real thoughts and feelings," I said with a loud voice to make sure she could hear it.

takes to make peace with my past. I want to find myself," she sounded very defensive.

"It will not be easy to run in the twisting labyrinth of your past, but I believe at the end, you will find your way out. You are only going to get better, Tatiana," I said decisively.

"May I ever be free from my suffering? If I could only get away from it!" she sighed.

"You have to determine your priority and decide what you want to analyze and discover about yourself. It will be a big job, Tatiana, you need to be very patient," I said.

As I spoke, Tatiana was softened in a moment. With a sudden movement, she bent forward and took out a picture from her bag, and placed it on the desk.

"I've got this picture to show you, if you don't mind."

"Let me see it," I exclaimed. I reached for the picture, and stared at it. Intrigued by how cool she could be now, I listened calmly.

Tatiana's expressions and gestures changed as she conjured the memories of her childhood, "In this picture, I was playing in the garden of my parent's house in Damour, a city coasting near Beirut. I was born to an extraordinary fate, and lived there until the civil war broke out and spread throughout the country," she told me with the greatest delight.

"It's a charming house," I said, as I kept looking at the picture.

After a short pause, the words popped out of Tatiana's mouth, "In 1980, at the time of the massacre, we had blackout nights when we pulled down our shades and turned down the lights in case an enemy plane flew over the city. I could hear the bombing and smell the smoke in the surroundings. They lastly bombed my neighborhood, and the entire region."

Tatiana fell into sudden silence. She looked down at the ground and said nothing, her eyes filled with hot tears. Then, she rapidly brushed them away with the back of her hand, and she resumed the conversation by saying, "My homeland demolished, knocked down and became a ruin. I don't like to think about it, you know."

"And what happened to your house? It's still there?" I asked her with great difficulty.

"Oh, they bombed it. I still can't sleep. I have to get up in the middle of the night and turn the lights on, and look up around me. I recall seeing people wandering the streets with no food, and bodies all over the place. Orphaned children were walking desperately around the city, looking for their parents. You can't imagine what it was like. We were hardly hit by the war. How could these things happen to us?" she sighed faintly.

Tatiana stopped and looked at me with an expression of deep thought and sadness. I made no comment. She kept looking at me with a questioning expression. I opened my mouth to speak even though there was nothing to be said, but Tatiana did not give me time to start my sentence.

"As a child, I was angry at the way that my destiny had rewarded me. One day, I sat in a park bench for hours, waiting for God to reveal himself so that I could talk to him. I thought that he might listen to me and give me an answer. I begged him for an answer, but I could not hear his voice. There was no sign of God, he never answered."

My lips were moving, but I made no sound. I remained quiet and let her talk.

"Do you believe in destiny?" she asked, as she put the picture back in her bag.

"Yes."

"What is most remarkable is that what we decide in life, and what the destiny decides for us," she smiled slightly.

"Yes," I repeated, and before I said another word, Tatiana interrupted me once again.

"How many times, I had to make important decisions in my life, but unexpected circumstances occurred and made it impossible to pursue what I needed to do. There is so much about my destiny that I can't control. Everything was written before I was born. Now, I realize how little I am in this extremely vast and gigantic universe!"

I nodded, and said nothing.

Tatiana's voice was perfectly calm as she resurrected her childhood in silence. A feeling of sadness swept through me. She looked at me seriously and continued, "The war had changed everyone's life. We didn't know how many people had died, but when I heard the numbers, I thought that my city was full of ghosts."

"I'm so terribly sorry that you had to go through all of that. But that's life, Tatiana. You have to accept, leave it behind and live it."

"You are amazing! You talk about it so well. It's easy when you say it," she exclaimed.

"It's all right now. The war seems very far away now," I told her, which was not, when I thought about it, the most comforting thing that I could say at this moment.

"Right," she simply articulated, as she shut her eyes and pushed on both temples.

A little later, Tatiana looked at me sadly, she sighed as she went on, "As sensitive as I was, this war implanted fear and terror in my delicate soul and my fragile body. Even today, after so many years, whenever I feel the insecurity in my life, I'm still seized with a great fear and convulse, feeling a violent and brutal movement in my frail body."

I looked at her with intensity. Once again, there was a silence for a couple of minutes. Now, Tatiana was speaking to me in quiet tone, as tears filled her eyes, "We decided to flee, to leave Damour, yet we could not believe that it was all real. I moved to Beirut, known as Paris of Middle East, with my mother, a very strong and extraordinary woman. We joined my grandparents, and six months later, we bought our little house."

I looked at her, listened to her words, and took a few critical notes. I did not ask her any further question. I just let her talk unreservedly, without interrupting her.

Tatiana's voice went on, "It was a cozy and charming house, especially in summer when geraniums cascaded from windows at the balcony. There was a small pond in the middle of the garden that reflected the sky, and in the center of it, a fountain making a melancholy sound. Each morning, the aroma of the coffee that my mother used to prepare woke me up."

We both looked up at the sky through the windows of my office; it was not snowing anymore. The late afternoon clouds had already begun to scatter. Tatiana glanced at her watch and after a quiet moment, she continued, her eyes continually swimming with tears, "For me, the hallucinations began after the bombardment in my homeland, on the day I should have died. I started having flashbacks, and I jumped at noises. I rarely slept and when I did, I dreamed of blood and body parts. My doctor diagnosed me with post-traumatic stress disorder, a condition characterized by flashbacks, and feelings of hopelessness, which sounded logical. I was only five years old."

Tatiana's voice was quiet, but sharp. She fell silent, staring at the ceiling. Shortly after, she clasped her hands on the desk, and laying her head on them, she burst into tears like a little girl crying.

I let her cry. I thought, it was good for her to cry.

"My nerves are on the rack. But frankly, I don't understand why suddenly I opened up like this? It's nonsense!" she said as she raised her voice, her green eyes shone bright.

"Why do you think it's nonsense?" I interrogated as I thought she might attack me again.

"Because everything seems to be foolish and futile in my life," she replied as she overstrained herself to a weak smile.

I listened to her attentively, stunned by the volubility and the metamorphosis of this beautiful young woman who talked sincerely. Sitting back with closed eyes, Tatiana tried to think of ways to speak her mind, "Sometimes, I'm so fed up with my words, especially when I describe my past."

"Like it or not, the past is always within you, even if you don't want to remember too much of it. We all have painful moments, it's therapeutic to face and understand them. You should change your attitude with words."

Judging from her face, I did not believe that she heard a thing.

"I often asked myself why God brought this war to us. Why?" she looked at me sadly.

"Tatiana, God doesn't bring the war," I said softly.

"So, who is responsible? This thought has often crossed my mind, you know."

"Men, the leaders, and the politicians are to be blamed. When the material side and the ego are very strong in men who have a certain power, they become greedy and selfish, then, they go to war."

"Right, it makes me rebellious when I see that all these Middle-Eastern countries, with all their natural resources, cultures, and old civilizations are unstable. As you know, the foreign dominators and leaders exploit them for their own ambitions and interests. It's so sad! Really sad and depressing! It makes me sick," she said.

I agreed and approved with a quick nod.

"The world is so corrupt and so unfair! What was the true lesson of the war in Vietnam, or the war in Afghanistan and Iraq? Why should billions and billions be spent on the War? War is a crime, isn't it? And yet, poor people are starving for daily food, and unknown artists are craving to be discovered. It makes me really sick when I think about it. I can't get over my fear of everything that is connected with war, such as shooting, machine-gun fire, and bombs. These are words that terrify me with horror," Tatiana expressed sadly with a face distorted by rage.

I felt that she could hardly get her last words out of her mouth. But to my surprise, she made a little effort and continued, "So whom can you trust? What can you believe? I'm having an identity crisis; I'm a lost soul. And I suppose this is what I unconsciously felt when I decided that I needed to see you in order to understand myself, and to find myself."

As time went on, Tatiana's speech began to falter, and she passed suddenly from one subject to another. She followed my gaze, pointing out at Celine's photograph.

"It's that your little girl? How old is she now?" she asked me; perhaps she wanted to change the subject of our conversation.

"Celine just turned seven in September. She is a sweet and happy little girl," I said.

"She has a kind face, exactly like you. She looks like you, and she is gorgeous," she said with a smile, leaning close to the picture.

"Perhaps," I said, thinking about it.

"You know, your natural look and your simplicity make me think of Sophie Marceau."

"Thank you."

"As I'm aging, I also look like my mother, more and more. I admit that she is a beautiful woman, but I just want to be me," she said thoughtfully, with a face as white as death.

"Is that a problem for you to look like your mother?" I inquired softly.

Breathing heavily, she looked confused, perhaps sad. Here, she stopped suddenly, and appeared to think that perhaps she talked too much. I was sure that she had something more on the tip of her tongue, but she said no more.

Tatiana got up from her seat and turned away to the window, and I could feel that she was shaking. Why? I wondered.

There was a pause, she searched for the words, "And darkness is stretching at the horizon; there won't be much time for answering your question. This is a very long story. I'll tell you all about it some other time."

"Okay."

The silence returned. She studied me with her eagle and warm eyes.

"Do you want to add something else?" I said, as I glanced at my watch.

"No, I better stop now, but I don't understand why I told you about all this? It's not important anymore. Thinking about my past is worse than physical pain."

"It's not important? Quite the contrary," I said, as I stopped taking notes.

"I mean it's an old story. When I think about my past, I become dizzy, as if from the top of a high-rise building, I look down on the street," she said, as she rose to her feet.

"I understand."

"By the way, everything that I'm telling you here is confidential," she said.

"Absolutely, you can rely on my discretion, Tatiana," I assured her.

"Thank you," she said, as she moved in a perfect rhythm, and slid into her mink coat. Then, she made an appointment for the following week, and turned away contentedly.

As I walked her to the door, Tatiana glanced around and said, "Your office is one of the most beautiful offices that I've seen. It has soul and character."

"Thank you."

"And I'm intoxicated by this unfamiliar scent; I bet it's your perfume."

I shook my head and smiled.

"You made a good impression on me. You seem calm, cool and open," she declared.

"Thank you, I'm very flattered, see you next time."

"See you next week, same day, same time. I promise I'll not be late," she uttered, slightly smiling.

A moment later, I heard the loud pounding on the door; Tatiana was out of my office. I was pleasantly surprised to find that my new patient was unbelievably smart and intelligent, but I had absolutely no idea that unlike all my other patients, Tatiana was going to become of crucial importance in my life.

I had no more patients after that. I entered the kitchen where Celine was drawing a picture of a beautiful house and a happy family: The father, the mother, children, and a little dog. When she saw me, she moved with quick steps toward me, and hung on my neck and said, "I love you mom."

"I love you more than anything in the world," I said.

She was charming with her blond curls, her blue eyes and her rosy cheeks. I spent the time until dinner in assisting with her homework and in reading the notes and the letters that had accumulated on my desk.

It was a quiet evening at home and I loved it.

FOUR

Over the ensuing days, as I worked in my office, I often found that I could not stop thinking about Tatiana. Sure, she made a good and unusual impression on me.

The weather was still dreadful. This morning, the raindrops pelted against the windows of my office. It did not stop raining until noon. Then, the heavy rain turned to snow, and suddenly around three o'clock, the weather broke. The dark clouds had rolled at the horizon, and the light became perfect, making the sky look almost clear.

My buzzer sounded. Tatiana's visit to my office took place that following Tuesday at three o'clock. I got up from my seat and let her in.

"Hi Tatiana, come on in," I said, smiling.

"Hi," she said, and she sat in her seat, her lips curling into a light smile.

She looked at me fondly, and I thought that she seemed pleased to see me. I sat down opposite of her. We both were silent for quite a time. And she did look glamorous, elegant, and even a little severe, in her skinny jeans cropped, and tailored black jacket.

However, in spite of her smiling face, I noticed an odd and funny expression, hard to describe. I desired to find out, trying to form an opinion about it.

"Is anything the matter with you?" I asked gently.

"No," she replied, making an effort to look cheerful.

Trying a new approach today, Tatiana was the first to express her thought; "Do I seem like the same person as I did the last time?" she turned to me with an anxious, fearful look.

She seemed genuinely curious to know the answer.

"Yes, you seem exactly the same," I replied, smiling.

"Good, I thought I wasn't," she said, as she let out a sigh and straightened her back.

"What makes you think like this?" I asked.

"I don't know. I'm afraid I'm becoming crazy. Am I chemically unbalanced?" she wondered, smiling bitterly.

"You shouldn't think of such negative things, you must opt a positive turn of mind."

"I know, but I can't help it, I'm constantly terrified," she said desperately.

The prevailing wisdom about her, both outside and inside was that in spite of her great wealth and her considerable beauty; she was incredibly down-to-earth.

She pondered in silence, looking at me sympathetically, without saying anything more.

This was a terrible time for her. Two months ago, she had almost died, and now she was stuck having to face life again.

We looked at each other for a moment in silence. Tatiana forced herself to keep a straight face, resting her elbow on the desk. I felt now distinctly that she had nothing to tell me. Sure, she would like to say something, but she looked unsure about what to say.

"Sorry, I'm a little nervous."

"Now, tell me what are you up to?" I tried to be very casual.

"Everything is just the same. How do you want me to stay calm when I have to deal with all kinds of problems in my life? I'm in real pain, do you understand?" she looked at me nervously.

I looked at her and remained silent. I saw perceptibly that she was truly unhappy inside.

"Do you really understand?" she repeated, stressing each word.

"Of course I understand. Whatever is your problem, I can help you," I said steadfastly.

"I believe that no one can help me," she said with conviction, looking around the office.

The silence returned and lasted for a few seconds; an uncomfortable silence.

I serenely waited; trying to analyze her expressions. I noticed that Tatiana, looking over at me and biting nervously her lips, was introverted, timid, and very reticent about her life.

"You must understand that I'm here to help you, not to judge you," I said kindly.

She did not react. The silence grew.

Casting around for some subject to talk about, she said in a quiet voice, "Sorry, I don't know what to say to you. I'm surprised to realize that it's not easy to speak at all."

"You must not be so nervous with me. You can say anything."

"Anything?" she interrogated; her eyes filled with wonder as she gazed at me.

"Yes, anything that comes into your mind. Please talk to me. You are a brave woman."

"I just can't think of anything, not even a single thing," she said desperately.

"Just tell me the first thing that pops into your head," I said insistently.

A frail smile played on her lips, and she tried to find a subject of conversation. She pondered for a while and suddenly a thought came to her. She said, "Three colors that would describe me the most, are the black and the white, the obscurity and the clarity, the light and the shadow. I also like the blue since it's linked symbolically to the sky, heaven and water. I believe that blue is the warmest color," her voice sounded weary and tired as she spoke.

I nodded silently.

"What are your favorite colors?" she asked me.

"Same."

"Really!"

"Yes."

She blinked. We glanced at one another. A look of hesitation came back into her face. Tatiana stared at me suspiciously.

"Why do you look surprised?" I asked, smiling.

"Never mind; colors make everything look different; they are a means of guidance."

"You are right."

She did not answer my question. I knew that whatever she might say to me, she would not say all that she had in her mind. Tatiana sighed, and some kind of sadness came over her. I felt that in the depth of her soul something very important had to be put in its place.

"Are you all right?"

"Yes, I'm fine, just fine," she said apathetically.

But I realized that she was far from what she said. I put myself together and uttered, "You don't look yourself, Tatiana. Now, tell me, what's going on in your life?"

We had another moment of quietness.

"Don't you think I'm better off not talking about my negative experiences?"

"Are you afraid of facing them?"

"No. Yes. I don't know," she answered indifferently.

"If you want to move past the unpleasant events in your past, you have to look back as if you look at yourself in the mirror. You will not only accept them, but also you will have the opportunity to gain the power to understand them with a new attitude."

Now, there was a long silence, I found her quite uncertain. It was hard to know what she had in her mind at that moment. I waited calmly, and a little later, she stopped hesitating.

A look of fear crossed her face, but she immediately took control of the situation and said, "My memories of the past just began to haunt me, memories of my childhood and my love for my father, the only true love that I've ever known," she uttered with a trembling voice.

"Yes."

Now, Tatiana's face was calm, her expression stern, but her smile very sweet. I did not react; everything seemed to be under control. Tatiana went on after a short moment of pause, "My education began at the laique French school in Beirut. I was a shy, introverted child. Even now, by nature, I'm not a talkative person. I just get tired of talking. But whenever I start talking, I talk too much and far too long," she said, smiling with an air of great innocence.

I smiled too.

"I remember being in the first grade and my mother telling me that my teacher repeatedly reported to her that it seemed as if I were always off, preoccupied, unfocused, and distracted. But every time she called on me, I had the right answer. I could not pay attention by focusing like this, listening was unbearable. My mother worried for me because she didn't understand me. She had always wanted me to be someone else, and she considered me a difficult, rebellious and a different child compared to my classmates. Nobody could really understand me and my feelings."

Tatiana looked at me sadly. I put my pen down, and instantly became suspicious. I asked, "Did something abnormal happen between you two?"

"No," she mumbled almost inaudibly as her face turned white.

I smiled with relief and elation. But deep down, I fully understood how hurt she was. I felt her body was shaking; I could not say anything else in opposition to her.

"Do you really want to know about all this?" she asked.

"No, if you don't want to," I said coolly.

"It's funny to talk about myself this way. Okay, as I said, academically, I was smart and intelligent, but I couldn't concentrate. Instead, I took a great deal of time reading serious books, and saw movies. Pleasantly, I could get lost in a movie. There were days that I stayed in my room and barely moved, and no one could understand that I was able to live in my own world."

"Yes."

"I lived in my head, and would wander into my imaginary world. It was a safe place to be, you understand?"

"Yes."

Tatiana stopped; her face took on an expression of sadness. Then after a short moment, she closed her eyes. She pretended to be asleep. I thought that she would continue to talk after a few moments of silence. There was nothing to be done; I had no choice but to wait.

I waited tranquilly; there was such full silence. I raised my eyes from my notes and looked through the windows. A ray of sunshine appeared momentarily between the tall trees of avenue Foche.

Moments later, Tatiana opened her eyes and turned towards me and muttered, "I'm emotionally and psychologically distressed. I'm a slave of painful memories. I'm flawed, since I struggled with my choices in my life and I made mistakes. You should know that I'm the painful incarnation of my own mistakes. Sometimes, I wish I just could forget all of my errors and start my life fresh again."

I narrowed my eyes on her and said, "I'm sorry! Nobody wants to make mistakes and some are worse than others. But one thing is for sure; we won't make the same mistake a second time once we learned a lesson."

In spite of this pessimistic and despairing conversation, Tatiana's expression softened.

"Yes, you are absolutely right," she said, shaking her head, after a deep silence.

"Now that you are aware of your past mistakes, Tatiana, you should avoid them in the present and the future. And if you are conscious of them, you should be able to change your ways of life."

She nodded.

The silence returned, and underneath of all this deathly silence, I felt that Tatiana was very bright, quick, sharp, smart, and even beyond that. She long waited for an opportunity to break this silence between us that seemed to be a little easier now.

"But you should know that I'm not always responsible for all of those mistakes. It's Tina who is brainless and does stupid things," she said apprehensively.

At this moment, I stared at her, not comprehending her for a very short lapse of time, but next I understood, "Tina?" I asked tenderly.

"Never mind, well, here is a thing," she said in a sudden panicky tone, but then, she said nothing. She blushed, with a puzzled expression.

We remained silent; both of us looked at the windows, and gazed at the changing sky. A sudden violent noise of thunderstorm shook the air and flashes of lightening broke crossways. A heavy rain began to pour down.

"Your secret is safe with me, Tatiana," I assured her.

"It's guaranteed?"

"I promise."

"Speaking of Tina, I don't like her. She hurts me, you can't imagine how often I've tried to push her away, but it never worked," she said innocently.

"Yes, I understand," I expressed sadly in a low tone.

Again we were both silent. After a brief pause, Tatiana went on, "Since my childhood, my imagination never stopped wandering beyond me and the world that surrounded me. Consequently, I've played a series of characters according to different circumstances of my life."

"You mean fictitious characters?" I asked warily.

"Half fiction, and half real; but you should know that Tina is not a character, she is real and she lives within me. She drives me nuts."

"Yes,"

"I liked to play characters since I could barely stand the reality of my life. My life is insupportable! I always dreamed of a different life. I think I was born naturally as an actress, but unfortunately God, the most famous director of Hollywood at all times, tragically granted me only sad parts to play," Tatiana said, with an ironical smile, her eyes flashing malignantly.

I listened attentively, taking notes with more details. I did not say a word.

Tatiana fell in a morose silence.

Dead silence. We both listened at the drops of rain that were streaming down the windows; strange feeling. She moved slightly in her seat and leaned back. I felt that she was having trouble breathing. Then, she quietly burst into tears, hiding her face into her hands. I advised her to relax for some time, and for a moment she did so.

Moments later, Tatiana inhaled deeply and said in a low voice, "Sorry, it's never easy for me to talk about all this. It's more difficult than I thought."

"It's okay. I think you are doing a great job. Calm down! What you need to do is just to relax, and be yourself," I advised her.

"How do you want me to be myself? What are you talking about? You don't understand that I can never be myself. In fact, I'm here because I'm determined with your help to expose myself nude, to lay bare my heart. I want to avoid lies and to elude artifices. You know, I always took refuge in lying, most of the time without any good reason."

"Yes. I'll help you to get away from all your tricky behaviors and actions," I said.

"I want to be free of everything that tormented me in the past. I want to make peace with myself, and the most important of all, I want to be myself. Who am I really? Am I Tatiana? Tatina? Tina? As you can see, I'm a terrible mess," Tatiana had gradually raised her voice; she could not control herself. Her voice echoed in the silence as tears trickled down her cheeks, she wiped them away angrily.

Outside, the rain kept falling. Tatiana seemed so sad and miserable that I did pity her.

"We will work on that. It's very important that you are willing to improve your life and move on," I told her nicely.

"Yes. In my desperate and unhappy life, I played characters. It seems to be funny, but I painfully carry these women with me and I'm confused. When I approach a character, I'm always looking for how we are similar. But I'm trying, now, with your help to protect that tiny space of me that's not the character."

"Okay."

"But I'm not sure how I can find myself just by talking to you? I've never been used to sharing my problems and my thoughts with anyone," she uttered sadly.

"Very often, there is some hidden meaning behind your words," I said carefully.

Tatiana looked into my face, surprised. Her eyes flitted around the office, and she seemed to be preoccupied with other things. My mind began to wander, but for the first time I thought she seemed to make herself very clear. I was pleased.

I stopped taking notes. Since Tatiana described to me the shades of her mind, I took this opportunity to talk to her expressively and openly of the situation. I turned to her, "Transparency is crucial in therapy. Being transparent means that you allow the light to pass through you, so that the thoughts and feelings inside you can be seen clearly and the truth easily perceived. You can't cheat yourself and you can't lie to me," I exclaimed seriously.

"I'm not sure that I can understand you," she clearly did not believe what she said.

"Tatiana, if you open your heart and your mind; you can uplift and transform your life. These sessions of talk therapies require you to be completely honest with yourself, and that can be difficult."

"What do you mean?"

"I mean that you have to face to your fears and worries, recalling distressing and painful memories and talking about your intimate thoughts and private life. Am I clear?"

"Yes, but it would be impossible to describe what I truly feel," she objected.

"Impossible is not French! I believe that everything is possible if you want to."

She shook her head silently.

"I'm not sure if I can ever get there. I'm mentally weak and I don't have the will power. My mind is deranged and unbalanced. I think I've been lying so much that darkness overtook me. I'm unable to be transparent, I can hardly see the light and I can't allow it to pass through me. And for this reason, I think people can't see me without obstacle. I'm not easily understood in society, because I'm unable to reveal the real truth. I never took my life seriously; I believe that this absurd life can never be accomplished successfully. It's a failure, and I'm a failure," her voice was vibrating with fear and emotion.

I listened to her words with attention and continued to write down more observations.

Tatiana fell silent. Sitting back in her chair, she was in a state of great anxiety. She slowly wiped away the sweat on her forehead, and pondered with a bitter smile. Her pale face betrayed bewilderment and pain.

"It's not to be wondered at, that I'm mentally and physically ill. You have no idea what it's like. An unknown voice sobs constantly within me, "look at you; nobody likes you and cares about you, you are not interesting as a person; and all because you don't open yourself up, you are not honest, and you never speak the truth." Oh! I would love to be honest, outgoing, get social and make friends, but it never worked for me, and I know why it does not work."

Tatiana stopped talking. I got this opportunity to ask her, "And why do you think it's not working?"

"I personally don't want to put up with people in general, because nobody understands me. They always misinterpret my thoughts, my feelings and the most important of all my words. They make me terribly worried."

"Okay. But if you try to be less reserved by showing your real feelings, people will have a different approach with you," I said firmly.

"I'm dreadfully afraid of being ridiculous," she said coldly, scanning me.

"Your fear comes from your insecurity, you should have self-confidence. Look at you, Tatiana, you are young, so pretty and intelligent!" I said cautiously.

I saw the coldness of her eyes, and as I studied her expression, I could tell that she did not hear a thing. I put down my pen, and turned to her, "It doesn't surprise me that you can't see the light. You manipulated so much the reality of your life that everything is disordered in your mind.

But don't worry, with patience and determination, everything is attainable with enough hard work once you find yourself and you understand your true objective in life. Tatiana, you are going to have to work on this, it will be difficult but not impossible," I said quite sternly.

"I'm afraid that I don't have that kind of strength for it. It's so hard for me to be myself. I vainly made such an effort to be what she wanted. Tatina is sincere, honest, open and straightforward, not me!"

She was afraid of continuing, and said no more on the subject. The words froze on Tatiana's lips. There was fear and terror in her voice; I could feel it by far.

At this point, I understood perfectly the gravity and the magnitude of the situation. It was such a bitter reality, but I thought that despite her psychological and emotional state, Tatiana maintained an amazing strong character.

"It's not only a question of strength, but also a question of time. You need to be patient, and you have to keep thinking positively for a life of harmony and fulfillment."

"Okay," she simply said as she exhaled fully.

"Don't forget that you can overcome negativity and bring out the unlimited potential within you for getting away from your pain and agony. Tatiana, you are strong and you have to arm yourself and be patient."

"Okay, but it will be difficult when I'm so troubled by all these injustices of the universe. I'm disgusted by the corruption, the lack of morale, and the deep difference between the social classes. The more I know of the world, the more I'm convinced that I shall never be happy."

"You can practice spiritual exercises to overcome your negative and destructive thoughts."

"Really! All this is factually new and original to me," she said gently as she nodded. She became quiet, and then she added, "I admit it, I admit everything you are telling me, and I know that there are many things in my life that I will never be able to forget."

Now, the sound of falling raindrops broke the silence of my office. Tatiana and I stared at each other mutely.

"The air smells incredible here, it's a very special fragrance!" she said, smiling.

I probably could have said something to her statement, but did not. Instead, fixing my eyes on my watch, I said, "It's time, we must stop now."

Suddenly, she got up and went to peer through the window overlooking the street.

"I love the clouds, the clouds that move silently up there. My time is up; I got such an awful headache anyway. I'll see you next week. Actually, I have to say next year."

"Merry Christmas and happy New Year," I said as I escorted her to the door.

"Merry Christmas to you too; you know, I've got so much that I want to share with you."

"It sounds good!"

"All my life, I was desperately in need of a confidante. I swear; I'm not making it up."

"I believe you."

"I need some air; it's hot in here. It's almost the beginning of the New Year, and who knows what the next year will bring to us. 2015 is meaningful to me," Tatiana said as she walked out the door.

"Poor soul," I thought, as soon as she was gone.

As usual, this session lasted forty-five minutes. I was tired, it had been a quite long day after all, and this last session was particularly tense and difficult. I was glad it was over.

I walked in Celine's room. She talked to me about what she had done that day in school. She had many friends, but she did not have a best friend. She felt very isolated in her own way. But at the end of the day, I guess she knew that she was still mummy's girl.

FIVE

JANUARY 2015

Blue skies stretched to the horizon. The sunlight woke me a few minutes after dawn. It had rained all night, and as the clouds were dispersing across the sky, the sun appeared. I tried to go back to sleep, but I found it impossible. I wondered how many more years I could continue to work like this.

After I practiced my yoga, I walked into the kitchen where mademoiselle Solange had already prepared the breakfast. I sat down at the kitchen table with her and as I drank my coffee, we chatted for a few minutes.

Having finished reading my morning paper and my second cup of coffee, I began making plans for my day, hoping for a nice weather.

This particular day could have passed like others, but as soon as I turned on the TV to listen to the news, I was horrified by much of what I watched. I heard the headlines, and caught the name of Charlie, Charlie magazine.

The Charlie Hebdo shooting was a terrorist attack, which occurred in Paris on that day, January 7, at about 11:30 in the morning local time. It began with a massacre at the offices of satirical magazine Charlie Hebdo; that had published controversial Muhammad cartoons.

A few minutes later, the president François Holland addressed a speech about this mass shooting. Like everyone else, I was paralyzed with grief of what had happened, and I shared the same state of depression and shock. My stomach lightened and I was nauseous at the back of my throat.

I listened helplessly to this tragedy and knew immediately that this was the topic story that would captivate everyone's attention all over the world.

Quickly everything took a different view, and a few hours later, people's voices "I'm Charlie" rose across the world. I desperately wished that France would be transformed for the better, for the freedom of speech that belonged to its great land.

It was three o'clock, when Tatiana entered the office. I instantaneously noticed that she looked different. I did not know whether she looked good or bad, but just different. Her hair was not as wavy as it was at the previous sessions, but it was still strawberry blonde. She had no make-up on, her eyes were larger and rounder and her nose more pronounced. In fact, I had never observed any of these before.

She wore a loose black jacket over a neglected long skirt, and she carried a big bag. Tatiana failed to take proper care of her appearance that day. Definitely, I thought that there was something really weird and creepy going on with her.

While she sat down, she breathed in deeply and said, "This morning I woke up in a state of great agitation. Did you hear what's happened?" she said in a low but distinct voice.

"Yes."

"It's terrible. What a world we live in? The whole fucking world is completely upside down. I only wish I could live in a better and healthier world," Tatiana said angrily.

I shook my head.

"I don't want to live in this chaotic fucking world any longer," she said as she frowned in disappointment.

"I understand your feelings, but what can we do? We have to live it and make the best of it. Don't feel burdened by the world, Tatiana," I advised her.

"You must be joking! How can I live in peace? It's crazy out there," she said, yelling.

"Meditation, it brings you serenity and tranquility," I said as I smiled at her.

"Do you believe in God?" she asked.

"Yes."

"Can you see him? Where is he?"

"He is here, he is in me, he is in you, and he is everywhere. You can turn to God at any time, and the more you give your love to him, the more you will feel him," I said.

Tatiana paused, staring at me. She remained silent; and seemed to be convinced by the sincerity of my words for a little time. Then brusquely, she raised her voice; "There is no justice in this fucking world. There has never been anything as horrible as this terrorist attack."

"Come on Tatiana, you survived a war!"

"That's true," she gave me a fond smile.

"It's important to face life with confidence and radiance," I reminded her.

"Okay, but the truth behind all events and actions is dirty, unfair, dishonorable, and vile. Don't you agree with me?"

"Tatiana, the world can't be a reasonable and honorable place, unless and until you begin to work towards peace and harmony," I said with assurance.

"And how would that be possible? How would that work?" she asked peculiarly.

"By removing hate and revulsion from your heart," I told her.

At this point, Tatiana did not seem to know what to say, she changed the subject and wished to talk of something else, "Do you mind if I look out your window?"

She walked to the window, crossed her arms and stared at the view. Was she pretending not to hear me? Was she trying to ignore me?

There was a long and strange pause, and in that awkward moment of silence, I felt Tatiana's pain. She was a fragile soul, I reminded myself.

"The world is unquestionably a more peaceful place without the Isis," she murmured.

"Sure, you are hundred percent right, and I do agree with you."

"It's a wonderful view, with the street lined with chestnut trees," she forced herself to say. She looked very preoccupied and pensive.

I looked helplessly out the window, and did not say a word. For a short time, I remained deep in thought.

At this moment, she gave me a fond smile, as she started walking backwards and forwards across the office, pausing for a short moment whenever she came to the window, "Never in my life, have I found it so difficult to stay calm as at this moment." Another pause succeeded, tears started from her eyes, then, she added in a low voice, "The sun is out, we shall have a beautiful afternoon," she murmured.

"Yes, the weather is remarkably nice," I said with pleasure.

Tatiana sat in silence, wrapped in her own thoughts. Looking in my eyes, she asked curiously, "Do you mind if I ask you a personal question?'

"It depends," I said as I narrowed my eyes.

"Don't worry! It's not about your love life," she said humorously.

"As you know, Tatiana, we are here to talk about you, only you. You are important, not me," I reminded her nicely as I emphasized on "you."

"I understand perfectly your point, and you will think that my question is an odd one, I dare say," she said as she laughed happily.

"What is it about?" I asked intriguingly.

"I can smell the pleasant aroma of your perfume all over your office as soon as I walk in here. I'm just curious; it's a very unusual and extraordinary fragrance, what is this?"

"Quelques Fleurs," I said.

"Quelques Fleurs!" she exclaimed, after a pause of wonder.

"Never heard of it?"

"Never," Tatiana said surprisingly.

"Sure, it's a very special perfume."

"Who makes it?"

"Houbigant," I said.

"I've been thinking a lot about how to ask you this question," she said as she looked enthusiastically at me.

"It's okay, don't worry."

"Yes, the scent of your fragrance perfumes the air all around us, and it's so feminine."

There was now a small glittering silence. This session went on in the most relaxed ambiance. Now, Tatiana started focusing on herself. I supposed that it was not easy for her to switch from this general conversation to what she knew she had to talk about.

"It's hard to remember the details of my past. It's especially tough for me to talk and describe people who have played an important role in my life; it's difficult, you know," she pronounced, and looked straight at me.

I shook my head, but did not say anything back.

"I'm much better connected with you than I've been with anybody else in the world."

"You have to be faithful to your words, Tatiana."

"Yes, magic words! I would love to have a friend like you. I've never had any friends, and believe it or not, my words are not empty," she said in a broken voice, staring at me.

I listened to her without saying a word. But Tatiana waited impatiently for a response. Actually, she waited long enough to know about my opinion.

I was filled with an extraordinary sense of confusion of thoughts. What would I say to her? Without any doubt, some kind of human warmth bound us together.

She waited a moment, and when I said nothing, she seemed disappointed. Tatiana cleared her throat and said, "No comment? Nothing?" she was biting her nails.

"Definitely," I replied quietly.

She seemed to read my thoughts, "Definitely what?"

"Definitely we are friends, Tatiana."

She smiled.

A few more minutes went by like this, then, she initiated a discussion. The subject that she started was running more or less about the same topic as on the previous session. Like all my other patients, Tatiana kept repeating herself over and over. Of course, I preferred not to cut short this conversation. I listened to her with great consideration and kindness, as long as she would be encouraged and stimulated to speak her mind. Revealing her deepest thoughts and feelings to me was definitely the essential key of this kind of therapy.

She stirred in her seat, shifting her pose and said, "Last night, I looked in the mirror, and said to myself, "You have to tell the truth," and that's what I'm trying to do now, tell you the truth. I know it's not going to be easy, but I made up my mind.

"I remember when I was twelve years old, I dreamed of attending one day the college and to study psychology in order to understand the origin and the nature of my issues. But I found it impossible, since I've been prone to depression. Even very young, I always felt that slowly my destiny was driving me to death. I constantly felt myself dying, but miraculously and unfortunately I survived."

"Yes," I alleged, taking my notes.

"I lived so very near to death, and I'm still alive!" Tatiana exclaimed.

After a very short break, she concentrated rigorously and said, "After the war, I began having flashbacks. I jumped at noises and I rarely slept, and when I did, I dreamed of blood and body parts. I've been having the same horrible nightmare since I left my homeland."

Tatiana's voice was filled with sadness. When she stopped, we stared at each other for a long time. Then something changed suddenly. Tatiana tried to articulate the words properly as she went on, "Have you ever read "Le bateau ivre?" "The Tipsy boat?""

"You mean the poem by Rimbaud?"

"Yes."

"And what is it about?" I said inquisitively.

"Well, I always desired to live my life like this tipsy boat. I want to take risks and go from one place to another without a settled route, itinerary or destination."

As she paused for a moment, I looked at her with a questioning expression, and then I went straight to the point, looking in her eyes, "Wandering about aimlessly? Tatiana, you wanted to study psychology, right? That could be a goal in your life."

She glanced at her watch and became quiet, finding no connection in her ideas. I thought that she was not at ease any longer.

There was a dead silence for a couple of minutes. Tatiana remained perfectly silent, looking at me with anxiety and worry.

I waited calmly.

She looked scary as she changed the tone of her voice, "See, you don't understand! You are not getting my point. It was Tina who wanted to study psychology, not me. I always dreamed of being "The tipsy boat." I was the one who had the spirit of adventure, not Tina."

I pitied her from the bottom of my heart, and I wanted to do all in my power to give her consolation, and peace of mind. But before I kept my mouth shut, I just said, "Sorry."

I felt that Tatiana hated to disappoint me, but she was clearly conscious that she had to speak the truth. At this moment, she turned her head away as she mumbled some incomprehensible and incoherent words. Next, she looked at me out of the corner of her eyes. I distinctly saw that her face turned pale with some inner pain.

I could not hear what she was trying to tell me, "Please speak louder what you want to say," I said softly.

Brutal and angry, she almost shouted out, "I admire Antoine De Saint-Exupéry, the author of the "Little Prince" who was a pilot and no stranger to fantastic voyages and adventures. The first time, he crashed in the Sahara and lived very near to death, but he survived. Years later, he took off from an airbase in Corsica and was never seen again." Tatiana looked at me, but her eyes seemed not to see me, "It was a noble death," she murmured, her eyes darkened with sadness.

I nodded silently.

While I focused on my notes, Tatiana was talking fast with a very particular, meticulous and expressive intonation, "You entirely misinterpreted what I said. There is this other woman who lives inside me and I'm afraid of her. Her name is Tina, and she is mean to me. You should know that I'm not that woman; there is no hatred in my heart," she said as tears stood in her eyes.

I studied deliberately the expressions on Tatiana's face, and saw nothing but sadness, anxiety, heartbreaking memories of the past, and apprehension of the future. All these terrible feelings reflected in her persona. I still did not say a word.

"I see that I'm frightening you, are you scared? Now, your turn to tell me the truth," she said in a melancholic tone.

"No dear," I said with an expression of serenity.

I wondered either she was a great actress or she was still in a state of critical and severe psychosis. It was hard to tell. It was important to stay neutral and observe different changes in her behavior and words that were inconsistent. I certainly could not come to the conclusion and take a quick action immediately.

I gazed at her pitifully.

Tatiana closed her eyes; she seemed to be tired. When she opened her eyes, she mumbled, "I'm locked in my own head and I don't stop worrying, do you understand?"

"Yes dear."

"The pain inhabits my every cell, and my anguish is poignant and worst of all, I have to bear it in solitude. I can't share it with anyone, not even my husband. It's a very painful situation."

"Why don't you share your feelings with your husband?" I asked.

"I don't want to tell him because he would never understand all the depth of my suffering."

"Are you sure about it?"

"Yes, and don't give me that look, please. I know what you are thinking."

"You can express to him your state of mind without telling him the details. I'm sure he will take your words in consideration once you share your thoughts with him."

"I prefer not, not now anyway."

"Okay."

At that instant, Tatiana started to cry very quietly, "Sorry," she said, looking inconsolable, "Fuck it," she uttered, wiping away her tears and forcing herself to stop. She made an enormous effort to stay calm. When she had recovered a bit, she explained, "Now, I realize that in some profound phase there are loads of things that I haven't actually dealt with. I've never really had a therapy before. Looking back on my childhood and my adolescence, perhaps I have been able to explore all these things that I buried within me, and that a great therapist would have made me deal with. I'm a great actress and I'm doing a very good job at covering it up. But when I'm allowed to indulge like I'm now, then this stuff does come out. It feels nice to be able to talk about my thoughts and feelings now," Tatiana assumed without looking at me, she sounded very sincere.

"You have to keep your commitment to these sessions. It's crucial that you confront your life honestly," I said, lowering my head. It hurt me to look at her anguished eyes.

"I will, even though I find it extremely difficult to show my emotions and feelings."

Now, Tatiana became quiet, lost in her own thoughts. She glanced one more time at her watch and said, "How slow the time is going today. I know I still have a few more minutes left. If you don't mind, I leave you now. I have to take a walk, and I need to take a deep breath, so my body can relax. Do you mind?" she articulated formally, and suddenly she got to her feet.

"It's okay," I said and I assured her that I would be available for her calls if she needed, "Whenever you worry about anything, just pick up the phone, day or night. You have my cell phone number, right?"

"Yes, thank you. You seem to be deeply concerned, I appreciate that," she said as she gave me a mysterious smile.

Moments later, Tatiana moved away without looking at me. I watched her go. Left alone, I got up from my seat, and began pacing up and down my office. Although I always tried to remain professional in my job, I felt profoundly sad regarding my new patient. I thought that Tatiana was a very special and extraordinary woman, out of the ordinary if not unique.

How would she be able to overcome the trauma lasting upon her? Surely, treating her with the greatest kindness and allowing her to speak freely about her intimate personal history, I certainly would help her to set the thoughts clear in her mind. It was imperatively vital that Tatiana grasp mentally that I did care for her, and she was under special protection.

However, to my long experience, the talk therapy would not prevent the chronic postponed phases such as visions, nightmares, and the regression within oneself. It would be indispensable for the patient to have a debriefing under the care of health professionals in order to take care of the scars of the soul. It was necessary that Tatiana felt secure in an environment with especially lots of love. She had to be surrounded by people who loved her truly, so that she would not feel rejected or abandoned.

Six

It was a gray rainy day. The sky was covered with clouds. In the fogs, I could hardly see the nearby buildings through the windows of my office.

It's interesting to see how life runs in full circles. I believed that I had my life totally under control in my work as well as my private life. In spite of my frail appearance, my patients think that I am as tough and firm as a crystal rock. I have to admit that partly it is true, but largely it is so wrong.

Frankly, when I get up each morning, I don't have at all the impression of being hard as a rock. I just perform something that I like to do, something that makes me really happy. My marriage with Christian helped me in a large extent to reconstruct myself. We had met at a party through mutual friends; it was such a romantic encounter! Two months later, we went to Tahiti for two weeks. Once back to Paris, we got married. Since then, we lived together side by side, enjoying each other with a profound love and a mutual respect. He had a different way of looking at life, and everything about him seemed so special and unique to me. He brought me serenity in life, and he allowed me to gravitate towards the intellectual sphere.

Christian's shadow was still there, and his remnants still lingered untouched in every corner of my home and at any time. He had eyes only for me and meeting him; it was like meeting someone out of my dreams. I knew that kind of love occurred only once in a lifetime. Therefore, I never expected to find that great passion with anyone else. Christian was the only man that I have ever loved, the only man that I ever wanted to love. I still missed his beautiful smile, the melodious sound of his voice and his brilliant mind. Alas, he left me too soon.

Sitting back in the seat of my office, I looked out at the sky, it was getting dark slowly. My four o'clock patient had still not arrived. The phone rang, I looked at the number flashing on the screen; it was Alexander.

"Hi love,"

"Hi."

"Is your time up with your patients?" he gently asked.

"Not yet, I'm still waiting for my last patient to arrive," I said.

"Maybe I could meet you early this evening for a drink."

"It sounds good."

He blew kisses down the phone, and I hung up. We agreed to meet for a drink at a bar nearby in avenue Victor Hugo. Now, it was five minutes past four, and my patient was still not here. Alexander's phone call brought me right back to the very first time when I met him at a fundraising benefit. My mind drifted back, and I believed that I had enough time to think about it before my patient's appearance.

⁕

Since Christian's death, I started to explore what my future might be without my husband who devoted his life as an ambassador to UNICEF. He was compassionate, and as a humanitarian, he had great gratitude and trust for what UNICEF does and what it means to children. Consequently for the same reason, I decided to make a deal with the universe and to follow in Christian's footsteps. I became devoted to helping the poor and innocent children, and to create a better world for all those who will one day take our place. Truly, the dream is that we should allow them to live decently, by offering them shelter, work, and accommodation to acquire knowledge.

For me, a happy soul and an inner peace come from performing estimable acts, helping those in need. When we all go to bed at night and turn in, it's just our conscience and us. Nothing else really matters; I like to sleep well, knowing that I have tried to make a difference in children's life in the undeveloped countries. By offering them the support, the security and cultural activities, we give them a deserving place in the heart of society.

It had been already six months since Christian's disappearance, I had made it this far, hadn't I? September 2014 merged into October, and I had not had yet any serious date. Sure, time does heal the grief, and I knew that one day I would get through this painful and depressing period.

It was the first week of October or so, when the wheel of fate turned and I found myself in a different direction.

The heavy and humid heat of summer was all gone, the air felt different in fall, it was lighter and crisper. The late afternoon sunlight filtered through orange and yellow leaves of the trees. The moon hanged low on the horizon and the fall breeze carried the nostalgic smell of chestnuts. Paris came back to normal life, Parisians returned home from their vacations.

On that breezy evening of October 2014, among the small crowd of hand-selected guests from all over the Europe, I slipped into a taxi, and made my way to the restaurant Bagatelle, where a private event promised to serve the particular common interest of children who suffered abuse, maltreatment, and abandonment with special needs. This sophisticated gathering was also meant to raise funds in order to promote the work of UNICEF.

I arrived at Bagatelle later than the other guests. Candles flickered in the darkness. As I stepped down the stairs to the reception room jammed with guests, I looked at the crowd and did not recognize as many people as I thought I would.

I remember what I felt when Alexander looked in my direction. When I watched him moving his eyes on me, it stirred something amazing within me. It was flattering and I just let myself go. I did not look away.

He wore a blue shirt that tended to flatter and reflect his blue eyes. He also wore leather black jacket over his shoulders, and this casualness gave him a theatrical air. But it did not matter, since his code had a style.

As he walked towards me, I had no idea of what I would say to him. My gaze was still on him as he approached with a glass of champagne in his hand. When he was near enough, he said, "I'm glad to meet you."

Did he already know me? I wondered.

"And you are?" I inquired. I was the most probably the only one in the room who did not know who he was.

"Alexander Lacroix," he said, as a smile of pleasure lighted up his face.

He was a big name. He was not especially good-looking, but he had a certain class, charm and elegance.

When I extended my hand to shake his, he took it in both his hands and held it for a moment. Alexander had his eyes locked on me. As he stared, a sensation of joy and delight filled my whole body, Jesus, I felt so good! We both felt a spark pass between us.

"Alexander Lacroix?" I thought about it, and I wondered why did this name sound so familiar? But then, I knew. I remembered the reviews were all tremendously positive since his prospects and work projects seemed to be promising, clever, and brilliant.

He was a major producer-director who had won several academy awards. He was in the press constantly; his films were sold all over the world, making him famous and well known. Wherever he went, he was pursued by reporters and journalists.

Tall with wide shoulders, he seemed to be eccentric, unconventional, and intelligent enough to catch my eye. And oh yes, he looked also sexy, very sexy. I found his Parisian accent of the upper classes very appealing. Alexander seemed to know everyone who was somebody. Everything about this man intrigued me.

When the chairman of the fundraiser commenced his speech, "I'm privileged to witness the integration of the new members to this foundation and the strength that this association brings to our great country. This is a grand opportunity for us to send our peaceful message to the world and…."

I heard the hysterical applause from the audience. Despite the chaos of the crowd, Alexander and I managed somehow to find a quiet corner where we could talk calmly. Almost everyone there looked in our direction, since we had to withdraw from the circle.

"Here, let's sit down," he said.

We sat at a cocktail table. Waiters in white coats glided around with trays of mini sandwiches. We toasted, and a lively conversation began which was interesting to both of us. We discussed every imaginable subject. Since he was smart and very cultivated, we were drawn to each other precisely because we shared so much in common.

"I heard a lot about you, I'm delighted to hear of your successful career," he said, staring appraisingly at me.

Our faces were so close that I could feel the heat of him. Obviously, such an opinion coming from him was agreeable to me.

"Thank you."

"Maybe I should keep you humble and not to tell you," Alexander said, smiling.

There was a spark of humor in his eyes. I could not remain indifferent to the compliment. As I finished my glass of sparkling champagne, I asked with interest and no preamble whatsoever, "Married?'

He was amazed that I had the nerve to ask him a personal question. He frowned as if the question was too tough. "You guess!" he said.

"I don't know. I asked you a simple question; you can give me a simple answer."

"I'm free and happy, but why this question?"

"I'm not interested in married men," I replied softly.

"I'm free," he repeated, and slowly he emptied his glass of champagne.

A waiter passed by with a tray of drinks, and Alexander leaned over and took one.

"Free?" I said, piercing him with my eyes.

"And happy," he repeated, laughing only with his eyes.

Then, he moved smoothly so close to me that our faces were almost touching.

"We should hang out some time. When shall we meet? May I have your contact information? I really would like to get to know you," he said with a sweet smile.

I was charmed by his direct approach. He spoke to me warmly in a friendly way, and took my hand in both of his and held it for a long time as he spoke.

"Okay, here is my cell phone number."

"Let's dine together next week. Are you free on Friday evening?'

Moments passed in stillness; I enjoyed his attention. Did I really know what I was getting into?

"Stop thinking, be happy," he said in an informal and conceited manner.

"Yes, I think so. I have nothing very particular that night," I answered after a short pause, not thinking of what I was saying. Sure, I found him very attractive and at that moment, I believe that I only hoped for a physical relationship.

51

The evening ended; Alexander escorted me home. He asked me if I would like to see him again.

"I don't know," I replied teasingly. When I left him that evening, I had no doubt that I wanted to spend my free time with him. Perhaps when I met him again, I would not find him very interesting. But what if I did? Then what? I was not sure if it would be wise to invite him into my life to get over the loss of Christian. I also thought that this was my moment only to look for some kind of tranquility, not adventure.

Despite my confusion, I began to see him. The following week, on Friday evening, I arrived at the restaurant "La Société" at nine o'clock. It had been Carla Bruni's favorite restaurant and everyone else's since.

I had done my hair, put on some light make up, and dressed with excitement, wrapping a silk purple scarf around my neck. Looking in the mirror scrupulously, I was satisfied with myself.

I saw Alexander at the bar waiting for me. I had not been this excited about anyone since my husband's death. When he saw me walk in, he caught my eye, waved me over to the bar and smiled.

"Delighted to see you, I'm very happy that you have come," he said, staring at me with a significant air.

Minutes later, we were comfortably seated. We began with fresh oysters. The waiter uncorked the bottle and poured the sparkling fruity wine into the glasses. The restaurant was filled with appetizing aromas. The conversation flowed with ease over a nice relaxed dinner.

We both genuinely liked one another, and Alexander flirted excessively. Ours fingers intertwined as we talked about our favorite books, movies, and the latest exhibitions. We both had the feeling that something between us had already been speaking for years.

"So, how is life treating you, Amanda?"

I told him about my husband's death, my daughter, and my work. He listened carefully.

"Are all your patients crazy?" he asked, laughing.

"Don't laugh, please. They are not crazy, they are lost souls," I said seriously.

"And how do you cure them?"

"It depends; every person's therapy is different. But generally speaking, I talk to them about spiritual life, meditation, and what they can do, so that their lives become meaningful," I said.

"Are you religious?" he asked.

"Religious? No, not at all, I'm spiritual. Now let's talk about you. Are you dealing with crazy actors? I'm sure, they are more fun," I commented as I laughed.

"Yes, most of them are full of themselves. They have big egos."

"Narcissism! But I guess there is nothing as exciting as making a movie," I exclaimed.

Alexander nodded, smiling. And for a while, he remained motionless, watching people.

The stars were blurring through the windows, the wine bottle was empty, and I was feeling warm and comfortable. Alexander put his arms around me, drew me closer to him and gave me a long and searing kiss.

The evening passed smoothly. It was past midnight as we wandered through his apartment located on the busy street of Faubourg Saint- Honoré.

"This is our love nest where our bodies twine and connect together," he said as he pulled me in his arms and kissed me passionately. I pressed myself against him and started kissing him fervently.

"May I get you something to drink?"

"A glass of wine would be nice," I said.

Warmed up by the wine we had drunk, we kept kissing. I instantly felt his tongue moving round inside my mouth. He knew that I loved his way of kissing. Everything about that moment was just breathtaking, so wonderful.

Alexander started to unbutton his shirt; I took off my dress. He unhooked my bra skillfully; he had a sublime touch. Then, he pulled me in his arms, kissing my lips, my hair and my neck. And before I knew it, I found myself in his king size bed. As he rolled on top of me; I sensed the heat of his body; his chest was firm and so were his arms.

"It's too dark here," I whispered.

"So?"

"I can't make love in the dark," I said.

"It's okay," he said, and he switched on the lamps on his bedside table, as he laughed.

I laughed too.

"Sure, it's more exciting, is it okay now?" he murmured after a short moment.

"It's much better, but what I really like is the light of candles," I whispered.

"Next time, I promise," Alexander said tenderly.

We made mad and crazy love to each other. There was never a pause to take a breath. We knew too well that we could not stop; we should not stop. I guess we must have desired each other equally. We squeezed each other's hands and smiled between kisses. Alexander liked my body, and I liked his. We were both free spirits and we had an amazing sexual chemistry.

As he was inside me, he looked into my eyes, and whispered: "Amanda, you are so hot!"

"You too," I whispered.

Sex with Alexander was entirely new and special; I had never had an experience like this with any man in my life. I felt that I was like a drug to him as he moaned exquisitely, when he came in me for the third time that night.

"Now, you are mine," he said, his voice was warm and soft.

We lay for some time in ecstasy, trying to slow our breathing. It was as though we were in seventh heaven. Alexander smelled curiously the scent of my perfume wrapped around my body, my neck and my hair. I heard the magical sound of his voice murmuring sweet and wild words, "I would never think it could be like this between us. What perfume are you wearing? It makes me crazy," he said, looking at me with concern.

"Quelques Fleurs," I whispered.

"It's a delicious smell."

"Thank you."

"I've never heard of it."

I nodded against his chest.

"It's phenomenal! I had never been so happy with any woman in my life before. Sure, there is something magical about all this. What is this, Amanda?" he said, as he buried his face in my hair.

Needless to say, there is something quite chemical that happens when people meet and are attracted to each other, and scent is most probably part of that. On a more personal level, smell is extremely important when it comes to attraction between two people. Research has shown that our body smell; can help us subconsciously choose our partners.

I thought the smell of my perfume captured Alexander's feelings. He felt wonderful as he discovered a new powerful aroma that night; I believe it was seduction.

I did not know what was happening to me? Was it love or sex? But whatever it was, I never wanted it to end. I stayed with him for a long time that night.

"I would like to see you again," he said as he pushed my hair out of my eyes.

"Do you want to see me again? I thought it was all about a one night stand," I said teasingly.

"You are so very well experienced, Amanda."

I smiled.

"Please, spend the night with me," he begged.

"Stay with you! It can't be," I declared.

Alexander wished I could stay with him and get up in the morning under one roof. But it was impossible since my daughter liked having me to herself with no man around to share with.

"I don't want you to go! I want to be able to turn my head on the pillow and speak to you."

"I have to go," I said seriously.

While I was getting dressed, Alexander demanded gently my scarf.

"Why? Tell me why on earth you want my scarf?"

"It holds your scent, Amanda. I want to keep your smell for eternity."

"It sounds good," I said as I laughed.

The traffic was light. It was three o'clock in the morning when he dropped me off in front of my apartment building.

"Would you like to see me again?" he asked, holding his breath.

I hesitated for a while, "Yes, I would," I said as a final point.

"Amanda, it was the most exciting night of my life," he said with enthusiasm.

In my room, I undressed and walked immediately in the bathroom, and treated myself in the luxurious bubble bathtub. At this moment, I could feel my husband in the silent space.

Minutes later, I went to Celine's room to check on her. Thinking that she was sleeping, I adjusted the blanket, bent down and kissed her on the forehead. To my surprise, her eyes popped open in the darkness. She put her arms around me, laughed, and pulled me very close, "I love you mom," she whispered, and kissed me sleepily. In a moment, she closed her eyes and was fast asleep.

I felt so deeply happy. This love that I was feeling for my daughter was the deepest love that I could have imagined.

When I had this flashback on Alexander's first encounter, I glanced at my watch, it was twenty minutes past four, and my patient still had not appeared. I heard mademoiselle Solange's voice as she stepped in my office, "Your patient just called and canceled her appointment for today. Apparently she ran out of gas and got stuck in the traffic. She is not coming."

I heard the door gently close behind her. Minutes later, I saw her standing in my office doorway.

"Would you like something to drink?" she whispered calmly.

"No."

She was a serious and responsible assistant, and my relationship with her was so special. I also thought that she was a beautiful woman with a nice figure and her blond hair, often tied back in a bun.

"You look pensive."

"I don't know. Yes, maybe you are right, I'm deeply thoughtful," I said.

SEVEN

It was snowing outside and the temperature dropped considerably. I stood by the window of my office; looking out at the flakes of snow spread out all around, it was magical.

I thought that my relationship with Alexander worked perfectly for me. I liked being in control of my own life; he did not monopolize my existence. I could count on seeing him one or two times a week, and I still had enough time for my work and my daughter. It was exactly what I wanted, an open relationship. However, it may have seemed like any other normal relationship to some people, but to me, I was simply in great company.

From the beginning of our liaison, I told him that besides my daughter, my work was my top priority, a fact that would not change whether I wore my engagement ring or not. For me, the most important thing in life is being passionate about what I do. Most people spend a lifetime searching for what they want to do with their lives. So I feel very lucky; I don't live my life in regret. I don't look back and think that I should have done this or I should have done that. It is very important to know that my choices in life had been the right one.

Two weeks after I met Alexander, whereas our relationship had commenced, he looked into my eyes and said, "Amanda, you are my type of woman, and what we have together is just perfect."

"What do you mean exactly?"

"You know what I mean; you have such an innate simplicity of taste that makes you so different from other women."

"Is that a compliment?"

"Sure, you are fiercely independent and you have charisma; this is what you can't learn in any school," he said in a tone of affection.

There was a lot about me that he liked. I was a serious and intelligent woman with a booming career and highly respected, and there was nothing arrogant about me. In spite of my successful career and even the books I had written, I was very humble, and he liked that about me.

Alexander and I were both comfortable with the way that things worked out. He respected me, and my daughter adored him. The first time when he came over to dine with us, he was holding a single red long-stemmed rose. He said hello to Celine and smiled. He gallantly gave her the rose and said, "Celine, I'm very happy to meet you, I've heard wonderful things about you, and your mother loves you very much."

Celine was instantly fascinated; she smiled back, thanking him.

In my cold manner way, I loved Alexander. It might not be the kind of love that people in general understand, but that did not matter to us. What we shared together was good enough for both of us.

It was freezing in Paris. The traffic was crazy as horns sounded continuously. I glanced at my watch; I still had a few minutes before three o'clock. I picked up the phone and checked my messages, then quickly returned two or three calls.

Shortly after, my phone started ringing. I looked at the screen, it was Alexander. I let it go to my voice mail since the door flew open and Tatiana stepped in my office.

Once she was seated, she made a frail smile and gave me the impression of being agitated and perturbed. She wore an elegant black dress with white polka dots, a white beret and matching gloves. She had utterly different outlook, an unusual approach and attitude that day.

There was a pause that seemed to go on forever. What was up with her? I wondered. The silence grew heavy, almost unbearable. God, she looked terrible now. I decided to break this stony silence, "How was your week?"

"Nothing exciting," she said.

"You okay?"

She suddenly became vigilant, ready to talk, "No, on my way to your office, I stopped at Starbucks to buy my cup of coffee. While I waited on the line, my phone rang. It was my cousin calling me from Chicago. I spoke Arabic spontaneously, and I immediately observed that people were looking at me in an odd way. What was wrong? After all, I chose neither my life nor the country of my birth, my religion or even my sex."

Suddenly a strange feeling stirred within me. I felt bad and in spite of myself, my feelings showed on my face.

Tatiana looked lovingly at me and asked why I acted so sad. I thought a moment, then I said, "I don't know," and I kept my head down. I was perfectly aware that professionally, I should not cause any kind of discomfort and confusion. I did my best to maintain as low as profile as I could, but she read the thoughts in my face and gave me a sad smile.

I sighed and said nothing.

Tatiana's face remained expressionless for several moments. She wrapped her arms tight against her chest and went on, "I don't like my life and I can't change it. If I had the power to write the script of my destiny, certainly it would be different. But unfortunately, I'm not the one who decides it. I'm only an unknown actress playing my part in this fucking world."

"Yes," I simply said, not wanting to interrupt her.

Tatiana paused shortly before she continued, "These sessions of therapy are a lot harder than I thought there were going to be. They allow me to travel to some faraway place. Sometimes, I'm melancholic but most of the time, I'm very sad, so sad that I become disoriented in my current life."

"I understand."

"Now, I feel that I'm getting completely lost in my past, since I'm diving deeply into it," she said as she stared at the ground.

"Maybe you need to get lost in order to renew your life and find yourself," I exclaimed.

"But therapy just by talking and talking isn't a waste of time?" Tatiana's lips hardly formed the words.

"The talk therapy focuses on the unconscious aspects of your personality, and your words determine your emotions and behavior," I said.

"Just talk and talk...?"

"Talking about your thoughts and feelings can help you deal with moments of your life when you felt troubled, anxious and worried. If you turn a pain over and over in your mind, the pain can grow and develop in your fragile soul. You have to take care of it, and talking about it can help you to search and explore what really is bothering you, so that you figure out what you could do about it."

"But my words have no meaning!" Tatiana said; her tone was troubled.

"How could such a thought occur to you? Your words have a great meaning, Tatiana."

Silence fell upon us once more. We exchanged a little smile, staring at each other.

"I don't know what's gotten into me?" she said, wiping her tears. "I'm sorry, I can't help it," she added, with a choke in her voice, trying to make me believe that she was drained.

She closed her eyes just for a moment and muttered, "I feel so much safer this way."

I lay back, breathed, lifted my eyes to her face and studied her for a few seconds.

There was a long stretch of uncomfortable silence between us. Tatiana flushed and tried to force a smile, "My words have meanings, but they are ugly," her face grew serious.

I frowned at her words, trying to make her understand that it was incorrect to speak like this, "Tatiana, my dear, you have to understand that you need support during your emotional breakdown. You have to try to be positive and patient. Let patience be your key word."

Before I had a chance to utter another word, she pushed her chair back, moved her lips but no words came out. Tatiana had withdrawn into sullen silence. Then, a little later, she said, "Why my life does feel so empty? I feel that my whole life has stopped. Slowly I got into this profound hole and it looks like I'm never going to be able to get out of it. I'm desperate, and I believe that everything the therapists are supposed to practice with their patients, it's not working, that it's bullshit."

"Well, I don't know about your issues yet," I said as I looked at her with compassion.

"Do you really think that I can overcome my pain if I tell you my historical origins?" Tatiana asked nervously.

"Yes, you have to be willing to look at the situation honestly. In this mechanism the truth may be distorted, your attitude is everything. It's very important to talk about your childhood and adolescence; because that is usually where the problems exist and continue to live."

"There is plenty of work to do. How long does it take the whole process?" she asked.

"It takes time, sometimes it takes years in psychotherapy to dig around the trauma and start to get to it. Tatiana, we have to get to the source of your problems," I said.

"It's difficult for me to show my real feelings. People think that I'm strange, mysterious and distant, but I'm not. The truth is that I don't know how to communicate; I don't know how to connect. They start by looking at you, then they study you and they end up judging you," Tatiana had inclined her head, and in the midst of her conversation, she happened to glance at me, giving me a look of anger and fury.

Her eyes filled with tears, she could find nothing more to say. Now, she was crying convulsively and dabbing her eyes with a little handkerchief.

"You should know that I'm not here to judge you," I declared.

"I'm dull and boring, and I would talk only of the weather or food to people, I mean banal and uninteresting conversation. I envy people who can express their emotions."

"I know what you mean, but now you are open and sincere!" I said, smiling.

Moments later, glancing at me continually, she manifested openly her thought, "you know what, and sometimes I like to go with my mood. Right now, I'm in bad temper and I don't want to talk to you," the words came low; her throat was dry. She was on her guard.

"It's okay, don't worry," I said.

It seemed as if she carried a great turmoil in her mind, she could not think at all, "I'm feeling restless. It's really okay if I leave you now?" she asked without looking at me.

"Yes."

She looked at her watch and her face lit up, "it's about time, I better go now. When I'm feeling blue, I like to walk along the Seine," she said as she stretched out her arms.

We exchanged a little forced smile. What could I do or say? I could not force her to stay.

"You okay now? Just go home and get some rest, it's the right thing to do," I said.

"You are right, I'm not feeling well and I should go home. You know, I hate to be morbid, but I'm sad at heart because I want things to make sense in my life, but nothing looks or feels right. Do you understand? This is what it's all about," she said with a melancholic tone.

"Try not to be sad," I just collected myself to say something positive.

"I'll try."

Moving slowly, she went out of the door without a word. I watched her go. I hoped that she would recover her sense of balance. It must have been something extraordinary obnoxious that could make her leave so suddenly. I wondered what it could be.

Tatiana haunted me with her pain for the rest of the day. As these sessions of therapy went by, I learned that she was intensely vulnerable, emotionally unbalanced, moody, and exceedingly passionate and difficult. Subject to melancholy, she was enduring and sensing distress and pain. Tatiana suffered deeply from a mental disorder marked by feelings of dejection. Capable of great kindness, she never found in life what she wanted, what she desired.

EIGHT

It was Tuesday, fifteen minutes past three and Tatiana was not here yet. She was expected at three o'clock, but still it was no sign of her.

"Call her," I told mademoiselle Solange.

"I keep calling her, but she is not answering," she said with a calm face.

"Did you leave her a message?"

"Yes, of course," she replied.

I picked up the phone to call Alexander, but as soon as I dialed the first two numbers, I had to put down the receiver. Tatiana appeared; the door burst open and she stumbled in.

"Sorry for being late, I just can't help it," she said; her voice sounded exhausted.

She had pulled her long hair back and twisted it in a knot; she looked pale.

An absolute silence fell between us.

"One thing puzzled me last time," I said to her, looking thoughtfully at her.

"What?"

"You left so suddenly."

"Yes, almost escaped. I escaped my shame about some serious stuff," she blushed.

"Okay, but that wasn't how I felt," I said casually.

"I'm really sorry; I've spent a lot of time trying to understand why I behaved like this?"

"What is that?" I asked.

Tatiana stared at me for a moment, and then said, "This is going to sound strange, you will think I'm crazy."

"I would never think of that."

"I confess that my conscience twinges constantly all the time, and I'm ashamed to admit it. I escaped carrying painfully my shame with me," she said with a note of sadness in her voice.

Tatiana's smile disappeared; she lightly shifted in her seat and shrugged. It took her some time to find the words, "In life, there are scars that as leprosy injure and damage your soul. They are so painful and they can hurt you drastically. However, you can't discuss these unpleasant scars to anyone, because people are accustomed to associate them to strange events. And if someone makes an effort to describe to them the nature of these disagreeable scars, they pretend to understand with a questionable and an ironic smile. But the truth is that nobody understands. Oh well! I don't know what I'm saying anymore. Today, I'm drugged and drowsy, I feel that I'm empty-headed and my tongue doesn't belong to me anymore," the words came out fast but she spoke slowly, trying to stay calm.

I turned my full attention to her and followed her words closely, taking a few notes. I had to take those words seriously; they seemed to have a great importance. In fact, these were Tatiana's coincidental words pronounced distinctly and correctly that gradually revealed her whole story over the following sessions.

"I'm wondering if my words could possibly have meaning for you or they are only a mix-up of confused and strange sounds?" she frowned.

"On the contrary, your words are precise, deep and meaningful," I articulated softly.

Then, I looked at her straight in the eyes and said sympathetically, "When the pain hurts your soul which is the most delicate part of you, Tatiana, you have to take care of it. Should it be otherwise, it can cause you severe injuries, mentally and physically," I said, pencil in hand.

Tatiana looked greatly disturbed and uneasy. I got the impression that she totally lost control of the situation. Without any doubt, she humiliated herself at what she had said, and that, I thought, exasperated her all the more.

We remained together in silence. For the next several minutes, Tatiana looked very severe and said nothing, not even a word escaped her mouth.

I continued to take a few notes, and then I turned back towards her. I caught her still staring at me. Her eyes were all over me.

"Please, talk to me about your own scars, Tatiana."

She smiled bitterly and pretended not to hear me, turning her head to the wall on purpose.

"I want you to talk to me about your own scars..." I repeated seriously.

Tatiana cut me off, waving her hands in the air. She said in a humorous tone, "What about my scars?" And she began mimicking me. I supposed she did it to be funny, but she annoyed me.

I stayed cool and tried not to lose my self-control and my temper. She leaped to her feet and walked to the window. Tatiana stood there, and looked back at me. Her face was pale and motionless; she was reduced to silence.

"I want you to talk to me about these issues seriously. It's very important that you take care of your scars," I said in a gentle voice as I sneaked a look at her. This statement could not have been any more honest on my part. It was essential to get know the origin and the nature of her problems. I absolutely needed to know.

Tatiana sat down, sighed and blinked her eyes rapidly, but made no comment.

I looked into her frightful eyes.

She looked at me appalled; her face contracted.

The silence felt heavy and painful.

Not knowing what to do or what to say, I waited patiently. I certainly was not going to become enraged at her.

When finally Tatiana decided to speak again, the color of her face changed as well as her voice, "It always scares me that I will become insane and end my life in a psychiatric hospital," she said in a trembling voice. The tears that she could hardly hold back flowed slowly down her cheeks.

"Tatiana, you should not think of such a thing. This will never happen," I secured her.

"What is the point of living? Life is too painful," she said with a wobbling voice.

"Life is a remarkable and wonderful gift," I affirmed, smiling lightly.

I believed that Tatiana was so distracted and preoccupied by her own thoughts, and so emotionally and mentally unstable that she was not listening to me any longer.

"I can't describe to you what my feelings are; I'm in denial about myself and my existence. Why should I live longer when I don't attach any importance to my life? I live under the shadow of death," she said as she sobbed, covering her face with her hands.

I let her sob.

"Am I going to go crazy?" she said as she lay back and closed her eyes, smiling resentfully.

"Oh, for heaven's sake, Tatiana, what are you saying? No, of course you are not!"

"I'm seriously discouraged, I feel I'm getting nowhere," she said, raising her voice.

"With this attitude, you are not going to make anything better. Lots of people at some point in their life feel darkness around them, but they can find their way back again."

Tatiana looked directly in my eyes without being able to make a connection. She was still pale; all the muscles of her face began literally to tremble. I looked at her, dazzled.

"I have a lot of questions about your scars," I repeated firmly.

"Unfortunately, I don't have any answer for you. My words can be only the source of misunderstanding," she said, as her tears would not stop.

"Okay."

"I know deep in my bones that my future is hopeless," she said in a shaky little voice.

"You must be tired; you don't realize what you are saying. Let's be calm and then, we will have to work on all of your scars," I said calmly.

Suddenly, she pulled back, as if she were afraid of me. Her eyes avoided mine; she looked perplexed and confused. I waited for her to react somehow, and I felt that with great effort, she finally concentrated on what I had just said.

"Do I look mysterious? Sometimes, I look in the mirror and I don't recognize myself," she said as she made a funny face. Then, she rose and I was afraid that she was about to leave too.

"Won't you sit down?"

Tatiana made a small noise; she muttered a few incoherent words that I was unable to hear properly. Obviously she was very nervous, and she did not know what to do. What was it that made her so nervous in my presence? What was she hiding?

"There is nothing so terrible that can't be said, my dear," I reassured her.

Tatiana returned carefully to her seat and glanced at me with a loving smile. This time, I saw the kindest smile that I had ever seen from her. I knew what she was going to say.

"You have no idea how important you are to me. You want me to talk to you about my scars? These scars are part of me. Will I not appear to you to be deliberately perverse?" You know, I decided never to look back at my past, there is really nothing to be proud of!" she said as she wiped away her tears, and blew her nose.

Sure, I was delighted with the praise that she addressed to me, and I understood perfectly how difficult it was for her to make real contact with me. As time went on, and as these few sessions ran more or less smoothly, I also noticed how well she knew to twist and manipulate the words to hide her deepest secret. After all, she was an actress, wasn't she?

"Talk therapy is not just talking about your problems; it is also working towards solutions. Tatiana, it will be helpful if you would only talk about your wounds and scars."

"It will be helpful…" Once again, she started about making droll face and she could not help mimicking me again. She thought it was really funny, and burst out laughing.

I looked straight in front of me; I could hardly hold back my laughter. Tatiana turned her eyes towards my face; she felt worried and a little ashamed. She moved on quickly to general topics then, mostly about her compassion for animals, and her great passion for books and movies.

When I raised my eyes after taking a few notes, I read Tatiana's thoughts from the expression of her face. I focused on the unconscious aspects of her personality to determine her emotions, feelings and behavior.

"You have a very kind face, and I totally trust you now. But I'm not really sure if it's a good idea to talk about my past, I better bury it. Don't you think so?"

"You can bury your past, but that will hold you back in life," I said assertively.

"Can I change my past? Can I heal my scars?" Tatiana asked desperately.

"You can't change your past, but you can look at it with different eyes," I replied sharply.

"How could I possibly change my attitude regarding my past?" she asked.

I looked directly in her eyes and said, "Please talk to me, it will help to talk. When you uncover the negative patterns in your life, you will not only learn how to move on in your life, but also we can accelerate the therapeutic process once we collect enough information."

She nodded, and plunged deeply into a reverie that lasted for a long time. As usual, I waited calmly. I found that she was unable to talk; instead she only stared at me. I was deeply touched by Tatiana's unhappiness, and I wanted to do my best to make the situation better.

"Don't you want to improve your life? There is another way of looking at your past. You can look at it from a different perspective. I'm serious, Tatiana, and I'm talking here about a major change."

She paused, deep in thought.

"Think it over, then," I said sternly.

"Do you really think that you can heal my scars? You know, they are profound and old; they grew with me and they are a part of who I am. I believe that I can never burst my bond with them. This rupture may cause an explosion in my system and is dangerous. I can never rip apart from my scars, do you understand? Besides, you know only a fragment about my past, don't you? I cannot go any further, sorry," her face was white with fear and worry.

She became quiet.

After a pause of a couple of minutes, I broke the silence to comfort her, "There must be no secrets among friends," I said in a low and sweet voice.

Now, Tatiana became more thoughtful and silent than she had been before. Gradually, a bit of color returned to her cheeks as she exclaimed, "I want to talk to you about my past even though the thought of it is horrifying. But I'm awfully tired now, that will be for the next session, okay?"

"It's okay."

"And I have a terrible headache," she said, trying to convince me why she needed to go home at this very instant.

"Just go home and get some rest."

"I will, see you next week, same day and same time."

Minutes later, Tatiana left the office with a smile of satisfaction and contentment.

Left alone, I sat a long while in complete quietude. I thought Tatiana's case would not be easy. She was keeping a very important part of her life secret and she was not still inclined to let me into it. I tried not to think, but she intrigued me. She had been hanging round here for some considerable time now. However from my long experience, I knew that soon the real words would be revealed. It was only a question of time and I had to wait.

I sent my email to doctor Luciano, explaining psychologically the condition of the patient as an exceptionally intelligent woman with a brilliant mind who had the capacity of controlling perfectly the situation. I insisted about what was to be done medically in order to maintain the balance of the nerves.

I took a moment to see Celine as soon as I let myself in the main house. I was so overtaken by fatigue that I had to lie down immediately. I stretched on my bed, almost chocked by sadness. Tatiana left me alone with my thoughts. Though I admired her strength. To me, there never seemed to be any spontaneity especially with her words. I thought whenever she spoke to me, she had already planned her words perfectly. My head was spinning and I felt I was going to burst, I definitely needed some air.

Moments later, I tiptoed into the kitchen to find mademoiselle Solange cooking the dinner. She was an amazing woman, I thought. Strong and independent, she always fulfilled her life as a woman.

"I'm just going out for an hour," I said.

"Dinner will be ready then."

"Okay," I said tiredly.

"Are you okay?" she asked me worriedly.

I said nothing; obviously I was unable to. I knew too well what had gotten into me.

"Don't worry! Next week, Tatiana will be a different person with different character. By the way, have you heard the story of chameleon that can change color according to its surroundings?" mademoiselle Solange said, trying to comfort me as usual.

"What about it?"

"The chameleon turns red on the red carpet, it turns green on the green carpet, and it turns yellow on the yellow carpet, and so on. It's unpredictable and frequently inconsistent and variable, never stable," she said, amused.

"You are absolutely right, and I have no doubt about it."

NINE

In the following days, I could not help thinking about Tatiana. I wondered either she was a great actress or she was still in a state of critical and severe psychosis. It was hard to tell. It was important to stay neutral for the time being, and only observe the different changes in her behavior and words that were inconsistent and contradictory. I could not come to any conclusion and take action straight away.

The next session with Tatiana was kind of a challenge. It was Tuesday, and in spite of the low temperature, the sun was bright. At three o'clock sharp, the door of my office made a sudden sharp explosive sound, as she opened the door and walked hurriedly in.

I thought she had a beautiful figure in her ripped jeans and a simple black pull. Her hair tied back in a bun; she looked absolutely gorgeous, but again different in so many respects.

Tatiana was the first to speak, "It's really cold out there, the sun is shining bright but it's freezing," she said as she collapsed in her seat.

"Your cheeks are pink from the cold," I said, smiling lightly.

"I know! I should have stayed home, but I feel that I have become addicted to these sessions. Before I had nobody to talk to, and now I have you," she said with joy.

I smiled.

"Since I started my therapy with you, every Tuesday at two o'clock, I start getting excited. The more my watch gains each minute, the more I feel happy," she said gladly.

Shortly after a brief silence, she knew that it was essential to talk; she began to speak fast about irrelevant things. Staring at her with the eyes wide open, I listened assiduously. When she stopped talking, we were

70

engulfed in a total silence, watching the sky through the windows. I did not want to take the initiative to say anything whatsoever.

The silence lasted for at least two minutes.

I waited.

"Sometimes I sit down in my room and think about my past, but ironically I find myself in an empty space, my mind goes blank."

"Yes," I confirmed.

"And some other times, I'm painfully haunted by echoes of my childhood and adolescence, it's driving me crazy. For instance last night, I couldn't stay home, so I walked out into the street. It was eleven o'clock; it was dark, cold and quiet by this time in my neighborhood. You know, I wasn't scared, I walked and walked, I would escape myself forever because I could not stand myself."

I remained silent.

"I lied a lot; I was the biggest liar that my mother had ever known. But you should know that I wasn't responsible for all these lies because every time that I tried to tell the truth, I got severely punished."

I listened to her with attention, and nodded silently.

"But she was a terrible mother too; she would never take my words seriously whenever I was telling her the truth."

"Yes."

"For the most part, I took care of myself as a child. My mother was a strong character, she was very smart and intelligent, but in spite of her terrific capacity, she did not know how to compromise," Tatiana stopped talking for a moment. She could hardly breathe.

"I was so happy when she took me to the movies and theaters. I recall seeing "En attendant Godot" by Beckett, and Faust when I was only ten years old," she went on.

"Hmm!"

"What is your favorite word?" she asked me all of a sudden.

I waited for a moment; it was an unpredictable question! And then I said, "Love," the first word that came to my mind.

"It's a beautiful word, love is the very essence of the soul," she said with sorrow in her voice.

"What is your favorite word?" I asked curiously.

"Forgiveness," she exclaimed promptly with sadness, in a tearful voice.

Tatiana's word came very fast; she did not have to think to answer that question. I thought about it, and I sensed that one of the keys of the locked door in her life was there.

"It's such a kind and comforting word, isn't it?" she added with conviction.

"Absolutely," I said with certainty.

A dead silence fell between us; we both kept looking in each other's eyes profoundly.

"I admit that what I did would be neither forgiven nor forgotten," Tatiana said sadly.

The church bells began to ring. She suddenly changed her mind; rose rapidly from her seat and walked towards the large French windows. Deeply wrapped in her own thoughts, she contemplated the street with admiration.

"I still think that Paris is the most beautiful city in the world; it looks like a museum," she said pensively, and stayed motionless for a few moments.

"I totally do agree with you."

Minutes later, Tatiana started walking hastily up and down the office. I watched her and said nothing. I felt that she was uneasy and anxious. Was she going to leave me now? I wondered. But to my surprise, she began to talk in a low tone, "You need a big heart for love, but a boundless golden heart for forgiveness," she said gloomily as she sat down disconsolately. The tears came and she could not hold them back.

"Yes, perhaps this word might be the key to unlock one of the closed doors in your past," I said cautiously.

"Now, wandering in the strange and terrifying labyrinth of my past, I speak words which I buried deep within my heart for a very long time," she confessed, "How odd, indeed!" she murmured within herself.

I took my pen and nodded silently to approve her comment.

"Now, I want to face myself in a way that I never did before," she declared decisively.

"It's very impressive; it's a courageous decision to make. I'm pleased at your strength."

"Thank you."

"Yes, I can only help you if you want to face yourself in the mirror," I said softly.

"So much happened in my life; I played different roles and pretended to be at one time Tina, and at other times Tatina. My soul fell apart in pieces, and I'm a lost soul. Now with your help, I'm trying to put these parts together into a whole. I want to free myself from the ghosts of my past and to give a sense to my life," Tatiana said as she dried her tears.

"Okay, I compliment you on your decision," I said, articulating every single letter.

"There is so much to tell, it's hard to begin. My story has a beginning but not an end," she said with such an air of mystery. Her face turned red and she looked upset, anxious.

"Try your strength, you are a brave and strong woman," I exclaimed firmly.

"I'm not sure if it would change anything, probably not," she contradicted herself again.

Tatiana believed that she could not make progress, recover her perception and her balance. I was quiet for a second as I listened to her, then I said, "Talking about the darkest moments of your life is difficult but important. When you look back at your negative thoughts and feelings, you just don't revive the pain but also you learn a lesson and you become stronger in life. Tatiana, you can't change your past, but you can have a new outlook and change the meaning of it. You can make a difference in the outcome."

An interminable pause fell upon us.

I saw her opening slowly her lips as if she decided to speak. I knew what she was going to say before the words came out from her lips, "I've been waiting so long to get all of my feelings out, but now for some reason I feel that I'm stuck. I'm having difficulties to let myself go, do you understand?"

"Yes, but you should not keep yourself back by delaying the improvement of your health. There is nothing to be scared of!"

"I'm not only scared, you know. Unconsciously, I'm trying to avoid the shame. I would like to think that I have nothing to hide or be ashamed of in my life, but that's not my case."

"There is nothing to be ashamed of! When you look back at your past, it helps you tremendously to better comprehend yourself. Then, you will figure it out how to live your current life."

She remained quiet without speaking or making a sound.

Tatiana smiled, rubbed her eyes and turned her face to the window. Perhaps, I gave her a sense of peace that she had not felt before.

"If you knew what a consolation and relief it would be to me if I only could talk to you about my past in greater details, and particularly my scars. You know, these scars are terrible, so awful and they hurt me. God, that really hurts! You understand? I admit I waited long and my wounds became septic and filled with pus. By now, they might be healed after all these years, but my scars are aching and so very painful. I promise, I will open my heart to you soon," she said looking at my face; her eyes were full of meaning.

I put down my pen, smiled and said gently, "We should take care of your scars, Tatiana."

"I'm afraid I have to leave you now, if you'll excuse me," she said with apology as she stood. She looked around the office with sadness; her eyes were full of silent tears.

I looked at my watch; we still had fifteen minutes left. I surely understood her plea. There was so much that I wanted to know about her scars, but I knew I had to be patient.

"Sometimes, it's hard for me to remain sitting for more than twenty or thirty minutes, I can't concentrate," she explained as she shot me a look of panic.

"Whatever you say, I understand. But you should know that it would be an enormous liberation and assistance for you to talk to me about your scars," I insisted once again.

"I'm aware of it," she said, and then, she talked fast about a variety of things not very important. She spoke casually for a little while. Her face was pale, and her mouth dry.

I listened quietly, shaking my head, eager to hear her story, the truth of her life.

"How wonderful your office smells! It's a very particular aroma," Tatiana said.

I forced myself to smile, and said nothing.

"What a hard day! I'm worn-out. See you next week," she said, and moving rapidly, she raced out the door. There was still a hint of melancholy in her words and manners.

I watched her walk away; I thought she was an extraordinary woman as I made my way back inside my office. Would I be capable of opening any doors for her? Could I really help her? Could I?

I felt that I was blocked on Tatiana's case for weeks now. Every time I sat down at my desk and thought about her, I found myself staring into space. She was haunted by echoes of her childhood and adolescence, and I knew I could not assist her to solve her problems until she came to terms with them. I needed the key to unlock those closed doors and I had not found it yet.

TEN

During multiple following sessions, Tatiana still refused to open her heart to me, and speak her mind. Throughout this time, my mind was greatly preoccupied by the important secret of her life, and my heart was filled with pity.

Sometimes, she spoke to me about her childhood in general, her love for her father to the highest degree, and her ambiguous relationship with her mother. Spinning like a top, she repeated continually herself, and expressed the same thoughts and feelings in so many different ways.

Unaware of how all these factors would determine her feelings and behavior, Tatiana's repetitive words helped her at some point to set in a secure position and to feel at ease and comfortable in my office. And the most important of all, she began to trust me relatively. She felt safe with me, which was so crucial to her. Also her physical and mental health showed slowly and moderately a bit of improvement; since she committed herself to attend regularly these sessions.

This type of talk therapy demonstrated how Tatiana's unconscious thoughts and feelings of her past affected the current patterns of her manner of bearing and comportment.

Since her childhood, apparently nobody did really listen to her and much less understand her. Didn't she remain isolated to the point where meaningful and daily communication failed her? Tatiana could not connect instantly to the world around her straight away, and she missed this essential mechanism to communicate to people, effects and most important of all her own needs, desires and requirements.

During these sessions, I also noticed that her attitude might not be always very reasonable when she found herself face-to-face with me.

However, she was perfectly capable of maintaining her strength, controlling appropriately the situation and specifically her words. So far, she decided to keep her secret deep inside, and I could not hold it against her.

I listened and stayed neutral, trying not to show my frustration, I had to control my feelings, and even though my personal values differed significantly from those of hers, I was never influenced by her words or judged her. I should wait and see whom I would meet in the next sessions. Was she going to participate and reveal her truth to me? Or was she going to beat around the bush just as the previous sessions?

There was so much that I liked to know about her, and I hoped that with time she would speak openly about her scars, so that I would get to know the nature and the origin of her depression, fear, and anxiety.

ELEVEN

It was a beautiful day and as usual I had been very busy. Since I had an interview with the daily paper "Le Monde", I had to cancel all my appointments in the morning. I only showed up at fifteen minutes to three at my office. I gave a call to Alexander to see how he was doing. He sounded very critical of me, since I was never around the way that he wanted. He told me that I was incredibly selfish, and I conceded that he was not so wrong.

"There are your emails, and here is your coffee," mademoiselle Solange said as he placed the cup on my desk. Serious in work, she was full of life and seemed always to be happy. She liked to talk and tell jokes, I was blessed to have her in my life.

I began going through the stack of letters, and as I took a big gulp of my coffee, the door flew open. It was three o'clock sharp, and Tatiana just arrived in time.

I stood up behind my desk, and smiled at her. She wore faded jeans and black cowboy boots; the Hermès floral scarf went twice round her neck. She looked good, and I assumed that sometimes her mental condition had nothing to do with her physical appearance. Regardless her beauty, there was something about her that made you look twice.

Tatiana smiled back and uttered right away, "Some edginess has just taken me over."

We both sat in silence.

All of a sudden, she took her head in her hands; ignoring me. Tatiana's unhappy face struck me, "What is the matter with her today?" I wondered as I looked at her.

Moments later, she lifted her head and gazed at me.

I broke the silence, "How have you been? Tell me how you are feeling now?"

"I'm not quite myself, how can I be well? How in these days can anyone with feelings remain calm? I can't pretend that everything is okay when it's not, I'm going through hell," she said with eyes open wide.

At my continuing silence, Tatiana stammered insignificantly a few words, and she blinked. I stared at her. She got up and began walking with a slow and regular pace across the office.

I could not understand why she was so agitated and troubled. Ultimately, I still did not know much about her. "Will that be all?" I thought. Tatiana looked at me warily, assuming that I had read all the thoughts in her mind.

"You are my confidante, nobody knows I'm seeing you, that I'm subjected to these sessions of talk therapy," she said honestly.

I felt a great complicity and involvements were established between the two of us, that was a very good sign, and I was pleased.

"Even not my husband, he doesn't know that I'm seeing you," she insisted in a different tone.

"Okay."

"I'm afraid that my way of thinking would be radically opposite to yours, and that we would get lost in translation."

"Don't worry, I understand your way of thinking," I said with confidence.

"I witnessed a series of violent fights between my parents, I was frightened and I felt insecure. I didn't have a happy childhood, do you understand?"

"Yes." I looked at Tatiana who was drying her tears, still standing next to the window.

After a long silence, she sighed and said, "When was the last time that I was really happy? All my life I've been struggling and seeking to find a path to be happy, but in reality it never happened to me," she turned and walked back to her seat, straightening her shirt.

In the silence that followed, Tatiana was not looking at me; she kept her head down with her eyes fixed on the floor. And the words just poured out of her mouth before she knew it, "I'm interested in family trees and I did search about mine, but I don't want to discuss it here, not now anyway."

"Okay."

"My mother was very young when I was born; I weighed four pounds and looked gorgeous. She was very happy to deliver a healthy child. My parents never asked me if I wanted to come to this world, they just made me, just like that. They should have put a tag on my forehead, "made in hell," I wish I was never born. My parents never loved each other, and their marriage was a disaster. I'm not the fruit of love, and for this reason I'm so degenerated, I'm a bad lot."

I listened to her, taking some notes. I did not ask her any questions, I knew that her childhood years were the most poignant and could often explain a lot about her current mental condition.

Lowering herself; Tatiana repeated with horror, "I'm one of these people who carry bad luck." And as she sighed heavily, she went on, "My mother was beautiful but she was very tough, egocentric and self-centered. She fed me with her own milk, something to be proud of! When I could walk, she took me to the park in my neighborhood once a week."

Tatiana paused.

I stopped taking notes.

"My mother thought she knew me, and that she could control me with her authority, but in reality she was indifferent to my inner life. She was a social worker and her salary had never been enough to pay the bills. We counted pennies to put food on the table. I hated the lack of financial security more than anything. When I was old enough, she taught me everything that I had to know about life."

Tatiana spoke like an actress rehearsing her part. Whenever she spoke of her mother, her face assumed a deep expression of sadness. I said nothing and looked indifferent.

"As her only child, I always had to help her to prepare meals and clean the house. Sometimes, it didn't seem fair to me. I was unbelievably clumsy and so unsure of myself. I constantly suspected myself of having done something wrong. I still have real self-esteem issues."

"Yes."

"I'm so ungraceful in my movements that every so often I really hate myself."

"Please, can you be more precise?"

"Sure, I knock things over, spill a full glass of wine over a white table cloth or drop a cup of coffee on the floor. Even now, it happens to me time to time; whatever I see is blank..."

Tatiana stopped in mid-sentence and looked deeply into my eyes. She remained for some time silent and dull; it was evident that she was concerned and worried.

"Whatever you see is blank? Please, can you explain it to me?"

"Shall I tell you?"

"Yes."

"Okay, for instance I look at my watch but I don't see the numbers on the watch's face. I can't figure out what time it is," Tatiana said as tears were flowing down her pale face.

Once more, she looked back on her childhood as a period of despondency and desolation. Her voice had come out shaky; she frowned, closed her eyes, and dropped her head again.

A dull silence followed. Now, all was silence in my office. I could easily sense the pain inside of her; she was trembling. I looked at her with compassion and empathy; we were silent. Neither of us felt like being the first to speak. I did not want to cause an interruption in the train of her thoughts; therefore I preferred that Tatiana led the conversation as usual.

Minutes later, she opened her eyes and said in a sweet tone, "Of course everything that I'm telling you about my childhood is absolutely not interesting. Actually, I don't know why I'm talking to you about it?"

"Not interesting! On the contrary, it's very attention-grabbing and important!"

Tatiana's beautiful green eyes shined brightly as she said, "What is important about all this? But it's okay; let's talk. In winters, my mother and I would sit around the fire, and she would tell me stories about her noble family. In a few words, my grandmother was a Russian immigrate, the daughter of an aristocrat intellectual, very famous and well respected. She left Russia right before the revolution and since then, she could not go back home if she wanted to."

Tatiana paused a moment.

"You certainly know that Russia is well known for espionage?" she exclaimed.

"What do you mean?" I asked innocently.

"Well, for instance they can intervene and hack the presidential elections in the foreign countries if they want to."

"Why would they do stuff like that?"

"You know! For their own interests; it's politics, and politics are dirty!" Tatiana said.

"Okay."

"Back to my childhood, my father, among others, was missing during the civil war period, one of the most tragic events. I often asked my mother about him, "When is daddy coming back home?" she never answered my question. Nobody was there to console me. My mother behaved as a stranger. I finally believed that I would never see my father again. For a long time, I simply lay sobbing on the floor; I felt pain in my whole body. Since then, I have a painful knot in my stomach from time to time."

Tatiana spoke very simply and naturally, but too fast. When she fell quiet, she rose from her seat and stood at the window and contemplated the park, "The sun is fading, whenever I'm sad, I walk on the bridge "Le Pont Mirabeau" to watch the sunset."

"Yes."

A few more minutes passed in silence, I put down my pen, and stopped taking remarks.

"Don't you want to sit?" I finally said, while thinking of other things.

"I'm not thinking straight and I'm too tired to think. Thinking about my father makes me only sad," she said, as she sat down unflappably.

Now, there was a profound and heavy silence in my office. As usual, I waited calmly. Tatiana looked worried and upset. She stared at me without saying a single word.

"I feel that something very important is on your mind," I said accurately.

Once again, silence reigned between us; no sound, no noise, and no motion.

"Yes, but I feel that I don't know what my words mean to me anymore," she said lastly.

I frowned as I stared at her, "I bet it's about your father. Emotionally, you were very attached to him, right?"

"Yes, but how do you know?" she raised her voice.

"I know; I just feel it."

"You are absolutely right, you can read my mind. We are gradually establishing a nice rapport and connection together. I see in the depth of your eyes that you are very close to me," Tatiana assumed delightfully.

"Yes."

"My father was my hero. He was such a true and honest man, with a heart of gold. He wrote good poetry, and he really cared for me. I always felt that he understood me in a way no one else did. My sad feelings stayed with me long after his death," Tatiana said proudly, and suddenly she wept and dried her eyes quickly with the back of her hand.

After a short pause, she went on, "I had heard of war, but never seen it. My own father going forth to war, it was the worst thing that could yet happen to me. I knew the war for what it was, it was cruel," her voice was low and shaky.

I remained calm.

"I wanted to know how my father died, the details, you know. I wanted to know what he looked like after he was dead. I felt so lonely after his death. I was left alone to cope with my terrible grief. My love for my father was passionate and beyond reason, I can never get over his loss."

"I'm sorry."

Now, Tatiana broke into sobs, but she forced herself to keep straight face as she continued, "My father used to sit me on his knee, his voice was low and warm, "Tatiana, you are beautiful, you will be the most extraordinary person, I love you so much and I worry what will happen to you when I'm gone?" he said to me one day. "And where would you go daddy?" I asked naively. And my father became suddenly very sad; tears filled his eyes."

"I'm so sorry," I repeated.

"Whenever I think back to that conversation, I sink into some deep depression that I can't escape. Life can be very difficult; it has never been fair to me. After my father's death, I didn't get the unconditional love from my mother; didn't I deserve it? I believe that God, if there is a God; abandoned me when I was a little girl."

Tatiana stared at me with hatred; her eyes expressed a feeling of despair and misery. I hated this look on her face.

"I understand perfectly why you have such ideas, but you should know that we all live in an imperfect world. Life is a battlefield, you have to be strong." Then, I told her how my husband who was young, healthy, and happy disappeared all of a sudden in a mysterious plane crash.

"This world is a jungle, and we are trapped in this jungle for the rest of our life," Tatiana said sadly.

At this moment, I observed that her eyes were not on me anymore, but straight up on the frame picture of my daughter, taken by my husband on a trip to New York several years earlier. With a shaky hand, she held it in her hands as she struggled to contain her exaltation. What was she thinking? I wondered.

"What was your daughter's name? I forgot," she said.

"Celine," I replied.

"What a beautiful name!" she exclaimed nicely.

"Thank you."

"Celine has lots of love in her eyes, just like you. I hope she is okay now, isn't she?" she inquired with a smile. She remained for some time silent and dull; it was evident that she was worried, "Please, tell me that she is okay," she insisted.

"Oh, yes, she is perfectly fine," I said, smiling.

She carefully put the picture down in its place and kept glancing at it. Tatiana turned to me and asked curiously, "And what did you tell her about her father's death?"

"I told Celine the truth as best as I could," I declared.

"Does she talk about her father sometimes?"

"Rarely," I said.

"She never asks you any questions?"

"Not really, but sometimes I feel that this silence is annoying her. For instance, a while ago on one circumstance, I saw that she was strangely calm and quiet, and when I asked her what was the matter with her, she refused to speak straightforwardly and I was sure that she had been thinking about her father for some time. Of course, I did talk to her openly and at this point; I realized she didn't want to talk further. I did not insist either; I wanted her to feel comfortable. I think it's the best way to cope with a situation like this." Tatiana nodded, but said nothing.

We conversed graciously for a brief moment in a relatively relaxed ambiance.

"Are you dating someone? Do you have a boyfriend now?" Tatiana asked kindly.

I remained silent.

"You are not answering my question?"

Even though Tatiana and I became sort of close to each other, I knew that professionally I had to keep some boundaries, "We are not here to talk about me, and it's all about you. You are the one who is important here, not me," I commented softly.

"Okay, I understand," she murmured, and pretended to ignore me for a short lapse of time.

After a brief silence, Tatiana transfixed on Celine's photograph once more, and without making eye contact with me, she uttered, "She is so pretty!"

"Yes, she is beautiful. She'd got the best bits of my husband and I," I said.

Several minutes passed in silence, and then out of the blue, she began unexpectedly to make some remark about my perfume. She turned to me as she said, "How intoxicating the smell of your perfume is, though. It leaves a trace behind, and it's so sexy!"

"Thank you, my perfume is a part of my identity. I don't really wear make-up but I would feel naked without it. I think there is something very poetic about it, isn't there?" I exclaimed gently.

"Absolutely," Tatiana said as she glanced at her watch, "Have we finished? What? It's already over? How fast the time is going today? Actually I feel good for having this opportunity to talk to you about my past, you don't have any idea how relieved I am," she said in a deep voice.

I smiled. It was a satisfying session; I finally got her to open up a bit and talk about her childhood with more interesting details. I rose quickly and walked her towards the door.

"Take care of yourself, Tatiana."

Suddenly, she slid her arm rapidly around me and gave me a quick kiss. I was stirred.

"I will, I look forward seeing you next Tuesday. You are the only person in this world that I can talk to. You know, I don't have any friends," her cheeks flamed as her mouth dropped open. Then, she added, "You are my only friend. We are on terms of mutual affection and respect."

"Yes."

"A friend in need is a friend indeed," she said, smiling.

Tatiana's words touched me deeply; I gave her a warm hug and said, "See you next week." I could feel warmth rising off her.

It was always a strange feeling when she said goodbye to me. Where was I at? I felt that something strange and meaningful had happened between us, I had to admit there was some kind of special and deep relation that connected us, and I never felt that way about any of my other patients so far.

I had a few minutes before my last patient arrived. I tried to gather my thoughts on a piece of paper: Tatiana suffered from serious disorder of multiple personalities, a very difficult childhood, a little girl whose beloved father was killed in a war, attempted suicide, psychiatrist hospital care and treatment. After all, I still did not know much about her. She was strong and extremely intelligent, and she could perfectly control her words. I certainly had to wait for her, and follow closely the unconscious factors in her speech and behavior in the next sessions.

Whom I was going to face?

It had been such a long day. When my last patient breezed out through the door; I headed down the hall and walked into the living room. Celine was lying on the sofa, watching TV. She had done her homework before I got there. No matter how bad and difficult my day was, finding my daughter with her bright and radiant face made me feel happy and instantly relaxed, she is the center of my existence.

TWELVE

It had rained and snowed often in December and January. The weather now was still very cold but clear. The bright afternoon sunlight poured in my office on this Tuesday. As usual, I had to wait until I had a free time, just a few minutes between my patients, to return my phone calls and to classify my notes.

I looked at my husband's pictures on my desk; his smile was so sweet and so real. Christian loved life and loved his family unconditionally. He was my husband, my lover and my best friend. We shared special moments together, and I had no doubt that we were made for each other.

I was checking my messages when my intercom buzzer rang; I hung up the phone and opened the door to Tatiana. I glanced at my watch; it was three o'clock.

As soon as she walked in, I was struck by her complete and radical change. She wore a tight blue top over skinny black pants. Also she looked pale and tired and had tears in her eyes. Tatiana appeared to be dull and lonely.

I took her by the hand and helped her to sit down. Tatiana grimaced and looked around my office nervously and said, "I didn't sleep well last night. I thought to cancel my appointment, but I knew too well that it's very important to see you and talk to you."

"I'm happy that you have come," I said, sitting behind my desk, opposite to her.

Tatiana placed her hand on the papers laid before me on my desk and said tiredly, "I'm just curious to read my file, what kind of note did you make and what do you think about my case?"

"You should know that these files belong only to me," I said kindly.

"I understand. Did I ever tell you that every time I come to your office, the smell of your perfume takes me to a different world? Yes, "Quelques Fleurs" has this incredible power. Did you know that?"

"Can you describe to me this world, I bet it's a better world," I said thoughtfully.

"Sure; it's an unknown world, tranquil and quiet where there is no war, no terrorist attacks, no racism and no poverty. People are real; there is love, much love. It's a beautiful world where flowers grow in abundance year-round; mimosas blossom in February, March is the time for camellias, magnolias and blue jasmines, while April glows with azaleas, peach trees and Japanese cherry trees in bloom.

"When I come to your office, I feel that I'm discovering a new life here, fresh and floral, not overpowering and aggressive."

"Interesting, it sounds like a fantasy world," I said, smiling.

"Yes, it's where I should belong to. Yet this unknown world is a far better place than the life I left behind. Do you understand?"

"Yes."

"And I wish that I were a little shiny star in the vast firmament of this world. You see, your perfume is unique," Tatiana said.

"What perfume are you wearing?" I asked.

"Fracas."

"Fracas de Robert Piguet?"

"Yes. If I decide to change my perfume one day, I'll definitely switch it to "Quelques Fleurs," she said, her eyes fixed on the floor.

"It might be a fine idea," I said, not knowing what I was saying.

After a few minutes of general conversation, she let out a long sigh and said, "I'm prepared for this meeting, you will be proud of me," she said as her eyes flashed.

"Excellent, I'm listening to you," I said as I thought that Tatiana was a great actress who never fumbled for words awkwardly.

"What can I tell you that would not sound like a fiction story? When I turned fourteen in that hot summer in Beirut, my mother got married."

"I'm sure that this had been very difficult for you," I said.

"Strange as it sounds, no, not at all," Tatiana said as a smile of happiness spread over her face.

"Okay."

"Tall, slender and handsome, Bernard, a government official of high standing was at least fifteen years younger than my mother. Enthusiast of Napoleon, the son of a French officer of the Legion of Honor, he was praised by everyone.

"He had studied in France and was knowledgeable about French art and culture. I could listen to him talk about anything. I found him very appealing and I think that's how it all started."

Filled with curiosity, I listened with interest and wondered what she was going to say and reveal to me, and above all, I was glad to see that Tatiana decided to express her thoughts and feelings explicitly.

After a short pause, she went on, "I began to fantasize what it would be like if I had a romance with him. In my madness of that time, I was watching him from the window of my room while he was watering the plants in the garden; he was muscular and sexy. I remember once I sent him a kiss; perhaps it was a teenage thing. He smiled at me and winked, and I instantly felt myself surrounded by this romantic ambiance. I saw a strange light in his eyes; I evidently understood what he meant."

Tatiana leaned against the back of her seat and closed her eyes for a couple of minutes.

I waited calmly and made some notes.

When she opened her eyes, she continued her story in a different tone, "In the months following Bernard's arrival, one day my mother looked at me directly and said, "Tatiana, it's very important that you keep your distance from him," I nodded, and in the next days, I tried really hard to distance myself as far as possible from him."

At this moment Tatiana made a short pause, rubbing her eyes, "Am I not boring you?"

"No, you do not worry about me."

"For the first two years, all went well. Bernard promised us to do everything in his power to provide us a comfortable life. I tried to connect him to my father who had disappeared when I was a little girl…"

Tatiana did not finish what she was saying; she heaved a sigh and suddenly stopped talking. I stared at her and felt devastated. She watched me in silence; I read the meaning of her eyes. Then, she stood up and walked to the window and opened it. What happened? What didn't she

want to talk about? I knew that she was holding something back; I wanted
to know what it was?

"I need air," she simply said.

When she closed the window, she looked at me perplexed, and
collapsed in her seat bursting into tears.

I tried to comfort her, "Are you all right?" I asked.

Tatiana nodded, but I could tell how disturbed she was. In Tatiana's
eyes, I read what I most dreaded. I felt her cheeks heat up. For a moment
no one said a single word.

Shortly afterwards, she spoke with a calm and quiet voice, "You know,
I'm going to speak more quietly for fear of being overheard," she said as
she made a soft-spoken sound.

"Nobody can hear you; Tatiana, don't worry," I assured her.

When she could breathe again, she continued, "At first, I was shy with
Bernard but little by little I got used to him and came to love him. He was
very approachable and friendly with fresh ideas. It seemed to be an idyllic
friendship."

I shook my head.

"I had the most complex feelings for him," she said with a severe tone.
Then, drawing a long sigh, she dropped her eyes.

I felt she was so anxious that she was unable to speak what was on her
mind. But to my surprise, she raised her eyes and went on, "During all this
time, I said nothing to anyone. And then, as strange as it might appear, I
felt embarrassment when his beautiful brown eyes caught mine. Bernard
excited me, but he scared me too. I had no idea what these confused new
feelings could mean, I could not discuss it with anyone," Tatiana could
hardly bring herself to say it.

We were silent for several seconds. She felt my fixed gaze, and
continued, "For the first time in my life, something very sweet and lustrous
was shimmering in my soul and body. I had a nice glow on my face, and
the impression that Bernard gave me made me so happy that I did not even
think what would come of it? He generally ignored me when my mother was
around; but as soon as her back was turned; he gave me such an intense
glance, which could only have one special meaning, I was flattered."

I listened attentively, taking a few more notes.

Another silence succeeded.

"I was jealous of my mother because I knew if Bernard and I had been together, we could have been happy."

"Were you jealous of your mother?" I asked casually.

She gave no answer; Tatiana's embarrassment lasted some time.

"Certainly, anyone who loves is jealous," she uttered as she flushed, "I always thought that my mother and Bernard were mismatched couple. I'm not sure how really they felt about each other. She took care of him and cooked usually his favorite food when he came home. But did they love each other? I can't remember them ever kissing or hugging in front of me."

Now, Tatiana stopped speaking, and while we stared at each other, I sensed that her eyes told me there was much more to this story than that. Despite my curiosity, I did not say a word. I remained calm and waited; I did not want her to feel any pressure or strain.

She twisted around in her seat and looking me seriously in the face, she said, "Will I ever be able to escape from my pain? You know, I'm bound forever to this wound. Do you have any idea what is that sting of remorse like?" her voice sounded pathetic, sad.

I started to reply, but Tatiana cut me short, "Will I be able to cut myself off from this world full of devils? As Jean-Paul Sartre said, "Hell is the others." I was in hell, Bernard drove me slowly to hell and I dived into it deeply. He was the cause of all my misery."

Silence returned; no movement, and no clamor. The strange expression on Tatiana's face showed a mixture of shame and anger. But she knew too well that there should not be any obstacle or barrier between us. She held her breath and turned back to me, "Transparency is important here, you see, my mind is perfectly made up today."

I smiled. I was fully convinced that she was telling me the truth. I was satisfied.

Tatiana made an effort to hide her agitation, and became quiet. She kept turning nervously round on her seat, and her face burning with the flush of shame, had already betrayed her. I looked at her and I knew that she suffered in so many ways that perhaps she would not be able to talk about it for some time. I saw fear in her eyes; her seriousness frightened me. I stayed cool and indifferent.

"I'm going to be very straightforward, I'll finish this conversation at another time," she seemed confused, distracted like she did not know how to explain her thoughts.

I was too astonished to speak; I said nothing. Tatiana could not speak and I did not insist; I felt helpless. We retreated into a comfortable silence, long silence, and a very long and smooth silence.

After we passed at least four minutes in this quiescent situation, the longest silence ever, I felt that she hesitated; she should speak or not speak? She glanced at her watch and gesticulated rapidly with her two hands, and I assumed that she would finally bring herself to confront the decision she had already made.

"Okay, I'm going to reveal my secret to you; even though it's very painful for me to speak the truth. Sometimes, revealing the truth can be a mortal blow, very fatal and perhaps mortal. Did you know that?"

"Yes, but you should know that my office is about intimacy and transparency. You don't have to wear a mask here, out there is different."

"I know that."

"You have to be honest to me or this is not going to work," I said nicely.

"Okay, I'll try even though this was meant to be a secret, and I'm sure I have kept it faithfully to this hour," she said cautiously, her voice trembled.

"Indeed, you have been very loyal and trustworthy for keeping this secret that long. I suppose you must know of what importance it is to you," I said carefully.

Tatiana remained silent for a few moments. I instantaneously noticed that when she articulated those words, her eyes and her face expressed clearly something very strange, and out of the ordinary.

"It's difficult for me to have to think about this again, but here is how it started. You know, I'm ashamed to have done it, I don't want to say a word about it," she said.

What was the real secret of her fear?

"But I don't understand what you dread?" I said deliberately, not taking my eyes from her.

Tatiana blushed and made no answer. She rose from her seat and started walking around the office. I gazed attentively at her face, she was giving nothing away. Was she already leaving me? But she walked nonchalantly back to her seat, and took one final look around and said,

"I'm sorry, I can't find the words. These words hate me and I hate them, do you understand?"

"Nothing makes you a bad person, and you are not supposed to be perfect," I finally told her as I gave her a sharp look.

"I'm too far to be perfect, I'm full of all kinds of flaws," she was visibly irritated.

"Nobody is perfect, you are a human being, Tatiana," I told her calmly.

Now, I understood that she was bursting to talk to me, but she was afraid of my judgments. I also thought that Tatiana's behavior might have had more to do with a mixed feeling of shame and guilt as well.

"Sure, I'm a human being! One of a kind!" she exclaimed sarcastically.

I remained silent, watching her every move and gesture. What was next? I wondered.

Suddenly everything changed and Tatiana went on in a low voice, "One night, I heard a gentle knock on my bedroom door, a knock, then a second. My heart was pounding as I tried not to be excited. I knew it was Bernard. I was lying lazily on my bed, reading my book. My face lit up when I saw him taking the first steps in my room. I almost died as he was getting close to me. I felt his breath in my nostril.

"Not knowing how to react, I only looked down shyly. He sat on the edge of my bed, I tried to push him away but he took me in his arms and cupped my breasts in his hands and kissed me on the lips.

"When he paused, I looked at him with a shy and malicious smile. I was really scared.

"Are you scared?" Bernard asked me.

"I'm not scared of you," and I insisted on "you."

"Then, what are you scared of?"

"I'm not scared!" I repeated with a trembling voice.

"Tatiana, I can feel it, you are scared," he said softly.

"I'm scared of love," I finally said.

"I was sixteen and I knew nothing about sex, isn't that strange? I was innocent about all this; I did not have any idea how to be with a man.

"Let me be the first," Bernard said gently.

"The first and the last, I don't know anything, teach me," I said to him, shyly.

"Bernard taught me how to kiss and how to make love. He undressed me slowly and caressed me with passion. Then, as he unzipped his pants and pulled out his penis, I did not know whether to watch or look away. He was looking at me, I tried to smile, but I was scared. I closed my eyes. He said nicely, "Tatiana, I won't harm you."

"And he entered me gently; I caressed him back and loved him. It hurt as I felt a slight sensation of burning inside me. He held me in his arms for a while to cheer me up. I felt instantly that he put a new heart in my fragile and delicate body. Moments later, I listened to his steps as he left my room. I feared we might be discovered. I knew that we both played with fire. Over the next few days, life around us changed forever."

Tatiana shot me a look of panic as she dropped back in her seat. Her face was pale, and silent tears of shame came into her eyes, "Perhaps I never should have mentioned this incident to you, this is an unpleasant episode of my life," she felt that the most terrible thing was said. Breathing heavily, she was not looking at me anymore.

I felt that Tatiana was full of remorse for having started this conversation with me. I knew so well what was passing in her mind. She wished she would not say this whole story, but it was too late now.

I froze in my seat and despite myself; I plunged into deep meditation. I always knew and I had no doubts that something disagreeable and repulsive had happened in her past.

"This was my secret, something buried within the deepest abysses of my heart," Tatiana uttered, and she dropped her eyes, not daring to look at me.

I looked at her piteously and sadly and tried to cheer her up, "We all have secrets, you should not feel bad about what happened that night," I said. I tried to understand what it must have been for her to keep this part of her life in secret for so long.

"You don't understand, it was about my mother and I betrayed her in her own home. I shattered her life. How could I bring myself to cause her such pain?"

"I understand perfectly your point, Tatiana. But you should know that you were very young and innocent."

"Do you really mean it?"

"Of course I mean it. You were not to blame; you should not let this incident trouble you."

Tatiana's embarrassment had now almost disappeared, "But this is so painful!"

I shook my head in approval.

Holding back her sobs, she went on as she raised her voice, "What more do you want to know? The day after we made love, I asked him, "Do you still love me now as much as before we made love?""

"Yes, but in a different way," Bernard replied.

"Why? Now that I'm profaned and vulgar, you don't want to love me passionately," I told him with a choke in my voice, I couldn't help myself.

"Not at all, I never had this feeling, Tatiana," Bernard stated.

"Be honest," I said firmly.

"Tatiana, you educated me in so many ways, and from now on, I think I'll adore you."

"I could see he felt guilty when my mother was around. I cursed my luck, not only did the first handsome guy that I had seen in my life was taken, but he was also my stepfather. Our burgeoning romance did not look at all promising.

"During that hot summer, we started seeing each other away from home at his sister's house, and my mother was still not aware of it. For the first time in my life, I had such a horrible thought; I wished that my mother were dead. I loved Bernard with such intensity that I wanted to spend the rest of my life with him. We made vows and promises, and we did make plans for an exciting future.

"Of course it was not easy for me to know about the world ahead of us, I could not even imagine, but I only wanted to be with him. Passionate about literature, he talked very emotionally about his favorite writers, all of them new to me, such as Proust, Stendhal, Flaubert, Camus and Omar Khayyam. So you can imagine how exciting it was for me to be the lover of such a brilliant man."

I smiled, shaking my head.

When Tatiana reached this part of her story, she turned to me and said, "Do you understand my feelings?"

"Of course I understand, I would like to hear the rest of your story."

"I should write a book about it," she said, smiling.

"You should."

"Was I really so vulnerable? How could I love him so strangely? I knew that it was a forbidden love, but this made our sexual life only more exciting. When Ivan Karamazov screamed, "Everyting is permitted," did he really mean that all our acts and behaviors are allowed? I suppose so."

I listened carefully and suspiciously, taking more notes.

"You see, I have the most complex feelings. I often think how strange I am that no one can ever understand me. Am I too complicated? Please, tell me the truth."

"You are different in so many respects."

"But am I still normal?"

"Yes."

"In the typical Middle-Eastern family, no one talks openly about sex, and I'm willing to explore this topic with you, but not now. At said time, I had no friends and I could not trust anyone but myself. I stayed alone with my secret that I didn't know how and for how long I could keep it."

A deep silence prevailed. What could I be thinking about? Like everyone else, Tatiana was looking for happiness, what else was I supposed to think at this very moment?

"We felt a strange happiness. For me, to have such a pitch of insolence and this kind of audacity to live my life clandestinely made me feel superior like the heroines of novels. At this point, I identified myself with Anna Karenina and Madame Bovary. I always liked to associate myself closely to the feelings and emotions of characters in films and novels; it was very exciting.

"Once a week, Bernard took me to the theaters to see movies, any movie, and mostly French movies. I had absolutely no idea what I really wanted to do when I grew up, perhaps an actress. I thought movies were where I belonged. I could imagine losing myself totally in the role of a different person. And I exactly know where this thought came from. When I'm acting, I act naturally, truly, and I'm completely myself. But in real life, I'm not entirely myself. For me acting is a necessity."

Tatiana stopped talking, her eyes bathed in tears. I had no idea what she was going to say next, I could not tell what to think myself.

We remained still, looking at each other. In this position, nothing happened.

After an overwhelming silence, she put her head back against the seat and continued, "I didn't know how we could go on like this? I begged him to leave my mother and run away with me. But he was convinced that it was not at all simple and he would put himself in a shameful position in society. I thought that he didn't have enough strength and courage and his love for me was not whole and real. Now looking back, I admit that as weak as he was, he had so much power in his job and perhaps it would be hard for him to give that up. It was too complicated; my case was a very unfortunate one."

"Yes."

"My words are like traveling back in time. I still remember that my mother disapproved him rigorously for being a part of an unknown and mysterious organization."

"What kind of organization?" I asked curiously.

"I don't know; he was very prudent and would never talk about it," she replied pensively.

Now, Tatiana fell silent once again, she glanced at her watch and said, "This session is over, Ouf! I'm exhausted and totally drained; I'm going to leave you now."

Shortly after, I followed her down the hallway to the exit door; she turned her back on me and said, "Maybe I should not have told you anything about Bernard. To me, it's like listening to someone else's life," and she laughed hysterically.

"It will help to talk," I said.

"I know."

"See you next week."

She gave me one final smile and breezed out through the door. When she left my office, I was in a state of shock by her tragic story; it was so unexpected.

I heard noisy talk as I walked to the main house. Celine was sitting in the dining room area along with her private instructor. I caught sight of her in the distance. She was practicing English, hardly knowing what she was saying. She made me laugh.

THIRTEEN

The phone was ringing as I opened the door of my office. It was fifteen minutes to three o'clock. I answered it, not even thinking that it might be Alexander again. He had already called me two times this morning. Since I met him, he seemed genuinely interested in my life and kept asking me what my days at my office were like.

"Hi love,"

"Hi, what's up now? Do you miss me?"

"Yes; I miss you too much. Where are you?" he asked.

"Where should I be?"

"Isn't there any way to see you? You said you were coming for a coffee. I'm here, in the coffee shop nearby," Alexander said.

"Sorry, I won't be there. I've got a lot of work that I have to finish, I have two more patients to see, and then; I have to take Celine to the dentist."

"It's really pleasant down here at this time of the day. I miss you Amanda, and I miss your smell, it had such an impact on me, I can't explain it. The other day; I was on the street and a woman just walked past, and she wore your perfume. Do you hear me? It was a flashback right away; I really need to see you."

"Sorry, I can't talk to you now, my patient is here, I'll talk to you tonight," I said as I hung up, and I did not wait to hear him say good-bye.

It was a strange day for me; I felt really depressed. I looked up at Christian's photograph; it seemed that his eyes stared at me and I could not hold back the tears. I felt a sharp pain in my chest, then, I remembered that it was our anniversary. It would have been almost twenty years since we met. Even though I had a busy life, Christian's long and interminable absence was deeply painful. I still had this feeling that one day he would be returning home.

Tatiana took a few steps into my office, stopped, looked around, and smiled. I shut the door as quickly as I could without saying a word.

She wore a white cotton shirt over a black leather skirt; her long and wavy hair was drawn into her pale face.

"Please sit down," I said.

She sat in her habitual seat, and she looked like she had lived a tough week. Her face had a deplorable and pitiful expression; I felt a sense of compassion for her. She began to speak, but all at once as she opened her mouth, she burst into tears. She prudently bowed her head down to hide her tears.

Tatiana was reduced to silence.

Shortly afterwards, with a sudden crack in her voice, she said, "You know, I'm not going to get anywhere with these sessions. I don't have the energy to go on like this. You told me to be patient; I've been patient. I need an update on how I'm doing? I don't see any major change since the first day when I came to your office. When will I get through all this? What can I do to make myself feel happy? How about six months? I need to know."

I shook my head and said, "It's hard to say, Tatiana. The length of a therapy varies depending on what type it is and on your individual needs. Some people have just a few sessions, and other people see a therapist a few times a week for several years. For your case, it could be one year at least, indeed it could be, maybe even longer, let say two years," I commented delicately.

I looked at her and saw that her face was more and more frowning. Her voice broke, and she sobbed like a little girl, she could no longer contain herself.

"It's okay, dear, let it all out," I said as I curved forward to hold her hand genially.

We fell into a profound, painful and excruciating silence for some time. I waited.

"So I'm hopeless!" she said with a shaky voice.

"You are not hopeless; you are a brave and intelligent woman. These meetings are your remedy, give it some time and you will see for yourself. Come on Tatiana, it has only been a couple of months; give me a break.

In the meantime, I want you to make notes of your thoughts and feelings every day, just like you are talking to me. It's almost like therapy, and you will get a certain power to comprehend better your current life."

"Intelligent? Yes, I was good at games and I was an honor student in school, the best in my class, all eyes were focused on me, but..." she fell silent as she wiped away her tears.

"But?" I said softly.

"But ...It doesn't mean anything; I had the blues all the time. I could not complete my studies; I wanted to become a psychologist like you, in order to discover the origin and the nature of my depression. It's such a shame! I was an honor student who ends up her life in hallucinations, isolation and drugs."

I remained still, taking some notes as usual.

"I don't have a degree, I left the school very young," she added, almost soundlessly.

Refraining herself from speaking, Tatiana looked at the window, and listened to the sound of the cars outside on the street.

"It's so noisy here, how can you work here all day long?" she raved after a pause.

"I know! I'm used to it," I said, smiling.

"What about me? Will I get used to my mood swings?" she said desperately.

"Oh! No, Tatiana, this is a bridge that you will cross when you get to it."

"But I'm unable to cross this bridge. There are many obstacles, and I only live in my imagination, I've lost my contact with the reality," she said violently and furiously.

"We all live in our imagination more or less, you are extremely introverted," I said.

"I've been concerned only about my own thoughts and feelings. I've never paid attention to people and things surrounding me."

"Your condition is extreme. Perhaps it's time to change your life-style like eating out more often, attending the theater, making friends, taking classes or even participating in social activities. Get social, Tatiana, you need to interact."

"I don't have any friends," she said sadly.

"You can make friends, it's very healthy to have friends," I said smoothly.

Tatiana stared at me with a cold expression and said, "Gradually I've become extreme in my condition since I felt rejected and abandoned. You know, I always have fear of abandon," tears were still standing in her eyes.

I listened to her and pitied her for the pain and suffering that she underwent.

"How can I make friends when I don't trust anybody?"

"I'm sure there are some nice people out there that you can trust. You have to open your heart. You have an amazing and incredible strength, Tatiana, and you should know that doctor Luciano and I are here for you. We love you and we do care for you."

"So you will never abandon me, right?"

"Right, I will always be there for you."

"Am I not deceiving you?"

"No, you never deceived me, Tatiana," I expressed honestly.

"You are incredible! You always make me feel good with your words and your persona, you are concerned and your vibes are positive. And the most important of all, the amazing smell of your perfume, which is unique. When I first smelled it, I thought that it really captured my thoughts and feelings as if I entered the world of my dreams," she said, smiling and relaxing slightly.

"It sounds great," I said and gave her an affectionate look.

"What time is it now? I forgot my watch."

"Twenty minutes to four."

"I still have time."

"And I'm listening to you. Tell me more about yourself, I need to know."

Tatiana took a deep breath, and the words poured from her lips, "Bernard and I started seeing each other away from home and my mother was not aware of my liaison with her husband. I was feeling ecstasy; I had never anticipated that my clandestine relationship with Bernard would bring me such a powerful energy in my life. He fulfilled me with happiness and we were happy just for being together. We talked about anything and everything, and I knew that I would never have those conversations with anybody again.

"A couple of months later, my mother became painfully conscious of our dangerous liaison. She was not blind of these changes in her husband and daughter's behaviors but she kept quiet. Perhaps she thought that I was only a toy for her husband and it was a temporary affair. She warned me several times that that union was strictly forbidden, but every time I began to think about it, I felt that it was too late. By now, Bernard had already taken possession of my soul and my body."

Tatiana stopped talking; her face was transformed gradually to an angry expression. She opened her mouth; was about to say something, blushed, and finally decided to say nothing.

In the silence that followed, she looked into my eyes and I saw that look of shame and guilt in her eyes, she was miserable and perturbed. I thought that perhaps for the first time, she lost control of the situation as if she humiliated herself of what she had said, and that exasperated her greatly.

Moments passed, Tatiana still paused in deep muteness. She had a feeling of uncertainty and doubt about how to act and what to say. She hesitated to break this silence. I preferred to wait and not interrupt the continuity and the flow of her story by inserting remarks.

"Over the next few months, I was starting to feel tired frequently. One day, my mother took one look at me and she knew instantly what was about to happen. She got furious and slapped me in the face, "Now, you are going to get rid of this bastard child," she said to me. I looked at her confused. The next day, she took me to her gynecologist who checked me and gave me a prescription of herbs to induce the abortion," Tatiana said, looking at the ceiling to keep the tears from spilling.

She paused in her terror and took a long deep breath before she went on, "I felt like a coward for trying to kill the tiny soul inside me, I felt the guilt and I humiliated myself. I felt what a murderer must feel."

I did not make any comment nor lift my eyes. I took a few notes rapidly as I heard something troubled in her voice. I looked at her and saw the expression of horror on her face. Now, she felt that secret panic within her once more. Nevertheless, she continued,

"In the days that followed, there was a terrible boredom and monotony inside the house. My mother would not speak to me and she would walk out of the room when I came in."

"And what happened to Bernard? How did he react?" I finally asked.

"He didn't seem to be concerned and supportive of me especially when my mother was around."

Tatiana stopped talking for a couple of minutes, then, she continued courageously, "As the days passed, the atmosphere of the house became slowly somber and lugubrious. Finally one day, my mother said to me, "You are a bad karma and I can't share my roof with you anymore. This is a scandal, my god! What are people going to say? Just think of this, in what a shameful position you have put me in the eyes of my friends and society? What made you do so? What do you want of him? And then she began yelling at me, "I have to resolve this terrible situation in the best manner, I'll let you know of my decision." My mother felt that there was no point to continue living together in the same house. Do you believe in karma?"

I put down my pen and gazed at her. Tatiana went on before I gave her an answer.

"I can't say how many days or weeks passed, the gloomy atmosphere of the house turned even gloomier, and my mother began talking of the preparations to send me to Paris, "The best plan will be for you to go very far away," she said in an icy tone. First, I was glad to get out of the house. There was a load of negative energy there; my mother's words brought only sadness to my heart."

"Yes, I can imagine how hard this situation might be for you."

"I needed to escape from there. I had never seen my mother so determined about anything. This is how the entire course of my life changed," Tatiana paused as if to catch her breath.

"And how did Bernard feel about you leaving for Paris?" I asked.

"He remained neutral and I hated him for refusing to own me, I desired intensely to be owned," Tatiana said as she turned her face away towards the wall.

I saw her miserable face suffering with pain. Her beautiful green eyes began to shine with tears, and I noticed that the whites of her eyes were slightly red; it might have been the after-effect of tears.

We stayed in a profound silence for some time. I stared at her with pitiful eyes; I profoundly sensed feelings of sorrow and distress for her and tried to stay cool and indifferent. Tatiana saw my expression and searched for the right words to reach me, "It was awful", she kept repeating with a bitter and forced smile.

I perceived the meaning and the importance of her embarrassment. When our eyes met again, it was clear that we perfectly understood each other.

After a few minutes more of silence, she said, "I remember those tears rolling down my cheeks, I was on my mother's knees expecting for forgiveness, but she was so furious that she refused to forgive me. I could see through my tears that her face was more anguished and tormented than mine. My mother did not know how to forgive me."

I shook my head sadly.

"I was ready to do anything that she wanted, but my mother said, "You are repulsive, you are not my daughter anymore, and you are a stranger to me, a perfect stranger. How could you do this to me? I would hate you forever for doing what you did to me," and she swore solemnly that she would never ever mention my name again. It was just awful!"

"Sure, it was a very nasty incident, but you were not to blame," I said soothingly.

"My mother hated me!" she said furiously.

"She didn't hate you, Tatiana. She was so emotional that she could not forgive you."

"Forgiveness was impossible, even though I did try with all my heart and soul."

"Sure, under those circumstances, reconciliation would be difficult. She was very upset and in a state of shock," I said tranquilly.

"Since then, I never listened for Bernard's footsteps behind my door, and my pillow was wet with tears every night. It was a very difficult position for him too. I felt that he closed his eyes and tried not to see what was going on in the house."

I listened, and said nothing.

"This is certainly the worst thing that I've ever done in my life. It was my fault! It was my entire fault and I had to take the consequences," Tatiana's voice was angry.

"Stop blaming yourself! You should not feel guilty; you were young and innocent. Bernard was responsible for all this mess," I said, trying to comfort her.

"You are quite certain?"

"Yes, Tatiana, you were a victim," I affirmed.

With the expression she had on her face, I saw that she was gladly praising me.

"Do you think there is a possibility that one day I can reconcile with my mother? Would I ever see her again?" she asked desperately.

"Life is full of possibilities," I said firmly.

Tatiana looked up into my eyes, astonished. Then, she stared at the window reciting some words, almost singing in a low and soft voice. Whatever she was singing, her words brought back tears of sadness and feelings of deepest grief.

At this moment, I could only watch her, helpless and silent. I tried to swallow the lump in my throat, but I couldn't.

"Am I still the same person in your eyes? You haven't told me yet how and what you think about me, I want to know," she asked me nervously; her breathing was irregular.

"You are still the same wonderful person with a beautiful nature, Tatiana. I always loved you and I love who you are as a human being, and if you love someone, you love the whole person. I love you just as you are and not as I would like you to be," I said.

"You mean unconditional love?"

"Yes."

"I'm happy that you can still love me as I am," she said, as her face suddenly lit up with a smile.

As I talked, I saw that slowly all traces of shame and guilt disappeared. Tatiana's tears dried and a sweet smile bloomed on her face. She made a show of noticing on her watch how late it was. We lingered at the door for a few more minutes.

"Next Tuesday? I look forward to seeing you," and with these last words, she almost ran out of my office.

Back to my desk, my phone started ringing. I looked at the screen; it was Alexander.

"Hi, how my love is doing?"

"Hi."

"You okay?"

"I'm just tired."

"Is Friday evening still on? I wanted just to make sure."

"Sure, I look forward, Alex."

After a short conversation, I hung up. I worked for the entire afternoon. I felt such a sickness at heart that I could hardly stay in my office. I quickly put on my coat and went for a walk to the park in my neighborhood. If Tatiana's story depressed me, sure, the streets of Paris did more to restore and bring back my spirits.

As soon as I entered the park, my phone started ringing, it was mademoiselle Solange.

"You have an appointment with the dentist, should I get Celine ready?"

"Cancel the appointment; I'm not in the mood. I'm going to take a long walk."

"If you don't mind, I'll take her."

"That sounds like a good idea!" I seemed pleased at this proposal.

"You are tired, aren't you?"

"Very tired," I said as I shut my eyes.

"Have a nice walk, see you then."

"Call me if you have any questions," I said restlessly.

"Don't worry, I know what to do."

FOURTEEN

All through the months of winter, Alexander and I continued to see each other nonchalantly in an informal way. He was very attractive, charming and oh yes, he was also a great lover. He excited me sexually, and I knew that he felt the same way.

Working in showbiz, he had the opportunity to meet numerous of beautiful women around him, but I was from a different world, not an actress, yet someone who understood perfectly his mind and his world.

On this Friday at five o'clock in the afternoon, I already managed to see all my patients for the day. Sitting back behind my desk, I looked up at the sky, the rain had stopped, the sun had gone down behind the trees, and it was pink and clear blue at the horizon. I made a few notes in my book and returned my last phone calls as quickly as I could.

I had a date with Alexander; he had suggested the bistro that was near my home to make it convenient for me.

The night air was cool and fresh from the rain and it started getting dark slowly when I arrived there. The ambiance of the bistro was pleasant, romantic and especially very intimate. Alexander was already waiting for me at a table in a quiet corner. Following my gaze, he stood up as I approached him.

He pulled me close and greeted me with a quick kiss on the mouth.

"I'm sorry, I'm late, I had a crazy day," I said.

"You look lovely! Your perfume has the power to pick me up," he said, as he exhaled.

"Oh!" I exclaimed.

"I mean your perfume is dark," he said gallantly.

"Dark?"

"Yes, but dark doesn't necessarily mean dark," he explained.

"What does it mean?"

"It means sultry, hot and sexy."

"Oh!" I repeated, smiling.

The waiter asked if we wanted to order drinks. We both ordered a glass of red wine.

"I miss not being with you as often as I want, Amanda. You are always so busy!" he certainly meant it.

"You are absolutely right, but I have so little time and I must get all this behind me."

"I know that! Busy, busy, you are so always busy, and I'm never included."

"You are right!" I looked at him with interest as I sat back, sipping my wine slowly.

The waiter came back with the menu; I ordered the organic grilled salmon with a side order of sautéed spinach. We continued to talk as we ate some warm crispy bread, with olive oil.

"As a child, I was fascinated by psychology, but as I grew up I realized that kind of job would only depress me since you have to deal with neurotic, alcoholic and crazy people. Sorry that's not a nice thing to say. I just prefer my job, what I do is more fun," he said.

"Sure, it's very sad to see all these desperate people with countless problems, and I admit that sometimes I'm depressed too, but most of the time I think I'm helpful because I try to listen to them and make a difference in their lives."

The waiter returned with the plates of hors-d'oeuvres. We waited for him to serve us and leave.

"Are you seeing someone?" Alexander asked discreetly.

"What do you mean?"

"I mean are you dating someone?"

"No, I haven't had a date since my husband's death," I said honestly.

Moments later, we paused as the waiter placed the food in front of us. Alexander had ordered lobster with cherry tomatoes. He took a bite of it, "This is really mouth-watering, and do you want to try? Here, taste this".

"No, thank you," I said while I was thinking what did I really know about him other than what he himself had told me.

"Now, tell me frankly…" I said as I drank from my wine, eyeing him over my glass.

He did not let me finish, his eyes sparkled more than usual, "Tell you what?"

"There is one thing that I want to know about you," I said, as I squeezed some lemon juice on my salmon, then, I reached for my knife and fork.

I guess Alexander knew what it would be; he laughed and raised his glass of wine.

"Are you married? Tell me the truth," I asked, smiling.

"The truth is that I'm free and happy," he said.

"That must be it. So you are married?"

"What does that matter?"

"Nothing; you don't have a wedding ring," I said as I gazed him, puzzled.

"I don't wear it anymore," he replied.

"Why?" I asked curiously.

"I don't know why," he said courteously.

"Well, that's the perfect thing to say," I smiled, then, I kept my eyes on my food.

"What is the importance?" he uttered angrily, as he looked up from his plate.

I told him that it was not since I knew that I wanted to be free and decided never to marry again. I wondered why such a simple question raised such an outburst of anger.

"Suppose I'm married but I'm fascinated by you. I like the way that you love me and I love to have sex with you," Alexander said austerely.

There was a slight air of mystery about his personality that unquestionably added to his charm. As he said this, I raised my eyes and half-smiled. He too, could not help smiling.

"So still we will see each other, right?"

"Perhaps I should reconsider," I said as I sliced another piece of salmon, holding it against my mouth.

"No, don't, come on Amanda, stop looking at me that way. We both are adults and we know what we are doing."

I looked in his eyes, smiled and shook my head.

Moments later, the waiter came back and cleared the table and asked if we wanted dessert or coffee.

"I'll have fresh mint tea."

"Just an espresso for me," Alexander said.

Did it matter that he was not exclusively mine? Yes, Alexander being married just did not seem important to me, and I know how selfish that sounds. We never discussed it again, and the subject never came up. What does that say about me? I don't know, perhaps I don't want to know.

"I want to get to know you, and I want to learn about each other," he said as he took me in his arms and ran his hands gently through my hair and down my back.

I felt his lips press against mine. We were kissing and I did not want him to stop. I saw the flashing light in his eyes and the smile of great excitement as he whispered, "I'm intoxicated with this pleasant aroma of your perfume, Amanda, and I can't imagine living my life without you. This situation is far more serious than you can imagine."

I simply nodded and smiled, but did not say anything. Perhaps I could not care less.

There was a long silence. The waiter passed by, and Alexander asked for the check. For the rest of the evening, we chatted easily and the conversation became animated and vigorous. We had a lot to say to each other, and we never seemed to stop talking.

As we talked, he took my hand and kissed it kindly, "Amanda, I'm so pleased to see your beautiful smile, you are driving me crazy," he said with a warm beam.

I threw my arms around his neck, and we dissolved into each other. We kissed like mad, until the waiter returned with the check. We stopped kissing.

The darkness was profound as we wandered out into the mysterious night air. During the short walk from the bistro to his car, he wrapped his arms tightly around my waist, pulling me against him, and showering me with more kisses. We walked silently in the quiet streets.

When we got in Alexander's car, we looked at each other and began to kiss passionately, avidly. His mouth was hot, sweet, and his kisses delightful.

"These kisses, Amanda, please don't stop. I've never felt anything this intense in my entire life," he said, holding me close and patting my leg.

I had chills through my entire body.

A short time after, we crossed the bridge. I poked my head out the window and looked up the peaceful Seine in the moonlight. Alexander headed to the left bank to show me the place where he grew up. It was very important for him and he got really excited, "Look up there, that's where I lived," he uttered with a dazzling smile.

I turned around to see the old building nearby. I felt it was a huge relief for him to share with me the memories of his childhood. He was enthusiastic about the whole thing: the conventional architecture, the old elevator, the stairs covered with red carpet, the grumpy and nosy concierge who liked to gossip about the tenants. We shared a smile.

Later in the evening, when he lastly pulled up in front of my apartment building, he held my hand and said, "When I'm seeing you again? We have to make up for lost time."

"Soon," I said vaguely.

"How about meeting me for dinner on Tuesday night?"

"I would love to," I said.

"La Belle Ange, I bet this is your favorite restaurant."

"Perfect, it sounds fantastic," I recalled that Christian and I used to go there all the time, it was one of his favorite restaurants, and had become mine.

Alexander opened the passenger-side door and I climbed out of his car.

"Thank you for this lovely evening," I said, absent-mindedly.

"It's my pleasure, Amanda. I'm so lonely without you tonight in my king size bed, sorry, but I can't keep my feelings deep inside any longer," he said gallantly.

I smiled and we kissed good-bye. I did not reply to his comment; I said nothing, I didn't utter a word. Did I feel sad or remorseful for just having him let go? What was wrong with me?

Thinking of whatever the next stage of my life might bring, I stepped in my building. When I turned back, I saw Alexander still standing in the dark; he blew me the last kiss.

FIFTEEN

Time had done nothing to diminish my memories of Christian, if anything; my feelings for him had deepened. Now, sitting in my office as the sun slanted through the tall trees of avenue Foche, I closed my eyes and sent a silent message to him. I still felt the emptiness in his absence.

My inner voice which always guided me so far in life was telling me to go slowly with Alexander, but I was quite uncertain about which direction that slow pace would take me.

It was ten minutes past three o'clock, and I was waiting for Tatiana. When I looked out through the window, I saw her on the street walking up fast, holding a cup of coffee in the right hand. Her mouth moved over some words that evidently I could not distinguish what she was saying.

Minutes later, she knocked on my door.

"Come on in, Tatiana," I said vociferously.

She pushed open the door with a disoriented sense and stepped inside my office. She advanced a few steps, and this time, she went right to the leather couch against the wall.

I could tell from her puffed-up eyes and dark circles that she had not slept well.

"May I sit here today, it seems to be more comfortable," she said, and she dropped her eyes as she took her seat on the couch.

"Sure, make yourself at ease."

"I need to drink coffee to clear my thoughts," she said as she stirred her coffee.

I nodded.

She took off her shoes and doubled her legs under her. After a few minutes of silence, Tatiana had enough time to collect her thoughts, "I hardly slept last night, I watched the clock tick away the minutes and seconds all through the night and I'm exhausted. The misadventures that happened in my life kept ringing persistently in my head. At sunrise, I felt drained and finally fell asleep, then, I had this dream," she said as she yawned.

She grabbed her cup of coffee and swallowed half of it in a gulp, then placed it on the floor. Lying down on the couch, she said after a pause, "My mind is becoming unhinged and crazy since I've been wandering in the labyrinth of my childhood and adolescence. If as Freud said, one can understand a person by the visions that they conjure while sleeping, then, I must tell you that I often have my recurring dream in which my mother is still angry."

"Yes,"

"Should I tell you about my dream?"

"Sure."

"It was a strange and scary dream. I dreamed of my mother; a veil hid her face. We were in our house in Beirut. "When did you come back?" she asked me. She spoke to me in an icy tone. "Never mind, I absolutely had to see you, mother. Do you still hate me?" she did not respond. She walked a few steps in silence, and then suddenly she stopped. I knew that whatever she might say to me, she would never forgive me. When her veil fell away and her face was uncovered, I saw a monster, a devil. My mother laughed, as I was frightened. It seemed as though she was happy being looked on as a devil."

Now, Tatiana sat up on the couch, put her feet down on the floor and dropped her head.

A weighty silence enveloped us at this instant; we could only stare at each other sadly. It was a painful moment; I felt sorry for her. I thought, "Why should that happen to her?"

There was a sob in her throat; I thought it was perhaps for the first time that she had ever spoken to me in such anger and rage. When she lifted her sorrowful head, the muscles contracted on her pale face. Tatiana remained thoughtfully silent for some time, and then she said, "I woke up unsettled, anxious, and I was shaking all over my body. I was sweating abundantly, I tried to get up but I felt that all my muscles were shutting down."

Taciturn and dazzled by her dream, Tatiana who was terrified stared sadly at me. As soon as our eyes met, she looked as if she might burst into tears at any moment. We remained quiet. The irregular rhythm of her breathing filled this mortal quietness.

"What do you think of your dream?" I asked softly.

"I don't know. Obviously she still hates me!" she exclaimed irritably.

"Tatiana, your mother doesn't hate you, and I promise that things will change soon."

"But what about this dream?" she asked desperately.

"Your dream is for the most part the reflection of your chaotic and muddled thoughts," I said, and I felt that I comforted her a bit in her mental distress.

Tatiana slipped her feet into her shoes and crossed her legs; she took another gulp of her coffee and remained silent.

"Don't worry, there is nothing to fear, this nightmare will be over," I said.

She said nothing, she only watched me silently.

Moments passed, I knew she was in pain. I came and sat beside her on the couch and put my hand on her knee. She immediately laid her head against my shoulder and closed her eyes.

"You love me," she said in a low voice.

"I sure do," I said smiling.

"You do care about me," she whispered and minutes later, Tatiana fell asleep.

I sat immobile and let her be. "My dear, it's all over now, everything will be over soon," I said, hoping that my gentle words would make their way to enter and permeate her unconscious mind hypnotically.

"I've been asleep," she said as she opened her eyes after a couple of minutes.

"Yes dear," I said as I got up and sat behind my desk.

"I liked having you at my side," she said, perhaps to make conversation I smiled.

Tatiana stared round the office and all of a sudden, the words leaped out of her mouth before she knew it, "Elements of that period of my life keep flashing back to me. I can't remember the exact moment that my mother decided that I should leave Beirut, but soon afterwards, I came aware that everything I had done for the several past weeks had been a preparation for my trip to Paris. I had to make a great effort to be strong and confront the sad reality that faced me.

"At that time, there was nothing better that I could wish for. In a way, I was content to escape anywhere, as far away as I could. But leaving my homeland had not been as easy as I had anticipated.

"My mother was convinced that this was the only solution to avoid a public scandal. The night before my departure, Bernard sneaked in my room and caught me packing my suitcase. He embraced me kindly and said in a low tone, "I love you Tatiana, but I can't be with you now, you have to understand that. I will find a way to be with you, I promise," and as he took one last look at me, he moved with quick steps out the door."

I shook my head and asked her, "And what about you? How did you react?"

Tatiana paused. Tears filled her eyes; it was difficult for her to speak. Her face expressed the mixture of hatred, fury and fear. I knew for a fact that she was terribly hurt.

"Did you believe what he said to you?" I asked, smiling slightly.

"First I decided not to believe him; I thought he did not deserve to be believed. But then, I never stopped trusting him. He was my friend, my lover and somehow he replaced my father. Who was going to replace him now? I found myself without a soul, without a life of feelings and thoughts. My inner life, on which I could live and in which I could take part was now stolen forever."

Silence reigned in my office.

Tatiana sighed and took the last gulp of her coffee, then, she went on changing the tone of her voice, "I knew that Paris was everybody's vision of nirvana, it sounded very exciting. I wanted to live in Paris since I was a little girl. I had a lot of postcards of the city, mostly black and white, and I always wanted to be in them.

"I desperately wanted to wear make-up and elegant clothes like Parisian women. Only they know how to look elegant, wearing outfits that reveal their shoulders and arms with the tops of their breasts exposed, sexy I mean.

"But somehow this sense of leaving my life behind would appear to me in my dreams again and again. Also this radical change brought me something new and very simple in my life that I had never experienced before, something very powerful, you know what it was? Tatiana asked me without expecting a response.

"No, what was it?" I wondered.

"Hope, but unfortunately this kind of feeling usually evaporates too quickly in the air. My hope turned out to be an illusion."

She continued with a serious and somber look. I listened carefully and warily, making more and more notes. I did not want to interrupt her. Suddenly Tatiana who was worried that she was talking to the full extent of her power, stopped, "Am I talking too much?"

Without waiting for my response, she went on and gave an answer to herself, "Now, I feel like talking, I have desperate need to talk."

"And I'm listening to you, my dear."

"Moving away from my homeland and my culture was heart- wrenching. What is your opinion?" she asked, as she pulled her hair back.

"About?"

"About change in general, what do you think? Usually I'm not good with change. I need a lifetime to adjust."

I raised my eyes from my notes and said, "Since you asked my opinion, there are times in our lives when change is to be expected, and there are things that we must face and cope with. My personal feeling about change is that is important for moving on. I always believed and I still think if you don't like something, change it and if you can't change a situation, perhaps it's time to change yourself..." I spoke quietly.

But Tatiana did not let me finish, she fell into a deep trance that I assumed perhaps she heard nothing of what I was saying to her. She looked miserably around and she uttered with a severe tone, "The day of my departure, I felt sad and empty. I became indifferent towards everything and everybody. I've led a pretty unstable life since I left my homeland. Long before I made France my home, I inhabited its culture, its literature, its poetry, its music and movies. But once I got there, I found myself in a foreign environment, unloved, as a total stranger who had left her roots and family behind."

"Sure, it was not easy at all to give away your childhood and adolescence like this. You were forced to live your country, and I understand perfectly your position," I stated.

"I was banned officially by my own mother," she said sarcastically.

"I admire your strength, Tatiana."

"The first years were a total nightmare. All I could see on the streets of Paris were people hideously deformed with distorted images. Did I suffer from a mental or visual problem? I had no clue. Panicked, I discovered that the reality of my life became gradually scenes of repugnance and aversion. I knew that everything was happening in my head. I felt myself trapped in a bizarre world, in the universe of Kafka indeed, essentially chaotic and hectic, I mean.

"At long last, I was left alone with my shadow in a cold and tiny studio outside of Paris. My shadow was my only and unique companion, the same shadow that was my playmate in my childhood and grew up with me. It will certainly get old and will stay my faithful friend until the end. We are inseparable.

"In the long silence of nights, I chronicled my destiny in a diary and I was amazed how so many scattered memories had come together in my tumultuous mind, thus, I filled hundreds of blank pages with my scribbling," Tatiana commented, in a state of confusion and disturbance.

There was another profound silence, full of meaning.

Minutes later, she cleared her throat and went on, "It was impossible for me to imagine how I would live there. I needed someone to provide me emotional support, to comfort me, to tell me how to live or how not to live. I could not make myself heard, much less understood by the world around me. I became gradually isolated to the point where meaningful human connection failed me."

"Didn't you want to get help at this time?"

"Sure, I started seeing Dominique Perrin; she is a therapist, a fifty-year-old woman. Have you heard her name? Do you know her?"

"No."

"Well, I didn't feel comfortable with her. Not only she was not a good listener, but she was very weird too, I mean a typical shrink. She looked like a detective, watching my words, gestures and movements. There was coldness in her manner that made me very uncomfortable. And since I was running out of money, I could not afford to pay her anyway," Tatiana paused and looked down as she said this.

I nodded and said no word.

"When I left home, I took all the money that my mother had saved for my dowry, but I lost it. And all because I put my trust in a man who stole my entire savings, leaving me with nothing, I felt like a fool."

"And who was this man?" I asked.

"He was my agent," she replied, as she managed a smile, keeping her head high.

"Were you in a relationship with him?"

"Yes, but nothing really serious. He was a kind of fool. The more I think about him now, the more I realize how stupid I was. At said time, my life was upside down."

"For how long did your relationship last with him?"

"Six months. What time is it?" Tatiana asked, looking towards the door.

"We've got enough time for the rest of your story," I answered.

We both stared at each other. I noticed that Tatiana, despite of her angry expression was perfectly at ease and in so many ways relieved and perhaps reassured. Was she free of anxiety so far? Beyond doubt, I was not convinced yet.

"Alone in Paris, without friends and family, with a melancholy disappointment in the past, I wished nothing, I desired nothing. I felt as isolated as a raft in the middle of a vast ocean," she commented sadly.

"I understand your feelings; all was strange and unfamiliar in your surroundings."

"Exactly, so you really understand my feelings?"

"Absolutely, I perfectly understand your situation, Tatiana."

"I found everything very expensive in Paris, so I moved to the suburb to cut down my expenses as much as possible. My life seemed hopeless. Now, in my solitude, I began to be more and more bored. I tried to change my look, I wanted to look like a fashionable Parisian woman, but I was not for the simple reason that I was a typical traditional Lebanese woman. I did not fit here in Paris," she said. Then, she moved rapidly to the window whispering some words within her. I could not detect what she was saying, but watching carefully the motion of her lips, I guess she was repeating to herself, "Poor Tatiana, poor me."

I put away my pen. She came back to her seat and looked in my eyes with eyes wet with tears. The more she talked of herself; the more I got the feeling that her problems ran deeper than I thought. I fully and clearly understood that without a stable home environment, Tatiana had difficulty to accept and cope with her new life in Paris at a very young age. She became gradually reclusive, and withdrawn. She struggled with depression, and for this reason she was unable to make friends. Slowly, she evolved into a melancholic state of loneliness.

Tatiana tried to relax on the couch. She sadly shook her head, and yet again, she went over in her memory concerning her relationship with her mother. She expressed her resentment for leaving her at a young age, "I wanted to see my mother and tell her that she could still forgive me. It was never too late to strengthen the rapport with loved ones. I just wanted her to understand my feelings; that's all."

Sitting still, I could not think of what to say. At this point, I could not separate myself of my deepest feelings. Suddenly, I felt that there were tears running down my cheeks. Without any doubt, there were silent tears of helplessness. My mind went blank and I felt my stomach contract with pain, "if only she would get well," I thought.

But I rapidly turned my head to hide my tears, I had to control my feelings and be in control of the situation at any price.

"As the years passed, as a consequence of my imposed loneliness and especially the lack of love, I became accustomed to my new life. Sometimes I was overwhelmed by my sadness, but I learned how to hide my feelings and emotions with calm."

Tatiana paused for a short moment, then she continued, "Like Albert Camus'Sisyphus who is doomed to hauling a rock uphill only to watch it roll down on the other side, I found myself faced with the fate of trying to obtain a measure of dignity for myself in this absurd fucking world."

I nodded and said, "You see, your strength is your strong point, you are amazing!" Tatiana did not say a word; she just half- smiled.

"I'm so proud of you! You are stronger than you think," I assured her.

"Yes, but I lost my identity, can you imagine? I felt terribly lonely and I had no one in my life to talk to. And worst of all, I could not trust anyone, do you understand?"

"My office is about confidence and transparency, you don't have to disguise, no masquerade, out there is different," I said with a comforting voice.

She shook her head in agreement, "Thank you, I appreciate that," she said in a low voice. Her breathless voice showed that she was no longer inclined to talk. Glancing at her watch, she murmured, "I suddenly have a terrible head-ache, I hope you'll excuse me, it's time anyway."

Tatiana stood and raised her arms to stretch her back. Pulling myself together for a few seconds, I got up rapidly, and accompanied her to the door.

"God, I feel dizzy," she said suddenly.

I thought her balance faltered. I grabbed her arm, "Are you okay?" I said worriedly.

"I'm not sure. Actually, no, I'm not okay," her words were coming very weakly now.

I helped her to sit on the couch.

"I can't breathe," she said, she was pale.

"What can I do for you? What will help?"

"Nothing, it happens sometimes, it will go away. I can't control it."

Tatiana suffered from physical pain; she was still hurt and mentally wounded.

"Try to relax and slow your breathing, especially when you exhale," I said calmly.

"Can you give me a glass of water, please?"

A few minutes later, I heard the click-clack of mademoiselle Solange's heels on the hard wood floor.

"Here, Tatiana, your glass of water, and take a deep breath, so your body can relax."

"Thank you for your kindness," she said as her trembling hand reached out to take it. She took a quick sip, "That feels good."

"I'm sure that you are still overmedicated. All these antidepressants treat only the symptoms and they come with great risks. They all have side effects and they can damage your brain function. I'll talk to doctor Luciano on the subject of all your prescription drugs; he should reduce the dose of your medication instead of drugging you too much with tranquilizers. In the meantime, you should exercise to kill your automatic negative thoughts."

"I'm stuck with my brain for the rest of my life," Tatiana said with a weak smile.

"You are not stuck with your brain, you can make it better. You can conquer anxiety and stress. Don't worry about anything, we will make sure that you are very well cared for," I said, trying to make her feel better by giving her special attention. I hoped that with our help, Tatiana would gradually begin to recover.

"Should I stop taking all my drugs?"

"No dear, that's not what I meant, you just need a moderate dose," I explained.

"I'm putting all my hope in you. Please, do everything you can to improve my health."

Moments later, when she left my office, I went to the kitchen and made some tea with a bunch of fresh cilantro leaves. There was still a long time before the dinner hour. My heart became so heavy that I could no longer sit tranquil.

I went to the park Monceau for a walk. I thought about Tatiana, as a result of a troubled childhood and adolescence, she was suffering from anxiety, panic attacks, night terrors and insomnia. I also thought that she was a remarkable woman and in spite of our differences, we became fond of one another.

SIXTEEN

It was too early when I woke up; I turned over for some time. The clouds had covered the sun that was shining now. Moments later, I put on my robe and walked slowly to the kitchen. Mademoiselle Solange had already prepared the coffee and placed the silver plate of croissants on the table.

Celine hitched her school bag onto her shoulder and headed off to school, only two blocks away from my apartment building.

It was ten minutes past nine and my patient still not there. I realized that this was the first time that she had been late without a phone call. Right after I checked my emails, Lilian showed up at the office. She was a writer and she had been often on tour.

"So sorry for being late," she said, and she sat in front of me.

"Busy as usual?"

"Yes, I'm going to Lyon first, and then to Grenoble for a tour."

"This is great, usually writers want a chance to tour their books and you are one of the few, you are incredible."

Lilian laughed lightly, and slid the magazine "Le Nouvel Observateur" in front of me on the desk; there was a picture of Donald Trump. I hadn't much interest in American politics but I knew who he was.

"God helps the world if he goes to the white house," she said sadly in a sarcastic tone.

"Too bad that president Obama's term will be over soon! He is so special!" I said.

She shook her head in agreement, then, after a general conversation, we started the session. I suddenly noticed that she was extremely uneasy and a bit nervous.

"Is everything okay?" I wondered.

"I'm not sure, I feel vulnerable and I'm a bit scared," Lilian answered apprehensively.

"Why?"

"Because everything that I said in my new book is kind of private, and now my words are out there in the world."

"So?"

"People will judge me."

"It's okay, you are a public image and people have different opinions about you."

"I see, okay." And she went on…

My session with Lilian ended at ten o'clock and during the rest of the day, I had a few more appointments and all I heard was blah, blah, blah, and it seemed perfectly natural to me. Some days were just like this and it was inevitable. Tears and grief for some, and forced smile for others.

There was a whole different universe here, and I found myself in the middle of it, cut off from the world outside with people who had a certain vision of life. I thought of those who spent most of their life worrying about their future; and others who were incredibly depressed and felt rejected and humiliated. Women who had to put up with the infidelity of their husbands, and those who had too much pride to stay in their marriage, therefore they decided to leave.

How many lives did I see here?

The sound of my buzzer made me jump. I glanced at my watch, it was three o'clock, and Tatiana was there. Once she shut the door safely behind her, she flopped in her seat, disheartened and dead-beat.

She wore blood-red lipstick and looked a little bizarre in her black leggings and long tunic. She managed to smile but I felt that it was only a smirk.

Tatiana was not in a good mood, "Oh God! What was the matter with her now?" I thought, looking at her stern and serious face.

"How are you feeling today?" I asked, alarmed.

Now, she was not smiling anymore, instead, I saw her sinking deeply in her black and momentous thoughts. She lowered her head, and her eyes dropped to the floor.

"Oh, I'm feeling much the same; as usual. I'm suffering but it doesn't matter anymore," she said, frowning gloomily.

Tatiana fell silent.

After a long pause, without looking at me, she contracted her face into a grimace expression and said, "I want to see you because I'm trying to make sense out of what has happened in my life."

"Of course," I said, looking at her distressed face.

"But I don't know how to put my own life back together. I feel that still it's not easy for me to express my feelings with words. Some words have no meaning for me, you understand, don't you?"

"Yes, and I think you are doing a remarkable job, Tatiana. You can express yourself with the right and exact words. We have a deep connection together, and as you know, this is very important in therapy."

"Sure, but I'm still in a state of excessive sadness often with physical symptoms. I have terrible headaches because nothing is going right in my life, do you really understand?"

"Yes, and I take your word for it. At this point, I know only half of your story, Tatiana," I said as I felt my face became excessively hot.

"You are right."

"Tell me what happened?"

"Today, on my way to your office, I had a sick feeling. I felt awkward about it and became clumsy," she said as she gave me an exasperated look.

"What happened?"

"I saw two shadows, it's hard to describe, you see! I'm fed up with these fucking words. Words matter and they can have tremendous consequences. I mean I have to be careful when I'm talking to you."

I remained silent.

"I saw two men who popped out on the street corner of the avenue of Victor Hugo. They were tall and they had mustaches, strange look, I mean. They followed me as soon as they saw me. Did they know me? I was scared. I refused to make eye contact with them, but I could hear their voices, they were so loud and earsplitting," she uttered.

Reduced to silence, Tatiana looked indifferent, and she was not looking at me anymore, but at the window.

"And what did they tell you?"

"They told me that I should kill myself in the metro, the perfect place to commit suicide. I started to run among people who walked slowly, blocking my way and making my movements difficult..." Tatiana fell silent once more, and even though she wiped her eyes, the tears kept falling.

"And then, what happened?

Tatiana had withdrawn into dour dumbness, just staring at me very deeply. As I waited for her to speak, you could have heard a pin drop.

"I was scared to death and at this point I thought they might want to kill me, you know. I kept running as fast as I could," Tatiana stopped, and sighed. She was pale, really pale.

"As I was running, a black dog showed up in the middle of this chaos and started barking and barking. I ran as rapidly as I could and fell down, I twisted my ankle," she wanted me to see her swollen ankle. She paused, and then continued, "The dog would not stop barking. My heart was beating faster and my head was spinning, I almost blacked out in the crowd.

"At this moment, I felt that I could not run anymore, I got locked into my motionless and frozen body, and I was out of breath. But I forced myself to keep going, be tough, and be strong. This is what I believed to have happened."

"I'm sorry." I was going to ask her a couple of questions, but Tatiana went on eagerly.

"Did I say a black dog?" Why did I even mention the color? A black or a white dog, what difference does it make anyway? Do you get my point?"

"Yes," I said, and I had to smile no matter what else I felt.

But Tatiana obsessed with the color of the dog, continued, "I mean a black dog is not wild just because it's black, it's wild because it's untamed, you know what I mean?"

"Yes; absolutely."

"A white dog can also be savage," she said with excitement.

"Of course," I said as I studied her expression for a moment. She still was preoccupied.

"Whatever, when I reached the street Paul Valéry, these two men had already vanished. But I'll never forget the humiliation of that moment, with everyone staring at me."

"I'm terribly sorry."

We remained silent, looking into each other's eyes. I opened my mouth to make my point of her story, but as usual, Tatiana did not let me talk.

"I'm in complete rupture with the reality, and only now I realize that everything happened in my head, I mean not the dog, the dog was real, but these two men never existed."

I was not surprised of what I heard; I knew that the whole story had been formed under her imagination. However I repeated, "And they never existed?"

"How incomprehensible are my thoughts and feelings! No, they never existed; only the dog was real," she exclaimed sadly as she dropped her head.

After a short pause, Tatiana lifted up her eyes and looked me full in the face. Her eyes were popping out of her head and every muscle in her face was shivering with nervous tension.

"Do you have any idea what caused you this incident?"

"No, I have no clue. It happened in no time, when I was not thinking of anything. And now that I know these two men never existed, I'm frightened. Am I out of my mind? You see, maybe a part of my brain is damaged or chemically unbalanced, I don't know. I'm hopeless and you know it. It's too late for me to improve my life. I'm condemned to live my life as it is and I cannot change it."

I drew a deep breath wondering what I was going to say, "It's never too late, Tatiana, you can get a new life; you can always start over. As I said before, these drugs that you are taking, they all have side-effects such as tiredness, headache, double vision etc....etc."

"I'll see doctor Luciano tomorrow," she said.

"I already sent him an email. Don't forget to tell him about all the medicines that you are taking. I'm sure he will reduce the dose of your drugs."

"I'll."

"And keep your spirits up and have faith," I said, looking straight into her eyes.

As a little smile played on her lips; she plunged in her thoughts for a while, ignoring me.

"It's damn hot here; may I open the window?" she asked me in a sweet tone.

"Sure," I said. I understood that she wanted to change the subject.

When she sat back, she glanced at her watch and dropped her head lower as she said, "Since my childhood, I've been blaming myself for what

I said, what I have not said or what I had to say, it's exhausting. I'm still young, pretty and intelligent but I have a mental block. Instead of feeling happy, I feel consumed by worry and panic.

"My head is an eternal disorder; I lose my things all the time. Last week, I lost my keys and got locked out."

Once more, Tatiana looked back over her childhood, being abandoned by her mother, unwanted pregnancy, leaving her homeland at a young age, the loss of her father, and being depressed and indifferent to anything. As usual, she liked to repeat herself and she liked being the eternal victim as the result of her inevitable fate.

She paused and then, the words flowed as Tatiana explained her situation, "And all this, what is it for? My whole life is a waste; I never have a moment of peace. What am I doing on this planet? What am I trying to accomplish with my life? I assumed that I would have a career and live my life happily, and now I feel empty. But what is happiness? And why have I been chasing happiness my whole life?" she interrogated.

"There is no absolute standard for happiness, you have to be content and satisfied with what you have and what you do. You can't envy somebody else's happiness either, you can be quite certain that you will not know how to use and apply it in your own life. Happiness is not a perfect silk outfit, which you can order especially from a factory made for you in a simple smooth-fitting design for a special purpose. So, happiness is relative and it depends on every person. We all search very hard for happiness everywhere, at every corner, but it's here, within you already. Tatiana, you do not worry, you will get better and you will enjoy your life."

Glancing one more time at her watch, she said desperately, "I hope so."

"You should think positive, your attitude is very important in therapy," I reminded her.

"Okay. As usual, the scent of your perfume brings a peaceful, natural and earthy element to me; it's very pleasant. This is certainly one of my favorite scents. For how long have you been wearing this perfume?"

"Forever, French women change the men of their life and their job very often, it's not a problem. But when it comes to change their perfume, they hesitate and think twice, it's a very big deal."

"Really? I didn't know that."

"Yes."

"It's about time now; I see you next week," she said.

Next, I rose from my seat, gave her a big hug and told her that she was the most wonderful person that I had ever known. I could perceive easily the sympathy and kindness in her beautiful green eyes. She smiled and nodded a muted thank you.

I followed her down the long hallway decorated with French and Italian paintings. Just after she darted out of my office, Tatiana observed the works of art on the walls, she exclaimed, "All these paintings are so stunning, but I have to tell you that the works of the expressionists make me sad somehow. To me, they only show the painter's inner chaos and anarchy."

I shook my head, smiling faintly, "That's true," I agreed.

Then, she spoke so passionately about art in general that she amazed herself.

"You are very special and..."

She left her sentence unfinished, and almost instantly she turned in the doorway, knowing that my eyes were on her.

"Thank you."

"And these delicate petals of roses are so beautiful in this Lalique crystal bowl over there," she said cheerfully, pointing at them.

"Thank you," I repeated.

"Your office is aesthetically pleasant," she added.

I smiled.

"See you next week."

"Take care," I said tiredly.

In spite of everything I might have imagined or suspected, I thought Tatiana was beautiful inside and out; and incredibly bright among all my patients at all times. She had a special place in my heart.

For the rest of the afternoon, I returned my phone calls and checked my emails. Then, I walked in the kitchen. Celine was taking small bites of her pizza and chewing slowly.

"Mom, are you okay?"

My heart flattered when I heard her voice.

"Yes sweetheart," I said as I took a sip of wine, feeling warmth at my throat as it slid down.

"I love you mom," she said, wiping her mouth with a napkin.

"I love you more," I said with a brilliant smile.

SEVENTEEN

I was sitting behind my desk and reading my patient's files, when I heard a tap at the door. As Tatiana opened the door, I was shocked by her new look. But indeed she was quite another woman! I thought. When she entered my office and moved a few steps towards me, I was very surprised and kind of shocked only for a moment at seeing her.

I saw a radical change in her physical appearance, she had good color in her cheeks, and her hair was white, silver white, straight and short. Of course, it looked fake and I assumed that she wore a wig.

"How do I look today? Do you like my new look?" she asked me with excitement.

"Different, you've done something different to your hair," I replied.

"I look attractive and sexy, right?" she said, her eyes sparkling.

It was hard not to be impressed by her passion, enthusiasm, intensity and her strength.

"I feel that I'm a real woman today. White hair is the sign of a formidable freedom, and it allows me to be distinguished from others. It also permits me to establish my position and to confirm my state of being glamorous. I can affirm my elegance and without any doubt my strong character," she spoke to me in her most pleasant voice.

"Hmmm!" I exclaimed amazingly.

"I love to look totally unlike myself in every respect," she was so pleased with herself.

"Okay."

"I think sometimes I can do anything that I like to do. I decided to live my life in the way that I think is right. All I want now is a quiet and peaceful life."

"Yes."

Surprised, I kept silent. There was not much that I could say. I thought with the influence of the wig, Tatiana's personality had also undergone a total change.

"I look like this American singer, shit, I forgot her name, lady Goya, no, lady Gogo."

"You mean lady Gaga?"

"Yes, lady Gaga, a close resemblance, right?" Tatiana insisted.

I kept quiet.

She took a mirror from her handbag, looked carefully at her face, and smiled lightly.

"I love acting so much, I explore different sides of myself as I get into frustration, vulnerability, fear or joy. There is something therapeutic about getting emotional and being relaxed, I mean stress-free," Tatiana explained, still holding the mirror.

"Yes."

"I made a choice to start acting, and even though I've not had a successful career, I never really changed my mind," she said as if she were talking to a part of herself.

"Okay."

"And now I'm trying to find who I am as a person after having played so many characters in my life," she said seriously.

"Okay," I mumbled, as I kept watching her silently.

Then, Tatiana brought the mirror to her lips, kissed gently her reflection, and smiled.

"But it sounds so unreal when I'm talking to you about my past, it almost looks like someone else's life, not mine," Tatiana said, as she got up from her seat and dropped lazily on the couch.

"It's so comfortable here! You know, my mind is not clear today."

"Are you tired? Maybe you didn't sleep well last night."

Lying comfortably there, she closed her eyes for a little while. Tatiana's face, which had been so radiant, was suddenly changed. Her eyes grew large as she opened them, filled with tears. Suddenly, she looked somber, and her face took on a sad expression.

In the silence that followed, I saw her crying calmly, "As usual, I'm in a constant fight for my life," she said with a shaky voice, curling up on the couch.

I remained silent.

"I have mood swings. Sometimes, I'm in the mood to be good, and sometimes I'm in the mood to be naughty, just like him, you know," she added in a broken voice.

I listened to her with great attention and concentration, making a few more notes.

"I loved Bernard in a strange way. He was sort of part father and part lover for me. I looked up to him as someone who was very experienced. It was only with him that I could have a real conversation. I watched with him the "Umbrellas of Cherbourg" and listened to Charles Aznavour and Francis Cabrel records.

"I loved him obsessively, I would still wake up in the middle of the night, and I immediately have the image of him in my head. I can't get him out of my system. He could put up with my moods because he too was moody and cranky, just like me," she murmured, her voice was low and strange.

I put away my pen and looked at her. How bizarre everything seemed to be all of a sudden! For some short time, I failed to comprehend her.

"When I left my homeland, I felt neglected and unloved, I never really felt at home in this country. I missed my charming little house in Beirut. I remember whenever I was bored by the monotony of life, I went to the pond surrounded by the lawn, bent forward and watched my reflection in the clear water. But unlike Narcissus who was fascinated by himself, I was frightened by my reflected image in the water. Do you realize what that means? Can you imagine what might have happened if I drowned? What's my life worth anyway? Really it had no importance and I didn't give a damn," she said indifferently as she began to wipe away her tears.

I took my pen and started to take additional notes with details and particular facts.

After a short pause, Tatiana lowered her voice impulsively, shrugged her shoulders and continued, "I also liked to go to the roof top and feed the pigeons that cooed; it was fun. My life was monotonous, but no matter how lonely I felt, it would still be my home, I was in my homeland," her face was buried in her hands and she was crying openly.

I shook my head sadly but said nothing; I did not raise my eyes from my notes.

At this moment, it was a profound silence that lasted for some considerable time.

Tatiana stared at me blinking, and trying to get my attention, she went on, "I remember I was really needy as a teen and my mother was not there for me. In fact, she was never present in my life, you know. She did not want to spend time with me; she never made an effort to understand my thoughts and feelings."

"Maybe she made an effort but you had never noticed it," I said softly.

Now, Tatiana replied quickly, with no hesitation in her shaky voice, "It's true that sometimes I have a spotty memory. There are things that I can't recall about my life, but no, no, my mother never really felt responsible for me, she abandoned me. I think she made a terrible mistake. Will I get over all that one day? I doubt."

"I'm sure she loved you in her own way, and I bet that she still loves you," I said smoothly.

"No, I'm sorry. I don't agree with you."

Tatiana nodded and went on, "What parent abandons her own child? Wasn't she aware in her heart of a filial sentiment and duty? Not too long before, I read in Shah-name "Epic of the king," written by Firdowsi, one of the greatest classics of world literature, the story of the great warrior hero Sam whose wife gives birth to an Albino son.

"We learn that Sam, finding his worldly ambitions, frustrated and in fear of becoming an object of ridicule, resolves to abandon the child in the Alborz Mountains. Simorgh, the fabulous mythological bird, adopts the child and raises him to become a wise and powerful hero."

At this moment, Tatiana abruptly stopped talking; striving to smile, but tears sprang in her eyes. As usual, she impressed me with her deep knowledge about books; she was amazing.

"I mean I wasn't a child when my mother abandoned me, I was sixteen years old, but I think it was very inhuman to send a young girl so very far away from home, I still needed her," Tatiana added warily.

"You are absolutely right!" I said.

"She was frightened of becoming an object of scandal! Was I an Albino? Speaking of my mother's inhuman behavior, I'm speechless. In fact, we were exact opposites in everything you can imagine. I wanted to look at her as a mother, but since she made it practically impossible, I accepted to be my own mother.

"I longed to have a mother, a real mother who understood me and my feelings. At the age of six or seven, I realized that she would never listen to me and she would never become my best friend. I felt so terribly lonely; I had no one to turn to until Bernard appeared in my life.

"I never dared to open my mouth, because whatever I said, I was misunderstood. Slowly Bernard drew me towards him; we talked about the most private things. Unlike my mother, he was a great listener.

"How was it that my mother was never a support to me? She never shared anything in life with me; on the contrary she pushed me away from her. When I became aware of that, I was very disappointed; it was really painful.

"I don't even know what name to put on her. Sometimes, I can't remember her face. Then, I look at her photograph for a few minutes, and I think that I don't know such a person; she is a perfect stranger to me. But then I think that I'm absent-minded. It's a confusing feeling, you understand?"

During all this time, Tatiana spoke about her feelings for her mother over and over. In fact, this crucial subject came up foremost repetitively in the previous sessions. But only now, I discerned that she thought about her not really with anger but with despair.

"For my part, I have forgiven her for who she is," she said with a cold, incredulous voice.

"I'm very proud of you! You have an excellent quality, free from pettiness and meanness, you are so very noble, Tatiana," I commented.

Next, I asked her a few questions, but I found her at this instant in a strange state of mind. Tatiana answered randomly to my questions.

"Sometimes, my memory is blank. I'm so frustrated that I can't remember anything of my past. And some other times, the memories of my earlier life frighten me, and then I panic. Do you think I'm becoming nuts?"

I put down my pen and stared at her, "Of course not!" Your thoughts may not be always very coherent, but you are very lucid and logical. Tatiana, you are doing much better than you think so far. Willing to talk to me explicitly about your deepest feelings means a lot."

"Do you really mean it?"

"Yes dear, you are incredibly staggering, and I really mean it," I said with assurance.

"I enjoy the time that I'm spending with you. I have plenty of time and I'm bored, I don't have any friends. I don't want to lose you for anything in the world, I need you. I was wiped out when I came to your office, but now I feel better," she said, her eyes never left me.

"This is so wonderful," I stared at her and said no more.

"You know, it's extremely hard to watch things and people that you really care about so much being taken away from you," she interjected sorrowfully.

"Yes."

"I mean, you can replace things but not people, especially those who are dear and precious," she added.

"You are right."

"I usually don't think about people in general, but you are constantly in my mind."

I smiled and said, "But it doesn't mean that you lack empathy, compassion and understanding towards people."

"I get to know a lot of people, but it's only on the surface, nothing deep and serious."

I studied her face and remarked that despite this upsetting session, she felt calm and serene.

"It's time for you to do different things and discover new worlds," I told her.

"It sounds good to me, there is a great deal to be learned and enjoyed, and I'm determined to make the most of my life."

"It's terrific," I said.

She glanced at her watch and said, "I'm leaving you now. I'm going to walk along the Seine, I like to sit on the dock by the river and watch the sunset."

"It's very romantic," I declared.

"Yes, but it's too sad to watch the sunset alone, and I also hate contemplating the full moon all by myself, especially when it's shining behind a dark cloud," she said, as she took a long deep breath, expressing sadness.

"Right," I sighed and made no comment.

"I used to watch the sunset with Bernard. Also he made me see once the mystical rainbow with its most brilliant colors that I had ever seen. I don't think I've ever been that happy in my life before or since. I find myself thinking often about him and what he taught me about love and life. Now, I understand better the meaning of his words. I can't deny that I loved him and thought very highly of him."

"And what your feelings are about him now? Do you still love him?"

"I still do," Tatiana replied as she nodded, and could not help laughing. I laughed too.

"Okay, I'm leaving you now; I'll see you next week."

"Enjoy your walk, and have a nice week," I said.

"Your office is fragrant of delightful scent of your perfume, it's breathtaking and out of this world!" Tatiana said as she walked out quietly.

"You are certainly right, I'll think about it," Tatiana said.

Tatiana became silent as the tomb. I waited a moment in quietness, taking notes.

"I spent many years recovering or perhaps trying to recover from a shattered heart and in many ways, a shattered world. Enchanted by the movies that I watched while growing up in Beirut; I always dreamed of becoming an actress. I remember cutting my hair short with bangs like Audrey Hepburn. I wanted desperately to look like her; she was stunning. I saw her in "War and Peace", "Breakfast at Tiffany's", and "My Fair Lady," when I was very young. She was breathtakingly successful, she acted from the inside out, and I loved her for who she was as a person.

"Just a few months after moving away from home and surviving a war that could have easily taken my life, I felt conflicted with the career that I wanted to work as an actress. As you know, I never attended any acting school. I was naturally born as an actress. I kept crying and wondering what the meaning of my life was when I was going to the auditions. I didn't understand the purpose of what I was doing after seeing so many losses in my life."

"Well, I still don't know your whole story, Tatiana, but I think that you've done okay for yourself so far. You are a strong person; you have survived hardship emotional and financial. Now, it's just a question of being explicitly positive, leaving no room for doubt, insecurity and uncertainty," I said, trying to seem relaxed about everything.

She said nothing; she only smiled. She would have said something, but kept quiet.

The silence stretched on for a little while.

Still staring at me in the same manner, Tatiana said, "It seems that you do believe in me, right?"

"Yes, but the most important of all is that you have to believe in yourself," I replied.

"At that time, I was alone and I doubted myself. I was convinced that I was worthless, and my life was over and I accepted it. I wish that I didn't feel so lonely; I remember the pain of knowing that I had no one to turn to and talk to. The idea of being ignored during such a traumatic time was devastating."

Once again, Tatiana went back to the time when she left her homeland, forced exile. She lived a miserable life in Paris when she was lonely and desperate enough to try anything; she was literally disconcerted in her surroundings. I thought that this prominent period of her life had left distinctly deep marks on her fragile and sensitive mind.

"Paris certainly had its appeal, the energy, the architecture, the light, the colors, and the spirit. But I always dreamed about Hollywood. Los Angeles is the city I really wanted to be at said time. Hollywood was the place to be, that's where all the famous actors are. Since I was so broke, I could not even give it some thought and consider it seriously.

"In the evenings, I wanted to go to bed earlier, not because I was tired, you know why? Because I wanted to dream earlier, and in my dreams I wanted to find my mother and get the two of us back together," she calmly pronounced her words.

"Now I understand," I said sadly in approval.

Tatiana sighed, and shook her head regretfully. The words rushed into her mouth, but she swallowed them back. She became silent.

In the silence that followed, we exchanged a smile. I stared at her and said, "I'm sorry."

Minutes later, to my great surprise, she went on courageously as she changed her position, "In fact, I wrote many letters to her and expected her to answer to me. I waited, year after year for a sign, but nothing. How could she be so cruel? My mother hated me like she had never hated anyone in her life."

I was afraid that my bitter exaltation would be reflected on my face, so I quickly covered my cheeks with my hands and said, "You two need to get together and talk."

"Yes, you are right, maybe I should take a trip to Lebanon after all," she uttered.

"But the barriers that you faced Tatiana, millions of women worldwide in all cultures and countries face as they try to improve their lives especially in a foreign country. This true fulfillment in life is not just about surviving, it's about growing prosperously and to be successful, it's especially about believing in you when nobody else does. You should never be afraid of anything. You must dig deep inside you to find the inner strength to fight your deepest fears."

Tatiana listened to me with the strangest expression on her face and

I got up too, letting her pass before me. I felt good to stretch my legs even though the tension in my neck remained.

"You take good care of you, try not to worry and have faith," I said.

A moment later, Tatiana was almost dancing as she went out of my office, slamming the door. I looked at her and shook my head with a smile.

Outside my office, Celine seemed to be waiting for me. She hugged me and we walked to the kitchen. Mademoiselle Solange had set on the table a bowl of guacamole; it looked delicious.

"How was your day, sweetie?"

"Good."

"Just good?"

We kept silent for about a few moments.

"Mom, I have something to tell you."

I was instantly worried, "What honey?"

"I'm sad, I miss daddy."

All of a sudden, my heart sank.

"Oh sweetheart, of course you miss him. I understand perfectly your feelings. I miss him too."

"Mom, could you get a dog for me?" she asked me immediately.

"Of course, I love dogs too, sweetie."

"I want to have a white poodle."

"Definitely, you will have one soon, very soon."

"Do you really mean it?"

"I promise."

"I will call her Charlotte, and she will be my best friend," she said, as she started jumping around the kitchen with excitement.

NINETEEN

Spring was here with sweet-smelling flowers. On an unseasonably sweltering March afternoon, I was sitting in silence behind my desk, marking spidery notes in the margin of a few sheets of paper.

It was almost like summer in Paris. The weather changed unexpectedly from winter-cold to temperatures in the 80s, and the sky turned blue and bright.

I leaned into the window to get a better view when I saw Celine standing outside in the park. She seemed to be keeping an eye on my window. Sparkling with laughter and amusement, she tried to catch my eyes and gave me rapidly a twinkle of the eyes. Then, she got happily onto her bicycle and pedaled away.

I glanced once more at the messages on my desk before Tatiana showed up on time.

She looked very cool and fresh in her linen blue dress, and she did not put on much make up. She slipped her phone back into her purse and sat down. She appeared courteous and quite open to conversation. Over the last couple of months, our relationship had just transformed into some kind of friendship that I did not want to lose.

"It's awfully hot and humid outside, my dress is sticking to my skin," she said.

Then suddenly, she began to speak to me in an angry stream of words as, "I don't have any clear ideas in my head, and I'm sorry," a melancholy expression came over her face.

"What happened? Did you get a good night's sleep?" I asked.

"This morning, I was awakened by a horrible nightmare which had recurred several times in my dreams. I got up and the images were still there, as they happened in real life. It took me a few minutes to realize that it was only a dream. It's more and more difficult to tell what is real and what is a dream," Tatiana uttered as she closed her eyes.

After a lengthy and painful silence, I cleared my throat and said, "Don't you want to talk to me about your dream?"

She opened her eyes and turned her attention to me, "Sure, I was in front of my parent's house in Beirut. I saw my mother who followed me while cursing; it was pain in her voice. She was holding a knife in her right hand and swinging it at me. What was going to happen? Was she going to kill me? I screamed for help and tried to escape, but my feet refused to move. My senses numbed with terror, I had no energy to run away. I often see this image in my dreams."

Tatiana paused as tears began to trickle down her face. She could not move from fear, she covered her face with her hands.

I could only wait in this silence of complete emptiness. Neither of us spoke for a couple of minutes.

"I was too frightened, too vulnerable to do anything as I woke up this morning," she said as she looked down; her sad expression showed on her face.

"What do you think of your dream?" I asked her softly.

She remained silent, and then she said, "I can't think, I don't know. Actually I do know; my mother is still resentful, offended, angry, and she hates me."

"Tatiana, you are stuck with this thought that your mother hates you, and she doesn't! If you really want to get over this issue and move on with your life, you need to see her."

"Okay, I'll think about it," she pledged, shaking her head.

"This is a big issue and you don't have to live with it for the rest of your life," I said. At this instant, there was a brief silence, and Tatiana seemed to be meditating calmly.

"How peaceful everything is around us!" she exclaimed out of the blue.

I smiled and stayed calm.

"The aroma of your perfume is spread in the air as usual," she said passionately.

"Yes."

After a pause, Tatiana sighed and all of a sudden, her voice changed and she expressed herself quite differently, "Once I arrived in Paris, I dreamed of another world, but soon I realized that this world didn't exist anymore, and perhaps it never existed. I thought of Paris as the promise land but it was only a mirage, a phantasm. I hated my mother for sending away the daughter, whom she was supposed to protect. I was alone in a city where I had no friends, no acquaintances. What was next? What was I going to do?

"I knew that I would have to meet people if I wanted to get on with my life, but it was not easy. I wanted to be an actress; movies had always been spaces of refuge for me, just like books. For a few harmonious hours, I could escape my reality of being a girl living on the margins. Movies transported me from my poverty to a land of possibility, where I could surrender to dreams.

"In Paris, it was impossible to get auditions; I only had a bit of experience. What was I going to do with my life? There was nothing that I really wanted to do besides of acting, and anything that I thought of; I was not particularly good at.

"I was an unknown actress, and I enjoyed no special privileges. My world was confined to my tiny studio and occasionally the market. I needed to pay my bills; it was then that I started working in stores, wrapping packages. The working conditions were terrible with low-paid salaries.

"I was too frightened of my future, but I knew one thing for sure, I was conscious of my beauty and I was attractive to men. It was during this difficult time that I met my husband," Tatiana said with a sheepish smile. "Okay," I smiled too.

"Miracles really happen when you least expect them. Do you believe in miracles?"

Silence prevailed for several seconds. She looked at me with strange eyes whose expression I could not understand. Not knowing what reply to make, I shook my head dubiously and skeptically.

She fell into a deep silence.

Yet, Tatiana had really never said anything to me about her husband, and I hoped that she would talk about the situation with him, it was important to know. Once, she only mentioned briefly that she wanted these sessions of therapy being kept secret from him. There were so many questions going around my head that I felt swamped.

She talked to me with great pleasure as she went on happily, "It was around this time that I was in Marrakech. Ultimately, life is anything but luck and coincidence. I was there for a shooting, a commercial hit, a broadcast advertisement for the perfume "Fracas." I had to pose nude, it was okay since it was all about art. This was an opportunity for me to learn new things."

I remained silent, making a few short notes.

"Since then, I've been wearing "Fracas." You see; I'm faithful to my perfume too, just like you. Do you know what Fracas means? It means a battle, a conflict; it's this battle that I carry within me. It's about my mental disorder due to stress in wartime combat; it's my opposition and disagreement to life. Fracas means also a noisy quarrel, to break off friendly relations. But you should know that I personally never ever broke up with anyone. My mother did, not me.

"It was Easter Sunday and there was a wedding happening nearby. What I loved about it was that it was a small celebration, and all the guests were having lunch at a long table with a little tent, it was wonderful.

"It was my first trip to Morocco; it's unlike any country that I've ever known. Have you already been there?"

"Yes, and I love it too," I said, smiling.

"Marrakech is populated with a large number of artists, designers, writers, photographers and film makers. It's a place where the air is always scented with orange blossoms. The Moroccans are a loving and graceful people who warmly embrace the foreigners; their music is an expression of the soul," Tatiana commented in admiration.

I nodded.

"So, when I got married, I had a small wedding at my husband's beautiful villa in Marrakech, and we had a long table in the garden with roses, jasmine, and citrus trees especially orange, tangerine and plenty of lemon trees with their shiny leaves. There was a marble fountain in the center, and all was hidden behind tall compound walls.

"We started our life in this idyllic spot. Though, I felt sad that my family could not be there with me, but I thought I was getting a new family the very same day."

Tatiana spoke the truth of her happiness. After a very short pause, she interjected, "It was so special."

A moment's silence followed. Suddenly, I missed my husband very much. I tried not to show my sadness as I was having a flashback to my own wedding. It was divine, it was a fairytale, it was truly special, it was the most elegant wedding ceremony that anyone could ever have had; roses and orchids, champagne and laughter. I still treasure that day. I recalled my first dance with Christian as a married couple; we were both totally enveloped in a veil of happy tears. Now, sitting in my office, I felt a tear at the corner of my eye, and I began dabbing at it gently with my hand.

Tatiana and I looked at each other and we just sighed. It seemed that we understood each other perfectly well. I watched as her body language, and her facial expression implied that she was still thinking and enjoying her wedding ceremony.

I remained quiet and let her meditate and enjoy.

Moments later, she said thoughtfully, "It was my strong desire to stabilize my life; I never imagined I would move to France one day and marry a French man. It was difficult for me to believe that I might be loved again. I felt that I was happy for the first time since I left my homeland. I had lost all my hope, but I put all of my trust in him."

Now, I thought that there was a life; a spirit in Tatiana's eyes, and her smile was so sweet. She paused shortly, and then she rapidly went on, "I didn't sleep with him until I got married, I told him that I would only go to bed with my husband, it would certainly be the best way, I thought at this time. All I could think of was being married to him, that was it," Tatiana said, clasping her hands, "It's simple being in love, I don't mean marriage is simple, but the dynamic of marriage is two people in love.

"Everything worked out for the best on my wedding day. The weather was perfect, temperate and fine for mid-May and it was warm enough to eat outside in the garden as we had hoped. God, we were in high spirits," she went on happily.

Engulfed by a calm and relaxed ambiance, we said very little.

"My husband was very kind to me and I found him very attractive. It had been a long time since a man had made me feel like a woman, but I felt that way now. I was metamorphosed in every sense of the word. I felt that I was a happy woman without any past. I felt that my life had just started in the paradise of Marrakech. How nice it all was!" Tatiana sighed with a quiet and satisfied smile. She looked happy, pleased with herself.

In the silence that followed, we both looked at the sky. In spite of the hot weather, the rain started falling lightly outside the windows of my office.

A moment later, Tatiana began to speak faster in her nervousness, "My husband didn't get any support from his family; I mean his mother, when he decided to marry me. She treated me very coldly."

"Why?"

"As you know, I'm Muslim and my husband is Jewish on his mother's side, but he really never had a Jewish education and he didn't get a Jewish name either. I personally never care about such things. His family celebrates the Jewish holidays. They fast on Yom Kippur and celebrate Passover and they would light Sabbath candles on Friday nights. He talked to me of the holocaust and his relatives who had died in the concentration camps; I was deeply moved.

"What is wrong with being a Jew or a Muslim anyway? There was a time not long before, that I read "Le Traité sur la Tolérance," by the great French philosopher Voltaire, it was fascinating. He said, "What! My brother the Turk, the Chinese, the Jewish, the Muslim and the Siamese, we all are created equal. Yes, without any doubt, we are all children of the same father and creatures of the same God. We are all one, and we are the human race. We need one another or we crumble to pieces." Tatiana fell silent, she could no longer look at me, and she gazed down with sadness.

She paused, sighed, and went on as fast as she could with a different tone, "From the poor and starving people in Africa to the rich and wealthiest people with an extravagant and lavish life, we are all human beings; only some have the privilege to survive better than others, that's all. We all have anger in our souls but love in our hearts, we are all people and we love tolerance and freedom," she articulated passionately.

Tatiana's words sounded like sweet music to my ear. I listened to her with pleasure.

Sitting still for a moment, without speaking, I watched her and noticed a strange and wonderful expression on her face.

"I have the feeling that I've been telling you the story of someone else's life, not mine. But believe it or not, it's my life, my own life," she confirmed ardently.

"Of course, and I have no doubt about it," I exclaimed.

Outside, a fine rain was still falling even though it was bright and sunny.

"Well, the weather is nice, but it's still raining. My mother always said that rain is a gift from God, and water is the symbol of the paradise," Tatiana uttered, wanting to talk, but not knowing really what to say.

"Yes."

"The rain gives me that earthy and pure smell. Before it hits the ground, rain is just water, but after the drops hit the ground and interact with dirt, we get a fresh and almost sweet fragrance, I love it."

I shook my head but said no word.

"This heady and delicate scent reminds me of rose water somehow, and I just love it."

"Okay."

"Do you know why?"

"Why?" I wondered.

"Rose water is my mother's favorite perfume and this scent reminds me of my childhood," Tatiana said cheerfully.

We sat in stunned silence for a while; I sensed that she was lost in thought for a moment. Looking at her watch, she rose quickly, "I must be going, and it's four o'clock. By the way, I won't be here next week. I decided to take your advice; I'm taking a short trip to Lebanon. I feel that I have to go back especially now that I'm wandering in the labyrinth of my past."

"How exciting, Tatiana! This is a great idea, this trip would probably make you feel better," I thought that it was important that she confronted her mother; she may come to the realization that she had been too judgmental about her, and she eventually needs to step back.

"I made up my mind, I thought about it for a week, and I think I'm ready to go back. Actually, I can hardly wait to leave," Tatiana had a great satisfaction in saying that she was going back to her homeland.

"Are you indeed going back there?" I was really excited for her.

"I can't go on with my life until I see my mother and have a conversation with her. That's what I wanted for so long. I've been craving for her to forgive me."

"Forgiveness is your sacred word that you carry within you," I told her.

"Yes, one day she will die and I'll feel more guilt than I can imagine," Tatiana said with a beatific smile.

"Have a nice trip."

"See you in two weeks."

Moments later, I heard Tatiana's high heels that clicked as she closed the door behind her; she was gone.

TWENTY

Weeks turned into months, Alexander and I fell into an agreeable routine of seeing each other for a drink or dining together once or twice a week. He made a habit of showering me with beautiful flowers, expensive gifts and passionate sex. He was always curious about what I was doing, but I decided to see him in a casual way. I did not want him to take control of my life.

However, I had to admit that this informal and unofficial relationship changed my life completely. I did not know what would come of it and frankly it did not really matter to me at this point in time. What I desired most was to enjoy fully my free occasions with euphoria and elation as it occurred. Was I living my life in a prohibited and dangerous territory? Should I have been cautious and distance myself? There was something about him and I found it impossible to stay away.

It was nearly five o'clock when my last patient had left. I rushed to the salon nearby to get a quick blow-dry. The guy named Bruno gently massaged my scalp for half an hour. It felt good and I especially enjoyed it after such a long working day. I exited the salon, feeling relaxed.

Then, I tried to figure out what to wear. I just wanted to be myself, simple and feminine. I slipped on my gray dress and applied carefully my red lipstick to match the color of my nails.

It was eight o'clock when Alexander came to pick me up in front of my apartment building. He got out of his car to open the door and smiled warmly at me. As I climbed into his car, he took my hand and squeezed. Suddenly something like an electric shock ran over my whole body. I instantly felt this incredible sexual attraction between us. My body heated as I held my breath.

"Amanda, you look stunning, and the exquisite smell of your perfume intrigues me."

I managed a smile.

"How was your work?" he asked with a slight smile on his lips.

"It's been a long day as usual," I said as I buckled my seat belt.

There was a moment of peaceful silence as he drove towards the left bank. The light of the moon illuminated the Seine River; it was delightful and the scenery very enthralling.

Within half an hour, we stepped inside the crowded room of "Ralph Lauren" restaurant, dimly lit. The staff greeted us warmly, and the maître d' in the tuxedo escorted us to the table.

We sat comfortably in the main room.

"Wine or would you prefer champagne?" the waiter asked politely.

"Wine is perfect," I said.

"Do you prefer red or white?"

"Red," I replied.

"We would like a bottle of Château Margaux, and we want you to bring us a variety of small dishes, it's more fun," Alexander said to the waiter.

That evening, we both enjoyed a pleasant time. We began talking about whatever came to our mind. Sitting next to me, he buried his face in my neck and whispered, "I don't think I've ever met anyone like you, Amanda. I've never had such a strong desire for any woman in my life as much as I'm longing for you, and you are so special."

"Thank you," I said apathetically.

The waiter arrived with our first course; I treated myself to oysters. We clinked our glasses.

"This is so tasty!" Alexander said pleasantly.

"Yes, it's very delicious," I confirmed.

"Marry me, I'll divorce my wife," he said unexpectedly.

Never in my wildest dreams in a million years did I imagine that I would be marrying someone in show business. I looked at him; the lights of the candles illuminated his face.

"So, what do you think?" he asked as he reached for my waist and pulled me towards his warm and well-built body.

"I don't know," I said as I put down my fork.

"What do you mean? Amanda, we only live once," Alexander said seriously.

"So?" I uttered in a strangled voice.

"I mean, we should be together," he said, and wiped his mouth with a napkin.

"We are together," I exclaimed and looked away. I thought that my heart stopped a little bit at this moment.

"Are you kidding me? We just see each other once or twice a week."

"We both are very busy."

"You are right, we both are busy but we can change things."

"Tell me how? What is it exactly that you want, Alex?"

"I want to live with you under the same roof," he declared.

"You can't be serious!"

"I've never been so serious!" Alexander said gracefully.

"But I don't want to live with you," I said bluntly.

"Why not?"

"I just don't want to. No, I don't want that."

"But why? Tell me why?" he wondered, as he shook his head.

"Because…" I felt my cheeks warming up.

"You should know that my marriage is not a success. I'll divorce my wife; we are not right for each other. There is absolutely nothing between us, only the routine of life and affection, and these are two enemies of love," he said as he took a sip of his wine. Then he added, "I'm craving love, I'm craving you, Amanda."

"Don't you want to go for counseling?"

"Don't play the psychologist here, not with me," he said as he raised his voice.

"I'm so sorry," I whispered.

"Don't be sorry, I'll know what to do when the time is right, and perhaps that time is not now," Alexander said as he stared at me with his searing blue eyes.

Then, he dropped his eyes and concentrated on his food. He looked like an unhappy man; there was a depth of sadness in his eyes.

We sat in silence for a while. I broke it by saying, "Well, I guess there is nothing more to be said, is there?"

"No, but perhaps I shouldn't have bothered to bring up the subject," he said gently.

"How can you say such a thing? I do care for you, Alex, and I enjoy your company very much," I told him kindly.

Alexander did not comment; he looked away.

Now, there was a deep silence between us. At this moment, I had no clear idea what would come of my relationship with Alexander.

His gaze startled me; his eyes were wounded and cold. But suddenly he turned to me and said, "Maybe we should just enjoy the moment, my love."

"I like this plan," I insisted with a smile.

When our eyes met again, I found a mixture of strong desire, sexual attraction, love and sadness in his gaze. I could not deny that in spite of his difficult situation, he had such an invigorating and energizing effect on me.

Late in the evening, slightly tipsy, we were the last to leave the restaurant. Once we were on the street, the sky threatened rain. We walked fast in silence as we made our way to his car.

It was past midnight when we stepped through the door of his apartment. Alexander was instantaneously on me as soon as we reached the entrance. He covered me with kisses and said, "You look gorgeous, Amanda, and every time I see you, you look prettier. Don't you know that? What is the secret?"

"Great sex," I murmured, smiling.

"I would like to keep you here forever, my love," he said charmingly.

"We have these lovely moments and we are together, Alex, that's all that matters. So many people never get the chance to experience this," I expressed sympathetically.

"Amanda, I want to be with you more often, I'm serious about you. Do you have any idea how much I love you," he said as a half-smile appeared on his lips.

"I feel that I'm factually disrupting and distracting your whole life," I said.

"Yes, but in the best manner possible," he said as he turned to me, his eyes were intense.

I remained silent, staring at him. "Don't you see that I need to get a life?" he continued eagerly.

We had sex, so much sex, and we did it everywhere, on the sofa, on the floor and on his bed. Every time he rolled on top of me, he whispered, "We are so right for each other."

Next, soon after, he vanished for a short moment, and when he reappeared, he pulled a Bulgari box out of his pocket and handed it to me gracefully.

I opened the box carefully and saw a diamond ring set in a platinum band.

"It's beautiful," I said. Tears came to my eyes; I had not been expecting this at all, since I did not take his words very seriously, I was stunned.

"This ring is to seal our beautiful and unique love affair," Alexander said excitedly.

I slipped it on the third finger on my right hand, "The size is perfect," I said as I kissed him.

"You must promise me that you'll never take it off. Will you promise?" he said, staring at me fixedly.

"Yes," I replied, and I continued to kiss him passionately.

"You smell so good, it's hard to resist," he murmured with enthusiasm.

Did I want to be Alexander's lover forever? Certainly, after my husband's death, I had to face a different challenge. I was not afraid of being alone. I was married once and I loved my husband; that was enough. Now, at this point of my life, I wanted to live my own life. I wanted to be free, I wanted to spend time with my daughter and I wanted to write more books. Therefore I decided to keep things like this with Alexander.

The sunrise started to appear in the horizon when he drove me back home. I barely opened the door and began to slip out of his car in front of my apartment building, when he grabbed me by my arm and stopped me.

"Amanda, I love you just the way you are. When we can see each other again?"

"I have to check my schedule first, I'll give you a call in the middle of next week, thank you for this charming evening," I said warmly.

"My love, I want to spend more time with you, once a week is not enough for me. Now I see, you don't care about me, do you?" Alexander said, as he looked deep into my eyes.

"Don't say that! I still want to see you, but you have to understand that I'm almost never free during the week. I promise to call you and make a plan," I said lovingly.

"It sounds good."

The next morning, mademoiselle Solange came into my office to bring me my mail, she sounded like a control freak as she said, "You must be tired, and you came back home kind of late, last night."

"Yes, I'm tired, I spent the night with Alexander," I yawned.

"You decide, I just feel protective of you, and I don't want you to be hurt," she said.

"Thank you, he seems to be a nice man."

"I'm sure you know what you are doing. After all you are the one who is helping all these people with their lives," she was trying hard to choose her words carefully.

"We will see," I said quietly.

"Perhaps you two will get married."

"Marry him? Come on."

"But aren't you happy with him?"

"I certainly enjoy his company, he is interesting, but we are different."

"What do you mean?" she asked curiously.

"He is married," I stated.

"Married?"

"Yes, married."

"Oh, God!" she said, her eyes were wide open with disbelief. She paused, and then she added, "But you deserve to be happy again."

"I'm happy. I have my daughter; my work, and I have you. Isn't that enough? I said, smiling.

"No, it's not enough, you need more than that. I don't know him, but I have the feeling that you two make a great match. I haven't seen you like this since your husband's death. But I don't want you to cope with emotional issues," she said affectionately.

"Neither do I."

Since that night, Alexander repeatedly asked me to marry him, and he became inquisitive, attempting to take control of the situation, which made me pull away even more. Also, in the following weeks, his wife suspected that something different was happening in her husband's life. She realized that he was not having just another flirtation; she became insanely jealous.

TWENTY-ONE

The windy and cold winter was finally over. The spring sunshine brought brightness and freshness as all the trees of avenue Foche turned entirely emerald green.

Eyeing my watch, I saw that I still had a few minutes until my next appointment. As usual, I went through my patient's files and returned my phone calls.

It was three o'clock when Tatiana stepped in my office, she seemed happy to see me. Exhaling fully around, she sat in her habitual seat and said promptly, "Here is what I want you to know."

"What?"

"Your perfume is a super feminine composition that gives a nod to vintage floral, the air smells incredible here."

"It could be," I said as I moved my head as a sign of agreement.

"And I bet that the top notes of your fragrance are orange blossom and bergamot," she said with excitement.

"Yes, you are absolutely right."

"Bergamot is so pleasant to smell. This fruit's scent is somehow bold yet subtle, crisp and sweet. If one day my struggle with life will end, I won't wear "Fracas" anymore. I'll go for "Quelques Fleurs." Would that be acceptable to you?"

"I didn't know that my opinion would be taken into consideration, Tatiana."

"Of course, and that is why I'm asking you now."

"Absolutely, if it makes you feel happy, why not?" I said kindly.

Now, Tatiana was not looking at me, in fact, she did not seem to be looking at anything.

"How was your trip?" I asked.

"My trip was kind of strange to me, and I felt that I visited the country only in my dream," she said, and she gave me a tired smile.

"I want to hear all about it."

"Sure, I had been away for so long, I didn't feel like home really. It was harder than I thought it would be. I stayed there one week, strolling up and down the ruined city. But the smells of cinnamon, cumin, saffron and cardamom were still in the air; I kept crying."

"I'm sorry."

"Much of the damage of the city's buildings and monuments had been repaired. The cobblestones ripped from the streets had been replaced. In many ways, Beirut is remarkably changed. There was no trash and the city's parks compete almost with any other in Europe. But if you look more closely, there are still vestiges of the war.

"When I arrived there, however the city that I remembered no longer existed. Most of my cousins, those who survived the war, had been married and moved away. It was painful to see that my childhood had been destroyed, this is one of the biggest sorrows of my life."

"I'm terribly sorry to hear that, Tatiana."

When she spoke a line to her satisfaction, she became silent and punched the air. When she was frustrated with her words, I felt that she would get down on her knees as if she would pound the floor.

Tatiana dropped her head lower and raised her voice, "I don't mean that I had a happy childhood, I'm just saying my childhood, you know."

"Yes," I acknowledged with a quick nod.

"My father's death really weighed on me and caused grave problems. I can still recall the days when I was sitting in the doorway, and waiting for him with tears. I lived my entire life clandestinely in the shadow of his image," she said sadly.

Suddenly, Tatiana stopped talking and burst into tears. Her face became pale and she refused to meet my eyes, she looked down at the floor.

Now, there was a deadly silence in my office, I waited, making a few more notes. In spite of Tatiana's stillness, I believed I understood perfectly her feelings at this time. I felt our connection was stronger than before, and I wanted things to make sense more than ever. I broke the silence, "Did you visit your parent's house? And tell me about your mother. Did you get a chance to see her?"

Tatiana rubbed her nose, nodded seriously but did not say anything.

I felt my chest contract. I knew with absolute certainty that to even try to push her to talk would be a mistake. I swallowed hard and stayed quiet.

Moments later, when our eyes met, so many words sounded monotonous between us.

"My words are repetitive and tediously uninteresting, aren't you bored?"

"No, Tatiana."

"My childhood is like those stories that never end," she said.

"But I like to hear about your childhood," I said tenderly.

"I'm just collecting myself to say something amusing and interesting to you, but I can't help myself, this is my only story," Tatiana said regretfully.

"Sometimes sad stories are more appealing and they grab more attention," I expressed.

"That's true, just because they are out of the ordinary," she said.

"Yes."

"In fact, I found my parent's house shuttered, nothing looked the same, yet everything looked familiar, I walked to the park where my mother had taken me when I was a little girl. I sat on a bench for a very long time, and closed my eyes. The park was filled with bitter −sweet memories, it reminded me of so much. I listened to the songs of the birds in cages hanging from low trees in the park. I realized that the little girl's soul inside of me didn't know anything but war, loneliness, losses and sadness. I have to admit that I wasn't lucky to get know peace and harmony as a child."

Tatiana stopped, the tears came back and she let them run down her face.

"Do you regret your trip?" I tried to meet her eyes.

"No, on the contrary, I'm feeling a flood of relief. Did I answer all of your questions? I need some air, can I open the window?"

"Sure."

She stood up and headed leisurely to the window.

"Do you still feel close to this little girl living inside of you?" I asked.

"Interesting question; it's a very good point. I'm trying to think of what words I would say to you," she paused and went on, "Yes, I felt her strongly inside of me before I started my therapy with you. She often hurt me and I had to put up with her. But now, I feel that she is still there, calm and quiet, looking at me. I feel that the memories of that part of my life are too far back to cause me any harm," she said, still resting her hand on the handle of the window.

"Excellent, Tatiana, I'm so proud of you!" I said with a satisfying smile.

"However, I admire her energy and her strength," she added gladly.

"Yes," I nodded, thinking that she finally made peace with this little girl inside of her.

"Did you try to get touch with your mother?" I continued, as I was intrigued.

A sudden silence fell upon us. She seemed to be embarrassed and mortified. I waited.

Tatiana dropped her head lower and lower. She did not even glance at me for a few moments. Then, she understood that she should answer my question, "You might find it hard to listen," she said, nerve-racking. She became tense, edgy, and dreadfully upset.

"Perhaps, but it sounds like something that I wouldn't want to miss," I said sternly.

"I understand. The very next day after my arrival, I did all I could to find her, nothing, absolutely nothing. Then, I found out through her friends that she had lost her mental faculties due to early-onset Alzheimer's, and she lives in attended home.

"I went to visit her, my mother was still as beautiful as she had been, but the expression on her face showed that she had aged, her cheeks had been hollowed.

"I burst into tears when I held her in my arms; I was so pleased to see her. She smelled of rose water. I asked her, "Mother, do you remember me? I'm your daughter." She stared at me for a very long time. I suspected her that she had forgotten me completely.

"She didn't know who I really was. "Tatiana," she herself looked amazed as she said my name, she remembered me now after a short instant. Her memory came back just for a very short time.

"Are you okay?" I said to her.

"Yes, I needed to see you," my mother murmured.

"I could tell that she had a limited memory of the past, she was able to recall only indistinct periods of time. She had no idea for instance of how long she had been there.

"It's not fair," she said.

"What is not fair?" I asked.

"He ruined my life as well as yours," my mother replied.

"Nothing matters anymore," I said.

"Yes, nothing matters anymore," she repeated.

"The nurse who attended her told me that I look exactly like her, same cheekbones and same eyes," Tatiana said, still standing by the window.

"Don't you want to sit?"

"Sure," she said, and she lay back on the couch, gazing up at the ceiling.

Once more, we remained quiet in a pleasant and comfortable silence. She was relaxed.

I found that the expression on Tatiana's face was different as she spoke of her mother. There was a great deal of kindness in her eyes and her voice was soft. Maybe this reunion would give her a chance to move on with her life, I thought.

'I hated myself for leaving her so soon; I left Beirut with a heavy heart."

"You can always go back there," I said.

"True; and I'll go back."

"Tell me about Bernard. Where is he now? Did you try to see him?" I asked curiously.

As I mentioned his name, Tatiana's face grew red. She paused for a very long time before she said, "Vainly I tried to trace him, but nothing. He had disappeared and I don't know what has become of him?"

"It's all okay, I would not speak another word to him for the rest of my life," I told her.

Tatiana's expression changed suddenly, "Yes, it's okay, it's not important anymore."

Yet, I felt there was a great deal about Bernard that Tatiana was determined to keep hidden. What was it? I decided to remain silent.

"You have gone through a big challenge," I said.

"I've learned a lesson from my trip, it's important that we live in the moment, nobody knows what the future will bring us."

I nodded, looking into her eyes.

"There is no question in my mind that there is a purpose, and things happen for a reason," Tatiana said.

I shook my head, and I thought that she finally made some kind of peace with herself.

"Contrary to what I used to think, God is not only in the sky, I began to see his light very close to my heart," she said, a dimple formed at the top of her both cheeks.

"Yes, it's a whole new life now, you have a lot to look forward," I said joyfully.

She was silent for several minutes and then said, "I feel that I'm not stuck with my past like before, even though I still have lots of issues. For years, I had to keep hiding my feelings for my mother; I hope this nightmare will be finally over."

"Slowly things are getting better in your life, and you will feel good," I said.

"Yes, how strange it is, a new world is opening despite the fact that I've been struggling with my marriage for some time now," she said desolately.

Her eyes met over me.

"This is a new subject, Tatiana, a whole different story this time," I said quietly.

"This is beyond everything else, but I don't think we should talk about it now," she nodded, without looking at me.

"Honestly I had no clue," I told her as I shrugged. I did not look at her when I said it.

Why did she suddenly introduce this subject after all this time? What was I supposed to think? What could I feel? Was she facing a crisis in her marriage? Was she dealing with the unpleasant and important topic of infidelity?

Tatiana made a weak smile, looking at her watch, "Time is up now, you'll excuse me," I'm dead tired, and still jetlagged," she said as she stood up.

"I'm really happy that you took this trip, take care," I said.

"By the way, if you don't mind, I'll see you two times a week, I would like to give it a try," she said tiredly, looking at me sadly.

"Yes, of course. It's okay, Tatiana, don't worry," I said very seriously.

She looked around, as if she had left something behind. The door slammed behind her as she exited without a word. I watched her leave.

TWENTY-TWO

"Good afternoon, Amanda," mademoiselle Solange said as she dumped a pile of mail and phone messages on my desk.

"Good afternoon," I said, as I turned to glance at her.

"Your patient just called, she is running a few minutes late."

"You mean Tatiana?"

"Who else could be? How is she doing now?"

"As brilliant as she is, I think she is doing great. I've never had a patient like her before, not that I remember."

"I know you are very concerned about her."

"Well, I care about all my patients, but Tatiana is very special and so challenging."

Then, she left my office as I heard the door close gently behind her. It was calm and silent, I returned to my paperwork, going through my patient's files.

It was quarter past three o'clock when Tatiana entered my office; she looked tired and pale. I sensed trouble inside her.

"Sorry for being late, I got stuck in the elevator of my building," she said.

"You okay now?"

"Yes, thank you, I'm fine."

She immediately decided to speak, "When I got married, my life had been irrevocably altered in a way that I had never imagined. My husband and I didn't make love until after we were married. He had been very patient with me. Usually men, the French men would walk away," she said, and then she fell silent.

Intrigued, I did not say anything. I did not want to show the least curiosity.

"But then I felt sorry," she mumbled.

"What were you sorry about?" I asked gently.

Two minutes, three minutes, and as the minutes passed, I kept waiting and waiting. She finally broke the silence, "Nothing."

"Nothing?" I said as I raised my eyebrow.

Tatiana heaved a sigh; she made up her mind to talk to me, "What can I say? We came from two different worlds, we could not understand each other's needs and desires."

"Okay."

"After just a few months of living together as a couple, we stopped having sex. I desired him less and less and he began making up lies about being tired more and more. Confused and frustrated, I wondered what was wrong."

"Okay," I said, taking a few notes.

"I really thought that we were bound to each other by the power of love, a platonic love, and sex didn't have anything to do with it. Even though we were physically attracted to each other, I felt that he had little sexual desire for me. My husband had no clue about what I was enduring," Tatiana uttered.

"You never talked to him about your past?" I asked, raising slightly my voice.

"No, he still doesn't know anything about my past," she said nervously.

We stayed motionless for a few moments.

"What about your sexual desire for him?" I asked.

"Psychically and physically I was locked up inside and outside," there was exasperation and frustration in her voice.

Tatiana paused for a brief moment and then continued, "Perhaps we were not matched sexually. I don't know; it's hard to tell. All I know is that we were bored with one another."

"I understand; but you were bored just after a couple of months?"

"Yes, I could never understand what he really felt."

"Did he understand what you felt?"

"How could I know? I only knew that for the first time in my life I didn't worry to pay my bills, the relief was enormous. I've kept this secret for me. Once again, I admit that I wasn't honest to myself."

"And not honest to your husband either, marriage must be built on honesty and trust," I said seriously.

"I played a silly game!"

"Didn't you get help at this time?"

"I went to a psychiatrist long before I met doctor Luciano; she rarely asked me questions and never made a single comment. I didn't feel comfortable talking to her anyway. What I needed then was some advice on how to live in my marriage. She intimidated me and I stopped seeing her after a few sessions."

Tears stopped her. She rose from her seat and headed towards the couch.

"It's much more comfortable here," she said with a shaky voice.

"Did you ever enjoy having sex with a man before your marriage?"

"Yes, with Bernard. We were as one when we made love."

"You mean your step-father? But your relationship with him didn't last long, right?"

Tatiana did not answer my question. Instead, she turned her eyes and said with a sheepish smile, "It was a forbidden love, but he was fabulous."

"You didn't answer my question, Tatiana," I insisted.

"I know, but I often wondered did I ever love Bernard as much as I loved my husband? Or was it really him that I loved all the time?"

She never answered my question and I did not want to push her further. I was puzzled; I could not read at all Tatiana's mind this time.

"You know, with my husband, everything was white, a platonic love. But with Bernard, everything was red, violent red!"

"What do you mean?"

"Red is the color of a great passion! Each color is created to have a certain signification. As you know, rubies symbolize passion and protection," she explained.

"Okay."

I knew that there was something profoundly not right about her, that she had always been different. Why she did not react and respond to my question? I wondered.

The tone of her voice was trembling with insecurity as she went on, "I knew that it was only me, and there was nothing wrong with my husband. Psychologically, I'm anxious, and since I always worry for a lot of stuff, I'm unaware and unconscious of my surroundings. I've always had this voice in my head, taking me out of my body during sex."

"You are oblivious to the point that you become insensible during sex," I exclaimed.

"Now, I'm asking myself, "Did I really love my husband? Did I believe in love? The era of "Romeo and Juliet" is over, everything has its time, and love is an illusion.""

"Didn't you love your husband when you got married?" I asked sternly.

Silence; this mortal silence lasted at least for some considerable time. I kept waiting.

"Sure, I did love him and to please my husband, I faked an orgasm, I just wrapped it up with a few moans and gasps, some excited body language and a languid smile afterwards. He felt the difference, but also I'd had enough and I felt empty. Pretending was the same as lying. So after that, my husband asked me to never fake again. You know, I didn't mean to lie, I just meant to make him happy," Tatiana admitted shyly.

"Perhaps you really don't love your husband; that you've never loved him, or perhaps you only hoped that he would take care of you so you wouldn't take care of yourself, honestly..."

Tatiana raised her voice to interrupt me, "That's not true, or maybe you are right, I'm not sure. It's a confused situation."

"You hoped that he would take care of you, not just materially but emotionally too."

"It's absurd, I did love him and I still do. But what do I know?" she asked herself.

I did not insist further even though I felt that Tatiana was looking perhaps for a sense of security with her husband. Sitting still, I listened with concentration. I knew that I had to remain calm and indifferent. The anxiety that she was facing at this moment made me wonder what it was that she was heading towards.

She stared at me nervously and made a strange and funny noise between her teeth.

"You okay?" I asked casually.

"Yes, but what I want you to know is that my husband loved me too, he would give me the moon and the stars to make me happy; I could not have wished for a better life."

"This is great! What more could you hope for?" I said, changing the tone of my voice.

"We loved each other and we decided to live by our own rules. We lived together under the same roof but we respected each other's freedom and privacy."

"I'm afraid I'm not getting your point, Tatiana. Can you please explain it to me?"

"Sure, my husband had his right to be free, and I was never jealous as long as I knew that he only loved me. I know it sounds strange, and I can't believe that I'm telling you all this," Tatiana said as she focused with an effort.

"So you gave him this freedom to have sex with any woman he likes? I said, my head lightly spinning.

"Yes, no if he didn't want to. Could I have, should I have done things differently?"

Suddenly, Tatiana fell silent again, and closed her eyes in a lethal silence.

It was all so very extraordinary and even strange that I had to laugh discreetly and subtly. I gave her a tender look; I knew no such case in my long experience. What on earth was I supposed to think now?

Shortly afterwards, Tatiana opened her eyes and turned to me. "I loved him enough to give him back his freedom and let him be happy."

We stared at each other without saying a word.

Tatiana was quiet for several seconds, and then she said, "Why am I telling you all this? I don't know, but if I don't tell you, whom should I tell?"

I made myself meet her gaze as I said, "You know that here you can tell me everything you want."

She shook her head and said, "As I'm saying all this, it sounds weird, but actually that's the way it was. I'm surprised to hear myself say it."

"But at said time you didn't think that it was bizarre and unusual," I said calmly.

She remained silent, looking at the ceiling. What was she thinking? I wondered.

"No, I thought it was normal since I could not have sex with him, so he had to look elsewhere," she said with a trembling voice.

"I see. Why didn't you leave him?"

"I would never leave my husband, I love him, he is a habit I've formed and he is security."

I nodded.

"Probably we should have continued to have sex just like other couples do, but it was meaningless to my husband. Also there was part of me that I hated. I hated myself for being not straightforward, I hated myself for being complicated and I hated myself for not being honest in my marriage. But you should know that it wasn't my fault."

"So whose fault was that?" I asked, slightly irritated.

"I'm sorry, I can't answer your question, not at this moment, not at this time," Tatiana said, as she bowed her head. When she spoke again, she said in a low tone, "Do you know what I am? I'm frigid. What do you think?"

"You can't be frigid, you are suffering sexual trauma which can lead you to the disorder and confusion. Sure, the drugs that you had been taking left you unable to maintain a normal sexual life. Don't forget that you were overmedicated, and that's why we needed to diminish your dosage significantly."

"So I'm not frigid," she said, looking straight into my eyes.

"You are so anxious that you look at many things mistakenly," I said.

Tatiana acknowledged my statement only by a slight nod. She spoke freely to me, but I still saw inconsistency and conflict in her troubled face. I also detected in her sad eyes this mystery that I was unable to comprehend, the mystery that bewildered me even though I knew that in one way or another she would reveal to me her real truth without restraint.

"I never considered all the aspects of marriage, you see, everything is a problem, better if I say I'm the problem."

"Don't forget that it was never a full marriage," I reminded her nicely.

"I anticipated a full marriage, but you are right, it wasn't a real one. Though, we were clear about what we were doing," Tatiana said with a brief shake of the head.

"Perhaps you should have been psychoanalyzed. Sometimes, for some women it takes a very long time to enjoy sex. Someone has to really know your body. You must understand that sex is not just about mutual orgasms. It's also about intimacy, and connection. Have you ever told your husband what you want and need?"

Tatiana lifted her head, looked at me with a forced smile and said, "I never discussed it with him, but now he is not interested in me anyway, and I don't like to be touched even though I still love him. It's difficult for me to describe the complexity of my feelings. There is something about having sex with him that makes me feel lonely afterwards."

"You are unable to get out of your head. You feel trapped in your mind and you can't connect with your body," I said.

"Yes, that is so," she admitted.

"I think you should be more active, you should exercise or perhaps practice yoga. Thus, you will help your body to respond more quickly and intensely."

"I started doing yoga," she said, smiling.

"When did you start?"

"Last month, and I already notice a lightness that I had never experienced."

"You won't regret it; yoga will make your mind clearer and more alert. You will perceive the true meaning behind life and it will build up your self-confidence. You will see Tatiana; your relationship to your body will change. You will learn to like yourself, take care of yourself and respect yourself," I assured her.

"Do you really mean it?"

"I guarantee. Through yoga, you can also overcome your anxiety, worry, fear and anger," I spoke with certainty.

"Really?" she repeated.

"Absolutely; yoga has been a great relief to many of my patients and to myself. It acts as a catalyst to psychotherapy, and it involves your connection with your deepest self."

"Yes, it's a soothing and relaxing experience, and I'm trying to keep myself on the track. I'm really working hard to put my life back together."

"I'm not surprised; I always knew that you are a strong and courageous woman."

"Sure?"

"I've never been so sure about anything," I said with conviction.

"So I'm not hopeless."

"No, Tatiana. I have one more question before you leave. May I?" I said as I looked at my watch.

"Please, I hope it's an easy question," she said, half- smiling.

"As I understood, you never said anything to your husband about your past, right?

"Right," she confirmed.

"Why?"

"I never told my husband or anyone who I really am. And now, I can't tell him anymore, it's too late. I'll become a stranger and I would put myself in danger if I told him about it. I would not allow him to hurt me, to judge me and to destroy me. What do you think?"

"It's entirely up to you; it's your decision, Tatiana. I don't know your husband yet, but I think telling him the truth, that will not harm you. On the contrary, you could have perhaps freed yourself of your anxiety and traumatism during your intimacy," I uttered.

"I'm afraid to let him in my past," she insisted.

"Talking is an important part of any kind of relationship. It can strengthen your ties with your partner or with other people in general. Talking can help you stay in good mental health. And being listened to; helps you feel that other people care about you.

"You see; I've not been honest," she admitted.

"From my perspective, honesty is the key of a real relationship and the most important element of true love," I avowed.

Perhaps we looked at the matter so differently that we might never understand one another. She did not oppose my comment, but simply listened and repeated herself, "I can't tell my husband the truth." Tatiana paused for a brief moment, closing her eyes.

"I don't want anyone to know about my condition," she said as she opened her eyes. She breathed deeply and immediately took possession of herself.

"Don't worry; everything you said here remains strictly confidential. This is the time and the place to discuss it."

"I'm glad that I could finally speak about it openly," she said calmly.

"Yes, this is extremely important in therapy."

She shook her head silently, gazing fixedly and kindly in my face for a long moment.

"I have a very strong connection with you, you make me feel comfortable," she finally said, smiling. Tatiana felt the emotion within her as she got on her feet, trying to move slowly towards the door.

"I'm happy to hear that this is your way of thinking," I said gladly.

"The air here is filled with the pleasant scent of your perfume, as usual," Tatiana said exhaling.

"It could be."

After a short time, when she was gone, I saw Celine who slid down the hallway silently, holding the little white puppy in her arms. The dog groaning faintly licked quickly her cheek, and jumped down.

Mademoiselle Solange appeared hastily. She took Celine's hand and said, "It's a gorgeous day, come on, we are going to the park. The air is soft and warm today; just a gentle breeze is blowing."

A look of happiness and delight showed on my daughter's face. The little dog, barking and moving with quick steps ahead, wagged her tail playfully. Celine took her in her arms and buried her happy face in her fur.

I looked at them for a long time before they left.

TWENTY-THREE

As soon as I entered my office, the phone started ringing. I looked at the screen; it was Alexander.

"Hi."

"Hi my love, I'm just wondering if you can come over for a drink."

"Sorry, I'm still working; I've got patients to see."

"You are always working, you never stop," he said.

At this precise time, I heard a noise behind the door. I glanced at my watch, it was three o'clock.

"My patient is here. Sorry, I have to go."

"Give me a call anytime you are free."

"Talk to you later on," I said as I quickly hung up the phone.

Over the previous few weeks, I had felt that Alexander had become more and more curious about what I was doing and whom I was seeing. I had wanted to see him in a casual way, but he had attempted to take control of my life on several occasions.

Tatiana paced around my office. Next, she sat on the couch and gave me an exasperated look, "As I told you, my husband and I decided to love and set each other free, but now..." she did not finish her sentence; she unexpectedly stopped and began to weep mutely.

A stunned silence fell in my office. I waited for Tatiana to talk, but she kept quiet. This silence lasted a very long time. She looked aggravated, and irritated. She gazed fixedly with the eyes wide open, and chewed her lips, "Men are bastards."

I watched her carefully.

"I'm so sorry; it's been a bad day. I can think of nothing to say, and I have terrible headaches because nothing is going right in my life these days," she said.

"What's wrong now?" I asked.

"You are French," she said.

"And?"

"French people don't overreact about infidelity," she said, stammering.
I felt myself getting warmer.

After about a few tense minutes, Tatiana said bitterly, "Today, my head
is fuzzy. You know, I often wonder why my husband ever married me!"

She tiptoed to the window and took a look outside on the street. She
looked stressed, uptight and apprehensive. After another short and uneasy
silence, she sat languidly on the couch and vainly made a great effort to
make herself at ease. All of a sudden, she began talking fast, and now, it
was as if she could not stop, "I just wanted a quiet life, but gradually it
has fallen apart. I hardly see my husband, he always pretends to be tired
or busy, too tired to go and see a movie, too tired to take a walk like the
old days, and too tired to go to restaurants. When was the last time that he
kissed me? I don't remember.

"I'm continually tortured by suspicions of infidelity. My husband has
not been very discreet about his lover's perfume which would hold on to
his shirt, his body and his hair," she said acrimoniously.

I witnessed the strangest expression on her face. Tatiana puzzled me
to such an extent that for a brief moment I forgot about everything she had
said.

"Really!" I shrugged and looked out. I sighed, and thought I was in a
difficult situation.

"Yes, I told you then what I had told no one. Now, I feel that I'm unable
to compete."

There was something about her eyes that frightened me. The heavy
silence thrived and I felt that my heart began to pump faster. I darted a
strange smile at her and said, "But you invented your own rules, Tatiana,
and I thought it was okay with you if your husband sees other women."

"Yes. But now, there is this other woman and I think that my husband
loves her. It must be so. His love for me is less now, I feel it. I'm consumed
with jealousy. I've never been jealous before, but this time it's different.
He might want to marry her, who knows? I'm worried, I can't take another
rejection," she said spitefully.

The blood rushed to her face as she went on, "Jealousy is an awful thing! I've seen so many women come and go in my husband's life and this time too, I assured myself that he would get rid of her within a few weeks or months, but I was so wrong."

Working with my patients was always a challenge. Tatiana had definitely gotten my full attention. It was the first time that she approached on this delicate subject. I wondered if this was really the main reason for her that a few months ago she attempted suicide.

"Honestly, I've never known that," I said bluntly. I was silent and surprised.

"Well, now you know; I hate to be jealous. Can you believe such a thing possible?"

I did not reply; I just kept quiet, making a few more notes in a piece of paper.

"Sure I'm not the first woman in the world who has been unhappy in her marriage. I remember how passionately my husband loved me, and how different he is now. Everything seems to be a mystery about him, I'm not just heart-broken but humiliated."

"I'm sure he still loves you in his own way, maybe you should fight for him," I said.

"It's too late for that, you know," she said as she began to keep her voice down.

"Nothing seemed permanent, you two need to sit and talk to each other," I said sternly.

"He never keeps me company anymore. Day after day, I realize that I'm much lonelier than before. Do you think I'm delirious? Please don't mock me, this is so painful!"

"Why would I mock you? That's not my way at all, Tatiana," I said very seriously.

She nodded, "I hate to hear myself talk this way. Did I ruin everything? Did I?"

Moments later, she lowered her head as tears stung her eyes. She continued with a shaky voice, "I'm afraid of being alone; it's painful for me to imagine living my life without loving someone ever again. I have a lot of love to give, no one likes divorce, and what do you think?" she asked me softly, blowing her nose.

"Generally speaking, divorce proceedings are agonizing and traumatic.

At a given time, you give your whole body and soul, your faith in love and your projects in life. You concentrate all your hopes and dreams on this one person. Consequently, taking away everything that you have already invested with your heart and soul is distressful. In many cases, even the person who decides to leave might live the divorce process as an abandon. It's important not to forget the dimension of human suffering," I commented calmly.

Lost and confused, Tatiana looked at me, obviously not really hearing what I had said.

"I have a nice life, but I spend all night long in a state of terrible anxiety. I'm sure that my husband is having a love affair," she said as she busied herself with Celine's photograph.

I could not put my thoughts together yet. After all, I did not know as much as I wanted. I could only picture her husband without knowing him as a man who stayed with a woman that he could have left years earlier, a disappointed woman with a fragile emotional condition who had trouble sharing his dreams.

"No one's life is perfect. Life has its ups and downs," I said, trying to calm her.

Now, staring in my eyes, Tatiana spoke again of her memories with her husband, "I still treasure the nights on the patio at my home. My husband and I would sit down for a long and intimate dinner, sampling as much delicious food as possible and drinking plenty of great wine. He gave me the most wonderful feeling of happiness and love. I felt so happy that nothing else seemed to matter. But this doesn't happen anymore. I want to have fun with my husband, doesn't every woman deserve that?"

"Certainly, and especially you, Tatiana, most of all," I said sympathetically.

"When I think it over, I come to the conclusion that there is a part of culpability and weakness, that make me vulnerable to be loved," she said frantically.

"I believe that this particular need can lead you very far away," I said.

"I thought it was a successful marriage, but now it's falling apart."

"Maybe only now, he realizes what he really wants and you can't give it to him. Don't forget, it has never been a full marriage, Tatiana," I reminded her once more.

Suddenly, her face changed, she looked straight in my face with cold eyes and said, "You are right, it was never a real marriage, but I wanted to believe that it was a good marriage. You know what, I should have died.

"A few months ago, I was deeply unhappy, and began quite seriously to think of suicide. I couldn't go on like this forever. I tried to convince myself that only death would rescue me from my misery and set me free from my depression. There is something wonderful about a death. Sometimes, I close my eyes and imagine how I would look when at last I'm dead. As desperate as I was, I attempted to commit suicide, but unfortunately it was a failure, my plan broke down."

Unable to restrain herself any longer, Tatiana burst into sobs. She could no longer speak.

My heart ached with pity for her. I kept quiet, making a few more notes as usual.

Next, she got up erratically, and headed towards the window, "Nothing is as exciting as death," she whispered.

Frightened by the desperate expression with which her last words were uttered, I said, "Sometimes, you get foolish ideas in your head and you don't know what you are thinking of."

"Do you really understand what I've been through?" she looked at me nervously.

"I clearly understand it now," I said.

"I wasn't afraid of death. Death for me means returning into the eternal source of love."

I remained silent, looking compassionately into her eyes for a very long moment.

"Tatiana, what you just said is full of meaning, so deep. Death is a part of life, and you shouldn't give that a trite subject; you can't ruin everything. You should be a lively and positive energy for good in this universe and embrace the mystery and grandeur of life."

A moment later, raising her voice and staring austerely at me, she said, "I feel a deep sense of insecurity about my life and my marriage. As a child, I always asked myself these questions: "Where did we come from? Where are we going? And why are we here? But I could never find the right answers. Now, I'm questioning everything again, I don't know what I am and why I'm here in this world. All I know is that I promised to love him for better or worse, didn't I? Now, worse is definitely here and I'm having difficulty coping with my position in life. How can I love him when his love for me ended?

I listened without saying anything and shook my head in silence. Tatiana was pale as a ghost, and seemed to be frenetic, and hysterical.

"Divorce is awful and so terrible to me; it will be such a blow to my life. I'm afraid of being left alone in this fucking world," she said irately after a short pause.

"You will not be left alone!"

I read in Tatiana's eyes the way that she felt, the lack of self-esteem, the feeling that she could not do anything right, the worry, the anxiety and the inability to get out of her marriage because of being dependent on her husband for support. I found that she was psychologically in a critical state of mind.

"Is your husband reliable?" I asked.

"Not really, but it feels good to have him around time to time," she said desperately.

At this moment, I was about to ask her a few more questions, but Tatiana, ignoring me, raised her voice and said, "People who commit suicide attract my attention, I can't help it. Some people hang themselves with a belt like this American actor Robin William, and others who shoot themselves with a gun like the prince Alireza of Iran who shot himself in his town house in Boston. Also there are those who kill themselves in the railway of the metro like that crazy blond woman who planned her death for months. She was a shrink, living like an eremite with no friends. I always wondered how she could help her patients. She had lots of issues and she needed help, but I believe that now she is finally in peace."

"How did you know her?" I asked.

"She was my neighbor, living next door to my condo."

"I see."

"I chose to leave this world peacefully even though it's not quiet and tranquil. You should know that I'm not afraid of death, I'm afraid of being tortured, I'm afraid of being alone and I'm afraid of getting old. I was so much in pain that I decided to leave my body, and set free my tormented soul. I didn't want to live anymore; I tried to take my own life. So I took a heavy dose of my prescription pills.

"When I was in the ambulance, I felt extremely strange with all kinds of chemicals flooding in my body. Doctor Luciano and his nurses saved my life by pumping my stomach. I felt I was buried alive in my own body; they did whatever else they needed to do to bring me back to life.

"When I found myself in intensive care, my husband standing there; was watching me compassionately," she said nervously as she wiped quickly the tears from her eyes.

Tatiana could no longer articulate the words; she hesitated for several times and stopped in the midst of what she was saying.

There was a profound silence between us. In this silence, I thought that after talking to me about her childhood during all these sessions, she finally got to the crucial point she was, when first she came to my office. It was time to come to the real point of having wanted to kill herself. The love affair that her husband conducted with this other woman explained undoubtedly Tatiana's attempted suicide.

I broke this silence that became intolerable and asked, "Have you done this before?"

"Of course not!" she replied.

Leaning her elbows on the desk, she gazed up at the sky through the windows for a short time, then she turned to me and said, "I wish that I would be cremated and my ashes buried under a weeping willow tree that sprout its leaves fully, so that I could grow with it and cast shadow for lovers to embrace under."

"Life is a remarkable and precious gift. There is something to be decided when we know more about this situation, I'm sure there is a way to get out of this mess," I said calmly.

"Do you really think I can get through this?" she asked, her voice sounded very weak.

"Tatiana, you are a valiant and strong woman, but I can't promise anything right now, since I don't know your husband. Together, we are going to work on your case, okay? Your case is universal; the infidelity in marriages is frequently so common and ordinary. Listen, I know that your life is filled with stress and worry, but you should know that all the medications that you had been taking could cause sexual dysfunction and suicidal thoughts," I said as I looked at her with questioning eyes.

Tatiana read my mind, and then she said, "I know that you are full of questions about my husband, but I told you everything. Besides, he still doesn't know that I'm seeing you."

"I wish I could get to know him, meeting your husband would definitely help me understand a lot of things."

"I'm not sure that's a good idea, it sounds sort of shadowy to me," she said nervously.

"Don't worry, I don't have the intention to meet him," I narrowed my eyes on her, and then I had my lips parted to say something, but suddenly stopped.

Shortly afterwards, Tatiana forced a light smile, glanced at her watch and said, "The storm-clouds are gathering, I had better be going home before it rains."

She got up quickly and pulling her hair from her face, she began looking carefully through the bookshelf.

"Have you read all of these?" she asked, as she waved her hand towards the books.

"Yes."

"Which one do you like the best?"

"All of them."

"All of them? She said, as she picked up one from the shelf and opened it.

When Tatiana selected the book, she came back to her seat and sat down again.

"I've always loved books, they are cold but faithful," she said, the book opened on her lap. She did not look up as she was turning the pages.

Five minutes passed in silence, I waited patiently.

"Can I borrow this? I want to read it," she said, looking inquiringly at me.

"Yes dear, that's for you. You can have it, take it home," I said, looking at her kindly.

"Thank you, what is it about?" she asked as she turned the cover of the book towards me: "The inner peace" by Paramahansa Yogananda.

I thought for a couple of seconds and said, "It's about how to find easiness and simplicity in every moment and face life with confidence and radiance. Each precious moment of our lives has either the potential to cover us in confusion and distress, or invite us into peace and happiness. It's also about how to overcome fear, worry, nervousness and anxiety."

"That sounds great, I think I should read it," she said as her eyes sparkled.

"Yes, take it home," I repeated.

"There is still so much to read!" she exclaimed, her jaw clenching.

I smiled.

"You read deep books, you are very profound," Tatiana said with an expression of sadness.

We exchanged a short glance.

"Are you able to bring all these subjects into your life? she asked impetuously.

I kept smiling.

"Hmm," said Tatiana, looking at all sides of the book, "Well, now I think I really should go. There isn't time anyway."

"Enjoy the book."

"I will," she said as she unlatched the door, thanking me with a nod of the head.

It was a disturbing session, and I wanted it to be over. I walked to the window and watched the rain falling.

At the end of the day, sometimes I like to sit in the living room with a glass of wine and a book. Then, I would have a bubble bath and eat the delicious food that mademoiselle Solange had prepared.

After having shared a few moments with my daughter that evening, I retired to my bedroom. I could not stop thinking about what Tatiana had mentioned to me about the perfume of her husband's lover. Why did she make me so uncomfortable? What was that all about? I wondered.

TWENTY-FOUR

My following appointment with Tatiana started not face-to-face and formally behind my desk, but in the most casual and comfortable position on the couch.

From where I was sitting, the daylight illuminating the expressions on her face, was casting a golden aura on her persona. In fact, it was the strength of this young woman that was very appealing and interesting in so many aspects. She looked beautiful, charming, attractive and perhaps a bit intense, just as actresses are.

Tatiana made me think of the poems of Charles Baudelaire, who gave these sensual and mysterious descriptions of women that I always found fascinating and very exciting.

She complained about the heavy make-up that she was wearing, "I feel like you can hardly see me, I'm not trying to hide myself behind it, but I'm totally in a different mood today. I would like to look different," she said as she smiled happily.

"You look stunning," I said.

"Thank you. You know, I wasn't in my right mind last week. I was very pessimistic and cynical. I only had a penchant for gloomy things, sorry, I could not help it."

"It's okay, I understand what you must have been through," I said.

"Do you really understand?"

"Of course I understand."

"Today I feel stronger, also in so many ways content and secure, I can't get it!"

"Excellent."

"I began to read the first chapters of your book. I read quite a lot of serious books but I have never read anything like this before. I absolutely felt compelled to read it."

"It seems great!"

"The subject grabbed my attention and at every couple of lines, I had to stop reading to marvel at how great it was. Now, I feel that it's possible to open the door to a new level of intimacy and love in our relationships," Tatiana said with a sudden sensation of peace and relief.

"Yes."

"For so many years, my life seemed blocked in a hopeless impasse, but now I think it's slowly moving forward."

"What do you mean?"

"I don't understand why I acted so strange when I talked to you about my mother."

"Can you be more specific? I'm not quite sure that I understand your point, Tatiana."

"Well, I don't see my mother that often, she is old now and a gust of wind could knock her over. I have to let her be, she is my mother; she is not a plague. I mean why I should conceive such a strong aversion when I admit that I was the one who caused her pain, it was my entire fault. You know, I mean her no harm. It really took me quite a time to realize that she is not a monster. The atrocities that she witnessed in life made her tough, cold and insensitive.

"I still love her, I plan to go back there and see her again. I want her to know that I'm happy in my marriage even if I'm not. She is still my mother that I loved, the mother who put bows in my hair when I was a little girl, and the mother who made me coffee each morning," Tatiana said as she dried her eyes.

"Yes," I affirmed.

"I admit that I've been mean and spiteful to her," she added, shaking her head.

With great effort, I concentrated on what she said to me. As she spoke calmly, she was conscious of the choice of her words. The little smile in her eyes gleamed more brightly than ever.

In the silence that followed, I smiled at her, understanding the psychological energy that helped her to explore the inner source of strength and the positive thinking, two fundamental qualities indispensable for a life of harmony and fulfillment.

"Is that how you feel now?" I asked her.

"Yes, it's the way that I really want to feel," she uttered.

For the first time, I was very satisfied and pleased to realize that Tatiana had undergone a staggering, an incredible and amazing metamorphosis regarding her mother.

After a brief silence, she asked, "What do you think of me today?"

"You are remarkable! You are mentally coherent, and your positive thoughts about your mother can lead you to inner peace. Now, your life should have more meaning and integrity."

"I've never pictured this moment, I definitely had to remove that widespread hatred that I felt towards my mother from my heart," she said coolly.

"Excellent, I'm very proud of you, Tatiana. Your life can't become peaceful and quiet unless and until you decide to live towards the peace and serenity," I articulated calmly.

She looked straight ahead and said, "I had lost the most important part of myself, and now with your help, I have the feeling that slowly this vital piece is coming back to me."

"No matter what is going on around you, you should try to stay unruffled."

"Okay, an unruffled composure!" she exclaimed with a very sweet smile on her lips.

"You can be happy in life if only you overcome the negativity."

"I promise I'll try my best. You are so French! You have an innate and natural way about yourself. You know how to look cool and be positive. You wear perfume that flatters you, and you know how to put things together and be sexy and feminine."

"Thank you," I said with a fixed smile.

"I don't believe in the concept of a beauty icon, the mysterious and attractiveness that you discover over the time, that is what's most powerful for me," she said.

I shook my head with a gesture of approval.

Now, at this moment, Tatiana and I were comfortably sitting on the couch in a meaningful silence. It seemed that we both understood perfectly each other and we had a great and systematic connection, this kind of correlation that ties cordially the patient with the therapist.

She crossed her legs and stared at me for several seconds, and then she said, "I had a strange dream last night, and I admit that it was kind of embarrassing. But I decided to talk to you about it."

"You know that my office is your sacred place where you can talk about anything you want without feeling awkward," I reminded her gently.

"Yes."

Tatiana became reserved and quiet, looking at me with feelings that aroused desire. Despite my curiosity, I kept my mouth shut and waited for her to speak her mind.

After a long pause, she said in a hollow voice, "Since I started my therapy, for the first time, I saw you in my dream last night."

"Okay," I smiled faintly.

"We were in this delightful little town of Montreux in Switzerland," she said shyly.

"Hmmm!"

"We stayed in the same charming hotel where Vladimir Nabokov, the author of Lolita spent his final days."

"Okay."

"We were there to assist at the golden rose festival. We crossed the lake and wandered down the narrow streets," Tatiana spoke with excitement.

Suddenly she fell silent.

"And?"

"Oh, I'm embarrassed, I can't tell you," she said as she blushed.

"Nothing ever should make you feel awkward or ashamed," I insisted.

"Nothing?"

"Yes; absolutely nothing." I repeated.

"Okay; and we dined in a picturesque restaurant. Then, we went to our hotel room and made love. It was the first time ever that I had a sexual act with a woman, and I found it magical. The smell of your perfume allowed me to liberate myself from my problems. It was a new feeling and I loved it," Tatiana spoke with vibrancy. When she said the last words, the embarrassment expressed on her face was even more noticeable than before.

"When I opened my eyes this morning, it took me only a second to remember my dream. I thought everything was so truthful, the scent of your skin that I like so much!"

I looked silently at Tatiana's face, stared at her, but said no words.

"You should know that I'm not a lesbian, I'm straight and I like men, but I go into ecstasies every time I see the naked body of a woman, of course when she has a nice figure such as Venus, the goddess of the beauty, love and sex for example."

I felt that my face wreathed in smiles, I kept quiet.

"What do you think of my dream?"

"What do you think? I reversed her question immediately.

"I mean what I really like, what really touches my heart is the intoxicating scent of your perfume, so new and original for me. And in my dream, the smell of your fragrance set me free from all kinds of problems that I'm facing in my life, it was fabulous!" she said after a pause.

"Yes, it must be so," I said, half-smiling.

I remained calm and indifferent. Tatiana uncrossed her legs and went on with completely a different tone, "Now, I'm ashamed to realize that I'm so unaware and irresponsible of my actions, I mean, really! No sense of decency, no respectable behavior."

"You should know that your unconscious, the part of your mind containing your thoughts not normally accessible to consciousness, is not on familiar terms with the sense of courtesy."

Tatiana said nothing, her lips began twitching nervously, and her expression changed at once as she changed the subject, "When I look back, I find it interesting to put the puzzle pieces of my marriage together. I've been trying to write my memories in long hand; this allows me to find a deeper connection to my words. I wanted to read you a few pages of my work today, but I could not find my notes this morning. It's not easy for me to find what I need in my place. My things are always missing: Keys, credit cards, eyeglasses, cell phone, books, you name it."

"You probably can't find them because you don't put them in the same place," I said.

"I don't have sense of organization, my place is always messy and it has become out of my control. I can't do anything about it. One day, my husband said, "Why should anyone keep all these things? This place is a chaos," and he packed his clothes and left. He made it clear that he was not happy and he preferred to live apart, but he would continue to support me financially until the end. Now, he is still my husband, but we live a separate life."

"Organization is a big part of your memory," I said.

"I know, but I can't do anything about it."

"What is the reason for you to accumulate all these things?" I asked.

"It's weird, but piling all kinds of objects gives me not only a certain power but also some kind of security, I feel safe and protected in a way," Tatiana told me.

We looked at one another.

"There is so much to take care of around my place. There is no space and the air is not circulating properly, since every corner of my place is overflowing with lots of objects, I call it the flea market. If you see my place, you understand my state of mind."

"Well, it's not healthy; it explains the chaos in your mind, your head and your brain."

"You are right, and I know it."

Moments later, Tatiana sighed deeply and went on, "My husband and I have always been radically different, so I suppose that it should come as no surprise that our differences have deepened. I still love him as crazy as that sounds, and I don't want to divorce him. I'm trying to visualize my life without him; what it will be like? I can't even imagine this.

"Like every woman, I want to believe that endless love is possible. Is my current situation my own entire fault? Could I have done things differently? My husband's affair with this woman is bruising me inside and out. I know he loves her, I feel it and I'm insanely jealous of her. I always thought that just having sex with someone gets them nowhere in life, but I was so wrong.

"There is no doubt that my husband needs sex, I understand that. Actually, I gave him the freedom to have sex with other women, but only sex. Now, I realize how much he wants to have sex with this particular woman and how much he loves her; that hurts."

"Yes."

"This is exactly what happened between my husband and I. Please, tell me what to do? I'm in desperate need of help."

"Are you sure that you still want to stay with him?" I asked her.

"Yes, of course. We are living separately anyway, but he is still taking care of my bills, and I'm filled with a great sense of protection, I mean financially. At first, I felt suicidal about my separation, and most of the time I was depressed. But then, I learned how to live alone. Divorce is very sad, and this is simply too much. Do you understand?"

"Yes," I replied, as I looked up at the sky, the pink and blue colors were slowly fading.

Then, I turned my attention to her and asked, "Did you marry him because you were in love or you wanted to shape your life and give a meaning to your existence? Perhaps you hoped that there would be a successful man to take care of you so you wouldn't take care of yourself."

There was a pause that seemed to go on forever. Tatiana did not move a muscle in her face. I waited, and then I repeated my question as I looked at her for some time, wondering what to say and what to do to help her. This question could not have been any more sincere on my part.

She finally pulled her long hair back and said, "At that time, he was good for my life. With him, my life was moving in a new direction, he stimulated me and brought me enthusiasm and excitement. I thought he was very wealthy, attractive and smart, and my life would be easy and this was my luck. I had to trust him and give him a chance, and I assumed that with time, I would love him," she controlled perfectly her words.

Tatiana fell silent. Perplexed; I could not really grasp the mix of feelings that she had for her husband. Did she know what she was talking of? Sure, at said time, she was desperate and perhaps she did love him too. Was she sincere with me? I felt that she misrepresented her truth by twisting and distorting the words, and she was so good at it. I was thrilled.

"How would I get through this? Nothing is in my control anymore. I can't discuss it with him, I would just give him an excuse to leave me, I don't want to lose him."

"Tatiana, one thing must be considered, your husband left you anyway. You two have a separate life now."

She nodded, tears dropped from her eyes and she pushed back her hair that kept falling into her eyes.

I stayed still, looking at her desolately.

"What would become of me? Please help me, what can I do? I need your help or I would not have told you. I've thought about everything that possibly can be done but I can't think of absolutely nothing. I was so desperate that I wanted to die, but my life had to be continued, and unfortunately I'm still alive."

Tatiana had this particular technique of repeating herself, and what she was saying was very important to her. I listened attentively to her as I always did, I was obviously interested in her every single word.

Now she collapsed into tears, and grabbed some tissues from the box on my desk. I waited for her to get a hold of herself.

"You must have had an emotional breakdown. When you are unhappy, you make some terrible decisions and then you get a huge moment of realization- like what was I thinking? - Look at you, you are pretty, intelligent and strong, stronger than you think. You've got so much to give," I said as I stared at her, making sure that she understood me.

"What would you do in my place?" she repeated, not hearing much of what I said.

"My advice, since you are asking me is patience, I would wait."

"Just wait?"

"Yes, we've got to figure this out, and it will take some time. I wish I could meet your husband, it would be a great help for me to assist you, Tatiana," I said, as I looked her eye to eye.

"My husband doesn't know that I'm seeing you. But if you meet him, I'm sure you will like him and you will be on his side," she said, as hate swelled up within her.

"Like him? Tatiana, you are my patient and you are important to me, not him. Everyone deserves a second chance, whether is in a relationship or in another bad situation."

"Oh, I'll forgive him."

"Do you have any idea who the other woman is?" I asked sharply.

"No, I have no clue; perhaps an actress, but I'm not sure."

"And for how long has she been in the picture?" I asked, intrigued by this subject.

"I think a few months, but I'm not sure," she said, ruminating.

"Well, logically for married couples who find themselves in the position you are in, we would recommend separation. But in your case, your husband left you anyway."

Silence followed; a very intense silence. The expression on Tatiana's face changed instantly, she bowed her head and whispered, "I don't want a divorce, period."

"No one type of solution works for everyone, and different kinds of therapy work well for different people," I explained.

Tatiana said nothing. She half-smiled, shaking her head.

It seemed to me that in Tatiana's case, divorce was out of question for the time being. She could not live her old life. Divorce meant to her to take away from her the last tie that bound her to life. As difficult and strange as her marriage has been, I could never bring myself to ask her to take the final step of filing for divorce under those dreadful circumstances. Given her fragile emotional state, I could not imagine traumatizing her any further.

"Marriage is not what people think it is. We want to believe that every marriage is the perfect balance, but it isn't. There are no guarantees in any marriage, but you do not worry. Somehow, we will figure it out when we get more information," I assured her with a smile.

"I'm such a failure," she protested.

"You are a human being, stop being judgmental about yourself," I said nicely.

Silence, and in this silence, tears flowed down both her cheeks as she smiled gloomily without speaking. Then all of a sudden, she changed rapidly the subject and said, "The smell of your perfume transports me to an enchanted world, it's incredibly true." Now, she was jovial.

I smiled too; I was filled with cheerful good humor.

"I'm breathing in your scent, and it's out of this world! This perfume is infused with notes meant to capture us. Perhaps I should change my perfume, I'm done with "Fracas," no more battle, no more struggle in life, the sooner, the better. What do you think?" she asked me as her eyes lighted up with joy.

"You have to decide for yourself, Tatiana. But since you're asking me, I would say that anything makes you happy in life, just go for it, why not?"

"You really don't mind? But this is your perfume, your identity, I mean," she insisted.

"It's okay," I said, and at this moment in time, I had absolutely no idea what I was getting myself into.

"Thank you."

"You look like you're going somewhere today," I said, smiling.

"I'm going to meet my husband; he is taking me to an auction. He doesn't have the courage to tell me that he is seeing this other woman. Her powerful perfume lingers in his clothes. If he really loves her, why is he afraid of telling me? Is he afraid of hurting me more?"

Suddenly something inside me made me anxious and uneasy, why? I wondered.

Tatiana's last words were a challenge that echoed through my office. As soon as I let her out the door, feeling more helpless than ever, I turned my attention to Celine who was hanging around with Charlotte. I could hear the sound of her angelic voice coming towards me. I walked with my light and rapid steps to meet my daughter.

TWENTY-FIVE

As time went on; a few more sessions with Tatiana ran more or less smoothly. In despite of the existing problems in her marriage, I thought she was doing better than I had imagined. Now, she looked at her past misdeeds with different eyes. She seemed unflustered about coming to my office and talking to me. I knew she still needed special attention and that was not unusual for patients like her.

Unlike a lot of people who decide to see a therapist just to be listened to, Tatiana anticipated the pleasure of speaking to me about her emotions, feelings and thoughts; but always she would ask my opinions. She was very reserved especially during the first sessions of her therapy, but gradually she established her position in my office and became comfortable with me.

Was she always sincere and truthful? Yes, most of the time. However, I understood that at some point, she had a certain characteristic and tendency to express herself in particular terms. Perhaps she specifically attempted to represent herself as someone slightly different. I believed it was perfectly comprehensible in Tatiana's case for the simple reason that she did not want to be severely criticized. Therefore, I consistently listened to her words carefully and suspiciously, and tried to select and gather the important hints and slight indications with the objective to come to a final conclusion.

Sitting upright at my desk, I was staring out at nothing in particular when my phone rang. I answered; it was Alexander.

"Hi love."

"Hi."

"I'm just wondering if we can have lunch so that we can chat comfortably," he said.

"I'm going to be working until four o'clock."

"No break for lunch?"

"No Alex, sorry," I said apologetically.

"What about a coffee?"

"Sorry again, I just can't today."

He remained silent for a moment, and then he said, "I've been thinking about you and I miss you."

"Okay."

"Just okay? Is that all?"

"What do you want me to say?"

"Never mind," he said.

"No, really Alex, what do you want?"

"I want you, I want to kiss you, and I want to make love to you," he said passionately.

A silence fell.

"So?" he said, as he raised his voice.

"Yes; definitely I want to see you too."

"Maybe we should get together for a drink after your work, let say at six o'clock."

"Okay, see you then."

Moments later, I heard Celine's voice that penetrated through the door. Next, she walked in my office; I glanced at her happy and glowing face and smiled.

"Mom, can we go to the park, it's a nice weather and I want to take out my little puppy."

"Sure sweetie, but not today, not right now. I have patients to see."

"I love you mom," and she hurriedly walked away.

I watched her lovingly as she went out the door. No matter how busy I was, I always made time to see her usually in the evening, if not between my patients.

I saw one more patient and then, at three o'clock, Tatiana took her seat on the couch as she looked around. She took out her cell phone from her bag and placed it next to her. She looked good, relaxed and calm as she stared at me in amazement.

"How have you been?" I asked.

"Fine," she smiled at me, clapping her hands.

"You look so calm and cool!" I exclaimed.

"Yes indeed. Do you want to hear the latest?"

"Yes, what is it?"

"It's something phenomenal! You shall hear it all," she said enthusiastically.

There was something strangely different about her today. In her beautiful green eyes, beaming with happiness, I saw all she needed to have in life.

"You look wonderful; now tell me what's going on in your life?"

"I'm perfectly happy the way things are," she said as tears of joy pearled in her eyes. Then, trapping herself into silence, she straightened her shoulders and stared at my face.

"I'm delighted for you," I said, even if I didn't fully understand what had happened.

Quietly seated, I was ready to listen to her.

Tatiana felt pretty much in charge of breaking this moment of silence. She shook her head, smiled at me and said, "I always felt safe and protected here, and this is very important. I know in my heart that you are essentially a beneficial power, a light in the obscurity of my life."

There was gratitude in her words towards me, I could sense it and was touched by it.

"I love my mother and I wouldn't do or say anything to hurt her," she murmured to herself.

"Sure,"

"Today is my birthday," she said gladly.

"Happy birthday," I said warmly.

"Thank you. Last night, I had a dream, but it wasn't a nightmare. It was a sweet and peaceful dream, so real," she told me in a mellow tone.

"This is excellent, Tatiana!"

"I was standing in front of my mother here, in your office. Her face was uncovered and she looked at me affectionately. She talked to me fondly; everything was as clear as it happened in real life. I felt so loved and so protected, I saw in my mother's face lots of love and warmth. "Can you forgive me now? It's my birthday!" I whispered to her. "I know, and that's the reason I came to see you, Tatiana. I forgive you, you are my daughter, my own flesh and blood, and I always loved you more than I had ever loved anyone," she said to me.

"Finally, I heard my mother talking to me with sweet words. There was pain in her voice, but under this pain, it was a deep love, true love. It pierced my heart. My mother threw her arms around me, and showered me with kisses and tears. I looked at her, stunned; I had never seen her cry like this. I asked her to stop crying, but she didn't pay attention to me. It's my birthday and I knew she would come to see me. When I woke up, I was wiping away my tears, there were tears of joy," she articulated with great emotion.

"Excellent, that's impressive, Tatiana," I said and looked at her very satisfied.

"It was the first dream of reconciliation with my mother," she said happily.

"Yes, now there is no confusion in your mind. Your birthday, the most important day of your life is the day of atonement," I commented.

"Yes, and I'm very happy about it," she said with pleasure.

As intensely as Tatiana had longed to be forgiven by her mother, she had not expected that seeing her in that dream would affect her so deeply.

"Now, I understand that the pain needs to be heard, my whole life was my secret. It was hard for someone like me who doesn't really like to talk, to share this pain with someone, but it was also too painful to contain. You have helped me a lot, only now I can feel all this pain attenuating slowly before my eyes," she said, leaning back on the couch comfortably cross-legged.

"It's time to move on with your life," I said.

"I shall no more talk about my mother with resentment, there is no need. I love her and she loves me. I certainly will go back to Lebanon to see her, I'm sure she will be happy to see me again."

"It's an excellent idea," I said.

"I finished the book that you gave me."

"The inner peace?"

"Yes, you've got a good memory."

"Did you enjoy reading it?"

"Sure, the book opened my heart and my mind to the joy and beauty and most of all love. Where is the author from? I've never heard his name before."

"Paramahansa Yogananda is from India, his life story has become a classic and has been translated into more than twenty languages," I uttered.

"Well, it's a great book, and I think everybody must read it," she declared.

This conversation went on for another ten minutes. I knew Tatiana's love for books, her passion for knowledge; she spent her entire life reading to the full extent of her power.

"I'm leaving you now, I have my yoga class," she said as she looked at her watch.

"There has been a positive change in your life, Tatiana, and your faith has become much deeper and stronger," I said gleefully.

"Yes, I also talked to my husband, I decided to become involved in children's rights and causes," she sounded calm and Zen.

"I think it's good for you to have such an activity in life. You are learning to get know yourself, and soon you will be perfectly capable of managing your life. You will be no longer afraid of this constant thought of abandonment and loss," I explained gently.

Minutes later, when I let her out the door, I thought that Tatiana was a very unusual patient in so many aspects: Hypersensitive, extremely intelligent and very knowledgeable beyond imagination, with a very strong character. She had a great passion for learning and had this enormous capacity of grabbing any information.

I walked back to the window of my office. The sun was getting gold over l'arc de triomphe; it was the most beautiful sunset. It was warm, just a perfect day. The streets were washed clean by the rain and the trees were in full bloom. Not being able to share all this beauty with my husband made the tears hover in my eyes.

TWENTY-SIX

I awoke; my face was wet with hot tears as I found myself thinking. It took me a moment to realize what it was. I dreamt of Christian, a dream of reminiscences and sighs, and a sweet and charming dream. I started having dreams right after his tragic disappearance, and I continued to have more or less the same dreams up till now all over again.

In my dream, Christian and I were taking a peaceful walk in a beautiful garden. It was as though he came back to me, it was so real. I could not forget the pleasure we felt and the transparent happiness. There were white and yellow gardenias floating in a pond with crystal clear water.

"Oh, thank God, you are finally here, Christian," I said to him.

As soon as I opened my eyes, I sat up in my bed and for a moment I saw my life without him. I felt paralyzed with fear. I took a deep breath and tiptoed into the kitchen and drank a full glass of almond milk. The phone began to ring; it was already eight o'clock. I picked up the receiver; it was Alexander.

"Good morning, my love."

"Good morning," I said with a low voice.

"Is everything all right? Did you sleep well? I just wanted to hear your voice."

I told him about my dream.

He listened, and then he said, "You have been working so hard lately, you need a rest."

I chewed my lip.

He asked me if I would like to spend the weekend with him in the Alp Mountains, "Why don't we go to Gstaad? I have a chalet over there."

I remained silent.

"You can relax and breathe the pure air of the mountains, it's so refreshing," he suggested.

I kept quiet.

"I mean just for the week-end," Alexander insisted.

What should I say to him? Part of me did not want to go but my inner voice said, "Take it easy with him and enjoy yourself."

"Okay, let's go," I said promptly.

Alexander sounded surprised. The excitement of his voice was palpable, "Amanda, do you have any idea how much I want you?"

It all came together very quickly; it was so rare for me to be so spontaneous. The same day I packed my clothes for my short trip and we left for the Swiss Alps.

Gstaad, surrounded by great natural beauty is a fashionable resort where celebrities from all over the world come to ski and be seen.

Passing through orchards, pastures and forests, it was Saturday at around noon, when we arrived at Alexander's chalet painted with red shutters, and loomed over the mountains with stupendous view.

He unlocked the door and with a movement of his hand, he invited me inside. I looked around the wooden chalet; it was cozy and serene. Very tastefully furnished, it was all about dark wood floors covered with antique Persian carpets. Several paintings of Picasso decorated the walls as well. To one side of the living room facing the green mountains was the bedroom, and on the other side was the kitchen overlooking a splendid landscape of the Alps.

The panoramic view was undeniably breathtaking and spectacular before me.

Alexander took my hand and led me to the sofa. Then, he pulled me in his arms and kissed me passionately.

"I'm so glad you're here," he whispered.

The air was chilly. He built a fire to warm the spacious room with wide views over the tops of pine trees. I wrapped my arms around my shoulders, enjoying momentarily the fairy-tale look of the landscape through the floor-to-ceiling windows, richly sculpted.

"I have all kinds of drinks, what would you prefer?" Alexander asked, standing by the bar.

"Wine is perfect."

"I assume red?"

"Yes."

He poured two glasses. Next, he sat next to me, lifted his glass to me slightly and said, "Cheers." I shot a glance at him over the top of my glass as I took a sip. He seemed to go into a trance.

"I'm absolutely crazy about you. The scent of your perfume is heavenly good," his words were seductive and his voice was soft and sensual.

Alexander put his muscular arm around my waist and pulled me close. We could barely keep our hands off each other. He started talking about his plans, movies and projects he wanted to accomplish for himself. Our conversation became intimate and passionate. I had never seen him so lively and enthusiastic. I liked the conversation, and I enjoyed the continuing silence after we stopped talking. I liked to listen to this long-lasting silence.

I felt that he needed my energy to stay dynamic, affectionate, loving and full of life.

"I'm so very comfortable talking to you, I want you to trust me," he said.

"I do trust you, but I want to get to know you better," I said as I took another sip of my wine.

"What do you mean to get to know me better? I know my life is a mess but I'm trying to work this out," he said as he raised his glass to me.

"Okay."

"I want to share my life with you; I'll find a way to make everything work. Trust me on that and this is the end of the discussion," his tone was serious.

Then, he kissed me on the cheek and started caressing me; I felt I was on fire. Every nerve of my body was lit up.

"Your scent is unique," he whispered.

I smiled and took another sip of wine; it was crisp and tasty. Alexander could not take his eyes off me; his gaze was very intense.

By the third round of drinks, he whispered in my ear, "I want you so badly and I know that you want me too," and suddenly he took my hand and led me through the living-room straight to his bedroom, looking out over the glorious mountains.

Leaning against the wall, he put his arms around me and pressed me tightly. I tenderly curled myself round his warm body. We started kissing again; I felt his tongue in my mouth. He was so hot; he took my breath away.

"I love the way that you kiss me, you are so sensual and I love you so much."

"Me too," I murmured.

We continued to kiss warmly and lovingly; I felt a blush rising on my face. The heat of his body warmed me all over.

Slowly, he pulled his pants down, gazing at me. As I took off my dress, he unclasped quickly my bra and tossed it on the floor. I started unbuttoning his shirt. He held me by my waist and moved his hands up my back. I felt myself melting under his gentle touch.

We kept kissing; the kisses were soft, then hard, very hard. I let myself fall on his bed. He collapsed on top of me, and I pleasantly felt his strong and firm body over me. He placed his hands on my breasts and caressed softly.

The glow of the candles threw shadows onto his body while he licked my skin wildly.

"The smell of your perfume makes me horny," he murmured as he came inside me. Moving in and out of me, he watched me with his piercing blue eyes. The sexual excitement was transcendent, inspiring, and exciting.

We had sex for a very long time.

Moments later, lying on bed very peacefully, with our faces only inches from each other, Alexander said without taking his eyes of mine, "We are perfect match."

"I know," I muttered, and that was exactly what I was thinking too.

"I'm going to take a shower. Would you like to join me?"

"I'm coming."

The stream of warm and clear water cascaded over us, I felt good. We had wild sex under the shower, and I thought that Alexander and I were all about the sex, which was perfectly fine with me.

Then shortly afterwards, I climbed out of the shower and grabbed a towel to dry myself. I unpacked the few clothes that I had brought, and hung them in the closet. I dressed quickly and walked to the living room.

"I made the reservation for dinner at nine o'clock, I bet you are starving. Here you go, Amanda," he said as he placed the plate of different variety of

Swiss cheeses and crackers on the coffee table. Then, he moved to the bar and poured wine into the glasses, "Here," he handed me a glass.

"Thank you."

"You will have to tell me about all kinds of things in your office," he said curiously.

"What is there to tell? I don't want to discuss work here. Besides, talking about my patients will only make me sad."

"Why a psychologist?" he asked me as he narrowed his eyes on me.

"Why? Why not?" I said, holding a cracker against my mouth.

"You are right, why not? I asked you a simple question, and you give me a simple answer."

We chatted easily for a few more minutes in a tranquil and cheerful ambiance.

"I read your book and I loved it," he said with delight.

"Which one?"

"Psychology in Paris," he answered. He paused and said, "You surely make a difference in people's lives, I'm extremely proud of you," he sounded slightly formal.

"It's not always easy, but I try. Now, it's your turn, tell me if you have already planned to produce a movie?"

"Certainly, but the project is going to take at least a couple of years."

Flames of candles flickered on the walls. He looked at me with interest; he grabbed my hand and pulled me to his side. His voice was low and sensual, "Your scent intoxicates me and it calms me too, I mean it," he uttered, and breathed deeply.

"This is a good point, Alex," I mumbled and started laughing hard.

"It's the first time I ever remembered being really happy," he said, his eyes dancing with amusement. He could barely contain his excitement.

I stared into Alexander's blue eyes and I sensed that something was up, but I did not want to ask him what it was.

"It's already twenty minutes to nine, ready for dinner? Let's go," he said.

The drive to the restaurant was not very long and we got there before we knew it. It was a rustic wood-paneled typical Swiss German restaurant. It was dark and cozy inside. The maître d' welcomed with warmth, holding his hand out for us to go first. We made our way through the tables and sat in a private corner.

I glanced around; it was a certain pastoral charm in this hidden place, and I enjoyed the unconventional architecture considered as avant-garde at the time of its construction. Moments later, the waiter strode to our table to take the orders.

"What sort of wine do you recommend to us?" Alexander asked.

"White wines are often remarkable here, and they are derived mainly from the Chasselas grape. The best-known and the most common wine is the fruity Fendant," the waiter explained.

"We would like a bottle of this fruity wine," Alexander ordered.

Moments later, the waiter came back, and poured the wine into two glasses. We clinked and drunk; it was worth tasting.

"Amanda, I'm just drawn to you," Alexander said, looking into my eyes. His face lit up with his radiant smile.

He was sitting across me; I slightly bent forward and kissed him on his lips. The feeling that he desired me so intensely was so wonderful and exquisite.

"I wish you could stay longer with me, Amanda."

"I would love it."

"This might sound foolish, but I'm crazy about you, and this has to be much more than a simple infatuation or just an obsession."

"I feel the same way about you," I whispered.

He ran lightly his hand through my hair and kissed me tenderly.

We could not stop kissing until the waiter interrupted us. He brought us raclette in a traditional way; a half-wheel of cheese was placed in front of a hearth, a heat source.

"Bon appetite," the waiter said gracefully.

The cheese had begun to melt and fell onto our plates, next to boiled potatoes, onions cured in vinegar, and tiny crisp pickles.

"This is very appetizing and delectable," Alexander said cheerfully.

"It's full of flavor, so yummy!" I said, as I took a long sip of my wine.

He looked at me and moved the hair from my face, "I love you Amanda and I'm falling for you."

"Oh no, not that again," I said nonchalantly, I was slightly shaking.

He lowered his head and put his glass down. Several seconds passed in quietness.

"What's the matter with you? Am I embarrassing you?" he said as he raised his head.

"No, Alex. I wasn't just expecting you to tell me this now," I said casually as I took my glass and gulped. I had a lump in my throat; I could not find a better answer.

The waiter hovered over us to fill the glasses.

We clinked the refilled glasses and Alexander ordered a second bottle of wine.

"So what do you think?" he asked inquiringly.

I closed my eyes for a brief moment, trying to keep my breath under control. When I felt calmer, I said, "This raclette is delicious, it's out of this world."

"You are incredible, Amanda, so very challenging. I like that, but you haven't answered my question."

There was silence between us, and I preferred to keep still. Did I try to ignore him?

I dropped my eyes in the continuing silence, and sipped my wine without looking at him or making any reply. I did not know what answer to give.

"No answer?" he said.

"Alex, what we have together is not love," I finally said.

"What is it?"

"It's sex, great sex," I said, and I was not going to change my mind about it.

"That's what you really think, Amanda?" he said with a warm and sincere smile.

"Yes."

"I deeply love you, I had never seen myself so committed into a relationship," he said defensively, as he busied himself with his drink, eyes down.

I smiled. I was unable to put any words or even any thoughts together yet. He looked at me, then took my face in his hands, and kissed me enthusiastically.

The waiter returned, interrupting us for a moment, "How was the raclette?"

"Delicious," we both replied.

Once he disappeared, Alexander made a face and frowned, he seemed to be uncomfortable. Perhaps it was not a satisfying answer, but it was probably the only one that I could have come up with at this moment.

We held hands the rest of the evening.

The waiter came back with fruit brandy, a common after-dinner drink in the region. Warm by the wine and slightly tipsy, I put myself together and said, "Alex, your words already mean so much to me and I appreciate that, but honestly what do we have in common?"

"We do have a lot in common, my love," he said, articulating his words clearly.

"Great sex," I repeated as I smiled.

"Stop it now, is that all you have to say?" he uttered, and gave me a long look.

My cheeks flamed as I whispered, "You know, love and sex are two different things."

"Yes, but they are subject to complete each other," he commented fervently.

"Sorry, I don't agree with you."

"You are very subjective, Amanda."

"And you are objective."

"You never told me you love me," he said nicely.

"No."

"Are you trying to protect yourself?"

"I don't know."

"Don't you trust me, Amanda?"

"This is not the point, Alex, I think I'm confused. I had not been with a man since my husband's death, maybe I only miss the excitement, and I'm not sure."

"I should not forget that you are a psychologist and you overanalyze everything."

"It could be."

Shortly after, he paid the check, and I thanked him for such a lovely dinner. We stood and Alexander held kindly my hand in his and squeezed, "Don't over think," he said.

We remained quiet on the drive back to the chalet, both lost in our own thoughts. When he parked his car in the garage, I reached for the door handle, but he stopped me instantly. He took my hand and put it gently on his pants, so I could feel how hard he was. Alexander turned me on. He hugged me in the darkness, and he said, "I've never known any woman like you, Amanda. You are amazing!"

As soon as we walked inside the chalet, he was all over me. We could not wait; we made love, crazy love on the kitchen table and on the carpet of the living room. Then, all night long, he held me tightly in his arms and told me how much he loved me.

The next morning, I opened my eyes; he was leaning over, gazing amorously at me. It was Sunday and already our last day. We wanted to enjoy every minute of it.

He made me a breakfast of organic rolled oats along with fresh berries that grow so well in the mountains. He served me the coffee with a small pot of cream. Alexander prided himself on his breakfast.

We spent the afternoon soaking up the sun in an outdoor café. Then, we took a leisurely walk in the woods and the countryside. Nothing would be easier than getting around this region. We tasted the local wine grown on a nearby hillside. We strolled nonchalantly in the center of town where we could find a shopping gallery, a covered market, a culinary book store and many bars and restaurants serving food from the four corners of the world, all under the same roof.

Strange as it seemed, it was a pleasure to be there with Alexander at my side. We talked and enjoyed the view of forests with larch trees that climb the mountainside of the Alps.

"I don't mean to judge you Amanda, but what you said last night shocked me."

"I'm terribly sorry."

"You should know that I've never seen you as a sex object, you mean so much more than that. You are a real woman of substance, and I'll be proud to have you as my wife. Sure, there is this strong physical attraction, but also this connection, this chemical thing between us, we cannot deny it."

I nodded and smiled.

"Your scent allows me to liberate myself from daily troubles, and I enjoy a sense of well-being and happiness at your side."

"Should I take this as a compliment?"

"You decide."

"Just kidding," I said.

However, one disturbing question kept running over in my mind, "So you mean that is all about my perfume. Is that really only for that you want me for?"

Alexander raised his eyebrow and smiled. I smiled too. I was pleased that he had noticed my remark; I just pointed something important out to him.

"Amanda, I know you are a psychologist but you need to change your mind," he said.

I shook my head and half-smiled.

"Your charisma and your sensuality are things that drive me crazy about you. Tu as du chien! And truly since I've been seeing you, I find it impossible to put up with my wife. We have a separate life anyway."

"What are you supposed to do with her?" I asked curiously.

"I have to leave her. I know it's not going to be easy but I need to get a life," he said seriously. Now, Alexander tried hard to keep the ambiance cheerful, but I got the feeling that he was sad and haunted.

We were quiet for a moment. This conversation made me uneasy. Sure, I did not want to be responsible for his break-up. Moreover, I thought it was very flattering that he was very open with me.

"You look different," his voice was soft.

"Maybe so."

"Why?"

"Why are you telling me this?"

"Amanda, I'm very happy to have you here, and I feel that I must tell you. If I don't tell you, whom should I tell?"

In the end of the day, we both admitted we had a lovely time and it was such a fine weekend. It was late in the evening when we reached the front of my apartment building. He switched off the engine; I unfastened my seat belt. He pulled me close to him and kissed me with passion.

"That was like a kind of magic! Will you come back and spend some time with me at the chalet? You can't imagine how happy I shall be, my love," he said passionately.

"Certainly; I will."

"And how long it will be before I hear from you?" he asked, looking at me anxiously.

"We'll talk," I uttered, and smiled weakly.

"Amanda, I know you've got a lot of work and you are very busy, but I need to see you. What are your plans for this Tuesday evening after work?"

"I haven't made any plan yet," I replied with hesitation.

"Why don't we go to Armani for an early dinner, the food is to die for, and then we'll go to see a play?"

"Excellent idea," I said as I grabbed my bag and popped out of his car.

Standing at the entrance door of my building, I remained there silent for a short moment, and then I headed inside the lobby straight to the elevator. I stood and pushed the bottom. Alexander, who had followed me, pulled me close and put his arms around my waist, "I love you Amanda, thanks again."

I smiled.

"Thanks for making my weekend pleasant, thanks for staying with me, and many thanks for changing my life."

"Oh!" I was slightly embarrassed.

"Really, I mean it," he said, and then, he headed out the door.

As soon as I stepped in my room, I started unpacking when I heard a knock at the door. Mademoiselle Solange stood silent in the doorway, smiling amiably at me.

"How was your weekend?" she asked smiling, trying to collect herself.

"Superb," I said.

She looked at me and smiled.

"I assume you're trying to tell me that you love him," she said, after thinking a moment.

"I'm not sure, I'm very confused. I prefer not to think about it."

"I understand," she said, nodding her head.

Mademoiselle Solange sighed and immediately stepped back and took a few steps toward the door. There was still a trace of sweet smile on her lips. Without a doubt, she tried to hide her disappointment behind her grin.

Twenty–Seven

Time passed, and Tatiana's sessions had been taking place more or less adequately. I had been working with her for a few months by now, helping her to express her thoughts and feelings. I tried to understand who she was regardless of her age or where she was from. Accompanying her step by step, I helped her to open up in a simple and easy manner. I always knew if she felt safe with me, she would feel good about herself and she would be relatively happy.

I also noticed that parallel to these sessions of talk therapy, some kind of serious spiritual changes were taking place in her life. After reading several books that talk about the work we are meant to do on this planet, and following regularly these sessions where at last she could free herself from her pain and anxieties, she drew up a plan to reach slowly the serenity and happiness in life. After years of terror, pain, disturbance and trauma, she had recovered little by little, and as a final point she started feeling peace and harmony. I was amazed at her determination and progress.

It was twenty minutes past three o'clock when Tatiana sat on the couch, looking bashful and apologetic for being late at my office.

"I think I know what you are thinking about me," she said.

"Why do you think that?" I asked.

"You know perfectly well."

"I honestly don't know what you are talking about," I said with great kindness.

"I don't know what's wrong with me, I'm late again, and this isn't funny anymore."

"It's okay. Tell me now how have you been?"

"Great," she said.

I could see the sympathy and kindness in her beautiful green eyes full of glee and joy.

"You look calm," I said.

"I am," she looked terrific.

I smiled, feeling happy at the same time.

She smiled back, looking me in the eyes, but said absolutely nothing. After a long pause, an idea came to her, "I had an amazing dream last night," she said sternly.

"Yes."

"It was such a beautiful dream!"

"Okay," I just said, trying to think what she was going to tell me next.

"I was in a desert; it was immense, vast and infinite. I enjoyed walking slowly on this barren and uncultivated land covered with sand. I walked and walked, and I was nude. Once I got tired, I tried to decide what to do next. I sat on the soft and warm sand; there was nothing else to do at this moment. I looked around, absolutely nothing. I didn't see anything and I didn't hear anything. It was calm and quiet, yet something vague and fuzzy, hard to explain, something inexpressibly stunning, and significantly admirable was shining in this mysterious and profound silence. I had never seen anything so wonderful, so breathtaking!

"The splendid and striking thing about all this was imperceptible. My most important point is that what was barely visible and almost unseen for my eyes, I could see it only with my heart. This had never happened to me before," Tatiana marveled.

We were silent for a moment, and when our eyes met, we stared at each other.

"The important thing about my dream is that it was crystal clear and so real. When I opened my eyes, I thought for a moment that I really was there," she commented quietly.

There was a moment of deep silence. Tatiana's dream captured my attention. I just heard the most amazing thing. I remained stunned and I could perfectly see a major change in the depths of her eyes.

"Tatiana, you felt something that you had never experienced before."

"Yes, I could not understand all this silence, but I discovered the light within me."

"I want you to tell me what you think of this dream?"

"Well, I could speak to God with a language without words, I felt the connection," Tatiana said, and she literally glowed.

"This is very impressive, so wonderful!"

"I know! This is a new feeling and I'm marvelously amazed."

Now, she seemed to be searching for words and ideas. After a short pause, she said calmly, "I feel that I live in a new world, a world having nothing in common with my past. I didn't know who I was and what I wanted. After all, what did I know about myself? Not as much as I wanted to. I only knew that I was a lost soul. Now, I feel that nothing in life is important. Why have I waited so long to get help?"

I smiled.

Tatiana went on, "I've spent many years living with my scars; I should have talked about my past much earlier. What an idiot I have been!"

"Don't blame yourself, it's never too late."

"I waited too long and my scars got deeper and deeper. You helped me find my place in this world, and you helped me to feel almost whole again. You taught me how to love life and have faith," she said charmingly. She looked very comfortable, and so at ease with herself.

"It's very important that you can look back at your past calmly," I said.

"For the first time, I committed myself to these sessions and I wanted to get help because you have this power to calm me down without saying much. It's about your aura and your persona, your voice is soothing and your smell is comforting. I can share with you my feelings and thoughts, and you listen to me and never judge me," she said with gratitude.

"I'm just doing my job, Tatiana."

"I did go a long way in the past few months. Now, the world that I know is noble and fabulous, there is no mess and the war is no more than a memory in my mind."

"Remember that nothing gives you peace but love and faith. Once you are on this path, your life will be much different, Tatiana. It will be a great challenge to think about things in your life in a different way. Now, I'm sure you are quite capable of taking charge of your life."

"Yes, I feel enough strength within me to take care of myself, and I'm not as obsessed as I used to be with my husband's lover, not that I don't care. It still hurts but I'm less concerned, I have different priorities."

"Keep in mind Tatiana, you are a strong woman."

"Thank you. The words that had been a muddle of confused and bizarre sounds; they suddenly became expressive and significantly full of meaning."

"This is fantastic and I'm so proud of you!"

"Now, I realize that there is nothing wrong with telling the truth."

"You are absolutely right, my dear."

"It's time now. Actually I stayed longer, and how much will you charge me for this extra time? I'm sorry, I overstayed," she seemed to be embarrassed.

I glanced at my watch; we both forgot about the time indeed. She had been talking softly and cheerfully for some significant time. I could hear the sound of peace and laughter in Tatiana's voice. I listened and paid special attention to her words, and perceived that something drastically delectable had happened in her life. Everything seemed beautiful and more serene to her. I got a feeling of great satisfaction from seeing her being in high spirits.

"It's okay, don't worry, I won't charge you this time," I said tiredly.

"Very well then, thank you. You know what?"

"What?"

"Shall I tell you?"

"Certainly; I'm listening to you."

"I decided to change my perfume," she said happily.

"No kidding!"

"So? What do you think?"

I stared at her without replying.

"No answer?" she frowned slightly.

"It will definitely be a new and interesting experience," I said, after thinking a moment.

"I'm going to Sephora to buy your perfume; it's still okay with you?"

"It's okay."

"Are you hundred percent sure?"

"Yes, my dear."

"It sounds delightful! You know, I don't look for my happiness outside, it's a completely internal state," she beamed at me, clapping her hands.

"That's right."

"I think the most important thing is authenticity, just being as real as

I can be. When first I came to your office, I was at a turning point in my life, and had a very difficult life. I had incredible challenges and ups and downs. I was hiding it, and I had a really tough time just being me. So now it's important that I'm just me. I'm not ashamed of who I am or where I came from."

"Being down, getting punched in the gut by life and coming back up, that's accomplishment, and this makes you feel strong."

After just a few minutes, Tatiana looked at herself in the mirror, stood up slowly and left my office with a big smile. I was happy to see that gradually she could gain her self-esteem, faith and the most important, her peace of mind. She progressively discovered something new within her, not yet knowing what it was. This new feeling was so scrumptious that it seemed to her incredible and far-fetched.

TWENTY–EIGHT

It was a nice and warm day. I took a look outside the windows of my office and enjoyed the green of the trees and the shining colors of the flowers in the park. As my two o'clock patient left, I started checking my emails when mademoiselle Solange walked in and announced, "Tatiana just called, she is running a few minutes late."

I glanced at my watch, it was already ten minutes past three o'clock. I continued to go through my emails; when the phone rang. It was Alexander. I saw his number and did not answer.

A few minutes later, I heard the sound of Tatiana's footsteps; I looked up. She stepped in hurriedly and closed the door behind her. She was in tight faded blue jeans, white shirt and a black cardigan. Her hair was loose and cascaded down her shoulders.

"Sorry for being late again," she said with a breathless voice.

I could hear her breathing; it was irregular and rapid.

"Please have a seat and relax." I paused and added, "Everything is all right?"

She let herself drop into the armchair and said with a happy smile, "Not bad at all! It's all right; I'm all right now. You mustn't worry about me anymore."

What struck me was the expression of her eyes, soft and serene. I had never seen her so happy. She looked safe and sound, so very clear and positive in her mind. I knew that something very important had happened in her life, but I did not know precisely what?

"You look so great, there is something new about you today, and what is it?"

She gave me a triumphant and enigmatic smile, "you are looking at me and wondering how I can be so happy?"

"As a matter of fact yes, and I'm listening to you. Tell me what's up with you?"

"I have incredible good news," she said, she could hardly contain her excitement and happiness.

"Okay."

"I've got some fantastic news, are you up for it?"

"Sure."

"If I tell you what happened, promise me you won't laugh."

"Of course I won't laugh," I said. I was dying to know what was going on.

"Something magical has happened to me, like a sweet dream," she said as she smiled.

I frowned to show her that I did not understand.

"Guess what?" she said.

"I think perhaps everything is settled between your husband and you," I said, feigning a guess.

"How do you know?" Tatiana asked me surprisingly after a brief silence.

"Just a guess," I said.

"You probably have a sixth sense," she said teasingly

"Perhaps," I said playfully as I smiled.

"What is happening to me is unbelievable, and it can't be true," she said seriously.

Sitting back straight, she folded her hands in her lap. Her eyes sparkled, and she tried to speak but she could not. Tatiana was too excited.

What was the matter with her? I wondered. I waited calmly to hear what she had to say.

"Something incredibly miraculous happened, you really did a good deed," she said blissfully. There was a smile of happiness on her lips.

I remained silent; I was thrilled and speechless. What was going on? What happened?

"You have done a splendid job," she repeated louder, staring wide-eyed at me.

"Don't be ridiculous, Tatiana," I said smoothly.

"I really mean it," she uttered sincerely as she kept looking at me joyfully.

We glanced at each other and smiled.

"The scent of your perfume permeates in every corner of my bedroom now."

"Oh! Is that what happened? Is that all?"

There was a pause; I could not exactly grasp what she meant.

"Do you know what makes my husband attracted to me again like the first day that we met? Strange though it may sound, it's "Quelques Fleurs," my new perfume. It turned out to be the right perfume for me," she said with a coquettish smile.

"Quelques Fleurs?" I said, opening my eyes wide. My voice had to be strange because I could hardly get the name of my perfume out of my mouth.

A sweet smile played around her lips.

Stunned and shocked, I stared at her.

"Yes, you can't imagine how absurdly it all came about. I only meant to change my perfume, and all at once everything turned out quite differently. There is something strange about my husband, and he loves me once again. I had never expected this to happen."

"Oh!" was all I could say at this moment. I looked at her in astonishment and did not know what else to say.

"I never in my wildest imagination thought that he would love me once more and would be sexually attracted to me again."

"Oh!" I kept repeating.

"What could be a greater miracle than that? But I've never seen a miracle happen so fast!" Tatiana said as a deep flash of pleasure came out on her face.

I froze in my seat.

We looked at each other for a few seconds and started laughing; it was an unforgettable and treasured laugh.

During a short pause, I kept my eyes away of Tatiana and thought of Christian and Alexander. They both loved the smell of my perfume. I turned back to her and said, "Men are crazy about this perfume, and I shouldn't be surprised."

She nodded, her eyes still fixed on mine.

"Love is the chemistry between two people and is chemical. It's the result of a particular scent," I explained.

"Yes," she said in excitement.

"Tatiana, that's fantastic! What could be better?"

"I can't think of anything right now; all this happened very fast and I'm worried."

"Yes, really fast. Does that truly worry you?"

"Yes, I haven't been happy for a long time, and that really scares me," she affirmed.

"You shall just have to make the best of it," I said after a moment's silence.

"Now, I admit all that happened between us doesn't matter anymore and I don't care about his lover, the woman who stole my life. I love my husband and I forgive him."

"Forgiveness is your favorite word," I said proudly.

"I enjoy the prestige of being his wife and wish nothing better than to live my life all over again."

"Your issues in life that seemed insurmountable and overwhelming are slowly fading."

"Yes, like all Lebanese women, I believe in magic, the good and bad kinds alike. If you believe in magic, then the supernatural pervades your life," she stated genuinely.

Despite myself I laughed; magic? What can I say? I'm not a full-blown magic believer, it might exist, and it might not. The truth remains a mystery. But I know that there is a rational explanation, based on reason.

The smell stimulates our senses. In fact, our connection with flowers goes much deeper. Psychologists showed that our intimate love affair with flowers has deep roots. It is born of the stimulation that these flowers incite in our brains, in particular in our senses of sight and smell as well as our emotions.

Smell is the most external part of our brain, and it often produces instinctive and emotional reactions and effects. Smells arrive at the limbic system, the most ancient and primitive part of the brain that controls emotions and is less subject to rational control. The kind of emotions that flowers trigger in our mind provoke positive feelings including pleasure, enjoyment, happiness and a sense of well-being.

Though it would be nice to say that the aroma of "Quelques Fleurs" had a positive impact on Tatiana's life, and it worked out for her in a way that no one would have or could have imagined.

We lingered for a few more moments, and after we exchanged some pleasantries, Tatiana got up suddenly from her seat and said, "I'm desperate for some air."

"I'm delighted for you, Tatiana. I want you to be happy."

"I'm afraid of my happiness, it won't last long," she said gravely.

"You must hope for the best, and the best is still to come."

"I hope so, see you next week."

"By the way, I won't be here next week," I announced to her.

"Where are you going? Will you soon be back? Please, don't leave me, I still need you," she exclaimed with a voice full of concern and trepidation.

"I'm going to Nice to attend a seminar, just for a week," I assured her.

Several minutes later, Tatiana's footsteps echoed away, she retired without a word.

The sun was almost set when I slipped on tiptoe in the living room and lay comfortably on the sofa, thinking of Tatiana. Soon after, I heard the door open gently and when I turned, I saw mademoiselle Solange walking slowly across the room, without making a sound.

"You look very tired," she said.

"I am tired."

"Coffee?" she mumbled.

"No, thank you."

"Perhaps a cup of your favorite tea will relax you."

Minutes later, she walked away, and when she reappeared, she was holding a silver tray with two cups. She joined me so that we could talk for a little while.

"I'm glad we have a moment to talk together," she said, pouring the savory jasmine tea into the cups.

"Where is Celine?" I asked.

"She is in her room, doing her homework."

"This tea is comforting, thank you." I said as I put the cup to my lips and took a sip.

"You look pensive, is everything okay?

"Yes," and I told her how the scent of my perfume shaped and changed Tatiana's life.

"Oh my god, this is quite a case!" she said after thinking a moment; and her mouth dropped open.

"Yes indeed. What a day!" I pondered.

"Are you serious? I've never heard anything like it," she said as she rolled her eyes on me, and she laughed.

I shook my head, thinking over thoroughly.

"It must be a relief for you. Don't you feel better?" she put on a happy face.

"I don't know, I really don't know," I said thoughtfully, looking affectionately at this woman who had been my best friend and confidante for so many years.

TWENTY-NINE

April has always been one of my favorite months of the year. It may have something to do with the changing of seasons, marking the arrival of spring. But it also has to do with the fact that my birthday falls on the first of this month. Yes, I have to admit that I'm officially an April fool.

I spent a few days in Nice to attend the French psychotherapy profession's most important annual seminar. The colloquium's topics were clinically depressed, suicidal adolescents, students with special needs, and gang-members. Since I had been seriously involved with several programs and research projects in those areas, I had been asked to deliver the keynote address.

I came back from my short trip one day earlier than I had planned. The flight to Paris was delayed by two hours. I squeezed my suitcase into a locker at the Orly airport, so I would not have to drag it with me.

The gray sky threatened rain as I said good-bye to the taxi driver and sneaked up to Alexander's building situated in "Square du Roule," in the corner of the busy street of Faubourg Saint-Honoré.

It was April first right before midnight, and I felt the cool night wind on my face. I punched out the digicode, opened slowly the iron gate and walked through the courtyard. It was the night that I had waited for so long. I finally decided to surprise Alexander and tell him that I loved him. Perhaps I should have told him before, but then I thought that only now, the situation and the timing would be perfect for telling him those extremely important and meaningful words. It was my birthday, a special night and I thought this was the moment to tell him that I loved him.

I wanted my birthday to be special. So here it was all, perfect time and perfect place. Since I had the key to his apartment, I took it out of my bag and slipped it into the lock with great excitement.

Alexander did not expect me at all that evening, and I wondered how he would react to see me. As excited as I was, I suddenly had a horrible feeling that something was amiss. The door swang open with a squeak, and I let myself in.

It was dark inside the hallway and I first thought that nobody was there. But then, I assumed that Alexander was asleep. I felt something strange engulf me. It was dark and for a moment, I could not see. It only took a few seconds for my eyes to adjust to the darkness.

I slid down the hallway silently, and as I reached the light switch, I pushed it. I listened and stood still, then, I continued my way through the deadly quiet hallway towards Alexander's bedroom.

"Alex," I whispered, walking noiselessly. "Alex," I repeated. I longed for a reply but nobody answered. "Alexander, do you hear me? Anyone!"

A faint perfume lingered in the air, and the closer I was getting to the bedroom, the stronger a familiar aroma that I could distinctly inhale, wrapped me like a velvet blanket. Now, the smell that I felt became physical, palpable and so easily perceived. It was the pleasant aroma of "Quelques Fleurs". I found the origin of this strange and magical comforting smell right outside Alexander's bedroom's closed door.

Suddenly a hot flash came over my face, my cheeks and my whole body. I nearly held my breath; affecting deliberately to be cool and remote. But then I found it impossible, since I could exhale and inhale systematically my perfume's scent in the air. I felt close to tears; it was hurtful to breath in this aroma. A few seconds later, I heard a low sigh.

I started to perspire and literally tremble. Had I gone insane? This had to be a nightmare.

A thousand questions leaped to my head, but what choice would I have now? What could I be thinking about? I forced myself to take a few more steps nonchalently. I felt a hole in my stomach and my heart raced at the idea of another human being in the house.

Trying to catch my breath as my heart shouted silently, I finally pushed the door open and tiptoed into the bedroom, lighted up by a single pink lamp with dark shade. I stopped in the doorway, I was afraid he would wake-up and be scared. I should not be there.

Now, the intoxicating aroma of "Quelques Fleurs" envelopped me amazingly. My legs felt shaky as I moved towards the center of the room. The lampshade gave off the glow of a fireplace, here, there and on the bed. I saw Alexander sleeping under the comforter, and I sadly discovered that he was not alone; there were two bodies intertwined.

I dropped my eyes to them carefully. It took me a second to get what was going on there. I forgot who I actually was for a moment. All I could think was how they would react when they see me there. It took me only a moment to reconize her, it could not be so! The woman lying next to Alexander was Tatiana, my patient. It was as though a violent shock of electricity passed over me. I was frozen on the spot.

I turned on the light and stared at them in wonder, and only at this moment I knew everything. "God, no!" I shouted as I covered my mouth. It took me an instant to comprehend the whole scenario. For just a moment, my heart stopped beating in my chest. And then, I felt everything else stop in that bedroom, "I shouldn't have come," I whispered. I felt numb from head to toe.

I could feel adrenaline flooding my body when they both opened their eyes. Nobody felt like saying anything; I stood and stared at them. It was a very unpleasant and nasty scene.

Now, they were sitting on the bed, both naked, and I witnessed the strangest scene ever. They both shook their heads, wide-eyes with shock. I saw Alexander's shameful face, he blinked, trying to grasp what was happening. I sadly flashed on the image of the two of us making love on that same bed.

Tatiana turned white as she wrapped the sheet tightly around her. She tried to say some inexpressible words, but her voice refused to utter any sound. I felt that her eyes were starting out of her head. She purposely avoided looking in my direction.

What was one to do in such a situation?

In the sudden rush of surprise, Alexander looked for several seconds at me, standing motionless in front of him. He could not pronounce a word or utter a sound, but just to say, "Amanda," he finally mentioned my name.

I nodded, as tears started from my eyes.

"What are you doing here? I expected you to be back tomorrow, did you change your flight?" he said in a broken voice.

I heard the wonder in his voice and took a half-step backward. I opened my mouth but I still was not sure what words would come out, "Just now," I heard myself say. I could feel the warm blood running in my cheeks. I took another step backward, still feeling a little quivering.

"Oh, I'm sorry Amanda, I'm most terribly sorry," he said politely.

"And so I am," I said, giving him back the key to his apartment. My voice came out shaky and raspy.

Everything happened so strangely like in a dream. This was a painful situation, and I wanted to cry but could not. At this moment, all I really knew was that I wanted to be alone. My feelings were in shambles; how would I get through this? I thought sadly.

The smell of "quelques Fleurs" perfumed agreeably the air around us. There were no words to describe what had happened and to discuss the matter was even further beyond the imagination. It was a mess and I had no idea what attitude to take with them. It was humiliating and so outrageous. How could this be happening to me?

I turned around, trembling. Then, I continued slowly to walk backward.

Tatiana was looking at me with hostile and intimidating eyes. I observed that she was longing to express herself regarding this situation, but Alexander carefully stopped her.

"I see you've met my wife. Have you two met somewhere before?" he asked as he glanced at his wife to find out whether she knew me.

Tatiana remained silent, staring at me.

"You know her then?" he insisted.

"Know her? To be sure I do," she murmured. She looked at her husband, still unable to hide his shock at seeing me.

"Amanda is my therapist," she said in a sarcastic tone, after a few seconds.

"Your therapist?" he muttered with a bitter smile; his mouth dropped open in surprise.

"Yes, but what has she to do with you? What am I missing here? Is she the woman that you have been seeing all this time? Is she the woman who stole my life?"

I waited for them to laugh in my face.

"We will discuss it later," Alexander said coldly, turning his scared eyes from one to other. And by replying in this manner, he also made me understand that he wished to be left alone.

"I'm afraid you both are not in the position to talk, I must leave the room," Tatiana said in a shocked tone, still staring at me in disbelief.

She seemed to behave with special dignity, and what a noble act on her part! I thought. But this was Tatiana.

"Please, no," I said with effort, since I had not the slightest doubt that it was my duty to leave. It was time to say good-bye to them. Unable to articulate one more word, I was anxious to escape. My inner voice said, "Get the hell out of here."

Turning my back on them, I moved rapidly, trying to suppress my nerves. As I was leaving the room, I felt their eyes follow me. They were whispering and talking as fast as could be. He murmured mysterious words to her that she understood and that calmed her. They smiled at each other, I was excluded. I no longer existed, and this was the end.

When I left them, I had a very sad feeling that I would never ever see Tatiana again. Running halfway down the staircase, I heard Alexander's voice through the sound of my own footsteps, "Wait a minute; I've been meaning to talk to you," and he went on, "I'm sorry if I hurt your feelings, just give me a chance to talk."

I listened, I could think of nothing to utter. I listened, but evidently I was not interested by it. What I did know was that I would not see or speak to him again. I looked back up the stairs and saw his pale face.

"Do you want me to drive you home?" he said, as if nothing was the matter.

"I'm not going home."

"Where are you going?"

"I think I'm going to take a walk," I answered carelessly.

"At this time? It's too late now. I can take you wherever you want to go."

"No, thank you. I need to recuperate my balance," I said, keeping my voice low.

"Whatever you want, damn it!" he grimaced.

Angry with myself, I ran down the stairs as rapidly as I could and got into the principle entrance of the building. I paused for a short moment; everything that I had planned turned out quite the opposite.

"Do you want me to call a taxi?" the doorman asked.

"No, thank you. I think I'll walk."

I took a step outside and pulled the door shut behind me. I crossed the square quickly and turned the corner. I began moving my steps into the profound darkness of a chilly spring night, alone. When I reached the cobblestone street of Faubourg Saint-Honoré, I took a turn to the right, but did not know what I wanted to do and where I wanted to go. I decided not to go home, I needed to be alone. God, what a night that was, and what foolish thing did I do? I wanted to have this nightmare come to an end.

I raised my eyes to the sky; the night was dark and thick; only a vague light appeared from the moon covered with clouds. Dragging one foot after another, I walked with my head down.

The spring air seemed chillier than usual. Wrapped in the air's moisture; I kept walking like a robot. I did my best to act brave, trying to swallow my shock, but I suddenly felt numb. Unable to bring myself to keep on walking, I felt I was paralyzed, that my legs would not carry me anymore.

I crossed the Boulevard Haussman, and then I went to sit on the bench, clasping my hands together. I waited for the night to pass. I closed my eyes and opened them again. I thought I would remember this night for the rest of my life. "What a night! What a terrible night!" I groaned.

Everything almost impossible to believe; it was like every other unimaginable and unexpected mystery in life. Worst of all, this was not happening to my patient's lives, it was happening to mine. Although I was angry with Alexander, I felt ghastly for disappointing Tatiana. I knew how crushed she was when she found out that I was the other woman.

Did I place my career at some risk? For sure, I had no wish to compromise my reputation, and more than anything in the world, I did not want to hurt Tatiana.

Now, sitting on the bench, I found myself enveloped in the darkness with a hollow heart. The world had gone blurry through my tears.

Across the street, there were lots of homeless people sleeping on the sidewalk. When I was a little girl, I was proud of being a Parisian, proud to say "I'm French." Back in the old good days, we could walk into any café, sit and drink coffee, and have an agreeable time with friends. We could admire the beautiful and elegant Parisian men and women smoking cigarettes and laughing. We could really feel the cheerful ambiance of each Parisian café, we were happy to be there. There was peace, prosperity and joie de vivre.

But what made me really sad just then; was that things had changed dramatically. There was nothing we could do about it. Yes, Paris had changed, and with the globalization and the unification of the world through the technology, we had a new image of Paris as a multicultural metropolis, with a flourishing and booming entrepreneurial culture. And of course terrorism is a part of our daily life and became an important subject to talk.

Now, regardless of its monuments, Paris looked like a third world country with all these poor people lying there in front of my eyes. I forgot that this was my city, my country. There was no fulfillment and no satisfaction in anything; I found it so sad, so depressing.

I became nostalgic. I missed the golden time of Paris and I missed la France profonde!

Lost in my thoughts, I heard the sound of my cell phone as it began to ring. The ringing continued and I let it go on for a minute. Once it was finally quiet, I reached for it and looked at the list of missed calls from Alexander. I flipped the phone closed and dropped it back into my bag.

My memory flashed back over all that had happened. Every session of therapy with Tatiana stacked one on top of the other. I remembered them as though they had been filmed and I was running them in my mind.

Whom should I blame for disappointment and frustration but myself?

I looked up at the sky, dark clouds were gathering, "It's going to pour in a minute," I thought. Definitely, things could not have been going worse, and the worst of it was that I never suspected anything. How did I not realize that earlier? I just could not see the connection. I could not remember in all those sessions we had, that Tatiana did even once mention her husband's name. How could I know? How could I guess?

The rain started to fall, and I had not brought my umbrella. I got up from the bench and started moving down the street of Faubourg Saint-Honoré as fast as I could without any particular destination.

I loved feeling the raindrops on my skin, and I loved walking in the rain especially at night. Wrapped in the smell of wet earth and the sound of the rain, I started talking to myself, "You are so stupid!" Then, this little voice said, "You knew he was married." And this other voice told me for comfort, "But you didn't know that he was Tatiana's husband, you knew nothing about it." Next, I tried to console myself, "It's okay, calm down."

But at each turn in my walk, my conversation with myself continued, "This relationship is over, all is over, and I must put an end to it."

The rain was coming down, I got soaked. My hair was wet, and I liked the way that I looked as if I were getting out of the shower. I was in turmoil as I crossed the square Chassaigne Goyon, reciting this mantra deliberately to myself, "I have to forget all and put this nightmare behind me."

I attempted to maintain my balance and my regular pace, when I stepped in the entrance door of the hotel "Le Bristol." I headed straight into the bar. It was time for a drink, and I needed to relax and calm down.

People talked in noisy tones, they stared at me and kept on talking. I scanned the room for an empty place, and as I fell into a chair, the bartender asked, "What can I get you mum?" He was a man with a long beard with a handsome and arrogant actor's face. Among all those voices at the bar, his voice was noticeable.

The Kir Royal was cold and crisp, just right for this exact time. I took a sip of my drink and looked around. It had been so many years, I thought, since I had ordered a drink at a bar. Suddenly, I felt a tap on my left arm; I turned to see a man in a gray suit next to me. He threw a sympathetic glance at me and tried to strike up a conversation.

"Hi, I'm Claude, and I was just wondering if I could keep you company?" he said with a slight smile.

"Thank you, I'm not in the mood," I said firmly. Sure, I did not need this kind of attention right now.

"I'm really sorry, I didn't mean to bother you," he said politely.

"It's okay," I said as I faked a smile.

"Cigarette? Do you smoke?" he asked politely.

I smoked a cigarette, without pleasure. I never liked the taste of tobacco. I took the last sip of my drink; my hands were shaking nervously as I placed the glass on the counter.

I hated to think that my plan had fallen through. Tatiana's panicked eyes and Alexander's wide-eyed surprise; it was all getting under my skin. I looked down at the empty glass in front of me, and thought there was no way I could have predicted it. The bartender turned to look at me and asked, "Do you want another drink?"

"Yes, thank you, I would love another one."

Fifteen minutes later, I took a fifty-euro bill from my wallet and left it on the counter. Then, I walked through the lobby of the hotel with a thoughtful mind. I had to admit once again that I was officially an April fool.

When I found myself on the street of Faubourg Saint-Honoré, I knew that the evening was not quite over for me. I kept walking and walking, then, turned right on Rue Royal. Scrambling along this street, I dragged my sorrow as heavy as it was. I felt numb, mentally, emotionally and physically drained. I was not as sad about all this as I was angry. I was angry with myself, and anger was boiling inside me.

The tears streamed down my cheeks and mingled with the raindrops on my face. I walked past the hotel Crillon into the place de la Concorde, and headed towards the Seine River. I realized that it took me more than fifteen minutes to get there.

Moments later, when I finally reached "Le Pont Alexandre III," I came near to the end of the bridge and paused. The rain had stopped. Enveloped in the damp and clean air, followed by the refreshing rain, I tried to recuperate what was left of my equilibrium. I Gazed over the Seine river, the world seemed silent, except for the majestic bateau-mouche moving smoothly and nonchalently in the still of the night; it was so magical.

Lost in contemplation, I looked at the diamond ring that Alexander had put on around my finger as a symbol of love. The ring gleamed and shined in the darkness; I twisted it round and round, hesitating.

Then, I braced my arms straight against the balustrade and transfixed at the reflections in the water under the light of the magnificent moon. Bending slightly forward, I kept twisting the ring feeling uncertain and reluctant. I turned my head and looked on all sides. I saw no movement, heard no sound, only the sweet tones of a bird song. I lastly slipped off the ring gently and let it fall in the river. The ring moved quickly up and down and dipped into the peaceful water that flowed by.

I broke my promise to Alexander but I was finally at peace!

Being constrained to acknowledge the end of my relationship with him, I have not said yet my last word. It was only now as I watched the ring plunge in the river, that I realized I had never loved him more. I was certain of that and the realization was exhilarating.

The thought of not seeing him again haunted me painfully. Had he already gotten under my skin? It could not just be the sex, I wondered for the first time.

The moon lighted my way as I crossed the bridge and returned to place de la Concorde. The avenue of Champs-Elysées was lit and it was twinkling like fairy dust. I was too exhausted to walk back home; I made my way to the taxi station.

"Where can I take you?" the driver asked.

"Avenue Foche," I said tiredly.

I could not imagine going back home and having to pretend that the past few months had never been real. Would I be able to pretend that this part of my life never existed?

Perhaps a good night sleep would put an end to this terrible nightmare, I thought sadly.

Sunrise was still two hours away when I shut my bedroom's door safely behind me. I was happy to be alone. I felt I was alone, not a word of my real feelings was outspoken.

Without undressing, I collapsed on the bed embracing my pillow. I tried to sleep, but could not even keep my eyes shut.

Since my husband's disappearance, I felt anxious at night in my empty bedroom. He would sleep here, keeping me company and warming me up with the natural heat of his body. But now for almost a year, there had been no sound, no movement and no human's warmth. There was simply silence, a profound silence.

The strangest image that I last had seen; haunted me in my solitude in the silence of the night. I got up and started walking up and down the room. Thinking vaguely, I opened the window and looked out at the park bathed in the moonlight. I felt a strange feeling for not being able to take the opportunity to reveal my heart to Alexander. My voice faltered, and my words became so meaningless and futile. What was the point?

Suddenly I was surprised by a gentle knock on my door, and next I saw Celine standing in her nightgown in the doorway.

"Mummy, I've got something to tell you," she said as she took a few steps towards me.

"What?" I thought she was having a nightmare.

"Happy birthday," she said, as she ran into my arms.

I felt my heart jump as she hugged me warmly, and rested her head on my shoulder. She touched my heart.

"Mom, are you okay?" she whispered.

I was unable to think or to say anything.

"Yes sweetie," I said, as tears chocked me.

"But why you look so sad?"

"I'm not sad sweetheart."

"So what are you thinking about?" she asked me sharply.

"I'm just thinking about life in general."

"And what's wrong about life?" she snapped.

"Nothing," I stammered, hiding my feelings, as though nothing had happened.

"What is the meaning of life?" she asked me.

I looked at her, and I knew that the same question was expressed in my eyes. What is the meaning of life?

I embraced her warmly and held her tight knowing that she was the only light in my existence. There was a lot of magic between us and I was extremely fortunate and privileged to have her.

THREE MONTHS LATER

THIRTY

The pale morning sun threw a glare through the window of my office. It was an ordinary day, not really sunny, nor gray. Lost deeply in my thoughts, I was sitting in silence behind my desk with a stack of papers in front of me. I looked at the photograph of my beloved husband; keeping his memory alive made my life more agreeable. A big part of me still belonged to him.

In the weeks that followed that nasty night, I heard nothing more of them except Alexander's messages in my voice mail that I ignored. There were days when I missed him, and days when I did not miss him at all. However, whenever I heard his voice leaving me messages such as "I love you," "I miss you," "The scent of Quelques Fleurs sparks a memory of you," "I need you," "I can smell you anytime I want," "Talk to me," I felt like I was living in a bizarre and wonderful dream. Even though I had some lovely and wild moments with him, I did not want to see him again or hear about him, my pride prevented me doing so. I preferred to keep his image as he was in my memories.

Alexander had made his choice and I respected him for it. Perhaps Tatiana was the kind of woman he could settle with. Quite honestly, I hadn't thought about them every day, but not completely forgotten them either. Yet I wondered if I would ever run into them one day, in the restaurant, theater, and café or even on the street.

In the course of that period, I was working with intensity and the memory of that night did not occupy my thoughts anymore. I decided to turn the page and move on with my life.

It was two o'clock in the afternoon when mademoiselle Solange opened the door of my office and placed a newspaper on my desk.

"You'd better read this before anything else," the seriousness of her voice made me frightened.

"What is this?"

"Just read it," she said.

It was "Le Figaro," the daily paper and Alexander's photograph was on the front of it. I read the first page that described him as a talented director-producer. I turned the next page and read about him, he was quoted in this article: "He said that the scent of a woman had metamorphosed his life and inspired him to produce the movie "The Magic of Quelques Fleurs."

I had always tried to keep my name as low-key as possible. Terrified of what the French media might write about me, I turned the next page and read the entire article, but nothing informative and too revealing was said.

Shortly afterwards, mademoiselle Solange came back with my cup of coffee.

"Now tell me, what are you going to do about it?"

"What can I do?"

"I have no idea," she said.

"It's pointless talking to him; there is no way he is going to change his mind. He will produce this movie anyway."

"By the way, do you know who your next patient is?" she said, half-smiling.

"Who is it?"

"It's Tatiana, she is coming back."

"Oh! No. Tatiana?" I said surprisingly.

"Yes, she called this morning and said that she must see you urgently. I said you were booked for the day, but I could squeeze her in between patients."

"I have to talk to her, I can't see her anymore," I said firmly, deep in thought.

Tatiana came to my office when I was least expecting her. In theory, I should not have expected to see her again. She looked younger since our last meeting; she was tanned and had braided her hair. Impeccably dressed, she wore dark sunglasses.

I stood up as she came in and we embraced. We were both very excited to see each other after three months. I also thought we were both nervous as well.

"Can I sit on the couch?" she asked politely, not looking at me directly.

"As you wish," I said.

"I apologize for showing up without an appointment, and thank you for squeezing me in," she uttered courteously.

I responded with a nod of the head.

She sat quietly in one side of the couch, in a state of profound happiness. I tried to see her eyes behind her dark glasses to read her expression. What was she hiding?

"God, I'm so happy to see you again and thank you for having me. There is something about coming in here," she said with a trembling voice as she swallowed nervously.

"I'm glad to see you too. How are things with you?" I exclaimed with a weak smile.

She hesitated for a moment, and then she said, "I'm fine, just fine," her voice was frail.

A deep and meaningful silence reigned between us; we kept looking at each other.

"It's difficult for me to be here, but there is this powerful spiritual bond between us. Do you really think I could ever forget you? You are my only friend, it's sad to forget a friend!" she articulated strongly, after a long pause.

The openness of her tone made me feel grateful, "Are you sure of that?"

Persuasive, she nodded, and her expression softened into a smile, "How could you have not known? Whom else can I talk to? Here, I can let the rest of my world go away," she said.

I remained silent, studying her expression and body language. She seemed to be honest, truthful and straightforward.

"I had to see you again and speak to you; otherwise I shall not have a moment's peace until everything is clear, crystal clear. You can't have any idea of how I'm suffering," she uttered. The tone of her voice was so gentle and kind, which made me feel comfortable.

"I'm sorry."

"You don't seem surprised to see me. Did you think you wouldn't see me again?" she asked me as she finally took off her eyeglasses.

While considering Tatiana's question, I naturally thought about that night. I put myself together and said, "Honestly, I didn't think of anything," I felt my smile fade.

"I needed to talk to you on the subject of…" but she did not finish her sentence. She looked uncertain and very confused.

"Okay," I murmured.

Now, Tatiana smiled, and it was almost as if nothing had ever happened.

"This session won't take too long; I wouldn't take up much of your time; a little talk? Is that okay?"

"It's perfectly okay," I said reassuringly.

An unpleasant silence followed; the atmosphere between us was now a bit tense as our eyes locked. What on earth was she going to talk about? At this very moment, she asked my permission to go to the bathroom. A little later, she reappeared and sat on the couch.

In this meaningful and unendurable silence that lasted for some time, we stared at each other and exchanged a little smile. What was she going to talk about? I knew that she had a strong desire to bombard me with all kinds of questions.

I sagged deeper into my chair, looking down at the desk. The chilly silence that still reigned in my office kept the two of us mysterious.

Leaning slightly forward, Tatiana started talking, her head down. She began to ask me questions in her low and thrilling voice, "Are you still angry with me?"

"Angry? No, I'm not angry at all; Tatiana. On the Contrary, I think we have a very deep connection now," my tone was stern.

"That was an unexpected answer! Actually, it's a lovely way to say it," she said, gazing down at the floor.

"I mean it, Tatiana," I said, maintaining a straight face.

She nodded, and seemed to be content and satisfied with my response.

As we smiled at each other, I felt we both could not help thinking of that nasty night.

"For weeks and months, I've been asking myself whether I should call you or not," she said, looking attentively at my face.

I half-smiled, and remained quiet.

"We didn't expect to see each other that night," she articulated with a bitter smile.

"Life is unpredictable and strange, Tatiana," I said, smiling warmly.

She did not say a word; instead she buried her face in her hands for a short instant.

I admitted that I had expected a bitter reaction from her, but absolutely nothing.

"It was a bizarre coincidence, but I've forgotten about all that now," she said as she arched her eyebrow.

I managed to remain perfectly calm; I needed to be in control of myself. She crossed her legs and put her hand under her chin. She must have read something in my eyes because she hesitated.

"As you know, in France a French woman is to be known by her husband's name, but to keep a bit of my identity that I lost, I prefer to use my own name not my married name. This is very important to me and it would be a terrible idea to give it up," she explained.

I smiled and kept my mouth shut.

There was another pause now, it seemed endless to me. We still held each other's eyes as though talking seemed out of question. I could not guess what she was actually feeling.

"Were you jealous?" she finally asked me as she made a great effort.

"Jealous? That can't be, but I can't tell you what I felt," I protested, hesitating over my words.

Tatiana's face relaxed, she cleared her throat and shifted calmly in her seat.

"I always wondered about your life outside this office, you were mysterious," she said not taking her eyes off me.

She was right, in all those sessions, I had never ever had a personal conversation about my private life, not even once, and she knew absolutely nothing about it.

"Did you love him? Please be honest with me," she asked as she smiled ironically. Then, she nervously twisted around in her seat, watching carefully my reaction.

I struggled to answer her question, "We had been lovers," my answer was short, and I lied smoothly, taking a deep breath.

I searched her face for a sign of how she might react; her expression gave formally nothing away. Once again, we fell silent and looked outside at the tall trees, and the sky.

"Lovers! You are a typical Parisian woman!" she said coldly, and her mouth dropped open. She seemed to understand me with difficulty.

"And?"

"And I envy you. You are highly educated and you are a free spirit. I'm impressed by your confidence," she said as her eyes flashed with real enjoyment.

I smiled but did not comment. I only hoped that she would talk more about what was really bothering her.

Once more, the intense silence echoed and made the ambiance of my office stifling and oppressive. Tatiana looked questioningly at me, unable to hide her curiosity. I broke the silence and said, "Is there anything else that you would like to ask me?"

"Yes, there are only a couple of questions left, and I would like the answer to, but I don't want to embarrass you," she said cautiously.

"You are not embarrassing me at all, Tatiana. I'll be pleased to answer to your questions," I swallowed, my mouth suddenly dry.

"So you never loved him?" she asked me with a smile full of triumph, and watched my face carefully as she spoke.

"I just liked him, we had an open relationship," I said, struggling to find the right words. In the deepest depths of my heart, I was tormented by this question.

"An open relationship? You mean like Simone De Beauvoir and Jean-Paul Sartre? But there was another woman too; they had ménage a trios; so thrilling!" Tatiana said, never taking her eyes off me.

"Yes."

"Do you know the name of that woman?" she asked, as she smiled.

"Yes, her name was Bianca," I answered promptly.

"All right then, maybe we should live all together as well," she said as she laughed.

I laughed too. I could scarcely believe what I was hearing. Did she really mean it?

"You know, you were the only woman I was ever jealous of, because my husband loved you so much," she said.

What a lovely compliment! I thought, as I felt numb and insensitive with a little guilt. Did she realize what she said?

There was a pause, Tatiana's eyes were straight on me, but I could not bring myself to look at her.

"What gives you this impression?" I asked seriously.

"The way that my husband looked at you that night, I can never forget," she expressed, as she changed completely the tone of her voice.

I gazed at her indifferently for a moment, then, I frowned. She smiled weakly at me and went on, "last night, I dreamed about all of us, I mean the three of us, but I don't remember much. When I woke up, I wondered is it me that he loves or you?"

I did not make any comment about Tatiana's dream; I was too astonished and overwhelmed to speak.

"I want to look like you, I have a lot to learn in the way of how to dress and talk," she uttered desperately.

"You have to be yourself, Tatiana. Your husband loves you the way you are. Look at you, you are gorgeous!"

She shook her head.

"Did you know that he was married?" she asked after a brief break.

I made a backward movement, it was the question I had been dreading. Tatiana noticed that she would only get a response after a moment's silence. I whispered, "Yes."

"But you didn't seem to object," she commented, turning her anger on me just for a short moment.

"I didn't mind, since I didn't want to marry him. You should know that I never meant to ruin your marriage. Please, try to understand, Tatiana, I never intended to hurt you," I expressed, trying to keep my voice casual.

"But you meant a great deal to my husband! Sure, you two had a great sexual chemistry, right?"

From the look on her face, I could tell that she had asked me her most important question. I had certainly never seen her struggle for words before. At this point, I thought she overstepped boundaries. I stared momentarily out of the window, and then I turned to her, "What would be the point? The most important of all is that you began a wonderful new life with the man that you love; the rest isn't significantly important," my voice was quiet and serious.

"Yes, but perhaps you should have answered my question," she said as she gave me a bitter laugh.

"Listen, Tatiana, you have changed in so many respects and surely for the better. I'm really happy to see that you were able to overcome the pain of your past and turn your life around; nothing matters anymore. Now, let's get moving," I said gently out loud.

She listened silently and nodded her head in agreement. Yet she continued to stare at me incredulously. I knew precisely what she was feeling, and what she was thinking.

"For how long have you two known each other?" she asked inquisitively.

"For a couple of months or so," I said smoothly.

"And what do you think of him?

God! She was an inquisitor, but she finally asked me an easy question, I thought.

"What can I say? He is smart and confident. Does that answer your question?"

She nodded.

"I have one last question," she paused, and then she said, "May I?"

"Sure."

"Do you still think about him?"

"No," I said as I dropped my eyes in case she would notice the spark in my eyes.

"Really!" she exclaimed with an air of surprise, as if I was making up a lie.

"Yes. Now, let's move on, let's talk about your life here a little bit."

"But this is about my life, my own life! Don't you get it?" she affirmed strongly.

She was right; it was all about her life. I was certain that Tatiana asked me more questions in this session than in the prior times, since she started her therapy with me.

"Yes indeed! This is my life! But sadly I don't own my life, my life owns me. Do you understand?" she continued as tears stood in her beautiful green eyes.

Was she to be pitied? Much to my surprise, she did not interrogate me any further. Apparently, she could not think of any other questions. Tatiana never turned her anger on me, she seemed eager for me to like her. Why didn't she hate me? I don't know, but she never did. At this moment, I noticed the sincerity and the authenticity of her feelings. There was no resentment left in her expression.

The silence returned, and the atmosphere in my office had become quiet and normal.

"You uplifted my life; it always struck me how comfortable I felt with you. Please, continue to help me, there is still so much more to be done with me. I must complete my sessions of therapy with you, otherwise I started all for nothing. There is still so much work to do," Tatiana said, her words exuding gratitude.

"In my job, we have rules, and rules are rules and we have to respect them. I'll be happy to refer you to one of my colleagues since I can't see you anymore. I'm very sorry, but professionally it doesn't seem right. If I start breaking rules, where I'm going to stop?" I expressed seriously.

"What do you mean?"

"Tatiana, regarding the circumstances between us now, I can't see you any longer, it's against the policy."

"But I don't want to go to someone else and start everything all over again. It has to be you or no one! I mean it. I'll never have this kind of connection with anybody, please don't leave me, I need you," she said pitifully, and tears began to roll down her cheeks.

"What if I give you three months starting today, and then we will see," I said formally.

"Thank you, I appreciate that, you are a dear person," she said, and just as she was about to leave me, she suddenly looked puzzled, and worried.

"You okay?"

"Yes; better than okay. But the aroma of "Quelques Fleurs" is not in the air here. Did you change your perfume?" she asked anxiously.

"Yes."

"Why? What perfume are you wearing now?" she asked me through her tears.

I remained silent, staring at her. A guilty expression crossed her face.

"Why did you change your perfume? "Quelques Fleurs" was a part of your identity," she said as she bit her lip, her voice was filled with curiosity.

"Why not just put aside everything on your mind and be happy, Tatiana."

"You are the best thing that ever happened to me, and I hope we shall always be great friends. You can't imagine how much I missed you and longed to see you," she told me in a shaky voice, the tears would not stop.

"I missed you too, Tatiana," I said fondly.

She watched me affectionately and said with a warm smile, "I liked to be missed, I think it's going to rain. It's summer, the rain is soft and warm, and I like to breathe the freshness," she said happily, her eyes were clear, so bright and so challenging.

She took a few steps back and pivoted towards the door. We started walking silently through the door. When I let her out of my office, I heard her footsteps slowly getting away in the entrance hall; she disappeared.

Before returning to my desk, I spent several seconds staring at the closed door through which Tatiana had just exited. It seemed to me that this session lasted longer than usual. It seemed also that all was forgotten and forgiven. Tatiana and I were both quite ready to let go the unpleasant and obnoxious incident that had occurred to us three months earlier. Most important of all, I fully understood that I had not finished with her yet, perhaps I might never be. Did I already change my opinion? Yes. Did I refuse to be logical and listen to the voice of reason? Certainly. Was I going to break the rule? I presumed so.

THIRTY-ONE

Weeks seemed to have passed and so much happened in Tatiana's life. I continued to provide her protection, support moral, and assistance in order to show her some positive ways to cope with her life. I fully realized that she still needed me to give her care and attention. I kindly took these facts into consideration, so that she would get every loving personal attention possible. She had conflicting and inconsistent feelings and thoughts about her life, and it took me months to prove her otherwise. I tried to heal her wounded soul by helping her discover her inner strength and return to a deeper place of connection with herself.

It was summer and Paris took a completely different look when the sun came out, it seemed like Frank Sinatra's refrain. The streets of the capital, quiet and peaceful, had no longer the same color when the sun glowed on the café terraces. In the old days, Paris in summer was tremendously fabulous as the celestial Paris of nineteen century, Paris of Maupassant, Emile Zola, and George Sand. The photos on my desk attested to this bitter passage of time.

It was three o'clock sharp when Tatiana walked into my office. She looked pretty in her white linen dress, and her hair tied in a ponytail. As she sat in front of me, she took off her straw hat decorated with flowers and placed it next to her. She smiled happily.

I tentatively returned her smile.

"What's new?" she asked me.

"Not too much," I replied.

"It's a beautiful day; I strolled around Montmartre and had a vanilla ice-cream. Now, I feel guilty about it, I don't stop putting on weight."

"You look terrific, you look all different from a few months back," I said.

"Thank you; I'm opened now to a world of new emotions. I feel terrifically calm, my anxiety is enormously reduced, and my sleep has improved as well. Now, I realize what I actually went through; I could never bring myself to talk of anything serious because I lacked confidence. Besides these sessions of talk therapy, I think yoga has a lot to do with it."

"This is great, Tatiana. I'm glad to hear that yoga worked out for you."

"I feel really empowered like I can direct my mind where I need to. Suicidal thoughts stopped tormenting me, and my flash-backs began to subside," she sounded very confident and content.

"This is so wonderful; you are literally reprogramming your brain. What an accomplishment! Everything you have been doing acts not as a medication, but as a catalyst to psychotherapy."

"I feel like I'm stepping outside in a whole new world and breathing fresh air. Everything has a new meaning in my life; even a small pleasure brings me happiness."

"Wow, tell me now what's new with you?" I said casually.

Tatiana gave me an enigmatic smile, and suddenly her expression changed. She introduced a new topic of conversation this time; I listened carefully.

"I'm not quite sure how to begin, but something interesting happened."

"It sounds exciting."

"My husband is producing this film, a movie based on a true story."

"And what would this movie be about?" I pretended.

We both remained still, looking fondly at each other's face. Tatiana's face was white.

During a long silence, afraid to position herself, she could only stare in my eyes. It seemed to me that she became uncomfortable and mysterious of course. This silence frightened me. She lastly cleared her throat and said, "The title of the movie is "The Magic of Quelques Fleurs," and we think that it will be a hit," she said, marveling at how things had worked.

"Have you found anyone to finance this movie?" I half-smiled, and tried my best not to deceive her.

"Yes, my husband got the funding and I got the part for the leading actress. I've never had a part like this in a movie before. I'm so excited by the way everything is shaping up."

"Your role in this movie is what you always wanted to accomplish, Tatiana. Your dream is becoming reality."

"Yes, it's unbelievably true," she looked at me all radiantly.

"All this will be the beginning of your career, Tatiana," I said as I straightened my shoulders.

"I just wanted so much to have a part in a movie, and now I'm not sure if I can do this. But perhaps it will help me to learn so much more about myself and about how I deserve to be treated in life," Tatiana said nervously. She was anxious to reveal that she was still susceptible to the feelings of inadequacy and insecurity.

"I think you are perfect for this role, I have a feeling about this, and you do not worry."

"All right, wish me luck."

"I wish you good luck. It's the possibility of having a dream come true that makes life interesting," I said.

Tatiana nodded silently and described the movie project, "When I read the script, and I knew what the story was about, I hesitated at first because it's something that's very close to my life," she expressed, eyes down.

"This has to be a proud moment for you, this movie project is the key to everything you have wished for, and you should be very excited about it," I said kindly.

"It's too hot here, or maybe it's just me," she said as she rose from her seat and walked around the office. When she stood in front of the window, she whispered, "My life has been beyond all expectations."

"When are you going to start the shooting?" I asked curiously.

"We already started, and we will finish filming in two or three months. As a matter of fact, I must stop now. I'm running late to the cast meeting, I have to be there earlier for make-up," she said as she checked her watch.

"Truly I wish you the best of luck, Tatiana," I uttered from the bottom of my heart. Suddenly she stood and jumped up and down like a little girl. At this moment in time, there was really nothing complicated and thorny about her, I thought.

"I'm so happy that you have me here. You'll still come to the opening of the movie, won't you?" she asked sincerely, rubbing her hands together.

"Of course I'll be there; I wouldn't miss it, Tatiana."

"I'll let you know when I know more about it," her face was glowing with excitement.

"I look forward to it," I said, managing a smile.

"What a dream world I live in!" her voice strained.

"That's terrific!"

After a short moment of chattering talk, she got up shakily, and headed out the door. I patted her arm and interjected, "Enjoy the acting, it's an intriguing experience, and it sounds exciting."

"I sure will. I'm going to meet the makeup specialist, and I'm very content about the whole thing. I should hurry to the studio. See you next time," she spoke in a kindly tone, as her eyes glowed. Then, she put her arms around me and held me close.

I had seen her before expressing those warm feelings towards me; I gave her a brief hug and wished her luck.

Moments later, I heard music. I quietly made my way to the living room. Celine was at the piano, playing some melody again and again. Standing there, I watched her mesmerized. She was playing one of Beethoven's most prominent compositions. I knew that symphony; it enthused and stimulated something very pleasant in me. I suddenly ached for my husband to be there; alongside me to listen to it. We loved each other to a great extent.

Could I love another man that much?

Celine lifted her head and looked in my eyes for a brief moment with a sweet smile on her face, it warmed my heart.

Music can guide you into places you may not normally go, and it's so powerful because it changes your brainwaves and takes you to another state of consciousness. This symphony played by my daughter brought tears to my eyes. For a few happy moments, I lived in another time and place. I unexpectedly could see my beloved husband and all the vivid and colorful memories connected with him, I missed him.

THIRTY-TWO

The following week when Tatiana came back to my office, she was gentle and warm with me and she kept saying that all was forgotten. But the expression of her eyes was bashful and changed. Hurrying inside my office, she sat at the desk in front of me, resting her body more or less upright on the buttocks as though she would pose for a portrait.

I looked at her, she had entirely different look. Dressed as a gypsy, she wore bright purple lipstick.

"I've been trying to decide if I should come to see you today. Actually it feels good to be here."

"You okay?"

"I don't know."

"What do you mean you don't know?"

We stared at each other for a few comfortable seconds. Was she trying to hide herself in this silence?

Tatiana raised her chin and glared at me, "I still need to see you compulsively and I have a strong desire to talk to you. I'm addicted to these sessions, you are like a drug to me and I've become dependent on you. Am I normal?" she seemed to struggle for words.

"Yes. How do you describe a normal person?"

"A person who is normal is free from mental and emotional disorders," she said.

"So conforming to what is standard, do you think you are hundred percent free from any kind of disturbance of the normal working of your mind?" I asked cautiously.

"No, I'm still itching to talk to you until I free myself completely from all artifices," she said warily, staring vigilantly at my face to see my reaction.

I studied her face and wondered if she ever intended to mislead me somehow? There was a possibility and this was not unusual. I remained silent, looking at her indifferently.

"Last night I had a dream."

"Tell me about it."

"You know, I'm going to sit on the couch, it's much more comfortable," she declared.

"Okay."

She walked to the couch with slow and smooth movements and sat down, extremely in control of the situation. Her eyes roved all around the office as her lips went on, "In my dream, I was flying and it was such a pleasant feeling, I felt free from oppression and all kinds of tricks, deceptions and illusions. The scenery seemed to be such a part of a familiar landscape; I'm thinking of the mysterious black forest, but I'm not sure. It was a change of atmosphere, a comfortable journey, far from this dirty world based on lies.

"Wherever I was flying, I witnessed scenes of tranquil and breathtaking beauty. I was flying in clear blue sky; the spectacle was one of a kind, and the air extraordinarily pure and refreshing.

"I prefer to live up there; rather than here among miserable, hypocrite, mean and narrow-minded people with absolutely no solid values and substance. They constantly transfer their negative vibes to you. Nobody could hurt me up there, my energy level was incredible and I was full of positive vibes. When I woke up, I could not tell if the light outside was morning light or afternoon. That was my dream."

Tatiana paused, crossed her legs, and closed her eyes for a few seconds. There was a silence. I waited for her while I was thinking about her meaningful and redolent dream.

"What do you think of this dream?" I asked her after a short instant.

"I don't know. What do you think?"

"I don't know what to say, I don't interpret dreams really, but there is a sense of freedom, you will be free from tricks and artifices that wound your fragile mind."

"Free? I wish. I'll not be a slave or in the power of another human being. I'll be flying and moving freely in the air, this is fantastic," she said as she was laughing.

"There is something very poetic and evocative about your dream too," I added.

She looked me with a brilliant smile.

"When I took that trip to Beirut, I spent an entire week looking for him, but nothing. And just because I could not find him, it doesn't mean that he was not out there, at some place, I mean. I already told you about him, right?" she said, looking at me sharply, and expecting me to confirm whatever she was saying, but not waiting really for a response.

I shook my head, trying to understand her between the lines, "Whom do you mean?"

"Oh! You know whom I mean," she spoke with enthusiasm.

"No, I have no idea, Tatiana."

"I mean my beloved love," she said feverishly. Her answer was unexpected.

I half-smiled; remained silent; watching carefully her expressions with consideration.

"What do you think of me today? You may think I'm delirious," she said, laughing.

"No, you're certainly not hallucinating," I objected strongly.

"I'm sure you are thinking that I'm very strange. Oh, you don't know me yet. You think you do know me, but you don't. I'm multifaceted and more complex than you think," she said sarcastically, and eyeing me attentively as she spoke.

Intrigued by her words, I blinked in surprise and said nothing. I thought as soon as the words were out of her mouth, Tatiana realized her mistake and changed the subject on me,

"I finally consider myself as a Parisian woman, everything is about my life, my own life," she said. Now, she looked like she was pleased with herself.

"It sounds good," I exclaimed, not really knowing what she was talking of.

"You opened up an entirely new world to me, but the thing is I'm very inconsistent with my decisions. My feelings are at present in a state of complete indecision."

"Yes." What else was there to say?

"My destiny had been already written before I was born. Everything was meant to happen in my life, I wish I could write it myself," she said as she sighed.

"And how would you write it?" I asked gently.

"Pretty simple, I would live on the Island of Bahamas with my beloved love, and watch the boats sailing under the auspicious clear blue sky and the bright sunshine. And in the evenings, we would sit in the silence of the night under the moonlight and enjoy life with plenitude. I wanted a different destiny and a different life, and I knew it from the beginning when I stepped in this fucking world," Tatiana said very quietly.

I listened to her but I was not sure that I heard her correctly. Once the words popped out from her mouth, she wished she had never said them, but it was too late. I held my tongue in an awkward silence; I was rather puzzled.

In the silence that followed, I narrowed my eyes on her, and looked in her eyes in disbelief. What was all this about? Who was her beloved love? I wondered.

"I don't quite get it, Tatiana," I finally admitted.

"I know that in my words, there is an enigmatic and incomprehensible meaning."

Silent, I did not know what to say. I just wondered what would be the next chapter.

"Life is absurd, unfair, and wrong, you are listening to me?" Suddenly she sounded very aggressive apt to make attacks.

She kept moving her lips; I barely caught the rest of her words. Tatiana seemed to be talking to herself.

"I'm sorry," I said, trying to get a grip on myself.

"Maybe the best thing for me would be to move to another country and start fresh. But I never stopped asking myself where do I really fit? I've been misplaced since I was born. The truth is that I'm not sure if one day I would live a normal life. I don't know if there would come a day when I could think of my past with no regret."

She paused for a short moment, then, she went on, "Life will never be the same, I don't know whether to laugh or cry anymore."

I kept quiet.

"I'm afraid there are no more tears left in my eyes, my tears are dry. You know, the world of tears is so mysterious," she said sadly.

"Yes, I'm sure something happened in your life, Tatiana. You bring up the subject when you feel ready for it," I said kindly.

"Sure, but I'm not up to it yet. I don't want to talk about it, not today, nope," she said in a loud voice, rolling her big eyes on me.

Hadn't I already earned her confidence? She talked to me as if we were strangers. Did she have more secrets? She was good at keeping secrets if she wanted to, wasn't she?

"Whatever you decide," I said indifferently.

"Even if I decide to talk about it now, it would be practically impossible."

"It's entirely your decision, Tatiana. But why do you think it's impossible?"

"Because in spite of myself, I'm persistently in control of my words, every single word, and I'm scared to be judged all the time, I can't help it," she expressed in a pitiful voice.

"Did I ever judge you? This is not my style, Tatiana."

"You have to understand that it's not easy for me to talk about my greatest weakness."

"We all have weak points. Haven't I already earned your trust?"

"I do trust you, but still. Please, try to understand me."

"What is the big deal, Tatiana?"

"It's a huge deal, you may well be surprised!" she exclaimed piercingly.

Now, all I wanted was to catch my breath. I was frustrated and disappointed at myself. In spite of the progressive improvement that she had made through the year, I felt Tatiana's case was a failure. I thought she had advanced especially to a better state, I had seen her proceeding steadily, but now I realized how wrong I was. I remained silent.

What could possibly exasperate and wind her up to become so sensible, prudent and discreet all of a sudden? Hadn't she already revealed a lot to me about her life? Why this discretion? What did I not know about her? The words stuck in my throat.

After a long silence, she suddenly knocked on the wall to get my attention. I put down my pen and looked up from the page I was taking notes.

"I'm scared to lay myself open to criticism, do you hear me?" she was staring blankly on the wall.

"It's wholly up to you, Tatiana. After all, you are the one who decides how far you want to go with your analysis," I said sternly.

"For a long time I refused to be a victim of my destiny and as you know, I did my best and worked hard to prove myself otherwise. But at this point, I just prefer to stay the quarry and eternal prey being pursued and hunted by my unlucky fate," she said miserably, lowering her voice.

"I'm so sorry to hear that. I see that you are in pain," I said desperately.

Tatiana stared at me and I understood her silent statement. I remained quiet. I looked at her and saw her eyes full of tears; she turned away.

For the rest of this session, Tatiana hardly said another word. I refused to be an inquisitor, and did not persevere in interrogating her further.

Moments later, she was exiting, she paused with her hand on the door handle and turned to me, "You should know that last night in my dream, my beloved love was flying with me, I wasn't alone. I don't stop dreaming about him, I wonder why that is."

"I guess he is part of you. He is locked within you, isn't it? This love is too strong to be denied," I interpreted seriously.

"Yes," she said, and looked at me with her intense beautiful eyes, frowning slightly.

I half-smiled and stood mute.

"But never ever I will be his," she declared sadly, in a sudden moment of sincerity.

"Why? Can you please tell me why?"

"Because..."

"Because what?"

"Because he belongs to his damn organization, it's his top priority, over his own needs and those of other people. I'm sorry if I surprised you," she said, still standing in the doorway. She hastily took a few steps back and forced herself to a smile.

"Okay."

"Only God knows what will happen to me. I have a strong feeling that something will change soon. There will be a new beginning, a new chapter in my life. I hate to hear myself talk this way, but it all came as a crushing blow to me and I don't give a shit," she uttered genuinely.

When Tatiana left, yes, there was a new chapter, there was something unspoken between us. I reminded myself that she had been frequently fitful and erratic with a changeable character, personality and humor, often unpredictable, unstable and rarely constant and steady.

At this point in time, all I felt towards her was pity and a profound feeling of pure love and kindness. Nevertheless she struck me with wonder and conjecture once again.

THIRTY-THREE

The following week as Tatiana curled up on the couch, she squeezed her eyes shut. I noticed the dark circles under her puffy eyes for lack of sleep.

"This morning, I didn't know what to do or where to go, like a zombie," she mumbled.

After a few seconds, she opened her eyes and looked out the window for a few moments, contemplating the clear sky.

"Birds are singing all around us, it's so beautiful. Can you hear them?" she muttered.

"Yes."

Then, she turned to me, anxious to get my attention, "I'm not who you think I am, you still don't know the truth of my life, and I don't know how to tell you the truth. You think that you do know me, but you don't. Who am I?" she said, looking at me like I might be a perfect alien.

Puzzled by her words, I was surprised by her tone, and my mouth hanged open slightly with shock. This was so unexpected and unforeseen; I asked her what it was about?

"Difficult to explain," Tatiana said, as she lowered her head, and biting nervously her lips.

I kept silent.

She glanced piercingly at me and continued, "Why do you think people can't understand me? Sometimes, my words are ambiguous, and they have two or three meanings. Do you still think I'm normal?"

I gave her an approving nod.

"I lied to people I cared about for no particular reason and betrayed them. I promised myself over and over to stop, but I found it impossible,

I could not stop. I can't explain why? Can you tell me why?" she said laughing, an absurd laugh.

I thought about it, but I could not come up with an answer at this moment.

"It's disgusting, am I a monster?"

"No, you are not a monster even though you think that you did some hideous and grotesque things."

"But I did a lot of repulsive things, and I don't want you to know about that. So, you see, the truth of my life is different."

I kept listening to her and eventually took some notes.

Shifting nervously in her seat, she seemed to struggle for the right words. Tatiana could scarcely breathe.

"Are you all right?" I asked, as I clearly noticed the expression of fear on her face.

She shook her head, looking away.

"What is going on Tatiana? What is wrong with you? I don't understand," I inquired.

"Nothing," she said with trembling lips.

"Are you sure?"

"Yes, I don't want you to worry about me, everything will be fine," her voice sounded odd. She felt as if she were talking to a part of herself that she had not known until then.

The instant her voice broke off, I felt the dishonesty of what she said, it made me uneasy. I sensed that she was in confusion and even a little tense. Sure, she had something on her mind that made her so upset, and without a doubt, something very strange happened, something that made her feel uncomfortable, and something that she did not want to share with me.

"I was supposed to tell you everything, transparency is the key. I should have told you regarding my most intimate secret earlier. I'm horrible and I feel guilty about the whole thing," Tatiana murmured in her low voice, tears springing to her eyes. She spoke with a mixed feeling of guilt and shame.

I never imagined that she had still kept a secret from me. What really was her real truth? What could it be? What in the world was the matter?

Scribbling a few remarks, I tried in vain to calm my frantic mind. I stared at her, putting down my pen.

"You can tell me now, it's never too late," I said gently.

After a long and intolerable silence, she finally let out a bitter laugh and said, "But I haven't decided yet on telling you my deepest secret," she was agitated and anxious.

"You can tell me when you are ready, Tatiana. It will be a relief and you know it," I uttered tenderly and outspokenly.

She nodded; thinking of what it could be like to tell me her deepest secret; her face still looked tense.

I patiently waited.

"There is so much I wanted to tell you, and I believe frankly that I've been truthful and said the whole thing. But I always wondered how on earth I would say this one. So you can imagine how chaotic my mind is so far," she said bluntly, looking straight in my eyes.

I believed her sincerity and thought it was flattering that she was honest with me. I raised my eyebrows at her and said, "There is nothing to be afraid of! We are friends, aren't we? You already revealed a lot about you, Tatiana."

"Yes, as usual you are right. I've come this far, I can't give up now," she said broodingly.

I agreed and smiled.

"But not today, it's too late for all that. I have an appointment and I should get going anyway," she said, trying to keep her voice sturdy.

"Whenever you are ready, there is no rush," I said even though I could not contain my curiosity any longer.

"I owe you some kind of apology for not having opened my whole heart to you," she said, looking at me seriously.

"Apology accepted," I said, smiling.

"You must understand; it was not that I didn't want to talk to you about it, but it was impossible, simply impossible."

"I perfectly understand; don't worry."

"I don't mean to justify myself, but only now I'm ready to let you into my deepest secret. I just waited for the right moment, you know," she said catching her breath.

Then, she changed the subject and the conversation turned to more general matters, which gave her a pleasant feeling of her own comfort. She talked of her movie, the books she had read, and whatever else came to her mind. I listened and answered to her questions. We both loved our exchanges of ideas.

Within a few minutes, she suddenly made an excuse and got to her feet. I walked her to the door. Tatiana tiptoed out of my office without saying a word; I glanced at my watch; we had fifteen minutes left. It puzzled me how suddenly she left.

THIRTY–FOUR

Tatiana sank on the couch, pulling back her hair. I took a seat on the edge of the couch next to her. She lowered her head, and remained immobile for a few moments.

"Sometimes, I search for words in vain, I mean powerful words and then I stray and get lost," she said, her head still down. She had put on this gesture so often recently.

"Yes."

"I often lose my way to go home and I think it's funny," she said, smiling. I smiled too.

"You are my confidante and you revolutionized my life. I had been going through a very tough time dealing with my past trauma, and I can't thank you enough. I'm no longer ashamed of myself, I feel no need to do what I don't like, I'm reconciled to being what I am and I don't mind what people think of me," she said as she managed a laugh.

I listened with rapt attention, my eyes filled with curiosity and awareness.

"But I guarded my deepest secret from you, I know that sounds foolish. I should not have waited so long to tell you," she declared, as she raised her head.

Immobilized in my position, I felt out of breath. What was I supposed to say? I kept quiet and studied her expression carefully with interest.

"Do you know what I'm thinking? she said; her face was sad.

"What?" I looked at her without comprehending what she was thinking.

"Now that I'm sitting on this famous psychologist's couch, I feel obligated to tell you the truth or I shall no longer be your faithful friend," Tatiana exclaimed with a trembling jaw, as the color drained from her face.

"And I'm listening to you, my dear," I said softly.

"But I'm afraid I'm going to turn out to be a great disappointment to you," she shouted. Her whole body began literally to shake, and she lost completely her temper.

"Don't exaggerate, Tatiana. You did a great job so far, and I'm very proud of you."

"I don't understand how I kept it all to myself for so long, I should have told you my story straightforwardly right away," she said with a small strangle in her voice.

"I still don't know what it is all about? Perhaps you needed some more time to look upon this issue more seriously," I said with a forced smile.

At this instant I thought, "Now I've had enough of her secrets," but the next moment I said to myself, "keep calm," as I clenched my teeth.

Shortly after another moment's silence, I saw her eyes full of tears. She drew a deep and heavy sigh as she went on, "When I think over the many mistakes that I made in my life, I get so confused that I don't know whether to laugh or cry. I wish to be a different person from who I am," the tears ran down her cheeks as she laughed hysterically.

I nodded and said absolutely nothing.

"I often sit still in my room, close my eyes and let myself daydream about my beloved love," Tatiana said in a tearful voice, as she bit her lip.

"I honestly didn't know you have a beloved love, Tatiana," I exclaimed, and looked straight in her beautiful eyes filled with tears.

"All this time, I told you nothing about him, but only now I've got a great deal to tell you in the most dreadful confidence. I was hiding him from myself, so I suppose it's very natural that I hid him from you too," she said pensive, after a short silence.

I smiled and kept shaking my head in sign of agreement, closeness and friendship.

"I bet weaving a sexual relationship with a terrorist is the most exciting phantasm of every woman in every country, isn't it? In any case, it's mine. But even though he is very vulnerable to extremism in politics, he never wanted anybody's blood on his hands."

"Okay," I murmured. I was shaken, and stunned.

"I know, it's a taboo, a forbidden subject," she continued enthusiastically.

At this moment, the silence fell once more upon us; it was a moment of intense quietude.

"And it's at night especially and in my bed before falling asleep that I think of him," she said in a tiny voice, as her face turned very red.

"What I would like to know," but before I could finish my sentence, her eyes fastened with an awed and daunted expression on me and said, "How in the world I could have known that once again an unimaginable misfortune was awaiting me around the corner. Honest to God, I don't understand what I'm going through," she insisted on her last words, with a mixture of anger and irony.

I was speechless, I felt that Tatiana had a strong desire to express her feelings about this matter; I said nothing and let her talk freely. She had to liberate herself from all her sad and heartrending feelings, and she had to let go the heavy and agonizing thoughts.

"Last night I dreamt of him. He was so real when he held me in his arms and kissed me passionately. He was so real as we had sex together, and he was so real as he gave me an intense orgasm. I was entranced, enraptured. It was a wonderful feeling when I awoke in the middle of the night. Then, I remembered it was just the same dream that had haunted me since I left my homeland," she said with sparkling eyes.

I listened to Tatiana in a state of shock; I was stunned and worried. I had no words to say and tried not to show my feelings. After all, her deepest secret had been well kept all this time, I thought.

But who was he? Was he a terrorist? Where did he come from? How did they meet each other? I wanted to ask. Then I thought that perhaps all this was purely an invention of her own imagination and that there was no such person in her life. No, it could not be a terrorist. I could hardly believe this was true; it was beyond me and certainly beyond belief.

Tatiana stopped for a short moment, breathing heavily. Her eyes were blurry from tears; she lowered her eyes and said, "Only last night, he told me that he wanted to be with me forever. Well, you think I'm crazy, but I'm not. If you don't want to believe me, you don't have to say anything," she said excitedly as she wiped her eyes.

At this point, I did not say a word.

"This love sounds too passionate to be real. What a crazy world it is! We quarrel and argue violently. I bore him, he enrages me, and sometimes we want to kill each other. But then, whenever we stay away, I can think only of seeing him again. We love and hate each other. Whenever I see him on the cover of magazines and read about the myth that he created out of his own life, I tell myself I got the best of him," Tatiana said frantically.

"Yes," I agreed, my eyes widened and I felt that my head was spinning.

Suddenly and unexpectedly, Tatiana wrapped her arm around my shoulder. I held her as she cried. I thought only crying could calm her and bring her relief at this moment, "Cry dear, it will help to cry."

"I feel dirty for not being honest with you; and it was only to you, however, that I let down my guard and talked about my private life and emotions. Will you forgive me?" She looked at me with eyes brimming with tears; her face expressed only the desire to be forgiven. It was a heartbreaking moment.

"You don't need my forgiveness, Tatiana. You didn't do anything wrong, you just weren't ready to tell me the whole truth," I said kindly.

We were so close to each other that we could talk without raising our voices. When her tears subsided, she looked deeply in my eyes, "This dream means something, right?" she asked me, as her eyes flashed fire.

"Yes, of course," I stammered.

I searched my brain for a reasonable explanation, but Tatiana went on, "Will it be over? You know, everything is getting very complicated."

"What is it? How complicated could it be?"

"You know, this secret I've never told anyone," she swallowed.

"And I'll never tell anyone either," I pledged firmly.

After a short pause, she said, "Thank you, I really appreciate that," and she grabbed a tissue to wipe her nose.

I saw that her hands were shaking, and what struck me the most was the strangeness of what I heard. I looked at her questioningly and skeptically.

"I know what I have to do now even though it's too late," she told me.

"It's never too late for anything," I insisted.

"I want to tell you what really happened, I want to tell you the birth and the lives of an astounding love," a half-smile appeared on her lips.

As time passed, I realized that she only kept repeating the same idea over and over in different ways, which was not unusual for someone in her mental condition. She kept turning around the same point without changing her demeanor. At this moment, I could not control my curiosity any longer. I was afraid to ask, but I asked. It was a straightforward question, "Who is he? Who is your beloved love? Are you having an affair? Is he Bernard? Did you continue to keep closely in touch with him all this time?"

Tatiana became suddenly hostile and turned upon me for a good reason. Perhaps I should have not been so aggressive and persistent. Watching the ground with a worried look, she blushed when I mentioned his name. When she made eye contact with me, she said, "I don't know."

"Come on Tatiana, how come you don't know?" I said distrustfully.

"I just don't know," she repeated, looking in my eyes with a shy and malicious smile, not without sadness.

"When did you hear last from Bernard?" I repeated.

Tatiana became so deeply absorbed in her mind that she did not hear what I said to her. I was tormented by this baffling question, "I asked you when you heard last from your step-father?" I gave her a serious, inquiring look, trying in vain to find in her eyes the answer to my question, the question that besieged me.

"How absent-minded I am! For God's sake, please stop asking me questions and attacking me. It is impossible for me to talk about it now. Don't you get it?" she said perplexedly, and exhaled a long, audible breath, as in sorrow.

"Okay," I said, with eyes fixed on her.

In the silence that followed, I decorticated her and analyzed her words for a long time. I did not ask further questions. She stared at me with her pale face and imploring eyes. There was a certain weight, seriousness, and fret in her troubled eyes full of a heavy secret.

"Are you mad at me?" she asked all of a sudden, after a short pause.

"I'm not mad at you, Tatiana. I only want to help you."

Her face twisted by pain and rage, she began to stutter. She lowered her voice still further, until it was almost inaudible. I felt I could not get a single word out of her.

Tatiana fell into sullen silence. I put my pen down, and waited calmly for her to speak.

"I don't know where to start, I feel as I'm going to burst again, sorry, I can't help it. And I know that I would get better with crying," she said as she broke down in tears once more. A sob broke from her tight throat.

I felt terribly sad and tried to control myself, but I couldn't. The tears filled my eyes and poured down my cheeks. It was a tragic moment.

"Quite honestly, I never wanted to share my deepest secret with anyone because I wanted to keep the beauty of it just for myself. Is there anything more beautiful in the whole world than to have a secret beloved love? It's such a lovely feeling," she said proudly as her face relaxed into a smile.

Keeping quiet, I half-smiled and did not answer.

Now, Tatiana went on talking quite normally, "My longing to talk to you becomes more and more intense. This secret that I carefully kept it to myself for a long time, I can't keep it forever, I must tell someone. You are the best one to tell since you always keep my secrets," she said.

I was wordless; I just nodded.

A deadly silence hung in every corner of my office. Holding my breath, I waited for her to reveal her deepest secret. It was imperative for me to know what had happened. I remained in a state of suspense and uncertainty while waiting for Tatiana to speak her truth. I was still boiling with curiosity, and yet I could not show it.

"I'm thinking how to express my inexpressible secret to you. How boring would it be to listen to it?"

"You never bored me, Tatiana," I said quietly.

She muttered some words that I did not understand. After a short pause, she said, "I'm just thinking of what I shall say next," then she lapsed into silence again. A bit later, she murmured, "I'm terribly sorry," and became silent once more.

I waited for her to speak with a great patience and complete serenity.

Suddenly the words flowed, the right and precise words, "I don't want anything left unsaid between us, you are my only friend, my faithful friend. I want to be brave and it's difficult. I confided my private feelings and thoughts to you, and unveiled my shame and my mistakes in this sanctuary. And of course, all that made me stronger; I can't deny it.

"Actually, I feel strong enough to assume my weaknesses and to expose myself nude in front of you. Now, I can allow myself to approach the fundamental subjects as far as I'm concerned; such as my fears, my most private feelings, my inward thoughts, my relation to my childhood and at long last my culpability to love someone and to desire someone else. Whatever you think of me, yes, I have to admit that I love and respect my husband with all my heart and soul, but my body desires another man, a chap with a very strong ideology and beliefs."

I listened to Tatiana when she quietly pronounced her words. Everything turned round and round in my head. My mouth was closed and sad; I felt I was slightly shaking.

"I'm living a great adventure and I'm enjoying an ambiguous and uncertain relationship. How will I ever free myself of it? Will I ever be able to have a normal life?" she went on with a sadness that surprised me.

Tatiana's words were a great blow to me. I listened suspiciously as she continued, "The strain of maintaining a double life all these years, of dividing myself between my husband whom I love and my beloved whom I need began to seem untenable and shaky, it's very complicated and not very clear. Do you understand my position?"

"Yes, has something happened? Who is he?" I asked sharply.

"Oh! He is everything I've always dreamed of," Tatiana said softly, as she blushed.

A dim silence fell over my office, and just then, her phone rang, "Oh, I should be leaving you now, my husband is here," she looked at her watch, jumped up, and turned on her heal.

As she walked to the door, she said politely, "You have no clue how hard my situation is. I'm really sorry to have surprised you and thank you for your patience and understanding," she exclaimed warmly. She was pale as she excused herself. Then, she gave me a warm cuddle as she walked towards the door.

I did not know what to say, I nodded in a kind of trance and patted her on the shoulder and said, "Tatiana, make sure you take good care of yourself, see you next week."

We looked at each other for a moment, and smiled.

"I'll be perfectly frank with you, I'll tell you exactly what happened, and I'll ask you what I should do. I promise I won't deceive you anymore," she said amicably, even though a look of embarrassment and pain came over her pale face.

Now, I felt the shame within her once more. I didn't say much, I just opened my mouth and whispered, "Okay."

"Of course you can help me if you want to, I desperately want this misfortune to be over," she said, overwhelmed by her torment and agony.

I listened to her without saying a word.

"You know, I'm in a terrible situation," she added, her voice shaking.

As the church bells sounded outside, she turned the doorknob and hurried from the office.

Frozen in a great shock, I was petrified; I needed to be alone. I could not think; there was nothing to think about. I lastly discovered that Tatiana was still keeping a deep secret within; secret she had kept for so many years. I just wondered if I would ever understand her complex personality and character. Tatiana, this enigmatic and mysterious woman, full of secrets and contradictions, left me with a feeling of surprise mingled with curiosity and bewilderment.

THIRTY–FIVE

The afternoon sun streamed in my office. It was three o'clock when Tatiana opened the door and strolled in. She looked nearly dead in her black leather jacket over a long skirt. Her wavy hair cascaded down around her shoulders. I can never forget Tatiana's face and her dark humor the minute she walked in my office. But I did not think much of it, assuming that she was tired due to a miserable sleepless night.

"Would you like to sit down?" I waved her towards her usual place, smiling.

She plopped down in her seat and placed her hat on the empty chair next to her. There was something very frightening in her eyes; she looked worried and disturbed.

"What do you think of me today?" she asked harshly.

"You look tired, but I like your jacket. I think it's adorable, and very chic."

"It's just an old jacket! Sometimes I really don't care how I look like," she exclaimed.

"But it looks nice on you," I said, smiling.

We looked at each other for a moment in silence. This silence between us became sacrosanct, and I feared that it would never end.

It took her a couple of minutes to find her voice, "Please, don't ask me how I'm feeling today."

"All right," I said quietly.

"This is a scary world for me to be in, and I mean it," the color vanished from her face.

"What's the matter? You seem down," I inquired calmly.

"I don't know," Tatiana said as she flashed a glance of hatred at me.

Did I have to worry about her once again? I thought unpretentiously that I could help her if I could get her to talk, "What's wrong?" I repeated.

"I feel like my life is ending," she said sadly. She cleared her throat and looked away. For a moment, I looked at her as if I failed to understand her. I felt utterly stuck.

"You are in pain, Tatiana," I said after a short pause.

"Yes, I'm in awful pain," she agreed with a blaze of anger.

"This is serious," I said, and I felt that something inside me changed all of a sudden.

"I don't really feel like talking," she said as she shrugged.

"You don't?" I was struck dumb, "Why not?" I finally said, as my throat turned dry.

"I just don't feel like it," she answered as she quickly shot me a sad look.

Minutes later, I tried again, "Come on, Tatiana, tell me what happened?"

"I just don't feel like talking," she repeated, bursting out of anger.

Then, she looked up at me with a strange half-smile that I had never seen before on her face, "You know, I cannot demand too much from life, and it's okay."

"It helps to talk and you know it. Tell me what is going on?" I interrogated severely.

"I just went my own way," she said in the strangest voice. She took a long breath and straightened her shoulders, then, she continued, "Well, I'm going to tell you something important about my life. I don't want you to get a wrong idea of me from everything you heard."

Her eyes glanced momentarily at me, and for half a minute, there was not a sound. She waited a little longer, hoping that I would begin a conversation. I remained silent.

"Again, I made a terrible mistake," she said, shaking her head.

I thought she hardly knew what she was saying; I reached the point of believing everything and nothing about her.

Tatiana's eyes began to blink anxiously. She said after a moment, "I didn't lie to you; I would never lie to my friend, only I've kept something important in secret. So I thought you ought to know it, but you will hear about this subject next time, okay?"

"Okay."

"You know, it's something quite confidential," she said, as her lips moved silently.

"Tatiana, you can tell me any time that suits you best," I said coolly.

She looked around and smiled. I did not have the faintest idea what this matter was about. I wanted to know what she had to tell me, and I longed to find out the connection between her stepfather and the terrorist that she had mentioned to me. Who was the terrorist? Who was he? Was he real? Now, I was slightly annoyed and aggravated rather than curious.

"I don't need to worry about this issue right now, but before I start on this, something else. I've got to speak to you about something very important before."

"Okay."

"I had recurring thoughts of death as I was growing up, and later on, when I got married. I never felt compelled to talk about them because I never felt close enough to anyone. Now, since I've been seeing you, I had to deal with the fundamental questions of hope and despair, love and hate, doubt and faith, life and death, and I never expected to go so far in million years. Lots of things about me have changed, I could not have hoped for better. You are the only person in the world with the power to calm me, you are the only person who listens to me," she uttered, and looked at me with a grateful expression.

I smiled.

Tatiana, whose eyes were not leaving mine, went on, "I thought it was over, but these thoughts are coming back. The closer I get to the end of the shooting of the movie, the closer I feel to death. I'm feeling this panic and I can't help it. It seems that death and I are living at close quarters. For me, the end of the shooting means the end of my life, the death of my hopes. I really feel that I'm very close to death; I feel that something is ending. This must be a happy and peaceful period of my life, but it's not," she tried hard to formulate the right words to me.

Tatiana's eyes spoke of death.

"But you shouldn't feel this way; your role in this movie is an incredible accomplishment that you have achieved, think about it. Everything in your life is falling slowly into place now, you should be happy," I said, with a reassuring look.

Tatiana lifted her hand to keep me silent for a moment. She looked at me and grumbled,

"I don't feel this way, and my mind doesn't work in that direction. Why if I don't live long enough to see myself on the screen. I feel that the end of this movie will be a source of bitter disappointment and my world will turn upside down. I have the feeling that something is about to happen, it's a presentiment and I can't be wrong about it."

"You have a long life ahead of you; the best is yet to come. You should look forward to the glamour of a premiere and your first performance, Tatiana. Think of all the beauty in the world and be happy."

"You misunderstood me entirely. Perhaps I'm not explaining myself with powerful words."

"Your words are well enough spoken, you must be tired and you need a break," I said. I felt sad and tried not to think about what she had just said.

"I'm enjoying every single moment of the shooting and I don't want it to end. But I'm filled with a strange feeling, a feeling of uncertainty," she lowered her voice.

I shook my head. At this moment, as she revealed her thoughts to me, my heart started beating. I felt there was an upheaval, and it was not logical, it was instinctive.

Tatiana's eyes darted to mine, she felt frightened beyond belief as she continued, "My fear makes me want to scream out loud, I'm already halfway towards death, I'm not kidding! Where will I be two or three months from now? Before I didn't fear the death but now I sense it, and the idea of nothingness is tormenting my soul. It's your fault; you attached me to this absurd life. I just started regaining my balance, and now I have this intuition and I'm convinced that soon I will be dead. I'm more frightened than I had ever been in my life, and it's your entire fault. You taught me how to live and love life; and you tied me to this fucking world," she ranted.

"But you've got so much life in front of you, things are only going to get better in your life," I exclaimed in a comforting tone.

Now, Tatiana stared out the window with silent tears running down her cheeks. Looking at her watch, she said, "How much more time do we have?"

"We are okay," I mumbled, and smiled at her helplessly. I admitted that she was afraid of something.

"The world is harsh and ruthless," she exclaimed, expressing her strong desire for peace in the world.

At this point, nothing I could have said would have done any good. She seemed taciturn and voiceless, and her lips were moving with no sound. Her terrified eyes told me that whatever hope and whatever courage she had had, she definitely lost them at once.

"You are going to be okay," I said to her softly.

She either did not hear me, or pretended not to hear me. Tatiana shook her head disapprovingly and turned away.

"Nothing is okay in my head anymore, I know that I'll die of injustice of life, and this will be registered on my death certificate," she sounded tense.

My sense of helplessness was overwhelming; my opinion did not really matter at this point. I refrained from further comment.

"My mind is haunted by so many frightful thoughts that even the blue sky, the sunrise, the sunset, the moonlight, the shooting stars, the song of the birds and the colorful flowers don't bring me peace and tranquility like before," she stopped hastily.

After a prolonged silence, she went on, "Last night, I had a premonition, I dreamt of dark and somber places, I saw blood everywhere and heard gunshot. I woke up, sweating, crying and shaking. I saw everything as if it would actually take place in real life soon, and I feel it as though it will happen to me in next to no time.

"The world is changing into something horrific, the world is collapsing, and yet you remain indifferent," raving mad, she dried quickly her cheeks wet with tears.

"Oh, for heaven's sake, Tatiana, we will be fine, don't worry," I tried to calm her.

"I certainly won't be fighting for my life," and she let out a loud laugh abruptly.

Then, she locked herself in the silence, and this silence was heavy and oppressive. It probably sounded funny, but in this absolute silence, I myself began to have a sick feeling in the pit of my stomach. These black and sinister thoughts took possession of my mind slowly, and tears stood in my eyes because I felt weak and powerless to help her.

Tatiana broke the silence, "I always liked to play parts that have meaning to me, not just something commercial."

"Your role in the movie is meaningful since it's a true story, it's you, and it's your life."

"Yes, but I feel that something will happen to spoil my life," she said forlornly.

I checked my watch; we had less than ten minutes before the end of the session.

I wondered what were the particular effects and conditions around her disposition inclined to affect her fragile mind to such an extent. Why this sudden fear of death? Why this abrupt feeling of panic? Why? Why?

"Paris is dreadful, don't you think so?" she said wonderingly.

"Please Tatiana, calm down, everything seems to be fine," I replied quietly.

"No, no. Everything is depressing, and everyone is gloomy. Paris is dark, ominous, and the great old days are over. Don't you see that?" she said with nervousness.

At this point, I continued to listen, and I preferred to stay quiet. I just shook my head.

"No answer? Never mind, I just wanted to hear your voice."

We looked at each other. I still found it impossible to articulate anything whatsoever; I remained quiet, and perhaps mysterious.

"Will you be there at the premiere?" she asked nicely, her eyes were not meeting mine anymore.

"Yes," I immediately promised her that I would be there.

"Do you keep your promises?" she asked, looking straight in my eyes.

"Always," I said with a warm smile.

"A solemn promise?" she insisted as she smiled, but her eyes looked frightened.

"Yes," I said firmly.

"Good, I don't like broken promises," she said seriously in her usual tone of voice. A little later, she burst into tears.

"Me either, I promise I will be there, just for you, Tatiana."

"Time is up, I feel drained, really dog-tired, and I'm leaving you now. I'm afraid it's getting very late, and I need to be outside and take a breath of fresh air," she said. Her eyes wandered away, and a little smile slightly curled her lips.

I let her down the hallway and wished her luck, "Don't give up your hope, something always turns up. I hope you can change your mind."

"You have to understand that it's not in my power anymore," she whispered. Then, she stopped, turned, and looked back at me with a beautiful long smile. Suddenly she left my office like a flash, with a quaking movement.

With this smile, Tatiana made an unforgettable impression on me. When she slammed the door behind her, I could not stop thinking about her for a very long time.

I returned to my desk, feeling uneasy. I began to read my dossier, but I was no longer able to concentrate. I was tense and anxious. Tatiana's unexpected words were dancing in my mind. I had the sound of her voice in my ears, and the resonance of the terrific words that she had said to me, reverberated like the quivering sound of a thunderstorm in my office.

At this moment, I could not realize at all what was about to happen? Did Tatiana know what lay ahead of her? Did she have a foreboding of something dreadful? I don't think any of us were really prepared for what happened next. But what I did believe was that we both lived in a state of terrible insecurity and apprehension for some considerable time.

THIRTY–SIX

FRIDAY, NOVEMBER 13, 2015.

It was a normal and lovely evening, an evening like any other, and it was meant to be quiet and peaceful. Paris was calm and people were not scared, they did not have any reason to be scared. They all loved life. Some chose to attend the concert at Bataclan to listen to their favorite music, "The Eagles of Death Metal," played by Southern Californian band, and some went to see a match of foot in France stadium, while others just preferred to have a drink at the terrace of "La Belle Équipe."

It felt like a typical Friday evening, and as these entire innocent and happy people were just enjoying life, suddenly multiple, coordinated attacks took place on these sites and in other locations throughout Paris. There was bloodshed and violence; people pouring out onto the streets were screaming, howling, and shouting in terror everywhere. Everything caught fire, and they felt hopeless.

At first, I could not understand what happened at all, but suddenly I became aware of the situation, and it seemed to me as if the whole world had turned upside down.

A black Volkswagen Polo pulled up outside the Bataclan concert hall at exactly 9:40PM on this Friday evening, and three heavily armed gunmen got out. Less than three hours later, they were dead, having killed ninety people at the venue and critically injured many others. The Bataclan siege was the last of the six attacks carried out at different locations across the city.

What was happening to Paris? Suddenly, I remembered Tatiana's words, when she talked to me outrageously and furiously. I thought that she simply spoke nonsensically in delirium. But only now I understood that her emotional and melodramatic language was not theatrical, it was in relation to her presentiment that she had sensed and seen in her dream. It was all about her feelings based on intuition.

The News teams made the coverage of the scenes; it was a real nightmare, so horrible and so unreal. The paramedics arrived to assist people and the police were controlling the situation. The lucky ones walked and ran away, the survivors moaned lamentably, and there were spread dead bodies in the locations and on streets.

It was a few minutes past midnight when I turned off the TV in a state of shock. I headed into the kitchen to brew some herbal tea, and drank it to calm my nerves. Then, I took a shower, warmer than usual and wrapped the towel around me. Moments later, when I crawled into my bed, I sensed that my body collapsed due to mental shock. I slept very badly that night.

The very next day, we were informed that the Isis had claimed responsibility for all these terrible attacks. François Holland announced that Paris was a city under siege and this was the deadliest attack that Paris had seen since World War II. He ordered to close the borders to prevent any suspect from leaving the country, and the lights had been turned off on Eiffel Tower.

Once again, this news affected us very deeply and hit the world harder than I had imagined. Since then, nothing was like before; French people realized with sadness that the most outrageous attack against the humanity happened in their beautiful city.

I was still sleeping when my phone began to ring. Rolling over, I reached for it and turned it off. The first rays of sun were beginning to light up my bedroom, but I could not get up until noon. It was Saturday and at first, I could not think why this particular day seemed so different from any other. I ducked my head under my pillow to escape the sunlight. I was just about to fall asleep when I heard a gentle knock at the door. I opened my eyes and peeked at mademoiselle Solange who turning the doorknob, strolled in, and advanced a few steps towards me.

She brought me coffee and croissants on a silver tray. She shook her head regretfully as she slid the newspapers out from under her arm.

"Is something wrong?" I asked, picking up a croissant.

"I'm afraid I have some bad news," she said, her cheeks flushing red.
"What is it?"

"Something really terrible happened; you shall read it all."

I took the papers in both hands and glanced down at the front page of
"Le Monde" first and "Le Figaro" next. Apparently, to my great surprise,
Tatiana made the front page in newspapers all over the country. The
headlines could not have been worse. My mouth fell open, and I thought
I had seen wrong.

Sitting on my bed with the image of Tatiana on my lap, I turned
the pages and read this article carefully, "Tatiana Ayoub, wife of the
famous movie director Alexander Lacroix, was brought to hospital alive
but unconscious. Victim of the attack at Bataclan, she is suffering from
a major head injury and she is in critical condition, fighting for her life."

My hands trembled at the same time as I stared at Tatiana's photograph.
How could this happen? I lost all sense of myself, no, no, no way! This was
impossible; this had to be a mistake; I shook my head in disbelief.

I poured myself some more coffee, and then sat back staring at the
words in a state of great shock and incredible sadness, tears swam in my
eyes.

Mademoiselle Solange returned a moment later and interrupted my
reading. She looked at me anxiously, wanting more information.

"How bad is she?" she asked nervously.

"She is in coma," I said as my tears started to fall.

I could not read anymore, I had read the same pages over and over
again. I called the hospital and asked for the latest news. They said
Tatiana was in deep coma and they could not give me more details over
the phone. Unsure what to do, I hesitated, and then I decided to take action.
I showered, dressed quickly, ran a brush through my hair and made my
way to Georges- Pompidou hospital.

The ride took twenty minutes. I addressed myself to the front desk and
spoke to a young man.

"May I help you?"

"I'm here to see Tatiana Ayoub, I'm her therapist," I said, looking
really concerned. I thought that Alexander had registered her under her
own name to keep the press away.

"She is in intensive care, fifth floor."

"Is someone with her in the room?"

"No, but her husband was here this morning."

When I got out of the elevator on fifth floor, I looked around and saw the sign "Intensive care." I moved slowly towards the sign. I had been cautious about this visit, since I did not want to run into Alexander. A nurse appeared and offered her assistance, she gestured to me to follow her.

I followed her without saying anything. The idea of Tatiana in her last session crossed my mind; her face expressed the mixture of hatred, fear and terror that I could see now.

With a sudden movement, the nurse opened the door. I saw Tatiana lying there, pale, tubes up her nose and surrounded by all kinds of machines. I stood in the doorway and looked at her sadly, sorrowfully. She was not in this world anymore.

Tears were running down my cheeks. I asked with a shaky voice, "Is she going to make it? How much of her is left?" I felt the trickle of blood streaming down my whole body.

"The worst of her injury seems to be located in her brain stem, so it's hard to predict. She was unconscious by the time she was transported to hospital, with blood seeping from a deep gash in her forehead. She is fighting for her life, and it's impossible to tell when she will wake up. We must wait and see," the nurse said.

Standing still, I felt stunned, and voiceless. I could never ever imagine anything so dreadful; this could not have happened to Tatiana, "It cannot be!" I exclaimed aloud. Victim of a great injustice, she had been in the wrong place at the wrong time.

I cautiously took one step, then another until I found myself by Tatiana's bedside, "Ah! It's terrible, truly," I said to myself. I moved silently to watch her closely. I could still feel waves of "Quelques Fleurs," running through her body and hair. There was no movement, no noise, and no word. Her eyes were closed, no more tears. How many tears had been shed from her beautiful eyes? I wondered. There were no more pearls of teardrops to swim in her eyes as a result of continuing suffering and anxiety. Could her bewildered and fearful nightmares finally be over?

I felt a strong feeling of repugnance and hatred within me, why? Why that? Why her? What could I do for her? Why was she seized by such a terrible twist of fate? I watched her helplessly. I felt crippled, useless and powerless to take any kind of action whatsoever. I held her cold hand in mine and started talking to her about everything and nothing. I talked about her pain, her spiritual life, her movie and her premonition. I remembered she felt bitter to see me being so indifferent, "Sorry Tatiana, I'm so very sorry, but I'll always be your friend," I whispered, as I burst into tears.

Was it by pure coincidence that all of a sudden Tatiana's hand became animated and squeezed lightly my third finger? Maybe, but I was persuaded that only for just a few seconds we were deeply reunited, it warmed my heart. Shortly after, her hand relaxed and she left me to return to her own world, her planet like the Little Prince. Tatiana seemed to have taken refuge in a world where no one could reach her; she was finally in peace.

When I got hold of myself and I was leaving the floor, the nurse caught me and asked, "Are you Amanda, Tatiana's therapist?"

"Yes, would you like to talk to me?" I said hesitantly.

"Please wait, wait a minute."

"How can I help you?"

"Please, I would like a moment alone with you," she said shyly.

"Okay."

"Do you know someone by the name of Bernard since you are Tatiana's therapist?"

"No, I've never heard of such a person," I replied promptly without thinking.

"Bernard?" she repeated rapidly.

Suddenly, I felt my whole body tense up as the nurse kept repeating this name. Sure, I had heard this name before and it seemed very familiar to me. Yes, of course I knew who she was referring to. My mouth dropped open and I felt a pang in my heart.

"No," I repeated, as I took a step back. I was not going to give her any information; I remembered my promises to Tatiana. I assured her that I had never heard this name before. I absolutely needed to guard my friend's privacy. I did my outmost to make sure that Tatiana's private life would remain intact. I paused and asked the nurse, "What about him?"

"Never mind, Tatiana was found unconscious in his arms," she said sorrowfully.

My mouth fell open as if to utter, "Really? I didn't know he lived in Paris." But I kept it shut. What was all that about?

"Is he okay?" I asked quickly with a hint of a bitter smile on my lips.

"First, he was conscious when the ambulance brought him here. In his delirium he stammered, "I just want you to save my beloved love, my last wish," then, shortly afterwards, he passed away.

"Did he?"

"Yes; and the authorities believe that as an activist, he might be involved in the mass shouting in Bataclan; but of course they are looking for more evidence," the nurse said.

The thought of Tatiana with her stepfather at Bataclan was freezing somehow; I wanted to know how it all happened? How in the world could he have stayed connected to her? I turned it over in my mind and thought, "So, this is how her life ended. It sounded like they truly did belong together. Love conquers all, but what had really passed between them? Were they in love? Were they in pain or what? How long and how often had they been lovers? What had happened between them? I could not understand all this mystery.

As I left the hospital in a state of stupor and trance, there were so many questions left unanswered, and I could not get them out of my mind. The name of Bernard continued to sit enthroned over my head. Tatiana's mysterious life was a secret and I swore myself to secrecy. Therefore, I made no attempt to acknowledge what had happened between them. But perhaps I should have been more sensible about everything she said to me at her last moments. I was quite furious at myself for doubting her, when she delivered her final words. Only now; I knew what she meant by that. Why didn't I listen and give close attention to her when she said she was living in the proximity of death? She believed she was dying, she told me so, and I refused to accept it. I thought about this too. This melancholic thought gave me definitely the blues of missed acts at this moment in time.

Since then, I went back to hospital a couple of times and stayed with Tatiana for as long as I could. Looking down closely at her, I would hold her cold hand in mine and whisper as warm tears flooded down my cheeks, "Tatiana, we all love you, wake up, I want my friend back," or "Tatiana, I'm still waiting for you in my office every Tuesday at three o'clock," or "Tatiana, come on, you need to wake up for the premiere of your movie."

And every time, I walked out of the room with a heavy heart, and wiping my eyes. Tatiana never woke up. Was it possible that she stayed in coma forever? This kind of brain injury is very hard to predict, they all said.

In the following months, there wasn't any change or improvement in Tatiana's condition, and they moved her from "Intensive care" to a regular room. Nothing could be done medically to change the outcome of this dreadful and tragic situation.

Tatiana, the victim of unfairness of life, became now a vegetable living her life in a deadly and eternal silence. Once again, I reminded myself that all was written, Tatiana's destiny was previously determined, and unfortunately not happily decided.

In my rational mind, I gradually began to believe that nothing I had done or not done had either caused or could have prevented this terrible and obnoxious incident.

Therefore, I had neither thoughts nor words.

SIX MONTHS LATER

THIRTY–SEVEN

The spotlights and the photographer's flashes showered the night sky of the avenue of Champs-Élysées announcing that there was a big event happening.

I saw a huge mass of people pushing and screaming desperately for autographs from their favorite actors. I walked past the paparazzi; there were a series of flashes in my face. I made quickly my way through the packed theater, a few minutes before the start. I glided down the aisle, smiling at everyone I knew. There were only a few seats left, I slid into in the middle of the third and sank into the only empty seat, all by myself.

Although excited, I was nervous about seeing Alexander again. Was he still filled with nostalgic feelings or would he be cold and indifferent? I wondered.

Moments later, Alexander who was sitting in the first row, turned back and looked around the theater until he saw me. I knew it was me he was looking for. The instant he caught sight of me, he was evidently pleased to see me. My eyes locked with his. He waved me hello and gave me a dazzling smile, right before the lights dimmed and the theater went dark.

As the curtain opened, I found myself absorbed deeply in my own thoughts. People in the audience applauded as the title appeared on the screen "Alexander Lacroix in association with Ripol Production Company presents "The Magic of Quelques Fleurs," based on a true story.

People kept cheering and applauding.

As the movie began, Tatiana came on the screen; she looked amazing. The first scene commenced in the office of a psychologist that was being played by Sophie Marceau. The camera moved on Tatiana, and lingered on her face for some time so that the spectators could get to know her.

Holding my breath, I was transfixed on the screen as my eyes filled with hot tears. It was a touching movie, and at moments, it was very painful for me to watch the situations that had been so familiar to me. This was my story and this was my conversation with Tatiana in my office.

The movie audience loved the film, a combination of charm and magic. They unanimously admired the story of the young beautiful patient and her charismatic psychologist. When the screen flashed end, voices came from the viewers, "What a touching ending!" And they clapped; the movie grabbed the heart of the audience.

I clapped too, very hard, as tears brimming in my eyes.

As soon as the curtain went down, I began pushing my way through the crowd. I suddenly felt someone putting an arm around my waist, and I heard my name being called, "Amanda!" I turned; the man standing behind me was Alexander. Our eyes met.

"Are you still too mad to talk to me? I've been looking for you," he exclaimed.

"I'm not mad at you," I replied coolly.

"I'm glad I caught you, what a pleasant surprise! I saw you come late into the theater. It's a pleasure to see you again," his voice was warm.

"Thank you for inviting me. I promised Tatiana I would be here. Congratulations, you did a great job, it couldn't have been any better," I said as I took a deep breath.

"So you kept your promise to Tatiana?"

"I couldn't break my promise to her; I only wish she could be here."

"Thanks for coming anyway. God! It's so lovely to see you, Amanda."

"How is she doing?" I asked, stepping back to make room for people to exit.

"Same, life is going on as if nothing ever happened," he declared.

"I'm terribly sorry. God rest her soul in peace!" I said, looking in his eyes.

People approached him to say good-bye.

"I knew that I would run into you at some point. It's time for a drink; can we go to toast my new movie? I mean your movie, please." Alexander said, staring me in the eye.

"Did you say my movie?"

"Yes, your movie," he repeated, as he bent down and kissed my hand.

"I don't get it, Alex. What do you mean?"

"The best time of my life was inextricably connected with you. Amanda, you were my only inspiration to make this movie."

"Oh, I'm flattered," I said, smiling.

There was a part of me that did not want to go, but since I still felt that I enjoyed his presence at my side, I found it difficult to resist. After a short hesitation, I said casually, "It sounds good. Let's go and have a drink."

We moved slowly and made our way through the crowd. We paused as a photographer took a picture of both of us. We walked in silence along the avenue of Champs-Elysées, I felt my confused thoughts and feelings. What on earth I was doing with him now? Was I meant to be talking to him?

A few minutes later, we strolled in the crowded and noisy bar of Four Season's hotel. Alexander pulled me to the couch and we sat next to each other.

"I need to say something to you," he said.

"You don't need to say anything," I said very seriously.

"Yes, I do. You seem so abrupt."

"Sorry, I don't mean to be abrupt," I uttered; my face broke into a languid smile.

"You are so tough with me, Amanda. Come on, life doesn't always go the way that we plan," he sounded so very strange, but austere.

The waiter, tall and formal, pulled the bottle of champagne out of the ice bucket and served us ceremoniously, and then he disappeared.

We toasted and took a sip.

"To your movie," I said.

"To our movie," Alexander said, and after a short pause, he went on, "I never stopped thinking about you."

"I thought that sex was the only important part of our relationship," I said, as I struggled to smile with sarcasm.

As a matter of fact, I felt that the sexual attraction between us was buried, but still not gone. Alexander put his arm round my waist, and gently kissed me. As he held me tight, I could feel his heart throbbing fast against his chest. I rapidly pushed him away.

"There is something I need to tell you," he repeated, looking me in the eye.

"What?"

"I love you," he loved me and I could see that in his eyes.

Alexander seemed perfectly sincere as he launched into deep discussion about his love for me; his fantasies and our future together, "My feelings for Tatiana are about responsibility and compassion, but my feelings for you are about passion and love," he uttered, while he held me against him and kissed me on my lips. It all happened very fast. For a second time, I gently pushed him away.

In a moment, the waiter came back to fill the glasses. I slid back in my seat and took a sip of sparkling champagne. I did not feel that I had to make a comment. Instead, I started looking at the people at the nearby tables. For a third time, he put his arms around me and caressed my breast gently; it was as though we were still lovers.

"It's a special night, and how happy I am not to have to be apart from you at this moment," he whispered gently.

I nodded silently, and pushed him away once more.

"How do you feel about all this?" he asked, gazing attentively into my eyes.

Leaning back in my seat, I raised my glass to him, and then took a sip. I remained quiet.

"Is there any hope for us?" Alexander exclaimed questioningly.

"I don't know," I finally said in an icy tone.

Suddenly, he pulled me close and kissed me hard, "I love you Amanda, we can start all over again."

"Time is a strange thing, Alex. I don't think I'm ready now," I said quietly.

"You don't seem indifferent to me, I can see that in your eyes, Amanda," he said.

"Maybe so, but things have changed. We never should have started."

"But we had no choice, my love. We felt a strong sexual attraction for each other," he said, as he raised his voice.

"We are in a difficult situation now; there is no way of knowing what will happen next?" I said.

Tatiana's condition raised the question and we both knew too well that we would never have the final answer.

"It's possible that she stays in coma forever; only a miracle will bring her back to life," Alexander said.

I was not convinced, "What if she does? And then what will happen? She will need you more than ever; she is still your wife, Alex."

"She is a part of my past and she has ceased to exist."

"But she is still alive," I affirmed.

"I see what you are worried about, I set up a trust that would provide her with a comfortable income for living," he assured me.

"It's not all about money!" I objected.

"So what will become of us?" he interrogated sternly.

I remained silent for some time, so very perplexed. Finally I said, "I don't know."

We chatted for a few more minutes.

"What about us?" he repeated.

"I need time to think about all this, I can't give you a response right now, I'm sorry."

"Think it over then, you mustn't decide now."

Alexander stared at me, I returned his gaze in silence. Some fractured memories of that particular and nasty night came slowly back to haunt me. Of course, I did not mention a word; that seemed way out of line given those circumstances. But Alexander seemed to have read my mind, he put himself together and said, "I had absolutely no idea about you being Tatiana's therapist, she never said a word to me. I was as shocked as you were, Tatiana could hide her feelings and thoughts so well. I always knew that she wasn't sincere."

I shook my head thoughtfully, and took another sip of champagne, "She never pretended to be what she wasn't," I acknowledged.

We fell into a lively discussion. We talked like this for a while, and then we were not talking any longer. We were silent for some time.

Moments later, Alexander broke this silence, "You were a special friend of hers, and I mean you two were very close to each other."

"You are right."

"So how much do you know about this guy named Bernard?" he asked curiously.

"Sorry, Alex, I'm terribly sorry."

"Professional discretion?" he interrogated, laughing.

I nodded in confirmation, and murmured, "Maybe."

"You know her so much better than I ever did," he told me.

"In some ways yes," I looked at him with approving eyes.

"You can tell me so much about her. Who is Bernard?" he repeated.

I did not answer him directly, "Do you pretend to be a jealous husband?"

"No, I'm just curious. But forget it. Forget what I said to you," he said.

I could not give him any information; I did not want to say anything, since I was attached tightly to my promise of secrecy to Tatiana. In fact, Alexander did not really care how she conducted herself, if anything; he was pleased recognizing that her infidelity strengthened his position.

"You made me realize what life can be like, Amanda. But every time I was going to leave her, she got the idea to threaten suicide. Regarding her condition, it was too painful to her, she could not face the divorce," Alexander said, his tone was persuasive, and his eyes even more.

I nodded, and glanced at my watch, "Sorry, but I'm late as it is," I said apologetically.

"I'm going to walk you home," he said.

Minutes later, Alexander and I crossed the lobby of the four Season's hotel. We walked slowly down the street side by side, eyeing the stores and café terraces.

"I called you and left several messages, I explained everything. Did you ever listen to any of my messages?"

"No," I said, slightly lying.

"You okay?" he asked.

"I'm fine."

"You seem nervous."

"No, I'm not."

He squeezed my hand; I felt the softness of his skin. We walked in silence for several minutes through the narrow streets. I had no idea what I was going to say next. When we reached the entrance door of my apartment building, I thought perhaps it was time to say good-bye forever, but I decided to be a littlel cooler.

"I'm going to have to leave you now, thanks for the drink," I said.

He gave me a flattering smile, and took my arm to keep me from going away, "Wait, wait a minute, Amanda, I want to see you again. May I have a second chance?" he said as his arms went around my waist.

We stood there, at the doorstep of my building, just staring at each other.

"I love you Amanda."

"You do?"

"You know I do," Alexander said, smiling.

There was a reason I was hesitant and uncertain. I showed him my indecision honestly.

"But you are not totally free, Alex, I need to think about all this. I want to make the right decision," I said with a self-assured smile.

"That sounds promising! Whatever you decide Amanda; I respect your decision. But one thing I can never forget, you must know that," he gave me a fixed stare.

"What?"

"The smell of you perfume, "Quelques Fleurs" transports me back in an instant to all those exciting moments I shared with you," he whispered against my ear.

I immediately interrupted him, holding my hand up, and begging him to stop.

"I'm not wearing that fragrance anymore, I changed my perfume," I said with a shaky voice.

Alexander seemed to think about that for a few seconds, "Why? What perfume are you wearing now?" his face turned inquiring, he frowned, thinking and looking at me with great curiosity.

I actually had no idea what I was going to say to him. Unconsciously, I guarded my tongue and preferred not to be outspoken about my new perfume this time. I did not want to tell him or anyone what it was. I did not want everyone to get it, because then, it would lose its specialness.

We looked into each other's eyes for several minutes. Alexander knew that something special must be said under such circumstances. He came nearer to me and stared at my face, "You still smell delicious, I mean what really makes me want you so much is the inner aroma that you emanate like a perfume that spreads through the air, and is so divine. Your natural smell is fine and sophisticated. There is a sense of deepness about you, and there is something infinitely seductive in your persona. You make me want to be a complete man," he said as he stepped closer to me, with a voice filled with emotion.

Alexander uttered those words with a melancholic gentleness. In his look, I discovered the ecstasy of love. We exchanged a significant smile and threw a meaningful gaze at each other, but said no word. We spoke without speaking in a deep silence, perhaps the longest silence that ever fell between us.

"Amanda, don't forget what I've just said to you here and I'll stay in touch with you," he said as he took my hand and squeezed it. Then, suddenly, he turned and walked away, leaving me alone.

I watched him walking down the sidewalk into the darkness. Several times, he turned his head and looked back, waving his hand. I stood there without moving, looking at him until he rounded the street corner of Paul Valéry.

Did I restrain myself from revealing my real feelings to him? I was heavy-hearted. How could I explain my confused feelings to him? I searched in vain for the words to describe them, words belonging only to me, engraved with my blood in my flesh.

The sweet smell of chestnut trees lingered in the air. From the doorstep, I could smell their delicate fragrance. Spring was here. It was an amazing night; the sky was clear and crammed with plenty of stars with the silvery glow that whispered to me that I should live my life fully. But what is the meaning of life? I wondered.

Life is a complicated labyrinth, isn't it? Fate is nothing but a confused and complex set of connections and links between the paths through which it is difficult to find one's way. And fate is also this powerful force that controls all events in life. I certainly remain fascinated and overwhelmed by all these changeable moves in the universe. So how can I act and make a decision in a world where fate renders everything futile and meaningless?

I alone must make decisions, and I'm perfectly aware of it. How can I ever foresee and predict the result and the outcome of my actions? I certainly don't wish to be caught in a network of unpredictable incidents leading me to the gravest consequences. Therefore, I will be desperately trying to comprehend the world better by following the flow of life, the path that was chosen for me here on earth, my destiny.

Still standing there in the moonlight, I saw mademoiselle Solange who came to the window and stood there for a short moment, staring down. I looked up at her, "Is it all quiet up there?" I asked anxiously.

"Yes, it is very quiet, but you'd better come up and get some sleep, you have a lot going on tomorrow," she said, closing the window.

I shook my head.

Slowly I turned the key and opened the door and let myself inside, wrapped in my mixed emotions and feelings. Everything in my mind ended with an interrogation point. I thought, "Tatiana is in coma, but what exactly does that mean? Is Alexander a widow or a free man? Will Tatiana wake up and find her way to her husband?" I was feeling strangely perplexed, bemused and I needed to be alone.

Now that I am alone with myself, an absurd bliss runs through my heart in spite of the tears that wet my face. How do I explain this unknown, strange and sudden feeling that overcomes me at this moment in time? I desperately try to find for the precise words to explain the reason pro this ecstasy and rapture. Maybe I really don't need words if I can only see them in Christian's multiple photographs.

ACKNOWLEDGMENTS

First and foremost, I especially want to thank Karen De Sanctis, my American twin sister whose spiritual life, authenticity, and kindness inspired me to write this story. Dear Karen, I don't know how to thank you for the unwavering support that you continue to give me in life. I can see in you all that is noble in Amanda; you helped me unlock so many doors in this tale. I will always love you.

I would like to thank my dear Ladan for taking a chance on this book and giving me her valuable feedback as a psychologist.

I'm indebted to my family, my brothers and my lovely nieces for their encouragement.

Last, I'm grateful to my friend Nazi P. for her wisdom, understanding, and gracious ways of welcoming me into her office and assisting me with warmth. My dear Nazi, you are so special, and I'm very lucky to have you in my life.